HIGH PRAISE FOR LIAM CALLANAN'S

THE CLOUD ATLAS

"These are imaginative and entertaining and moving pages. Liam is a gifted and interesting writer, a writer to notice, a writer to watch, a writer any reader of serious fiction will be proud to have read."
—Alan Cheuse, NPR's *All Things Considered*

"Liam Callanan's extraordinary novel begins on the far side of historical fact and goes from there, skillfully working its surprising way through factual time and imaginative possibilities. A fine, rare achievement." —Beverly Lowry, author of *Crossed Over: A Murder, A Memoir*

"*The Cloud Atlas* is a tense weave of present and past, secrets and confessions. Liam Callanan has written an absorbing, richly layered novel about a vast and mysterious land and its well-concealed collision with history." —Porter Shreve, author of *The Obituary Writer*

"*The Cloud Atlas* claims its own and intricate geography; this is a little-known and less-traveled landscape, and Liam Callanan charts it expertly. A tautly woven tale."
—Nicholas Delbanco, author of *What Remains*

"*The Cloud Atlas* is an elegant, elegiac novel that turns one of the most bizarre episodes of American history into a fable about the collision of innocence and mystery, practicality and faith. A fascinating debut."
—Gary Krist, author of *Chaos Theory*

"*The Cloud Atlas* is an amazing first novel—a story of soldier-turned-priest struggling with life and death, a crisis of the spirit, and a rare and haunting love affair that remains in the mind long after the reader has finished this unusual novel."
—Susan Richards Shreve, author of *Plum & Jaggers*

"What a mind-bending novel this is. In this haunting story, Liam Callanan makes you believe that humankind really does have a chance to survive its own most sinister inventions."
—Stephen Goodwin, author of *Breaking Her Fall*

"Liam Callanan is a first-rate writer at the beginning of a long and distinguished career." —Richard Bausch, author of *Someone to Watch Over Me*

"Equal parts history, memory and vision quest . . . Callanan wears the burden of historical fiction with ease." —*New York Times*

"What stays with you is the great arc of a small man's life on the edge of the world, and of sympathy that resonates." —*Time Out New York*

"The first-person narrative moves. . . . Callanan has produced a genuine page-turner." —*Rocky Mountain News*

"Callanan is a mesmerizing new talent." —*Creative Loafing* (Charlotte)

"Liam Callanan's novel transcends the easily accessible to paint a compelling portrait of the tale's characters." —*Winston-Salem Journal*

"Callanan uses this little-known and shocking piece of American World War II history as a way to tell a more intimate tale of three people whose paths cross inextricably toward the end of the war. In doing so, he deftly weaves together a war story, a love story and a mystery."
—*Virginian Pilot & Ledger Star*

"This remarkable novel . . . will entice the book club crowd; the strong characterizations and moral dilemmas will leave them with plenty to discuss. Highly recommended."
—*Library Journal* (starred review)

THE
CLOUD
ATLAS

LIAM CALLANAN

DIAL PRESS TRADE PAPERBACKS

THE CLOUD ATLAS
A Dial Press Trade Paperback Book

PUBLISHING HISTORY
Delacorte Press hardcover edition published February 2004
Delta Trade Paperback edition November 2004
Dial Press Trade Paperback edition / March 2007

Published by The Dial Press
A Division of Random House, Inc.
New York, New York

This is a work of fiction. Names, characters, places, and incidents
either are the product of the author's imagination or are used
fictitiously. Any resemblance to actual persons, living or dead,
events, or locales is entirely coincidental.

Book design and illustrations by Virginia Norey

The Dial Press and Dial Press Trade Paperbacks are registered
trademarks of Random House, Inc., and the colophon is a
trademark of Random House, Inc.

Library of Congress Catalog Card Number: 2003053240

ISBN: 978-0-385-33695-6

Printed in the United States of America
Published simultaneously in Canada

www.dialpress.com

12 11 10 9 8 7 6 5 4 3
BVG

To Lucy

Would that I had
had such a map

THE
CLOUD
ATLAS

1

No morphine: no use, the doctor said.

The boy would die within the hour, and morphine was in short supply. He was saving it for the soldiers—for American soldiers, he added, checking the wall clock, then his watch, then me. It was four o'clock, 1600 hours Alaskan War Time, on July 6, 1945, a mere thirty-four days before fighting in Japan officially ended. The boy was Japanese.

When I was a boy, I was told a writer should date his age from the day he started writing. I can't remember why I was told this; I just remember that I liked it enough to repeat it over the years to those who might benefit from the wisdom. To anyone. To people like my drill sergeant.

He had a quick reply: a soldier should date his age from the day he started killing.

If that's so, I was even younger than the world took me for back then. An eighteen-year-old sergeant, I'd been in the army for ten months, waging a secret war, from Alaska, for six. I'd trained in bomb disposal. I'd learned to speak some Yup'ik, I'd fallen in love with a woman who talked with touch, I'd shot a bar glass out of my captain's hand.

And now, in that tiny room, in a mission infirmary just inland from the Bering Sea, the weather cool and wet, I was sitting at the side of a boy who was dying.

I was AWOL.

And for the first time since putting on a uniform, I was crying.

At eleven, the boy died. At midnight, I turned three days old.

CHAPTER 1

I'M A WANTED MAN.

That's hardly enough to distinguish me around here, of course. I've heard it said that a percentage of Alaska's population is always fleeing something—the authorities, spouses, children, civilization. By comparison, I have it easy. It's just a couple of old priests hunting me, and I know them both. I could take them if it came to that, and it won't.

I'll be honest up front. They're coming after me for the most mundane of reasons. The only thing slightly extraordinary is that they're coming at all. For a while, I thought they would just forget about me, and that I'd be able to live out my days like most fugitives here: not entirely free from want, but free from those who want you. But no, first one sent a letter and then the other: these initial letters just suggestions, of course. Then a second round, with a request. And the third round, with an order. Come home.

Now, I served in the army. I know what it means to disobey an order, even a bishop's, and yet I did.

Let them come.

They say they will. This Friday, two days from today. My superiors (the bishop himself, they'd have me believe, and his right-hand man) are flying all the way out here to my lonely home in the bush to haul me in for the crime of—believe it or not—growing old. Apparently you can't be seventy-three and live in southwestern Alaska, though this fact seems lost on a good portion of the population here in Bethel. But no, it's been decided. It's time I came in, returned stateside, or, as those here say, Outside. When I've asked what I'm to do in retirement, they've said, *Rest, write—almost sixty years in the bush, what stories you must have!*

A younger man will replace me, I'm told, but who are they kidding? Silver-haired fiftysomethings count as young priests these days. And the fact is, fifty may be too old—if the silverhair being moved here is from, say, Phoenix. Me, I grew into this environment. I came during the war, left for seminary, and returned to stay. I've had fifty-six years to get acclimated, and the hardest part of that acclimation came when I was young and could take it. Show me the golf-tanned, fifty-year-old suburban priest who will survive transplantation here—I don't care how carefully he parcels out his multivitamins.

There is a bit of mystery to their pursuing me. There's another Catholic missionary I know who lives up north on the banks of the Yukon, in much rougher conditions than the relatively civilized frontier life here in Bethel (which includes electricity, a hospital, even alcohol—though only by mail). This Yukon priest, he's eighty. Maybe ninety. No one's coming for him. And his parishioners don't even like him, at least not as much as mine do me.

It's why I didn't answer any of the letters I received. One, I've aged into a fine contrarian, but more important, I wanted these men to come tell me face-to-face that I needed to retire. That way, when they said, *It's because you're getting old,* I could study their eyes and see what the other reason, the real reason, is.

I have an idea.

It's not about the man I killed, or the boy I didn't save. It's not even about the woman I loved.

But the shaman—

Well. Yes. This all might have something to do with him.

* * *

THE LOWER PART of Ronnie's leg was not torn off by wolves, though that's what he tells most people. And if someone got to see it, which almost no one ever does, that person might come away thinking he was telling the truth. His right leg ends just above the ankle in a tight red scar, the exact size, shape, and color of angrily pursed lips. The skin around it, smoother than silk from all the creams and ointments medical staff insist he use, colors with the weather and hosts storms of its own: clouds of bruises—red, blue, and purple—gather, encircling the stump, spreading, growing darker, and then fading. The amputation is relatively new, the prosthesis even newer, and learning to walk again has been a battle for him. After watching more than one afternoon's practicing devolve from laughs and jokes to curses and grunts and perspiration and Ronnie begging, *Please, please take it off, let the swollen stump pulse and breathe as it wants to*—well, a person wanted those wolves. *He* wanted them. I wanted them, pacing, their fiery eyes sizing him up, but at least looking him in the eye, not like the diabetes that was truly to blame.

By some accounts, I should be glad that Ronnie—just installed in his room, at the end of the ward, with windows looking west—is ill; for years, he had been trying to kill me. Nothing special, just a shaman trying to roust a priest. But shortly after arriving in the hospice, diabetes flaring and pneumonia threatening, he summoned me to his bedside. Plans had changed, he said. He was no longer seeking my death. And to prove his sincerity, he gave me the talisman that he'd planned to use to speed my demise.

It resembled a voodoo doll, and it resembled me, as much as such a thing could: short and starting to stoop, gray hair, something like glasses. He had dressed me in my blacks, although I rarely wore or wear clerical garb out here in the bush. Such clothes aren't warm enough for winter, too scratchy for summer. Besides, people knew well enough that I was the local Catholic priest. Ronnie knew; that's why he wanted to kill me: my God and I had driven his people and powers away. We had

had this argument for decades, ever since I came to this part of Alaska to replace the previous priest, who had disappeared (some said literally, said they watched him fade away, limb by limb, until all that was left was a mouth in an O of horror, until there was nothing).

Ronnie liked to suggest that he had something to do with this disappearance. He was, then as now, the local shaman, a bit green for the role at the time, but few sought the job (Ronnie would claim the job sought the man). Ronnie himself wasn't a great advertisement. Whatever his success had been with my predecessor (who my superiors suspected had simply fled, hysterical, out into the tundra one winter night—we'd lost more than one man that way), Ronnie's efforts with or against me went unrewarded. Charms were tacked to my door; various sacrifices filleted and placed about my corrugated tin chapel; and, of course, much scheming and chanting and brow furrowing was done out of sight. All to no avail.

And for an interloper, I was, and am, innocuous enough. Better yet: I have had a positive effect. We missionaries all tell ourselves that, but I have, I really have. With the help of modern medicine, I have healed the sick; with the help of the bishop, fed the hungry; with help of wealthy, faraway, misty-eyed parishes, clothed the poor. I have insisted on saying Mass, but I adjusted my schedule to meet theirs. What's more, I've eaten their food, I've tried to talk their language, I've played their games with their children. The previous man outlawed traditional dancing. I've encouraged it and attempted to learn.

And I've blessed things. Babies, houses, holes in the ice. Dogs, and later, snowmachines. Outboard motors and cases of Crisco. Nets, knives, and sewing needles, yes; but guns, never. And once, a dead woman's stuffed parakeet, although that was more exorcism than blessing. Her widower had remarried; the man's new wife said the parakeet helped friends cheat her at cards. *Saint Francis,* I prayed, *it's not enough that this woman has to make a life in the subarctic tundra? With a husband who keeps his first wife's parakeet? Peace, Saint Francis. Go easy, O Lord.*

And this hospice, Quyana House. It's a curious, mostly empty place, located well outside of town. It blossomed on the grounds of an abandoned radar installation, and is supported almost entirely by a Seattle family whose son drowned here one summer while serving as a missionary-in-training.

THE HOSPICE IS OFTEN empty because it's hard to get to, and people don't quite trust this Outside generosity. (*Quyana* means "thank you" in Yup'ik, which is all well and good, since this part of Alaska is Yup'ik Eskimo, but people find it a strange name nonetheless: just who is being thanked, and for what?) Plus, the old and terminally ill usually die at home—or at the hospital in town. The hospital is known as the Yellow Submarine, but the way it snakes along the tundra, long and flat, its every corner rounded, it looks more like bars of soap smushed together, or maybe some Outside architect's idea for a hospital on the moon. It stands on stilts; just about everything in town does. Otherwise, buildings would melt the permafrost and slowly sink into the tundra. But the hospital's awkward seventies *Star Wars* design makes its stilts look like landing gear; the entire building seems poised for take-off, and there are those in town who sometimes wish it would.

The hospice, on the other hand, is a soaring structure, seemingly composed of equal parts glass and light. We all await the storm that will level it, but month after month it survives, and maybe I shouldn't be surprised: I've blessed the place half a dozen times. First, when they cleared the land for construction; second, when someone had fallen from some scaffolding and broken both legs; third and fourth came when a new wing went up and when it collapsed; fifth was the grand opening; and sixth was the dedication of the wing where Ronnie now lies, ready to discuss the terms of our truce.

I had put the doll replica of me in my breast pocket, taking care that the little arms and head were peeking out. At first, I did it as a joke, but then I had this sudden, inexplicable need to cough, and I thought: play it safe. I gave the little guy more room and Ronnie smiled. He knew I was thinking of the word, the word that's become a central tenet of my amalgamated Alaskan faith, a word that inevitably becomes part of any religion that spends too much time in the subzero subarctic dark: *maybe*. No one from Outside understands this law of the bush. No one understands how rock-solid principles can slide here; how black-and-white so inexorably mists to gray; how a priest, a true believer, a defender of the faith, a dealer in eternal truths, can find himself spooked by a makeshift voodoo doll. It can't happen. It's not possible. You repeat this like a mantra, and then you get back to the word.

Maybe.

For Ronnie, God bless him (if only either were interested), there is no *maybe*, only *is*. On those occasions when we do talk theology—which is seldom, sadly, now that he's more sober—Ronnie always taunts me with his trump card: proof. Show me proof of your God, this Jesus, he'll say; I usually respond with some version of the Apostle Paul's insistence to the Hebrews that faith is the evidence of things not seen. Ronnie finds this rather pat: his proof, he says, is in the stars, in the grains of snow blowing against the glass, in the salmon who return every year, in the Yup'ik people, who, despite everything, still walk the earth. All this is proof of spirits—his spirits—at work.

Diabetes, on the other hand, is proof of my work. Not me personally, not even my God, but certainly my people, he says. And it's true, junk food is replacing alcohol as the white man's new smallpox, and though it takes longer to kill the native population, the unhealthy shift in diet from what the land provided to what air cargo provides—Spam, Pop-Tarts, and worse—still takes too many lives too early.

Diabetes sent Ronnie to the hospital more than once, then trouble with his liver. For years, he drank too much, but as I'm down to one kidney, I'm not one to lecture him on that. He's been using the hospice for his health care of late. He likes it here; it's quiet, no one bothers him. But he bothers them, since they're not really set up to deliver the care he needs, unless he gets really ill. He used to respond that if they kept it up, he would be that ill, and for a while, that seemed funny. But now he's more sick, more often, and they just shrug and let him stay as long as he wants. I think he misses fighting with them. I miss it, too.

In the past, we'd talk and joke a bit whenever I visited him here. (Or rather, I talk, and Ronnie shakes his head and rolls his eyes: I talk too much.) Whenever he fell asleep, I would pray, as much a function of habit as anything else: when I first started visiting Ronnie back in the hospital, I would ask him to pray with me, and he would inevitably fall asleep. Eventually, it became a kind of ritual that soothed us both. I sat and prayed, he slept, and in this way, we visited.

The balance has shifted of late, though. He's dying. Or rather, he thinks he is and wants me to think the same. I'll admit: he is asleep more than he is awake, and when he is awake, it's very strange. He'll stop, mid-conversation, and search around the room: something is missing, or something is here. "I can hear him," he'll whisper. And sometimes, when there *is* something to hear—a distant moan or cough—he'll say, "Tell me how he died," which I never understand: Does he need a primer? What does he think he'd learn from the other patients? Then he'll look at me, and I can see in his eyes what he wants to say, what he's never said to me, not directly: *I need your help.* Help, real help, is back in town, back at the hospital. But whenever I ask about moving him there, he shakes his head.

"Everyone is gone, Lou-is."

Ronnie alone has never called me "Father," and whenever he says my name, he mimics the exaggerated, not-sure-if-you-speak-English pronunciation I used when I first introduced myself, what? Forty, fifty years ago? A century, maybe.

"Gone where?" I asked, and he nodded his head toward the window. "To the festival?" I said. He shook his head and stared outside, silent. One of the smaller villages upriver was hosting a gathering; as always, they'd scheduled it for the last days of winter, at just about the point when you simply couldn't take it anymore. Alaska's winter calendar is full of these events. They say that, in Anchorage, if you have a tuxedo, you'll have something to do every night from November through March; out here, the same is true if you swap the tuxedo for a snowmachine.

I don't have a tuxedo—clerical garb is just as black and much cheaper—but I do have a snowmachine, which I got from the high school shop class. They'd gotten it from the manufacturer, who'd donated it with only one condition (courtesy of their lawyers): students couldn't ride it, just take it apart and put it back together again. Which they did for ten years, before giving it to me, with, their teacher promised, the "vast majority" of its essential parts intact. But I take it out less and less of late. Not because of my body—though my bones do increasingly feel as though they were made of kindling—but my mind. The older I get, the more recent my youth seems, and the more I recall that first youthful trip I made into the bush. I was a soldier then, not a priest, and it was summer, not winter.

This is another reason why I always visit Ronnie. He's good at hauling me into the present.

"There's no one left," he said again. "No one for me, no one for you."

I shook my head, and he repeated the line, louder. My hearing is lousy; a wartime blast took half of it and age has slowly been claiming the rest. I compensate well—I'd understood Ronnie just fine—but he likes to have an excuse to shout. Sometimes I find myself shouting back; we've acquired a certain reputation around town.

"No one!" Ronnie shouted. But no smile.

"We have each other, Ronnie," I said, at a normal, chaplain-to-patient level.

No smile. "This is what we must talk about. You and me," Ronnie said, his volume falling all the while.

RONNIE WANTED several things. First, twenty dollars. Then, my signature on a form. And most important, my promise that I would help him die. I gave him the twenty. I signed the form without looking, but then took it back when he made that last request about helping him die. I may not be the Church's best priest—actually, there's no confusion on that point—but I wasn't about to help a man, my friend, commit suicide.

"Not suicide," Ronnie said. I was simultaneously trying to read the form and figure out what was going on. "This paper says you can tell the doctors what to do. And that paper is called a will," he said. "I'm leaving everything to you. If you help me."

"I take 'everything' to mean the twenty I just gave you."

Back in his drinking days—or, let's call them what they were, decades—Ronnie's anger was noisy and physical. But of late, his most serious weapon is silence. When he is upset, he closes his mouth and sometimes his eyes.

He started again. "This is what they told me: you sign this, you make decisions for me. When I can't."

"Like always," I said. Like when it was time to leave a bar. Like when it was time for him to finally see the doctor.

"These are my wishes," Ronnie said. "I wish to die. No 'ex-tra-or-di-nar-y measures.'"

"Ronnie," I said. "You're not dying. And I'm not going to let them kill you."

He waited a long time before replying. He closed his eyes, and for a moment, I thought he'd gone to sleep. "I don't want you to let them *save* me," he said, opening his eyes once more.

"Ronnie," I said.

I've introduced Ronnie as the man who was trying to kill me, but the truth is, he has probably kept me alive all this time, this far from the rest of the world. "Okay," I said. I handed back the form. "But if you die, you promise I'll get the twenty back?"

Absolutely not. He needed the money to pay for a special bracelet from Alaska's Comfort One program. The program is for the very ill; the bracelet indicates that you do not want to be resuscitated. Paramedics and other medical professionals have to honor it. I've seen the bracelets at work—it's like a magic charm. Say a crisis occurs. Say people automatically rush to deliver aid. Then they spot the bracelet, and it's almost as if they bounce off the patient.

Ronnie had ordered his bracelet C.O.D., the way many people shop in the bush. They go through catalogs, place orders, and hope the money will be there when the goods come. It is heartbreaking to see the pile of unclaimed boxes at the airport after Christmas. UPS sends a man out to haul it all back each January; I call him the anti-Santa. But Ronnie had planned ahead: he'd had the band shipped care of the church. Asking for the twenty was just a courtesy; the bill was already waiting for me.

I tried to tell Ronnie that he probably wouldn't need such a bracelet in the hospice, but if he was worried, we could talk to his doctor and make a note on his chart. I even knew the shorthand; I'd seen it on dozens of charts before: DNR, *Do Not Resuscitate*. Ronnie smiled, the smile he always used when he was reminded how much wiser shamans were than priests.

"It's not for me," he said. Then he took a deep breath, the effort of which seemed to drain his face of the smile. "It's for the wolf."

RONNIE'S PASSING WAS no minor thing, not in his mind. As he saw it, he was the last shaman, the last in the area to possess his gifts, or his knowledge. Generations of missionaries had driven what magic they could from the land, but the spirit had persisted. Now modern life— airplanes, college educations, government jobs—was removing what remained.

I told Ronnie that he didn't need to worry; Yup'ik traditions were preserved in books, on tapes (thanks in part to the boundless altruism of oil companies). And the tundra teemed with academics whenever the weather was warm. Some summers, it seemed a Yup'ik family was likely to see more anthropologists than salmon.

Ronnie never listened to me, and he didn't now. What he had to say couldn't be discussed in a classroom or read about in a book, he explained, between gasping breaths so theatrical I almost took them for real. But he persisted: he needed to pass along his *stories,* from one man to another, so they could pass on to still another, and another, so that the knowledge and spirit of the Yup'ik would not vanish from the earth.

And it was more than that. He had something to tell me, he said. A particular story. A secret. Something I should know, "after all this time."

He closed his eyes.

I patted Ronnie's hand gently and moved to go. I couldn't stay. Having witnessed the deaths of both friends and enemies, I know that it can be harder to lose a foe: you lose a boundary, a cause. And since Ronnie was both friend and foe, I imagined losing him would be harder still. It's a kind of love, I suppose.

"Ronnie," I said, but that was all I got out before I was stormed by a crowd of emotions, memories, old mental movie clips. Ronnie wasn't awake enough to see me rock back into my chair. This has been happening to me more and more, lately: a kind of memory-induced vertigo. It's disturbing, clearly an illness of some sort, something inside breaking down. The woman who cleans my quarters, a woman I myself baptized but who still believes in all sorts of spirits and magic, told me the problem had to do with a restless soul. She suggested collecting some *ayuq* from the tundra and making iced tea from it. *Ayuq* is called Labrador tea, Eskimo tea, tundra tea, or *ayuq*, depending on who's doing the calling, and the list of illnesses it cures is diverse as well. A tattered copy of *Reader's Digest,* meanwhile, told me the problem was corroded neural pathways and suggested I drink brewed garlic. I thought about distilling the best of both methods by taking up whisky again, with ice, but Ronnie lying here in this bed is evidence enough that alcohol won't work.

Ronnie's eyes opened, failed to focus, and then closed again. He spoke anyway: "In the beginning," he told his chest, "there was Raven."

I settled back. I have heard multiple stories of creation in Alaska, but in the beginning, there is always Raven. The version Ronnie tells is my favorite. In the beginning, Raven scratches at the earth with his claws and makes hills, mountains. The countless gouges his talons leave in the soil fill with water and become lakes, rivers, and sloughs.

Upon this land, Raven created a man of stone. Formidable and strong—a man designed to survive in the harsh climate of southwestern Alaska. But then spring came, and the snows melted, the soil turned to mud, and the stone man sank deeper into the tundra with every step.

So Raven tried again. This time he molded a man of clay, or dirt. More fragile, more vulnerable—true; but more adaptable and better suited to travel the land he had sprung from.

It's a sign of how long I have lived here that I know Ronnie and his stories so well. And while I was always more interested in hearing a new story, I was still intrigued to hear Ronnie tell one I already knew and see what use he might put it to. Did he feel like the man of stone now, sinking into his illness? Or the man of clay, so easily broken?

Or perhaps he and I were the two first men—but which of us was stone, which clay?

I asked him. He scowled.

"This is what I have said," Ronnie said. His breathing became his punctuation. "In the beginning there was Raven. And then, a family. A mother. A boy. Her lovers. His fathers."

"More than one?" I interrupted, still not understanding. "Sounds like quite a story."

Ronnie closed his eyes, and when he opened them once more, he spoke. "This is not a story. This is true."

A nurse arrived, bearing a syringe on a tray. Ronnie scanned back and forth: me, nurse, syringe. He settled on the syringe.

"You heard what I said?" he told the syringe as it approached. "You told the doctor? No painkillers. No sleep medicines." He pointed at me. "I have things I need to discuss. With my *priest*." The nurse nodded gently, and reassured him that his request had already been written down on his chart. Then she explained that she was just there to draw blood. Ronnie watched carefully as she cinched the constricting band around his arm, searched for a vein, and then drew what she needed.

"What she wants to take," Ronnie said, "is already gone." Which might have been true, considering that years of drinking had likely left his veins more full of Gilbey's gin than blood. When she was finished, he sank back into the pillow.

"Raven," he said.

"Ronnie," I said. "What are you bothering the nurses for? They're going to take good care of you. If there's one thing they do better in the hospice than the hospital, it's take care of pain. So if you're uncomfortable, let them—"

"What I need to say, I need a clear head to say," he said.

Now, a few years before, there's only one thing Ronnie would have said next: *So let us drink.*

Instead, he said something I'd never heard him say before: "Father." I tensed. Then another surprise: "I want to confess."

This was so startling I assumed we were joking again. "Oh, Ronnie," I said. "Let's just talk. Old friends."

"Enemies," he said, and smiled. "I want to go to confession."

"You're not even Catholic, Ronnie," I said, sure the floor was groaning and splitting beneath me like some last chunk of springtime ice in the river. Was Ronnie ready to believe? Had he finally found his proof?

"I don't have to be Catholic to tell secrets," Ronnie said. He drew a deep breath, and then another, and another, and in another moment, he seemed deep asleep.

RONNIE IS NOT CATHOLIC. Nor is he Russian Orthodox. Nor Moravian Protestant. Nor Baptist, nor a member of any of the other churches that crowd vulnerable Bethel. As a result, it was somewhat difficult for me to obtain for him a position as assistant chaplain at the hospice some time ago, but it was certainly easier than getting him a position titled, say, "staff shaman."

It's not that people would have frowned on the term *shaman*. (Or maybe they might have; it's a white man's word, and imprecise the way white men's words are. *Angalkuq* is the Yup'ik term.) Shamans, or *angalkut*, served many functions in times past, but a chief duty was healing, and even the hospital in town incorporates such traditional medicine into its care today.

But people did frown on Ronnie. He was, way back when, an *angalkuq* of some note. Mostly because he was a final, and absolutely unrepentant, holdout against the missionaries. As such, he merited a certain amount of respect, even from those God-fearing Natives who no longer sought his services—so much of the old ways had been lost, but in Ronnie they had a time capsule, a treasury, an unassailable fortress.

Until a tide of alcohol flooded it.

Ronnie's abilities had waned during the war, it was said, maybe before. Some said it happened gradually, some said abruptly. Some said Ronnie had done something, and others said something had been done to him. But every version of the story I heard turned out the same way: the war had brought soldiers; the soldiers, alcohol; and alcohol, for Ronnie at least, brought fleeting glimpses of the ethereal provinces he once visited regularly.

By the time I met him, he lacked both powers and respect. To my shame, I did nothing to help him. I thought an enfeebled foe made my job that much easier. Though Ronnie's various attempts to run me out of Alaska, or out of this world altogether, were occasionally frightening, withstanding them seemed to burnish my reputation in the community.

But eventually, I'd had my fill of respect. And I'd come to like Ronnie—in part, because no one else did. So I went to him. I worked with him, as much as he'd let me.

He should have been long dead by then, and I think he knew this. I say that because I can't think of any other reason why he would have let me help him as much as I tried to. Except for one. I'd suggested a dozen times he enter a treatment program, but he didn't agree until I— or a mischievous God putting words in my mouth—announced that if he stopped drinking, I would as well. I wasn't an alcoholic, but—well, drinking wasn't improving me, either.

In any case, I could see in Ronnie's smile gratitude for someone joining him on the difficult road ahead—and also delight that he had found yet a new way to discomfort me.

We've had a truce, a delicate one, with alcohol ever since. But a strange thing happened when Ronnie sobered up: he had nothing to do. He'd had nothing to do when he was an alcoholic, but being drunk was itself a kind of occupation: you had duties and obligations, like being disorderly, you had an office—in Ronnie's case, a jail cell—where you could reliably be found.

So for the past three or four years, before this most recent set of ailments put him in bed instead of beside one, Ronnie has worked with me at the hospice. I suppose I could have tried to get him a place at the hospital in town, but they were already staffed with Native healers (with far finer reputations than Ronnie's), and besides, I wanted someplace quiet. Out of the way.

Ronnie has insisted that his powers have dimmed to such a degree that he's of little use to anyone, but even I can see that certain patients, certain families, get a measure of peace from our visits. They don't look to Ronnie for a cure any more than they do the hospice. Rather, they just want some sort of assurance that the one who is ill will pass through death and into the next life more easily.

Unfortunately, other families want Lazarus-level care, and this leads to disappointments. I know—I thought we all knew—that sometimes people get better, and sometimes they don't, especially in a hospice, but I guess some people expect more of Ronnie. And so when patients he's visited with die—though they were going to die anyway (we all die)—it counts against Ronnie.

And lately, me. I'd thought my role was innocent enough, just nudging Ronnie into spending his last years more productively, more spiritually, but no. Ronnie visits, a patient dies—a parishioner, no less, albeit one who *always* dozed through Mass—and word spreads around town. Maybe two others outlive their diagnoses for a month or two, but another dies suddenly, maybe another, and maybe to those who haven't stood beside Ronnie and seen the—for lack of a better word— peace he brings, it all adds up wrong.

And so word travels, this wide-open land doing nothing to check its course, and the bishop hears one of his priests is aiding the practice of witchcraft, and an inquiry is made, and another, and these are ignored, and then you are where I am. At the bedside of a shaman, magic having failed both of you, at the mercy of gossips and gods and bishops and ravens.

So I sat with Ronnie for a while, waiting to see if he was faking sleep—or death. But his breathing settled into a quiet rhythm, and when a gentle snoring commenced, I rose to leave.

On the way out, I checked his chart for the DNR. I didn't see it. But something else was written there, two words that sent me back to my seat beside him and kept me there for the rest of the morning.

I WANTED TO CONFESS, too. I go to confession regularly, of course, once a year, at least, whether I need to or not. I usually avail myself of another missionary who's passing through (I prefer the foreign ones, whose faith is always stronger than their English), or I go during one of my visits to Anchorage or Fairbanks. But there, partly out of respect for my brother priests, I confess only what is expected: the petty excesses, errors, failures of daily life. I'm not about to saddle them with all that happened to me, especially during the war. It is enough that I should bear that: I don't want them to suffer with it as well. Wartime transgressions, I figure, will wait for my deathbed, for last rites, when I can cough them out in an unintelligible rattle, be forgiven, and then go on to my reward.

And this is exactly what Ronnie, my brother shaman, was doing. And that's how I realized what I was missing: release, reward. Oh, I'm old enough, have seen enough, that there have been times of late when I've wanted to die—long, dark nights of the soul are nothing new in a land where winter nights can last twenty hours or more. But who could wait, like Ronnie, until the precipice before death to talk? I wanted to tell *my* secrets, now, ones I have held fast for a lifetime. And who would listen? Ronnie.

No, I've not wanted to burden a brother priest with my secrets, but I'd happily burden Ronnie: he's dying, after all; he won't have to suffer me long. As I waited for him to reawaken, I began to draft my speech in my head. But the longer he slept, the longer my confession became. I worried I would never get it all out if I waited for Ronnie to reawaken. So I didn't wait. Instead, in low tones, mumbling to myself, to Ronnie, I started my story.

In the beginning, Ronnie had said, there was Raven, trickster and creator of the Yup'ik world.

My story also began with something that flew.

IT WAS A MOST INGENIOUS device. Leave aside the compliment implicit in *ingenious*—yes, yes, this was 1944–45, they were still the enemy—and for now, simply admire the handiwork, as I did, each time we found one intact.

A four-tier wedding cake, mostly aluminum, two feet tall. The top tier is a plastic box, a little bigger than one you'd use to hold recipes. Inside the box, a liquid solution of 10 percent calcium chloride, which insulates the small, 1.5 volt wet-cell battery, equal in heft to a good-size bar of soap. Two wires emerge from the box: follow them down. One disappears into a larger wooden box, the cake's second tier. This is where they housed the aneroid barometers: three smaller ones, each calibrated to complete an electrical circuit at a specific altitude, and one larger, more sophisticated, barometer that served as the primary control unit for the flight.

Okay, working our way down now, top to bottom, just like you would (and I did) in the field. Nothing explosive yet.

Next: the wooden barometer box is sitting on a large, round Bakelite platter. Innocent enough. But look beneath (or don't; it *was* unnerving, even for me, hurriedly trained in bomb disposal). Dozens of wires, all crisscrossing this way and that, many of them connecting to contacts on the bottom of the Bakelite platter, and still others descending to the cake's two lower tiers, the two round aluminum rings spoked like wagon wheels. I suppose I should be more exact. We're not following wires; these are fuses. Twenty-four inches long. Burning time of two minutes, sixteen seconds. Wired in pairs so that if one fuse failed, the other would finish the job. Smart. While airborne, the barometers set the fuses off during the final descent. On the ground, clumsiness or ignorance did the job equally well.

Bang: it wasn't the fuses you had to worry about, though, not ultimately. But they were connected to little—well, squibs is what we called them, because to call them what they essentially were, firecrackers, made it all sound like fun.

When the firecrackers popped, one of the thirty-two sandbags would drop, and as each one dropped, you got a better view (if you were watching this contraption in flight, but few were that lucky) of what all this fuss was about. Around the circumference of the ring dangled four or more 5-kilogram thermite incendiary bombs, which would explode on impact. And in the middle? In the middle dangled a nasty black 15-kilogram antipersonnel bomb, finned like a torpedo and filled with picric acid or TNT. When these exploded, you'd encounter debris scattered as far as a quarter mile away. And for variety, sometimes you'd discover some strange canister hanging there you didn't recognize at all.

Oh, and the flash bomb—250 grams of magnesium powder that you'd find if you followed the longest fuse—followed it from where it began, beneath that bottom tier, followed it to where it climbed, up, up, sixty-four feet, where it burrowed like a canker into the side of those magical balloons.

That's what they were, balloons.

Who wouldn't be curious coming upon one in a field, beside a road, among trees? Even deflated, flat on the forest floor like it was melting away, wouldn't you marvel at it? Thirty-two feet in diameter, one hundred feet in circumference, and the whole of it, most incredibly, paper, made from mulberry trees or rice, *washi* paper. Each balloon required forty to sixty paper panels, and each panel was painstakingly made by hand, in thousands of homes across Japan. Each household produced their share, then handed it up the line to authorities who handed it up to factories (in one case, a converted opera house), where women and children—girls, all who were left then, and who were found to be more skilled than the boys anyway—joined the panels with glue made from a potato-like vegetable. (The vegetable: *konnyaku,* "devil's tongue," quite edible, quite Japanese; to reply in kind, we'd have had to caulk our bombs with apple pie. In any case, with food growing scarce in war-winnowed Japan, workers began eating what glue they didn't use, and then, whatever glue they could find.)

A balloon of paper and potato glue, a wedding cake of firecrackers and aluminum. Designed to silently ride the winds across the Pacific, barometers triggering ballast drops when necessary, and then, finally, descend into the impregnable United States mainland, setting forest fires, killing soldiers, civilians.

Ingenious. Yes, I'll use the word. Considering that any one balloon, landing in the right spot, or even a wrong spot, could do an incredible amount of damage.

But the Japanese didn't just send one balloon. Over the course of a few months, beginning in the fall of 1944 and ending in the spring of 1945, they launched close to ten thousand bomb-laden balloons, an effort which, by its end, had required the concerted effort of millions of people.

I'm not sure what the word for that is.

Years after the war, I was on a retreat with a German Jesuit who had been in Japan when the atomic bombs were dropped. One night at dinner, it came up that I had been a soldier in the war. He fixed me with a stare, and then asked me a question he'd obviously been asking Americans ever since V-J Day. "Why?" he said. I knew better than to answer, but then he asked another question. "Why two?"

Why ten thousand?

But I didn't say it.

And in the end, of course, he was right. You only needed one, be it atomic bomb or balloon.

One balloon could halt the development of the atomic bomb, in fact.

And one did, temporarily, on April Fool's Day, 1945, knocking down power lines that led to the Hanford, Washington, atomic energy plant, which was producing materials for the bombs that would later be dropped on Japan.

Or—

One balloon could result in the only World War II civilian casualties due to enemy action on mainland U.S. soil.

And one did, on May 6, 1945, in an Oregon forest, where it intrigued children on a church outing. It exploded, killing all five, plus a young woman, pregnant, who'd been watching over them, while her husband, the reverend, was parking the car.

Or—

One balloon could carry a small life from one world to another.

It is this last balloon that carried me into this life, into this hospice, to this bedside, this mumbled confession.

Or it was all ten thousand.

It's simply a question of what you believe, or what proof you have, and I might have asked Ronnie what he believed, but I didn't; he was sleeping. So for a response, I was left with words scribbled in bold at the top of his chart, proof of Ronnie's wishes, words Ronnie thought would help ensure he said all he needed to say.

"NO MORPHINE."

CHAPTER 2

IT'S STILL WEDNESDAY. I'M STILL IN THE HOSPICE. IT'S NOT clear where Ronnie is. He's lying on the bed, same as he was. But with his eyes closed, his breath a series of uneven sighs, it's clear he's somewhere else. Not gone, but going.

I hadn't gotten too far into my monologue when Ronnie's nurse, a new one, came by. I had grown accustomed to the silence of Ronnie's room, how the light that bled through the shades made things more silent, and then this nurse came in, unable to stop talking.

Within five minutes, I had heard her life story, up to and including that very moment. She worked for a company called TravelNurse; the company sent nurses around the country, even the world, helping facilities fill gaps.

Fortunately, nothing about her monologue required a reply, or even much of a reaction, so I sat mute, my thoughts gone to fuzz while she talked. As she left, though, she suddenly turned.

"You can hold his hand, you know," she said. "Sometimes, when patients—sorry, loved ones—are too tired to talk, or even listen, you can, well, *communicate* with them just by holding their hand." I watched as she lightly picked up Ronnie's hand. He did not awaken for the demonstration. "It's easy," she said. "Well, maybe not for men." She smiled. I smiled. And then she laid Ronnie's hand back down, paused a moment, and left.

"Ronnie," I said, sure he was awake now.

But if he was, he made no sign of it. I settled back in my chair, but then a sound at the door made me start. It was just the nurse, checking to see if we were holding hands. We exchanged a smile again, both of us trying to out-pity or -patronize the other, and then I adjusted my chair so that I could better see the hallway. It wasn't the nurse's return I feared; I'd become jumpy at the thought that those coming for me would arrive two days early, and find me at the scene of the crime.

THE FIRST TIME Ronnie and I raised someone from the dead, it probably wasn't worth the effort.

Fats Haugen was about to achieve what his behavior suggested he'd always sought—death by drink. There were those of us who wished him well in his quest. A Virginia native whose first name was made even worse by the fact that he'd chosen it for himself, he'd come to Bethel in the 1950s, taken a Yup'ik bride, Mary, and acted wretchedly— especially to her—ever since.

But Mary was a saint. And beautiful. And it was because of her that I often attempted to reach out to her husband, to get him counseling, treatment, time, space—whatever he needed to return to humanness. Mary said he was Catholic; I urged him to come to confession. I'm always amazed what sort of healing confession can get started. But he spat it all back at me, sometimes literally. Mary came to confession instead, weekly, I think as a way to compensate for him, but she had to struggle to come up with any sins worth confessing. Instead of penance, I would sometimes send her forth to go kick a dog—and tell her not to come back to confession until she had.

But she never could or would, and so I loved her dearly and knew I would do anything for her. That's why, when she knocked at the rectory door late one night, eyes full of tears, and asked if I would come and "pray over" her husband in the hospice, I did not hesitate. And when she asked, mumbling, eyes averted, if Ronnie might come along, too, I still did not refuse. I loved her this much. I could have said "Ronnie who?" or "What are you talking about?" or "The rumors you've heard about Ronnie and me calling on pagan spirits to heal people aren't true," but I did not.

Which is how we came to find ourselves holding hands, Ronnie and I, and Fats and Mary, the door closed, lights dimmed, and Ronnie breathing an ancient chant in an ancient language, almost below hearing.

No, it isn't easy for men to hold hands. Fats squirmed, though he hardly seemed to have the strength to. I felt anxious, too, watching Mary divide her desperate looks between me and the door, where I'm sure she thought the devil would appear.

I prayed for Fats, but I must also admit that I prayed for Mary, for Ronnie, and most of all for me, because I knew what I was doing would get me in trouble eventually. Praying with someone in the hospice is one thing; laying on hands is another—though it has a long and honest Christian tradition behind it. But joining hands, participating in a rite that, Ronnie assured me, was all about Native spirits and had nothing to do with "*your* god"—well, this wasn't exactly what generations of missionaries before me had preached, prayed, and died for.

And then it happened. Fats stopped squirming; his eyes shut and his mouth opened, releasing a low moan.

"Tell me how he died," Ronnie has asked. Well, I would have thought it went like this. I have visited the dying for many years, I have administered last rites many times. I know what last moments look like. Fats was in the midst of his. But something happened.

Mary cried out: "Frank!" A perfectly lovely name.

"Come," said Ronnie quietly.

I checked the monitors. Ronnie was always in charge of whatever magic occurred. I took responsibility for the constellation of blinking red lights surrounding the patient. Fats's blood pressure was incredibly low, but climbing.

Ronnie repeated his instruction. Fats moaned again, a little louder. Then Ronnie looked at me and rolled his eyes, ever so slightly. "It's not going to work," he whispered. "He's not here."

"Who's not here?" asked Mary. Fats moaned once more, soft again.

"No one—" I started.

"My *tuunraq*," said Ronnie, quite nonchalant now, as though he were referring to his attorney and not his favored spirit helper, his animal familiar—a wolf, in fact, whose capricious absence Ronnie had been lamenting for some time. It was the *tuunraq*'s job to enter the patient and clear out whatever was bad—a bit like spiritual angioplasty.

"Father!" Mary hissed, letting go of our hands. I nodded Ronnie out of the room, and turned to Fats.

He'd stopped moaning, which wasn't too much of a surprise. While Ronnie wasn't always able to bring on a cure, his touch—the lights—the chanting—could all have a disproportionate effect on the susceptible mind.

When Fats opened his eyes, I paused. And then I made the sign of the cross and Mary followed suit, and then, much to our joint surprise, Fats did as well. "Pray with me, Fats—Frank," I said, not because he would, but because I knew it was Mary's heart rate we then needed to ease. I began a Hail Mary. And then Fats, God bless him, was finally moved to speak.

"Father," he said, "I want to confess...."

And that, to me, was magic.

I SAT THERE AFTER she left, Ronnie's TravelNurse, and stared at my own hands. And when the memories of what they had touched, held, let slip, grew unwieldy, I turned to Ronnie.

I stared at Ronnie's hands for a minute, small and muscular, the knuckles cracked white. Then I picked up the one closest to me, and held it, lightly, like the nurse had. And when he didn't reply with a whisper or *hoo* or squeeze or tap, I smiled again; he was sleeping soundly. Time for me to leave.

After a bit, I squeezed his hand to let him know I was going.

Nothing. I stood, drawing the hand up with me. I squeezed harder. And listened.

Nothing. Something was wrong.

With my free hand, I went for his shoulder; I kept clutching his dead hand with mine. He'd become his own, life-sized voodoo doll. I called out his name, louder and louder, and then I called for the nurse, and then I called for God, and then I called for goddamned Steven Gottschalk.

BEFORE THIS MORNING, I could not have told you what Ronnie's hand felt like—I could have imagined it, perhaps, but that would have been a feat of imagination, imagination driven by what visual details my mind retains. But Steven Gottschalk's hand, I remember every fiber of it, every whorl, and every second it took me to realize that what I'd found there on the ground was not a pink-black glove but a human hand.

It was our last week of bomb disposal school at Aberdeen Proving Ground, just inland from the Chesapeake Bay in Maryland, and I was holding Steven Gottschalk's hand. The rest of him had just been rushed back to the base hospital, though he would die before he arrived. Those of us who remained had been told to fan out over the frag—fragmentation—zone. We were looking for parts of the bomb he'd been working on. I didn't even know what I'd found until I bent down, and even then, it was a moment or two before the recognition took hold and I began to retch.

I was unprepared, in every respect. We didn't train with live ordnance; but in this case, a truck accident had left a bomb in a precarious spot on base, and Gottschalk, an instructor, saw this as a valuable teaching opportunity. He positioned us someplace nearby but safe, and then went to work. Later, they told us that that was how he had wanted to go, but I didn't believe it. No one wants to go like that, and Gottschalk had told us in the classroom how he had once dreamed of becoming a pilot. When that hadn't worked out, he decided to give bomb disposal a chance.

My career path was more direct. I'd earned my way into explosives training. In part because I was book-smart and good with diagrams, but more because I scored the absolute lowest—of any recruit, ever, I was told—in marksmanship. As one sergeant put it, me with a gun in my hand was a bomb waiting to go off—so why not volunteer to go to school where I could learn to prevent similar explosions?

I did learn. Quickly. And I became consumed with strange, twin desires. One, to prove myself so expert that those who once laughed at me would feel ashamed that they ever had. And two, to edge as close to death as I could as often as I could, with the faint, teenaged hope that I might just die—and those who had once laughed at me would feel even worse.

My drive was mistaken for talent and my recklessness for courage, and the result was that I was promoted rapidly (not such a feat, sadly, in bomb disposal, where sudden openings were frequent). I made sergeant in just a matter of months. But by then, my war—with those who had laughed—was over. My zeal went away with Steven Gottschalk's hand, just as surely as if he had reached inside me and pulled it out himself. But it was too late; my course was set. I finished training and received orders for the South Pacific.

As I was processing through the Fourth Air Force headquarters in San Francisco, however, an officer decided that I should "make the most" of my "layover" by undergoing some additional training across the Golden Gate, where the army had established a network of coastal artillery batteries and a small garrison, Fort Cronkhite.

Fort Cronkhite was an unusual place. Designed to help repel an invasion, it often looked as though it were being invaded. Soldiers in training regularly stormed the small cove where the fort was located, taking the wide stony beach and then working their way up the ravine behind, picking their way around the fort's tidy collection of red-roofed, white-clapboard buildings. Beyond the buildings, the slope climbed sharply into the Marin Headlands, grassy hills that formed that part of the continent's final defense against the Pacific Ocean. From a distance, it looked as though the Headlands ran parallel to the shoreline in a long, smooth ridge, but up close, what looked like innocent folds in the earth's fabric turned out to be countless ravines, great and small.

Viewed from the ridgetop gun emplacements, the fort resembled a California-style summer camp—broad, meadowed hillsides gone gold for lack of rain, the ocean beyond making a slow, vain, glittering entrance late each morning as the fog burned off.

Instead of training, I was given the duty of inspecting the gun batteries' concrete bunkers. They were fitted with clumsy booby traps, designed to explode if the positions were ever overrun. After the first day, I'd determined they were more likely to kill our boys—I was surprised, in fact, that they hadn't already. The colonel leading me around was so proud of the setup, however, that I knew I couldn't be candid. So, while he waited outside each bunker gloating, I went in and did my "inspections," which I performed by quickly and permanently disarming each device.

I was staring at my handiwork in the last bunker, trying not to think of Steven Gottschalk, when I heard shouts. I ducked back out and, blinking rapidly, tried to figure out why a piece of the afternoon sky had torn loose and was floating toward us.

"Stand by to fire!" screamed the colonel, but it was a moment before anyone moved. It looked like a balloon, and it swung toward us like a hypnotist's watch, an ordinary thing working some extraordinary magic. Once I separated it from the sun, I realized that it was a balloon, an unusual one, thirty or so feet in diameter, and slender. It was more than slender, actually: it looked starved and weak, a dirty gray. The bottom half of the balloon was partially deflated; a quick glance would mistake it for a parachute. But down beneath, where you'd expect some person to dangle, hung instead a kind of crate that hardly seemed worth the balloon's trouble.

"Weather balloon, sir?" asked another sergeant, squinting. "I dunno, I heard some guys down in Monterey got in some awful kind of trouble for shooting down a—"

"Stand by to fire!" the colonel shrieked, his voice getting higher instead of louder. The sergeant backed up a step, and then skipped into a slow trot toward his bunker.

But the colonel wouldn't issue the order to fire; he just stood there, same as me, and stared the balloon all the way down to the ground. I think we didn't move because it was so quiet: except for the moon, there's nothing in life that big that ever moved so quietly. Even a sailboat makes a sound—the sails, the rigging, the water roiling past. But these balloons, six or seven stories tall, sailed silently. The only sound they made was when they landed, as this one soon did. Its payload scraped into a fold in the hill a few hundred yards off, and for a moment, the balloon floated there, stuck.

"Stand down," said the colonel. I looked down the hill and saw that some curious soldiers were already climbing toward it. The colonel summoned a pair of binoculars and studied the balloon for a while, until a gust of wind came. The balloon popped free, dragged itself and its cargo a few yards up the hill, and then gave up once more. The colonel handed me the glasses, which I thought generous until I realized he simply didn't want to hold them anymore.

"What the hell can a balloon tell you about weather, Sergeant?" he asked, still staring after it.

"I don't know, sir," I mumbled, adjusting the focus. Finally, I found the curious soldiers. I scanned up the hill ahead of them, along the path the balloon had torn through the grass and brush, until I reached the balloon itself.

Something had pierced the envelope, and the balloon now lay on its side, seemingly gasping, as if it had beached itself.

"Look like rain?" the colonel asked, and answered himself by laughing once. "Sunny and seventy through the weekend?" he added, checking his watch. "Weather. Five bucks says this is a Navy toy."

I held my breath as I followed the balloon's shroud down to its payload. I'd never seen a hot-air balloon other than in photographs, and if anything, this balloon looked more incredible on the ground than in the air. The soldiers were almost upon it now, and I frowned, realizing that they would soon obstruct my view.

That's when I saw the fuse.

And then another, and another. And then a whole tangle of them came into view as I studied the payload more closely, and realized that each was a carefully wired charge—

"It's-a-bomb-sir," I said. I couldn't be sure—the soldiers were in the way now, milling about, but—it had to be. I'd never seen a weather balloon, but I'd seen plenty of bombs in the classroom, and they—

"Sergeant?" the colonel asked, as if I'd reported sighting a seagull.

"A bomb, a bomb, a bomb," I said, the words tumbling out so rapidly, it felt as though they were causing me to fall forward—and then I was—falling, running down the hillside toward the balloon.

I hadn't saved Gottschalk, hadn't even had a chance to.

As I ran, I stumbled, the binoculars caught me in the jaw; I tore them off and threw them away, yelling all the while. Behind me, the colonel must have been yelling, too, but I don't remember that. I only remember thinking, for a split second, that I had indeed fooled time, and that I was the only one moving. The soldiers, the bomb-laden balloon, the colonel—everyone was still, awaiting my intercession.

The first blast—just the noise, not the force—sent me to the ground. When I got up, I saw flames, and heard screams so fierce it was like I could see the sound. I began running even faster until I heard the second blast, tripped again, and lying there, finally realized I was too late.

One of the balloon's incendiaries must have detonated. It was later determined that the first blast had only wounded one or two of the soldiers, but the fire ended up claiming them all. The fire would have caught up with me as well, except that within a minute or so more of scrambling toward the crash, I was stopped by a steep, sharp ravine that had been invisible when I first started out. I picked my way down into it, but then discovered I couldn't climb the other side. Eventually, I had to follow the ravine all the way down to the beachhead, watching the smoke billow just above me, out of reach.

ANOTHER RAVINE, on the far side of the crash site, and a fire road—a hopeful name for a swath of bare earth—did more to contain the blaze than anything else. By the time they had figured out a way to pump water up the hillside, the fire was mostly out. That night, the bodies of the soldiers were recovered, and around midnight, a pair of military policemen pulled me from my bunk and drove me as far up the hillside as their jeep would take us.

They delivered me into the care of the colonel. Earlier in the day, during the cleanup, I'd offered my services but had been rebuffed. I wasn't sure if the colonel had summoned me now for apologies or blame.

"Turns out we lost two of *our* three bomb disposal guys in the fire," he said. "Third's on leave. So we've got you." He jerked his head up the hill, where gas-powered floodlights illuminated a still-smoking black field. Now I would say that it looked like lava, but back then, I'd never seen hot lava, not even pictures. Back then, it looked like what it was—scorched earth, a little piece of hell. "What happened?" he asked.

"Sir," I said, looking up the hill, "I'm guessing it was some kind of incendiary—"

"That's pretty fucking brilliant, Sergeant. What was your clue? The six-acre brush fire?"

Another jeep, and then another, arrived.

"Wait here," the colonel said, and I did, because it looked for all the world like aliens were stepping out of the jeeps. Six men in silver flash-suits and gas masks finished zipping up, checking gear. I'd seen fire-retardant clothing during my bomb disposal training—but nothing like these outfits, this late at night, lit by lights high on a hill.

"Who's in charge here?" said the only one of them not suited in silver.

"I am," said the colonel.

"You were," said the man, a captain, closing the distance. "We'll take it from here."

"I lost five men," the colonel said. "Is this your goddamn weather balloon?"

The captain nodded his men up the hill, and they began a surprisingly rapid ascent. Then he turned back to us. "It's mine now."

"Whose was it? Where did it come from? Why wasn't I alerted?" the colonel asked.

"That," the captain said, "is confidential." That clearly wasn't good enough for the colonel, but before the colonel could blurt out another question, the captain looked at me and asked, "Who's this?"

The colonel drew himself up. "This asshole, supposedly a bomb man, was the first to figure out that the balloon was booby-trapped."

"Bomb disposal?" the captain said, peering through the dark. "What's your name?"

"He was a little damn slow," the colonel said. "A few minutes earlier, he could have saved some lives."

I looked at the captain: "Belk, sir."

The captain barked a little laugh. "You don't say? Sergeant Louis A. Belk?" I nodded. "How do you like that? You're mine, too. Wait for me in the jeep."

I was glad to leave the colonel to him, and watched from a distance as the two officers argued. Finally, the colonel offered up a bit of a smile, and the two of them walked over.

The colonel regarded me, savored, and smirked. "You poor sap," he said. "Whose ass did you forget to kiss?"

I looked to the captain. He looked at the colonel and then at me. "I am carrying orders to remove you from Camp Sunshine here, immediately, and deliver you to Elmendorf Field, Fort Richardson, Alaska," he said, and then hiked up the hill toward his men.

"*Alaska,*" the colonel repeated, very pleased.

I watched the captain exchange words with his men, who now had their masks off. Then he walked back toward us and climbed into the jeep.

"Bon voyage," the colonel said to me.

"I'd keep clear of the area," the captain said. "Just in case." We all looked back up the hill, where the men now had their masks back on. The jeep sputtered to life and the captain steered us down the track he'd come up.

Hands on hips, feet apart, the colonel watched us drive away. I stared back at him for as long as I could, until I couldn't be sure if I was seeing or imagining him.

WHAT NEITHER THE colonel nor I knew at the time was that one of the most closely guarded secrets of World War II had exploded right in front of us.

The Japanese were bombing mainland North America. And the attack was far more widespread, and had gone on much longer, than the infamous raid on Pearl Harbor. In many ways, it was much more audacious. Certainly the censorship campaign that surrounded the bombing campaign was audacious: American authorities ordered nothing be reported. In the months to come, I would learn a little more, but only a little. The complete history—such as it is—I have come to learn only over the course of many years.

In mid-1944—not long after I enlisted, as it happens—a Navy ship made a curious discovery just off the coast of Southern California. The lookout first reported a downed pilot; what he could see through his binoculars had all the looks of a parachute. But there had been no word of any sorties being flown in their sector that day, and certainly no word of any mishaps. Upon drawing closer, the ship found no evidence of a pilot or plane, and when the material was hauled on board, it appeared to be a large hot-air balloon of rubberized silk. Instead of a basket, it contained a peculiar sort of crate, to which were affixed various instruments. One of the communications officers said it looked like a weather balloon. Thus mollified, the ship's captain brought the balloon and its crate home, where it was packed off to a warehouse in Long Beach. Word was sent to the weather bureau to come collect their fallen star.

The bureau had yet to reply when the authorities learned of an explosion outside Thermopolis, Wyoming (I'm fuzzy on some details, but not that one; my Alaskan missionary mind refuses to forget such a warm-sounding place). Residents had seen what appeared to be a parachute, rocketing toward earth with fatal speed. Shortly after came a tremendous explosion, and bright flames of a bizarre red hue leapt in answer to the sound. The next morning, locals set out to discover what had happened, and there, fifteen miles northwest of town, they came upon a great crater littered with shrapnel. There was talk of comets and flying saucers. The police notified the military.

Not long after, the Fourth Air Force, responsible for the air defense of the western United States, learned of a gigantic paper balloon that had crashed outside Kalispell, Montana. Its construction, though elaborately conceived, was somewhat makeshift, and authorities initially believed it had been assembled and launched from a nearby German prisoner-of-war camp or one of the Japanese internment camps.

But within the next few weeks, dozens more balloons were sighted. Some as far north as Saskatchewan and others just south of Santa Barbara. And while evidence of some of the early landings had disappeared in explosions, more balloons began to be recovered intact. (One western sheriff bravely, or comically, leapt after a balloon's trailing line as it neared the ground; it bounced and dragged him across the desert for several miles before he finally managed to stop and anchor it.)

The balloons found intact dispelled much of the mystery that had initially surrounded them. Since the Japanese had assumed any evidence of the balloon weapon would be destroyed in an explosion, they had done little to mask the weapon's source: serial numbers and other designations, written in Japanese, were printed directly on the balloon. Further evidence was found in the sandbags that served as ballast: government geologists determined the sand used was particular to the east coast of Japan's mainland, or largest island, Honshu.

Slowly, it became clear what was happening. Japan had developed and was deploying the world's first intercontinental warheads. And so far, America's defense consisted of tall trees and wide-open spaces.

CHAPTER 3

WE WERE IN THE AIR BEFORE SUNRISE, THE CAPTAIN, HIS men, their prize, and me all onboard a C-47 bound north. We refueled at first light in Seattle, and then started up to Anchorage. What takes three hours today took nine back then—or more, depending on whether the pilot had ever flown to Alaska before.

I wish the trip had lasted even longer. Three hours, nine hours— one hundred hours probably wouldn't be enough transition time from the Outside world to Alaska. But these are the illusions planes perpetuate: the intimacy of great distances, the seeming absence of life below, and worst of all, the notion that by flying over the land, you have somehow conquered it. I rely on planes now; we all do. But there is an aspect to them that I hate, and it is the distance they put between you and the ground. The view, of course, is gorgeous, but it is completely sanitized, static beyond the glass, sometimes hidden beneath clouds. It allows you to think of Alaska the way the rest of the world does, a gigantic, postcard-perfect park, its mountains and trees and glaciers, however distant, reassuringly reachable and safe.

I still remember that first trip, how strangely soft everything below looked, the towering peaks buried in snow and clouds. I would have stayed at the window the entire time, but the captain called me forward to hear my explanation of how I'd ended up at Fort Cronkhite. He offered no explanations of his own in return, other than to say that my leave had been canceled. He said I'd find out what I needed to know soon enough—both about my posting and our odd cargo. I asked if I could take a look at the wreckage stowed in the cargo bay, and for a moment, he looked ready to agree, but then shook his head and told me to catch some sleep. I went to my jump seat and closed my eyes, but all I could see was that balloon, floating there, closer and closer, bigger and bigger. I wanted to reach out and touch it, but I couldn't, even while dreaming. I finally fell back, frustrated, and let the balloon hang there in my mind, my arm lifted, hand outstretched.

WHAT I CAUGHT, instead, was a message delivered to me directly by the empire of Japan.

I'd gone downtown into Anchorage after we landed, and was standing on Fourth Avenue, screwing up my courage to enter a bar. I had plenty of choices. A low-flying plane buzzed overhead. No one looked up; enough planes were flying in and out of Elmendorf Field those days that the skies above were noisier than the streets below. But then we heard the rumble of antiaircraft guns, the whine of more planes. While my fellow passersby dove for the sidewalk—or the safety of a bar entrance—I stood there, stupidly, staring up, watching the sky fall.

The plane had dropped a barrage of leaflets, printed on very thin, rose-colored paper. For a few minutes, the air was full of them, thousands of slips dancing between those of us still standing, as though human speech had hardened with the chill and become visible.

SSURRenndderr, it began, and I remember the spelling very specifically, because it seemed like the writer was drunk—or that it had been written for drunks, in which case, it had found its target on Fourth Avenue. As other people bent to pick up the slips, I tried sounding out the word as it was written, but my efforts were drowned out by a tremendous explosion. I dropped.

It has always surprised people, especially later in life, that I am so skittish at the sound of an explosion—they think ice-cold stoicism was the first thing they'd teach someone defusing bombs. But the truth is just the opposite. You were trained to be afraid, to be cautious, to move slowly, and if you sensed a boom, to flatten yourself before the blast did. I wouldn't be surprised if they taught things differently now, but back then, we weren't really learning how to defuse bombs. In some cases, it didn't matter if we made mistakes or not—either way, the bomb would disappear. Whether or not we went with it was up to us.

The end of the message was more curious, just three words: *WOMAN! FAMILIES! FARMS!!!* It summoned up some kidlike frustration in me: I wanted to know what they were saying. Surrender, yes, but what about this last bit? Why one woman? Whose families? What farms?

I stayed down on the ground, even as I heard other folks getting up. I guess I was instinctively waiting for the all-clear signal from training days, and once I came to my senses, I slowly dusted myself off. When I heard nothing but voices, and in the distance, some sirens, I realized they'd gotten the plane. They'd shot him down, or perhaps he'd crashed—one of those then-bizarre "kamikaze dives" we'd heard happened much farther south in the Pacific theater. I read my slip again, said the word aloud, softly, felt my tongue flicker like a snake's: "SSURRenndderr." I wasn't much of a soldier. Just hearing the word—hearing me say it—made me shiver slightly.

Most other folks were laughing and yelling. One of the bar owners had burst onto the street shouting that he would honor the slips as coupons, each worth a penny before 5 P.M. Another door to another bar popped open with shouts of a better offer. Soon enough, the streets of Anchorage were overcome with the sort of riot that the pilot, gone to his glory, had intended.

* * *

I USED TO JOKE—I suppose you could call it joking—that the kamikaze pilot represented the whole of my Alaskan welcoming committee. He certainly did better than the Army, which did its best to ignore me during my first weeks above the sixtieth parallel, to such a degree that I eventually had wandered downtown in time for the kamikaze pilot.

For the rest of September and the first part of October 1944, I reported each morning at Fort Richardson to a Building 100, where I was supposed to receive my new orders. But each day I was told the captain I'd been assigned to was away, and I was dispatched to some service detail in his absence—unloading supplies, setting up tents, even directing traffic. Or I was simply sent back to the barracks. But I didn't like spending time there, since the barracks I'd been assigned was nothing more than a giant tent, half the length of a football field. It was dark and damp and had an odd smell that one of the guys said was mustard gas and another said was formaldehyde.

Of course, avoiding the barracks had put me downtown during the leaflet drop. I was a good Catholic boy and thus ascribed little to chance; God was obviously displeased I'd gone to Fourth Avenue, what with all its temptations. So when the next free block of time presented itself, I stayed on base. To prove to God I was starting anew, I even sought out the chapel.

Inside, I discovered just how upset with me God was.

"You're late, Sergeant!" Father Pabich barked when I entered. Tall, bearlike, and every inch the longshoreman he once was, Father Pabich, I came to discover, had a vigorous faith. He mostly saw me for what I was—a kid, scared and vulnerable and misplaced—and decided to do what he could.

"Sir," I said, lurching forward.

"*Father*," he said.

"Father, I—" I looked at my watch. "Late for what?"

"For Mass," he said, and walked back through the door he'd just come out of. He returned pushing a small cart and wearing a stole.

"You'll serve," he said. He looked at my name strip. "Belk?" he asked. "You're not a Jew, are you?"

I shook my head. "Catholic."

"There's no rabbi here," he said. "Shot down. Aleutians. No other rabbi for a thousand miles," he added, ducking below the cart, and slapping whatever he found there on top: a candle, a napkin, a breviary. "Don't light the candle," he said, and then darted back through the door. I stood there, trying to decide whether I could leave. But before I did, Father Pabich had reappeared, hands folded. He pointed me to my place with his chin and began the Latin. I didn't look up until it was my time to chime in. When I did, his voice paused as he evaluated my response, and then rolled on. At communion, he filled the chalice with wine, almost to the brim, and drank down half of it. Then he saw me out of the corner of his eye, and held the chalice out to me. I took a sip and handed it back. He looked inside and handed it back to me. I took another sip. He grabbed it back out of my hands and drank down the rest.

When Mass was finished, he told me to stay, and then rolled the altar cart back inside. He reemerged without the stole, carrying a package of cigarettes. He shook one out, looked at it a moment, and then lit it. I'd already prepared an answer for when he offered me one, but he never did. Instead, he sat there, studying me, until something over my shoulder caught his eye. He stood up.

"Too late!" he said. A couple of blond, young—very young—soldiers looked up at him, confused. "We're closed!" he said. They didn't move, so he stood. "I'm hearing a goddamn confession!" The two backed out. He sat down again. "So?" he said. I started to say something, but he held up his hand, took a long drag. He took the cigarette out of his mouth. "Your name was—" He squinted. "Bell? Belk."

"Father?"

"Mass is every God-granted morning at 0555." He looked at his watch. "It's now 1400."

"I wasn't even looking to—I didn't even know." I looked down.

"What are you doing here?" he asked.

"I was going to take—I was going to—pray."

He looked at my insignia. "Bomb disposal?" I nodded. "I think we'd all feel safer knowing you weren't relying on *prayer.*"

I looked away and said nothing.

"Oh, Lord," he said. "I understand now. Sergeant from the bomb disposal unit, in chapel alone, midafternoon. You want out."

"No, sir—"

"That's right, the answer is no."

"Father?"

"Every week, I get a nervous nellie in here, decides he doesn't like the way war smells, wants to transfer to the chaplaincy corps, or worse. They look like—they look like you, Belk. And here's what I tell them: no."

"I don't want—I wasn't looking for a transfer."

"You're not getting one, you especially." He paused. "Bomb disposal," he said, and shook his head. "Well, that's your lot, son: you're a kid, at war, in Alaska, the back shelf of the devil's own icebox, and you've been told to run after bombs the rest of us are told to run from. It ain't fair, but neither was the cross." He looked at me. "You want to know what's not fair? Three times, Belk, last week, I get on a plane, fly out to some god-awful piece of frozen waste, and say last rites for a guy who'd gotten blown up by a mine or a bomb. Two of those bombs were ours, by the way. One, Jap."

I waited.

"I couldn't do a damn thing for those boys, other than try to get them into something like a state of grace before they made a run at heaven. Jesus, Mary, and Joseph." He paused to shake out another cigarette and light it off the one he had. "Pray for us," he finished. "This army doesn't need any more damn priests saving souls, Belk. We need somebody who can save lives."

"Yes, Father," I said.

He waved this away. "Or take some lives," he said, hunching forward. "Then you come to me, Belk," he went on. "You shoot a few of those bastards for me." He stood. "Then we'll see if you want to be— or can be—a priest." I stood as well, thinking I was supposed to leave, but instead, he talked for another twenty minutes.

Anchorage, apparently, was a frozen Gomorrah, and Father Pabich was worried about me. Not so much that I'd damage my potential as a priest, but more that I'd "fall into the sins of distraction." And Anchorage offered many: bars, women, men—and, Father Pabich said, "magicians."

"I'm not much for magic, Father," I said.

"I don't mean card tricks," he said, "although you'd be wise to give cards a wide berth, too. I mean people who don't trust the way of God, people who see spirits, people who worship idols. Masons, Republicans, or strike-breaking Pinkerton men—you know who I'm talking about. Magicians: I'm trying to make it simple for you. People who put their faith in something other than God." He looked at me carefully. "Listen: people say God's got a lot of work still to do up here," he said. "I say, *we've* got work to do. Right?" I nodded. "Go in peace, son," he said. "Just don't go too far."

MAGICIANS: SUDDENLY, I wasn't worried so much about doing evil. There were plenty of others here doing it for me, and what's more, it sounded pretty damn interesting. Rather than striking fear in me, Father Pabich gave me a kind of fearlessness. As a stand-in for God, Father Pabich was of the roaring, Old Testament variety, but the cigarettes and swearing made me realize that, just like everything else, God operated under different rules in the Alaskan army.

Which is a long way of saying that I went straight back downtown.

But after Father's hype, downtown was actually something of a disappointment. Magicians: maybe I'd expected I'd walk down the street and be in the midst of a circus parade. But it looked a lot more like scout camp. Mountains all around, loud voices, uniforms, dirty faces, and everywhere, mud and muck. No girls.

Scout camp isn't so far from the truth, I suppose. Alaska was still a territory then, not a state, and Anchorage was more outpost than town, its civic boosters' and newspapers' claims to the contrary. Downtown, such as it was, looked like a city for a few blocks, but soon enough, paved streets gave way to gravel and, inevitably, mud. Much of it looked like it had been built by a film crew for a B-grade western—sagging wooden facades, peeling paint promising goods and services from another era. A source of great pride was the city's Federal Building, which housed the court and post office. It showed up on more than one postcard, looking quite formal and impressive, if a bit small—it helped that the various ramshackle buildings nearby were always cropped out of the picture.

Any magicians had been cropped out as well; from my walks around town, I determined that Anchorage's population consisted entirely of men and dogs, the dogs more likely to be sober. That's probably because dogs couldn't read the paper, where they'd find ads like the one I spotted that afternoon for the Big Dipper Liquor Store (conveniently located next door to the Big Dipper Bar). The type must have been four or five inches tall: "1 CENT SALE. GIN—RUM—BRANDY. Buy a Bottle at OPA Prices—Have Another for One Cent."

But it was a much smaller ad, in tiny type, that intrigued me. In the midst of the classifieds, which consisted largely of desperately worded ads seeking housing, appeared a section called "Personal Services." Here were found notices for professions that Alaska did not seem to need—professional tailoring, pet grooming, even a phrenologist. But, then: "Lily reads palms and tells fortunes in the Starhope Building, room 219, most days, 5–7. Careful and correct."

So I went. Of course I went. Out of curiosity, and out of respect to

Father Pabich, who I suspected would be disappointed if I didn't get in some kind of trouble downtown. And out of respect to a bomb disposal sergeant I'd trained under, whose three favorite words were *careful and correct*. It would be interesting to meet a woman who adhered to the sergeant's philosophy.

"First," she said. "The rules."

I had climbed the stairs of the Starhope, less sure with each step. Debris—paper, sand, bits of construction material—was scattered everywhere, as though the building were in the process of going up or coming down. The sounds of the street faded, the muffled din and occasional shouts now sounding like a far-off party that I'd been left out of.

I'd expected many doors—or at least nineteen—on the second floor, but found only three. One, missing a door, opened into a darkened office. More trash. The third door was locked. A smoked glass window gave no clue as to what lay behind it. The door to 219 was ajar. A bare bulb burned inside.

"No yelling. No laughing. No spitting. No taking your clothes off. No stupid questions." That all seemed easy enough, if odd. The only difficult rule was the last one: once my eyes adjusted, all I had were questions.

Lily—I assumed—stood beside the room's one window, which overlooked the street. My first question was whether this really was the Lily from the ad—the palm reader. I had no idea what a palm reader looked like, but I suppose I thought of them as being older, heavier, maybe wearing some strange getup. Lily was none of that, or rather, she was her own strange getup. She was tall, tall as I, and when she stepped closer, taller. She had long straight black hair, black eyes that didn't reflect, a wide, flat face, and—well, which of the most striking facts should I mention first? The one that surprised me more then, or the one that surprises me more now?

Let me share the one that surprised me then, since that does more to explain the mix of idiocy and naïveté that I was in those days: Lily—

was the enemy. It only took a single glance—at her face—to tell me this. Me, who had never exchanged a word with a Japanese citizen. No matter. I was a highly trained soldier. I'd seen newsreels. I read the papers. I knew, precisely and instantly, who or what she was. Japanese.

But the second surprise is better, and unlike the memory of the first, still brings a smile to my lips: Lily was wearing a man's shirt, long but not that long, a clunky pair of boots, and absolutely nothing else.

In that respect, in every respect, she was the most remarkable palm reader I had ever seen. And having seen her, I knew that I had to leave, immediately.

I ducked my head in a kind of goodbye, and then moved quickly to the door. Or I thought I moved quickly. But then there was some against-the-rules shouting—from her, I realized, but it took a moment because the noise seemed too loud, too off-key—and when the shouting was done, she was in the doorway, blocking my exit.

"Damn you," she said, staring hard, breathing hard. "You're not a damn cop, are you? Or an MP? Because they've been through. And things were *taken care of*." She'd been moving on me as she spoke, and before I knew it, I'd stuttered back half a step.

She frowned. "You're not a cop."

"Ma'am," I said, touching my hat like I'd seen the good cowboys do in the movies. "I'm sorry." I looked down at her legs. They started where the shirt stopped, and descended, smooth, brown, and, here and there, bruised, into those boots.

"I said no laughing," she said quietly. "I wear boots. So do you. It's cold. Welcome to Alaska." She scuffed at the floor. "Why do boys get so hung up on the boots?" she asked, and then left the doorway to walk around me. "There's a discount if you've got some cigarettes." I didn't. "And sometimes a discount if you're a gentleman."

That's when she saw my shoulder insignia: that bright red bomb, fat and finned and ready to drop. On a trip into Anchorage a few years ago, I saw the patch disposal guys wear now—our World War II–era bomb is still there, but smaller, crowded by a base of lightning and laurels. Naturally, I prefer the one we wore. Nothing but that bomb, the red brighter than blood. People's eyes usually caught there a moment, but Lily did more than that. She flinched slightly, like I'd raised a hand to hit her.

"Well, hel-lo!" she said, or stammered, unable now to meet my eye. I relaxed, sure that I was intimidating her rather than the other way around. A pause followed as we both tried to figure out something to say.

But a sharp voice behind me figured it out for us: "Problem here?"

I could feel someone step around me, and then, there he was: thin, taller, blond, milky blue eyes scanning Lily and me. "Young man getting out of line, Miss Lily?" he asked.

I could tell two things by his insignia: he, too, was in bomb disposal, but more important, he outranked me. Once he discovered the same, he smiled.

I shook my head, but turned to Lily: Had I been out of line, somehow?

"No," Lily said. She laughed weakly, gave me a questioning look—surely this man and I knew each other?—and then retreated deeper into the office.

"No," I mumbled.

"Good night," the man said, not even looking at me. I felt like I was moving out the door without really moving my feet.

"Right," I said, but by then I was outside, the door was closing.

Before it shut completely, Lily shouted for me to wait. The door eased open again, and I could see her rustling around in the room's pile of blankets while the man watched. As soon as I realized my vantage point afforded me a somewhat intimate view of her backside, I looked away. The other man did not. I looked again.

Lily came back with a closed fist, and pressed something into my left hand. "Your change," she said, waiting until I met her gaze before she let go.

I shook my head, but only slightly, and the man cut off any protest. "Make haste, young man." He drew back and looked at me with disdain. "Change?" He exhaled. "As for myself, I intend to get my money's worth." He turned to Lily. "Mademoiselle?" he said, and I left.

I DIDN'T REALIZE for several blocks that my hands were two fists in my pockets. Only then did I unclench, and only then, with a huddled display of instruments in a music store window looking over my shoulder, did I pull out my change and examine it. She'd given me a dollar. On it, she'd written a message. A very short message, actually, all she had had time to write: "11."

I looked around, refolded the bill, and continued down the street. For whatever reason, I started walking faster and faster, until I reached the main road out to Fort Richardson. By then I was running, sure in some vague way that someone was pursuing me. But when I finally allowed myself to glance back into Anchorage's blackout dark, I couldn't see anyone at all.

WHAT I FEARED then is what Ronnie fears now, and has feared for some time: the unseen forces that hound you through the night.

Old explorers who first witnessed this phenomenon struggled for words to describe it; eventually they settled on *arctic hysteria*. The affliction did not discriminate: both Natives and Outsiders occasionally succumbed to some force—often during this very time of year, deep winter, which is characterized less by snow than endless dark—that caused them to strip off their clothes and run outside, into the cold, into the tundra. If they're not caught in time, some wound up (wind up) running into the great beyond.

It's a story I like to share when people who have never been to Alaska ask me what it's like. This usually comes right after they've squealed something along the lines of "Alaska! It's so big!" as though it might fall on them. But they don't really want to know what it's like. For them, asking me about Alaska is like pressing "play" to watch a horror movie; they just want to be scared: *Alaska!* A short discussion of arctic hysteria usually satisfies them, as it has all the things they think an Alaska story needs: cold, dark, death. It's missing a bear or a wolf, but I have other anecdotes to cover that.

Years ago, when I asked Ronnie about arctic hysteria, he had a ready punch line: *Sometimes, they don't come after you.* Time was, he explained, before the white man, before Ski-Doos, before Village Public Safety Officers, before medevac helicopters—sometimes, they just let people run away and disappear.

He was trying to spook me, of course, but it didn't work. As it happens, I have found myself chasing after Ronnie a dozen times, more frequently of late. I'll hear him run howling past my window late some night and leave my warm bed to run him down. Sometimes I catch him, sometimes I don't find him until much later, when he's passed out, in the shelter of some truck or house or Dumpster, often on a night that's cold enough to kill.

Whenever he comes to, in a few hours or a few days, he rarely mentions just what drove him into the night. But sometimes the memory is fresh or frightening enough that he can't help but speak of it, and out it comes, a similar story every time: an eagle, a caribou, a bear, encounters him, alone, walking down some street in town. He's recognized, and the animal gives chase. And as the chase continues, the animal changes from one form to another, always drawing closer, closer, until finally it is at his heels, and then Ronnie knows, hears, smells, feels, who it was all along. "The wolf, Lou-is," he says then.

"The wolf," he says now, blinking awake, and staring straight up at the hospice ceiling. "The wolf, Lou-is, he's closer now. He knows. He remembers. The boy. His mother. The baby. The wolf. My *tuunraq.*" Ronnie turns to face me, to make sure I am listening, though I myself can't be sure. Am I listening? Or dreaming? I feel a kind of fire in my legs, an urge to run myself. "He's heard I've been acting as an *angalkuq* once more. Without him. After all these years. He heard I was working right here. This place. That's how he found me. He's coming now. I hear him. He's coming now. Lou-is. Tell me—"

CHAPTER 4

"YOU ARE NOT CRAZY."

First day, first hour of bomb disposal training, and a dozen of us enlisted were crammed into a makeshift classroom barracks at Aberdeen Proving Ground. Gottschalk was still alive. That first balloon, Alaska, Lily were all in my future.

First question: How can you tell the difference between a BD officer and a BD enlisted man? Some of the guys actually worried it out, raised their hands and gave answers about insignia or uniforms. One guy said something about the way a man stands, which caused another to mutter something lewd, and that's when the sergeant instructing us gave the correct answer: the difference between us guys and officers? We are not crazy.

Because it turned out there was a basic principle in bomb disposal, one they taught you before they taught you anything about bombs.

The officer defuses the bomb.

"Then what do we do, Sarge?" asked a guy nearby, whom I took to be even younger than I.

The sergeant smiled. "Grow old."

* * *

THIS DIVISION OF DUTIES was British and was already in the process of changing. Soon enough, both enlisted and officers would be trained to render bombs safe. But when I went through, guys like me mostly had just one duty: dig. Think about bomb disposal today, and you're thinking of ticking, wire-tangled things, hidden under a desk or a bridge. Maybe that sounds scary, but to us, something tucked under a desk would have sounded like roast turkey with trimmings. The bombs we went after had, for the most part, tumbled out of planes. Drop a bomb from that height, and if it doesn't explode when it's supposed to, all one hundred pounds—or five hundred or one thousand or more—of it disappears right into the ground.

That's when you start digging. Down a story or more, depending on the soil and the weight of the bomb. When you're not digging, you're timbering, to keep the hole from collapsing. To prevent anything from exploding too soon, everybody's using special, nonmagnetic tools and wearing cloth shoes without metal eyelets and belts without buckles—or that's what they were always doing in the training films.

Lit cigarettes are forbidden, obviously. They dangle from everyone's lips.

When you've finally gotten the ugly squat cockroach of a thing all exposed, you climb—carefully—back out, and call for an officer. He dusts off his hands (he's been eating, watching, trying to radio someone who can tell him more about where this bomb came from). Then he grabs his tools and goes down, taking his knowledge with him.

But you couldn't dig too many holes without learning a thing or two about bomb disposal yourself, and smart officers—older officers—always welcomed input from their crews.

AUGUST 1944. A B-17 is returning from a practice bombing run in the California desert. The story goes that they had had a lousy day on the test range, missing targets left and right. Then again, they may have been just holding their skills in reserve, because they hit their last target dead-on.

Officially, it was an accident. Unofficially, it was a miracle, because there's really no other explanation for a bomb falling into the middle of the Japanese-American Relocation Camp at Manzanar without killing anyone. It fell through the roof of a small building that was housing some recently arrived ceramics equipment. The equipment was destroyed—a true silver lining for internees who hadn't been looking forward to the prospect of the make-work pottery program, devoted to crafting lumpy ashtrays and bowls—but the bomb failed to explode. All five hundred pounds of it managed to drill through two packing cases, the pallet beneath, and continue on fourteen feet deeper into the arid soil beneath the floor.

My Aberdeen classmates and I had the misfortune of being relatively nearby, stationed just south of San Francisco at Fort Ord, waiting to be dispersed across the Pacific. Someone somewhere looked at a readiness roster, realized he had a BD crew in his backyard, and sent us off to put our newly completed training to use. It must have seemed ideal. Give some new guys a real challenge, with relatively low risks: it was our own bomb, right? Something we knew inside out? And ultimately, what's the worst that could happen? Some trainees die, maybe take a few Japanese with them.

Our detail numbered eight. A lieutenant, sergeant, plus six of us who didn't know any better, and so were excited, almost giddy, at the prospect of our first real job. The lieutenant was young, but again, that was to be expected in our line of work.

You did *not* expect the officer to be skittish, or for his eyes to be red-rimmed, even watery, but who knows where the lieutenant had been the night before. And you definitely didn't expect him to have a tremor in his hand, but no one else seemed to notice that, so I kept quiet. When it came time, after all, he'd be the one down in the hole, alone.

The sergeant, Redes, was the oldest of the group by far. He had plenty of experience but wasn't much interested in sharing it. He had just rotated stateside from France, and would only snort and roll his eyes if you asked him about his time there.

Before we arrived, camp security evacuated the affected area, save for a few internees left in our care, "in case there's any dirty work." Sergeant Redes took one look at them and then ordered them to guard the area's perimeter. "For starters, don't let that security officer back in here," he told them.

The hardest part came first. It was obvious where the bomb had fallen—the partially destroyed building was a solid clue, even to guys as new at the job as we were—but it wasn't so obvious where the bomb was now. Inside, amidst the wrecked equipment, or burrowed in the ground well beneath? Ordnance locators detected nothing around the perimeter; the bomb had to be directly under the building. The lieutenant and Redes talked for a while, and then Redes came over to us. Clear out the pottery equipment, he said, but slowly. "Don't go banging around in there," he said. "Pretend the whole building is a bomb." Then he lit a cigarette, while we all stood and watched him. "We're going to do this today, girls," he said, and stared at us until we moved.

The work went slowly, even more slowly than the sergeant or the lieutenant would have liked, but since they'd told us to be cautious, they must have felt they couldn't rush us. Once we'd moved out all the equipment and packing material without finding anything, we tore up what remained of the floor. Still nothing. Glad to discover the building wasn't sitting on a cement slab, we started digging.

We were at it for one hour, and then two, and when the third began, we'd lost almost all sense of the bomb—we were just here to dig, and keep digging until we were told to stop.

Clink.

I knew infantry guys who would always claim the bullet, or shell, or bomb that was actually going to hit you had a different sound, different from the bullets that whizzed by safely, I suppose. But in bomb disposal, there was only that one sound—*clink,* the sound of a shovel or pick gone too far—and if you heard it, you usually weren't around afterward to describe the experience in detail. Of course, the other reason you almost never heard it was because experienced bomb disposal men were more careful than I—probing first, then digging, probing, digging, never just diving in. I'd been probing, I promise. I'd been cautious.

It wasn't that loud a clink.

But this was a bomb that would not go off. It had fallen thousands of feet from a plane, it had broken through a roof and a floor and a mess of equipment for making pots, and it wasn't going to explode just because some trainee had nicked it with a shovel. It was designed for rough handling, after all—it had to survive transport from the factory, loading onto the airplane, and whatever rough weather the plane encountered.

Still, a bomb's patience was usually about spent by the time guys like us found it. So after my clink, none of us breathed, none of us moved, and none of us said anything, until someone weakly said, "Sarge..."

Redes was in the doorway above us before the sound had left the air. "Who's the dipshit trying to get us killed?"

I suppose I could have put down the shovel and pretended it was someone else, but I was still motionless, scared.

"Belk," Redes said.

"I was being careful, sir," I said, though I wasn't sure I had been.

"'Careful'?" To our great relief, he started climbing down into the hole. He wasn't scared. "Jesus, Belk," he said at the bottom. "'Careful'? What do we say?"

I wasn't smiling then, but I'm smiling now, because we said what Lily said.

We said: *careful and correct.*

Though Redes hadn't said much since joining our unit, he'd said enough that we knew this was a favorite phrase. I'd heard half a dozen instructors say it, but Redes made it his own through repetition and embellishment: you could be as *careful* as you wanted, he'd always say, but if you didn't follow procedures *correctly*, you could still blow your-self up—with great care. I should have been paying more attention. Watching the soil, stopping to test with the probe.

"Careful and correct," I said.

"Correct," Redes said. "Since you're the whiz kid, you've earned the prize of finishing this job off. The rest of you, out. Belk, finish exposing the bomb."

The rest of the gang climbed out, delighted to get away from the bomb and the sergeant's wrath.

Sergeant Redes descended and watched me dig for a minute or two before he spoke. "I did the same thing, you know. 'Clink.'" He looked up out of the hole and shook his head.

I thought he would get mad if I stopped digging, but I did anyway. "Did your sergeant get mad?" I asked.

"I was the sergeant," he said. "Last day before I left France. Right in the middle of the town square. Ten yards, maybe, from the front door of the church, which was a thousand years old or something. Every-body from my lieutenant to the monsignor to some passing colonel looking on, watching the experienced sergeant do his work. *Clink*."

"What happened?"

"Nothing. Same as here." He bent down, ran his hands lightly over the bomb, and let out a long breath before muttering, "This is odd." He studied it for a minute more, agreed with himself about something, and then said, "You know the lieutenant's got a sister?"

I didn't, but I knew enough about army life to brace myself for something coarse.

"Redhead," he said. "So I hear. Showed me her picture, black and white. Pretty. I suppose the lieutenant's a little red up top, too." He turned to look at me. "That's the thing of it. They were twins, he tells me. Boy-girl twins. Whaddya call that?"

I shook my head, and he turned back to the bomb.

"So she's a WAC nurse," he said. "Was. Died Monday. Italy. Jeep. Land mine."

"That's—hard," I said, and Redes waited for me to say something more, something adequate.

When I didn't, he turned back to the bomb. "They're not giving him leave till the end of the month. *That's* hard. Now give me a hand here." Redes had both hands on the bomb and was trying to roll it back toward him. We steadied it, and then he paused and looked out of the hole.

"You're my best student, you know," he said. "Or were." He smiled. Then the lieutenant called his name, and Redes told me to wait. He climbed up to the lip of the hole and told the lieutenant that he needed just a few more minutes to finish clearing the site. Then he came back down to the bottom of the pit, excited.

"So let's finish your training, whaddya think?" he said quickly. "What do we do next?"

"We, well, let's see. I go and get a couple of sticks of C2 or C3, run some blasting wire back clear of the fragmentation zone, hook it up to the blasting machine." I could see the little pages of my training manual flutter past in my head.

"What the hell are you talking about?" Redes said.

"I'm sorry, the, uh, *fifty-cap* blasting machine," I said. "I think."

"The what? Let's call it what it is, soldier. You're talking about the little box, with the plunger you push down and make everything go boom?" I nodded my head. "That's the hell box, right? Don't bother telling me they taught you something else in your fancy little school." I nodded again. "Okay," he said. "That's a lovely plan. But what's the problem with it?"

I was still stuck on *hell box,* so his question caught me off guard. "Not enough wire?"

Redes looked at me and then rubbed his hands together, slowly. "Right, not enough wire. Belk, there's not enough wire in the world for this job. The problem with that plan is, we blow this bomb where it is, we flatten the camp, which, since it looks like it's built with balsa wood, we could probably level with a couple of lit farts, for that matter. In any case, that all means we take care of the problem *here*." He pointed to the bomb. "So let's get started. There's something extremely strange about this bomb. What is it?"

I looked at it for a long time. It didn't look strange. It looked just like the bombs in the manual, markings and all. I shrugged.

"Where's the fuze pocket?"

I relaxed, glad to be back on familiar ground. This question was easy. Like most guys, I'd come into the bomb disposal squad thinking the business end of the bomb was always the nose, but that wasn't the case. Sometimes the fuze was in a cylinder, or pocket, embedded in the middle, as it was here.

"Right there," I said, pointing to the middle. "Transverse fuzing. German specialty." Sergeant Redes looked at me and waited. I waited, too, pleased with my vocabulary. And then I gasped. "This is a German bomb, Sergeant? The Nazis are— Sergeant? Oh my God." I was breathless; a German air raid over California?

Only now did Redes look concerned. "Not so loud, Belk. You already tried to set the bomb off, let's not try to set the camp gossips off, too." He squatted. "The truth—according to the lieutenant, who radioed the airfield—is that they've been using some captured Nazi ordnance out on the test range. Why waste good American ammo, and so on. Though the lieutenant doesn't quite buy that, and neither do I— for starters, they'd have the wrong damn charging shackles, though that's probably a good thing, because the condensers wouldn't—well. I'm guessing there's a pilot and crew who are going to have a hell of an interesting debriefing."

A German bomb. I stared at it. I read the papers; we had the Germans on the run. We'd landed in Normandy that June. We were going to win in Europe; I knew it. I thought everyone did. And yet here I was, in the middle of California, staring at a German bomb.

"But this is good news," said Redes. "Right? Because this is all I've seen for the past year or so, and it was probably all over your classroom, too, right?"

It certainly was. I could see the training films in my head.

If you had the right tool—and Redes did, I was surprised to see, a funny kind of two-pin wrench—you could unscrew the keep ring and access the fuze pocket. Then you could remove the fuze. You weren't quite done, of course. The fuze was its own kind of mini-bomb; screwed onto one end of it was a doughnut-shaped gaine, which was what provided the initial charge. Once you'd unscrewed the gaine, you could breathe a little easier. The fuze without the gaine was a like a gun without a trigger, and a bomb without a fuze was basically a mess of explosives in a handy carrying case. Dangerous, sure, but disassembled, you could toss the parts (maybe *toss* isn't the right word) into the back of a truck and cart it all off to some lonely pit and blow it up.

But you couldn't do any of that unless you removed or disabled the fuze, and only an officer could do that. Which is why I was surprised to see Sergeant Redes start in on the job, narrating what he was doing the whole time.

"Say what you will about your Nazis, they build a good bomb. Don't repeat that, there's no such thing as a good bomb. And every now and then, they get sneaky. That's not good, either. But the thing is, they're well made"—here he strained with a little effort as he got into a better position—"for the most part. Built tough."

He fitted the spanner wrench to the keep ring. I swear I could see him tense and hold his breath. I was already holding mine. Then he did something incredible: he turned the wrench. The ring resisted. He put a second hand to it, grunted, held his breath again, tried again. This time, the ring scraped open an eighth of a turn. He exhaled and smiled. "No, she's not going to give us trouble. Normally, you'd give a listen, but we know this animal, right? Hell, I've worked on lots more German bombs than American ones."

"That's good," I whispered, because that was as much voice as I could muster.

"Well, we'll see." He turned the tool again, and the ring scraped around a bit more. Finally, it began to move more freely. He turned it around and around until it was completely loose.

Now I was really scared. Not just because the most dangerous part of the bomb was almost in our hands, but because what we were doing was clearly against the rules as I knew them. One, the officer defuses the bomb. Two, only one man does the job, to minimize potential loss of life. I looked up. What if the lieutenant decided to peer over the side now? I felt around for my shovel. I was just digging.

Redes rocked back on his haunches for a second and surveyed his progress. "Now, American bombs. Fuze in the nose or the tail. Honest piece of business, for the most part. But you know what? I'm glad it's the enemy that's got to defuse them. Most of them, anyway." He looked at me. "Belk? What's next?"

"British bombs?" I squeaked.

"My whiz kid," he said. "No, what's next to do here?"

"Call for the lieutenant?"

Redes looked at me. "I thought I explained," he said.

I thought about the lieutenant's red-haired sister, tried to imagine what she looked like. His twin? I looked back up to the top of the hole, and then back to Redes. "Pull out, well, pull out the fuze," I said, "and then call Lieutenant—" Redes shook his head. I exhaled. "Remove the gaine?"

"Good boy," he said. He leaned forward to look at it a little more closely. He shifted to the side a bit, and motioned me over. "Let's hope it's not damaged. So what you're going to do now—" The sound of the lieutenant's voice, angry, cut him off. Redes yelled up a quick apology, changed his mind about something, and turned back to me: "—is watch me work very quickly." He slowly drew the fuze out of the bomb, found the gaine, unscrewed it, and delicately set it all beside the case.

"You see all that?" he said. "Get a good look?" I nodded. "Because you're not likely to see that again, something that rare. A precision-crafted German fuze, just *falling* out of a bomb like that, the gaine spiraling off it. Damnedest thing." He winked and then gave me a lift out of the hole just as the lieutenant looked over the edge.

"What's the problem here, Sergeant?" The lieutenant looked worse than before, if that was possible. His face was drawn and pale, his eyes sad and angry both. I almost thought he was going to spit on me as I climbed out.

"Well, sir, this *is* a funny one..." I heard Redes start to say as the lieutenant climbed down. I could hear their voices go back and forth after that, softer and softer, until I couldn't make out any words at all. Then it fell silent, and a long moment later, Redes's head appeared above the hole.

He put on an angry face for me. "What're you doing here, Belk? Why haven't you cleared to safety? Lieutenant's in the hole." He walked me back to where the group was waiting. When we were within earshot, he shouted out, "Nothing too tricky, boys, but the lieutenant's going to need a little time, little quiet before he's ready for us." A couple of the guys exchanged looks. One went over to talk with the internees. The sergeant stared back toward the building.

"Well, British bombs—to answer your question," he said. "They're respectable enough. Their bomb disposal crews? The best, no question. They have more experience than a man would want. But I tell you what: I'm glad I'm not over there clearing *their* beaches. Damn English land mines could kill a man." He allowed himself a smile. The other guys, catching a word or two, drifted closer to hear better.

But the sergeant stopped when he saw the lieutenant emerge, blinking, from the building. Redes told us to stay where we were and went out to meet him. After a minute's discussion, the lieutenant started off in the direction of the camp administration building, and Redes returned to us. He dispatched three men back to the building to figure out some way we could hoist the bomb out safely. Two others were sent to retrieve our specially outfitted truck, whose winch would provide most of the required muscle. That left me with no other job than to stand there, beside the sergeant.

"Careful—*and* correct," he said, pleased. "That's what we learned today, right?"

"Right, Sarge," I said.

He watched our guys file into the building. "Wasn't pleased about coming here," he said, "if you can believe that. Who doesn't like California? Me. I don't like California. Because it's too close to goddamn Japan. And if there's a bomb you don't want to mess with, it's a Jap bomb." We started walking over to the building. "Because they build a shitty bomb. Japanese military command, if you want to call it that, they don't exactly have the most respect for a man's life. Take your suicide planes, for example. Kids who don't know how to fly, screaming down into our ships." He cleared his throat. "So your Jap bombmaker, he's not thinking safety when he makes his bomb. He's ready to lose a man here and there. At the factory. On the runway. In the plane. You come across one of those bombs on the ground, you don't know what kind of shit you're getting into."

We were at the door to the building now, and he paused. He took a long look around the camp. "Now, then," he said quietly, "I've never handled a Japanese bomb. Course, that's probably why I'm still here." He looked around the camp one more time, and then ducked inside.

CHAPTER 5

RONNIE IS NOT IN A COMA, OR "NOT A CLASSIC COMA," AS A doctor just put it to me, as though there were comas one might treasure and frame.

After Ronnie had awoken to tell me about the wolf, he slipped away again, this time submerging so deep, I thought he had died. I held his hand, I called for him, and then called for the nurses. Ronnie didn't wake up, the nurses didn't come. I had to leave Ronnie there and go chasing down the hall for someone to attend to him. No one quite understood my concern—wasn't this why he'd come to the hospice?—and I tried to explain all the reasons why it was too soon for him to die. He had something to tell me, I said, and they smiled sympathetically. It was urgent, I said, and they began to look nervous. When I finally blurted out something about a wolf, they called the doctor.

But everyone at the hospital was busy with a snowmachine accident. Two kids were hurt, a third had died. No one could come to see the old, alcoholic *angalkuq* in his room at the hospice, not for hours.

Part of the problem was that Ronnie insisted on breathing, his heart insisted on beating. "Both pluses," the doctor said when he finally got to his bedside. Never mind the big minus, unconsciousness. The doctor didn't understand my concern, or why he'd been summoned. "I thought I'd been called to pronounce," he said, looking hopefully at the clock, as though there might still be a need to note the time of death. Then he looked at me, professionally, and asked how I was feeling.

I ignored him. The doctor didn't know Ronnie, or me—he's one of these hotshots from Seattle who come up here once or twice a year, get community service hours, and think they're saving the world. Some of them are good; this one was not. When he switched back to small talk and asked if I was a relative of Ronnie's, I knew he hadn't been examining him—or me—that closely. I was wearing my collar, for once. I pointed that out, plus the fact that I was white, and then the fact that I also served as the hospice chaplain. Now he looked truly surprised. Said he'd expect me to be a bit more "sophisticated," then, about "these things."

I made the mistake of telling him, sophisticated as I was, that I still needed a little help with fancy medical terms like "these things."

Then he got right to the point. Ronnie wasn't sick: he was dying.

What about the two pluses?

"He's not dying," I said, because Ronnie would have said the same if he'd been able to. He had something to tell me. And I him. "He can't."

"He can," the doctor said. "He will."

"Not on my watch," I said, trampling over what may have been an empathetic "sorry" dribbling from the doctor's mouth. I couldn't hear him very well.

"Then keep watching," the doctor said, and started for the door. "As for me, I'm on the eight o'clock flight."

"Godspeed," I said. When the doctor had gone, I turned to Ronnie and said something different. "Run," I whispered. "But don't outrun me."

EVERYONE IN ALASKA had a secret in World War II; most, like me, still do. There were plenty of men who had made their way to Alaska long before war had broken out. I imagine some came for a love of the wilderness, but more came for the vastness of it. Long before its official motto became "The Last Frontier," Alaska was just that, an outpost on the edge of the Arctic, the edge of the earth. Nowadays, people flock to remote places to "find themselves," but in the 1930s and 1940s, men, and some women, went to Alaska to do just the opposite: disappear.

Maybe you'd robbed a bank. Maybe you'd killed a man—maybe by accident or on purpose, maybe you couldn't say. Maybe you'd caught a man sleeping with your wife. Maybe a man had caught you with his. Maybe you were the wife. Maybe you were nothing more than a middle-grade con man, running out of luck and time, and so you fled to where the North American continent finally ran out of room. Maybe you just wanted an adventure. France has its Foreign Legion; we had, and to some extent, still have, Alaska—places you go to take leave of one life and start another.

Which, of course, is precisely what I was doing. But I was a kid then, eighteen and only getting dumber, and I didn't realize any of this at first. The longer I spent in Alaska, though, the more I realized—the more I read into eyes cast down, into conversations trailing off. No one had a past. And so while some initially feared the attention and excitement war would bring to Alaska, most grew to enjoy it. There was new anonymity amidst a growing crowd of strangers—and new chances to establish yourself, to craft a new history. War reset the clock for all of us.

In the Alaskan military community, the secrets ran even thicker. So many men were involved in so-called top secret missions that those who weren't, pretended. Ask a guy at a bar what he did, and he'd more than likely just roll his eyes and shrug. The modest would say something dismissive like "You know how it is"; the vain would look around and then whisper urgently, "It's *top* secret."

A few hours after my encounter with Lily the palm reader, someone was telling me just that—"It's top secret"—over a beer. We were in an unofficial Army Air Corps club just off base, which officers and enlisted shared, after a fashion—the officers had one side of the room, the enlisted the other. It wasn't a friendly place; everybody stared at their drinks, until they no longer could stare at much of anything.

I'd retreated to the club not long before. Shortly after arriving back on base from downtown, I'd bumped into a sergeant who recognized me from the daily visits I made to Building 100. My officer was back, he said. My official duties were about to begin; if I was smart, I'd grab a last drink while I could. Who knows where I'd find myself tomorrow. But when I'd asked the sergeant where I could find my C.O., he shook his head and said, he'll find you.

"*Top* secret," the man to my right said again.

I'd wandered in looking for a normal conversation, but was having no luck. My top secret companion at the bar had hands that were rough and callused and creased with dirt. I figured he was probably busy building base housing, and the only secret was when or if they would finish.

"What about you?" he asked.

I shrugged. "I—well, I work with ordnance. Bombs."

"Goddamn right," the man said, and pointed at my sleeve. "*Secret* bombs?"

I shook my head.

"They're not secret?" he said.

"I don't know," I said, looking around. Try as I might, I couldn't focus; all I could see was Lily's dollar, that magic 11, "careful and correct" (jarringly accompanied by a memory of Sergeant Redes), and then Lily, the loose shirt, the bare legs.

"Then *that's* a secret, eh?" the man said, and rocked back satisfied.

"What is?" I asked absently.

The man pressed on: "Who's your C.O.?"

I shut my eyes to erase Lily and opened them on my drinking partner. After a moment spent recalling his question, I answered: "Some captain." I knew his name well enough, and would be meeting him soon, but I didn't feel like saying any more than I had to.

" 'Some captain'—right," the man said. "Let's have it."

"Top secret," I said, and looked at the clock behind the bar. It was 9 P.M., but outside, it looked like 9 A.M. Some liked the way the sun shone late into the evenings; I came to feel, and still feel, it made one feel like a drunk. It felt odd to have a drink in my hand when the world outside looked like it hadn't reached noon yet.

My friend wasn't bothered by the time or the light. Perhaps he had solved this problem as I later learned some men did—they simply drank around the clock. That way, time and sobriety became irrelevant. "Top secret—*right,*" he said, frowning into his drink. Maybe the time didn't bother him, but I did. "You're just *fooling* with me," he said.

I stood up and put some money on the bar. "It's Gurley," I said. "Captain—Something—Gurley. I'm not sure of his first name." But it wasn't enough, or it wasn't what he wanted to hear—he grabbed up my hand and held tight. What startled me most was not the abruptness of the act, but the gruff tenderness of it.

"Best to keep *that* a secret, then," he said finally. He finished his drink and stood up without a wobble.

"Why?" I asked, looking at him intently for the first time all night. A gray hair or two poked out above the collar of his T-shirt.

"You know why," he said. "Or if you don't, you'll know soon enough." Push any man up here far enough, and you always reached this same blind alley of significant looks and silent lips.

"What the *fuck*?" I said, exasperated. But I swore so infrequently— I'm still pretty bad at it, at least in English—that my voice involuntarily squeaked at the novelty. A few people turned around. "Everybody's got a secret here. Everybody's a damn spy," I sputtered, though that's not what I meant, and my voice went soft as a result.

But the man took no notice, and just shook his head. "We all pretend to be," he told his empty glass. "He *is*."

The door opened with a shout, so sharp and loud I couldn't make out the word, only the volume behind it.

"And *here* he is," he said without turning around.

"Sergeant Belk!" my captain shouted. I had not turned to look at him yet. "Sergeant Louis A. Belk, if you're on base or in this bar, God *help* you if I find you before the MPs do."

My friend turned to me slowly, summoned what sobriety he had left, and squinted at my name strip, which I could tell he couldn't read. He stiffened up and looked at me. "Be glad you're not Belk," he said.

I swiveled around in my chair, and faced Captain Gurley for the first time. "But I am," I said quietly.

"THIS BAR IS CLOSED," Gurley roared, his voice more musical than loud. "The hour of judgment is at hand. Be gone, princesses of darkness!" Looks were exchanged, heads shook, but everyone filed out quickly enough. Even the bartender tried to leave, but Gurley stopped him—and me.

He jabbed a finger in my chest. *"Belk."* I can feel the force of that finger still; it's a chronic pain, actually, that flares up in times of stress.

Gurley looked at me carefully. "You're familiar," he said.

So was he: he had been Lily's appointment from earlier. He waited a moment, long enough for me to wonder if he remembered or not. Then he spat out my name again: "Belk!" He frowned, and then slowly knocked on the bar, twice. "That is one fucking lousy name, Sergeant." He looked for the bartender, and then spun back: "God above, what sort of faithless name is that?"

I said nothing.

Gurley leaned over and grabbed my chin with a bony hand. I later decided his strength was a mystery until you looked closely. He was tall and thin, but more than thin: skeletal, a look that makes some look emaciated and others as though they'd been hammered out of steel. He had an odd way of standing, too: he teetered occasionally, as though he were having trouble finding his footing. I wasn't thinking about any of that then, though. I was just trying to figure out why I couldn't snap my head out of his grasp. He kept talking, punching each comma and period: "A question requires an answer, Sergeant, not some subhuman gesture. Speech is what separates us—*most* of us—from primates. Are you a primate?"

"No," I said.

"I'm not sure you got that quite right," he said, somehow managing to squeeze harder.

"No, *sir*," I said.

"Better, but still, not enough," he said. "Are you a primate?"

"No, sir," I said.

"As in monkey, chimpanzee, o-*rang*-u-tan."

No.

"Mmm," he said, and then took a step back to regard me. "Lutheran?"

I shook my head.

"Methodist?"

No.

"I'm usually quite good at this.... Let's see... 'Belk'... Presbyterian?"

No.

"Not—Episcopalian? Couldn't be." He frowned, and then leaned close, put his nose at my neck, and sniffed. Once, twice.

"No," he said, stepping back stiffly once more, eyes wide with mock horror. "Good God, Belk, *Catholic?*" He looked me up and down. "A papist?"

"Catholic," I said quietly.

Gurley looked around as if to call someone else's attention to the zebra that had just walked into the room. "*Catholic*, then," he said, and knocked on the bar, signaling something to the bartender. "My family always, and I mean *always*, had Catholic servants. But that was us. Only the best. Silver spoon in my mouth and all the rest."

The bartender brought over a bottle of Canadian Club and a glass. Gurley nodded at him. The man poured. Gurley picked up the bottle, sniffed it, and set it back down.

"Go," he said, and the bartender was gone before I'd swiveled back around. He looked to me. "It's true. My mother had a preference for them—and so did I." I lowered my eyes. "Catholic girls, Belk," he said, and inhaled. "Are you Irish?" he asked.

"No," I said, and started to say something else.

"Alas," Gurley said. "There might have been the chance I'd ravished—fucked—a *cousin* of yours. Perchance a *sister*." He looked at me. "Quite sure?"

"Captain," I began, eager to stop him before his claims progressed.

"Sergeant," Gurley began again, and then changed his mind. "But you must excuse me. I am better bred than my babbling tirade betrays." He stopped. "Do you know what *tirade* means?" I nodded anyway. "Ah," Gurley said. "I see two things. One, that you do not know the word's definition, and two, that you are a pitiable liar." He drained his glass, then poured himself another two fingers and downed that, upper lip drawn back like he was swallowing vitamins. "So, knowing this, I am pleased to proceed with my experiment. Ready, Sergeant?"

"Captain," I said again, and that's all I said, because I was a kid and scared. I tried to think about what Sergeant Redes would have done. Earlier that day, I learned he had been lost at sea, and now realized some things are just out of our control.

"Are you a good shot?" Gurley asked. I could hardly hear him for my booming pulse. In the meantime, it was as if he'd invisibly handed something over, some sort of false courage that ran through me and made me want to deck him, ready to deck him, in fact, if he made one more crack about me or his servants. Before that, though, I'd do myself and my faith proud by being as obnoxious as I wanted. Simple enough.

"I'm a fucking *great* shot," I said, my voice bouncing a little less higher over the profanity this time. Then I leaned forward like I had a secret. "Sir," I added with a small grin.

Gurley broadhanded me with such force that I barked back into the bar and then to the floor, knocking over both stool and whisky.

"You *fuck,*" Gurley said. "Pray that the vessel containing that most precious elixir is not broken." He kicked me—gently, I suppose, for him. "Do go and find out." I looked up at him insolently—I had so much still to learn—and I could see he was about to swat me again. But instead, he gave another light kick and went to his glass, looking for another drop or two. Then he leaned over the bar and looked down.

"It's there," he said, pointing. "Re-trieve." I crawled to my feet with the help of a stool, and walked around behind the bar. I bent over to get the bottle and almost passed out, but caught myself. I put the bottle on the bar and began walking back around, but he stopped me with a hand. "That's fine. You're safer back there, don't you think? Bar between us?" I nodded. "Thomas Gurley, Captain, U.S. Army Air Corps, late of the O-S-S, Office of Strategic Services." He winked and held out a hand.

"Louis Belk," I mumbled. "Sergeant, I guess."

"My word, Belk, be sure about *some*thing." He examined his empty glass and then me. "Good. So you're a good shot, you daresay."

As I've explained, I was a terrible shot.

"Let's see if you can hit this glass," he said.

"With what?" I asked.

"With your *gun,* Belk," Gurley said. "Or—whatever. Your forehead. You seem like a bright lad."

"I'm not—I'm not going to fire a gun in here," I said.

"Of course in here. That's why I cleared the bar. So we could talk. Get to know each other. Kind of an entrance exam for your position. Includes a little target practice. Ready?"

"But I don't have a gun, not here," I said. I didn't have one anywhere.

"What?" said Gurley. "Maybe they didn't make it clear back in basic training—this is, in fact, a *war.*"

"A war," I repeated.

"A holy war," said Gurley, "a crusade, if you will." He unsnapped his holster and pulled out his gun. He laid it on the bar. "Lesson one," he said. "Gun. Colt M1911. Forty-five caliber." I looked at it. Gurley leaned across the bar, and before I could realize what was happening, he'd backhanded me again. My mouth was a mush of blood. He regarded this. "Swallow." I did.

And this is the point, were Ronnie awake, were he ever to awake, he would ask, Why? Never mind that avoiding that question is why most people come to Alaska; never mind that few questions are less answerable *in* Alaska: Why did I let Gurley abuse me so? Because Gurley was an officer? Because I was tired? Because I was a fool?

Why did I do what I did? For the same reason anyone in the army does what they do: because that's how you're trained. Now, it wasn't that I'd been trained to be a coward, and it wasn't simply that I'd been trained to follow orders.

I had been trained in the art of bomb disposal. Some guys might just take a rifle and shoot at an unexploded bomb to get rid of it, but that was artless (and in most situations, fatally stupid). No, what I did, what I'd been trained to do, was circle, study, plan, and when I was ready, move.

And Gurley, I didn't know him that well, yet. But I knew this: he could fume and rage and spit, but lay an ear to him and you'd hear it— he was still ticking. He hadn't gone off, not really, not yet. To haul back and hit him would have been like aiming that rifle and pulling the trigger. And then what would you have? What you always got when you didn't think ahead. Body parts, all over.

"Pick up the gun, Belk." And I did, though doing so gave me an almost physical sense of things flying out of control. I blinked, hoping to regain my balance, but it only made me dizzier.

"Now we're going to shoot."

I was surprised, and disappointed, that he was so obviously *not* worried that a man he had just struck, twice, might be interested in shooting him.

He held up the glass, and looked at me until I returned his gaze. "A moving target." Then he pointed down the bar. "Ready?"

I nodded, adjusted my grip. Circle, study, plan.

Gurley made as if to toss the glass in the air, but then rocketed it down the bar, a line drive. It shattered against a far wall before I had a chance to do anything, let alone shoot.

"You didn't even fire, *mon petit ami*," Gurley said with a smile. He knocked the bar. "Another glass." I drew a breath, found a glass, set it up. "Ready?" he said. I nodded and raised the gun. Another line drive down the bar, even faster this time. I almost squeezed the trigger, but held off when I realized I was far too late.

"C'm'ere," said Gurley. I leaned over. He took the gun from my hand and, holding the barrel, smacked the side of my head with it. For a second I couldn't see, and when my vision finally blinked back, I realized my right eye was already swelling shut.

"Second lesson," Gurley said. "Are you looking at me?" I assumed I was, and stared more intently. "Second lesson," he repeated. "Never, never let a man take your gun." He gave it back to me, and raised his hand to strike again. Reflexively, I aimed the gun at him. The hell with circling. Training can only take a man so far.

Gurley whistled low. "Third lesson," he said, hands halfheartedly in the air. "Never aim a gun at a man unless you plan on shooting him." I held my aim for a moment and then lowered the gun. "Good," Gurley said. "I'd hate for us to get off to the wrong start." He knocked the bar again. I set up a third glass. It rattled as I put it down and we both watched my shaky hand struggle for a second to release it. "Ready?" he said. I nodded. He reared back to pitch the glass down the bar.

I shot it out of his hand.

He staggered backward. His hand was miraculously not injured, and honestly, I don't think I was prepared to deal with the consequences if it had been. He studied his hand, as if trying to remember whether he'd ever picked up the glass, and then let a smile seep across his face. He reached across the bar and, as I flinched, clapped me on the shoulder.

"Nice, god, damn, shot, Belk," he said. "Maybe we'll make a warrior out of you yet." He bared his teeth; perhaps he thought he was grinning. "I'll be gone again, two days," he said. "Thus you can understand my eagerness to meet you tonight." I must have looked woozy, because he eyed me carefully. "Belk? Listen, now: you have two whole days to come to your senses. Meet me at 0800, two days from now, Building 520." I nodded this time. He smiled. "Building 520," he repeated. "And bring your gun, if you like." With that, he turned on one leg, wobbled, found his balance, and walk-swayed out of the bar.

CHAPTER 6

ELEVEN P.M., THE STARHOPE HOTEL.

It had taken me some puzzling over the dollar that Lily had pressed into my hand before I decided that what she'd scribbled on the back was an invitation. But to what?

I stood outside the building, looking up at the windows of Lily's "office" on the second floor, thinking about Gurley, Lily, and Lily's bare legs. Would another man be there tonight? Would another interrupt us?

And yes, innocent that I was, I even thought about her advertised business, those careful and correct palm readings: after all that had happened so far, I was more interested than ever in learning my future. Especially if that future included sex.

I apologize: there are certain words a priest can't say, like *sex*, or the proper names of various parts of the anatomy, or the improper names, or, of course, the full raft of obscenities, carnal and otherwise. I can't say these words not because I lack the nerve, but the audience. These are things people can't hear me say; that's why it's a pleasure to talk to Ronnie now, who apparently can't hear me at all.

Whom else could I tell what it was like to stand outside that hotel, looking up, sweating hormones, the tart, metallic taste of blood from the fight with Gurley only now going stale in my mouth?

Whom else could I tell that of everything I felt, the sharpest feeling was fear?

Damn right I was scared. Scared of Gurley? Maybe I thought that then, but that was a fleeting fear. You can't be scared of a car that loses control on the highway. There's no time, no reason: you just concentrate on staying alive.

No, I was scared of the woman up on the second floor. And it kept me standing on the street right up to, and then after, eleven o'clock. Five after, ten after. I couldn't bring myself to go in, although I decided I would rush ahead if I saw any other man make for the building. But in the meantime, I stood there, rubbing between thumb and forefinger the magic dollar Lily had given me, wondering as I did so what crime I might have already committed and what crimes I might soon commit.

Here was the problem. Lily was a woman, a spit-in-the-eye-of-God occultist (the distance between palm reading and worshiping idols seemed shorter in my youth), a siren—she was all this, yes, but what consumed me was that Lily was Japanese. And while that didn't automatically make her a spy, everything else did: her presence here, in Alaska, when all other Japanese had been sent to camps; this strange building; her dark office; Gurley's mysterious arrival; the dollar she'd given me—and, of course, the fact that she was supposedly a palm reader. She made no secret that she dealt in secrets.

"Boo," came a voice from behind me, and I must have leapt in the air, straight up, several inches, with my heart going faster and higher. "Don't turn around," said the voice, which was doing a fair impression of a movie hoodlum until it broke down laughing. "Boo," the voice said again between laughs, and I turned around to find Lily, grinning broadly.

"Hello," I said, using the biggest, most adult soldier voice I could manage. Lily imitated me—not very well, I thought, but she also found this funny, and laughed until I at least started to smile.

But when she finally caught her breath and focused, she stopped laughing altogether.

"What happened to you?" she asked. She started to extend a hand to the bruises on my face, and if she'd actually touched them, I would have counted the battle with Gurley as well worth the pain. But she stopped short, just inches from my skin. There was that kind of buzzing that comes just before a first kiss—yes, I know about these things, or knew—and I couldn't say anything, do anything. She'd immobilized me faster than Gurley, and panicked me just the same.

"I have to go," I said, and then started to back away.

"I should have warned you," she said, and my heart stopped beating while it waited to see if the next word out of her mouth would be *Gurley*. "Anchorage can be a bit rough on a new kid in town." She waited for me to answer, but I could only shrug. "Fourth Avenue, I'm guessing? I mean, you don't need to be a mind reader to see what happened to you. Bar fight—some sailors, likely, they're usually pretty pissed by the time they come ashore in Anchorage." She wrinkled her nose and started smiling again. "So I feel kinda bad. Sending you off to wander half the night. A kid like you."

She'd won me over again until she came out with that *kid*.

"I'm sorry," I said. "I really do—have to go. I shouldn't have—"

"Not so fast, soldier," she said, stepping after me with surprising speed. "You owe me something?"

"I—I don't owe you anything—I left before—"

"You left carrying something of mine. Something like—a dollar." She waited for a response. "You think I'm a magician *and* a palm reader? I smack my palms together and the money comes out? Let's have it." Her hand darted to my side. I felt something and then nothing, like a mouse had scurried into my pocket and then—*pop*—disappeared. She held up the dollar: "And I got another problem, sailor. What time is it?"

"Soldier," I said.

"You're late. Note said eleven, didn't it?" She followed this with a friendly, weary frown, as if we always argued like this. Then she started inside.

"I'm not sure I should go in there," my voice higher, age lower.

Lily just looked at me. "I think you should," she said. "Seems pretty clear you're not safe on the streets," she added, and then smiled. "Besides, how else are you going to get your wallet back?"

UPSTAIRS, ALL WAS as it had been before. The door was ajar, the single bulb still burned overhead. Still no furniture, still the pile of blankets in one corner of the room. My wallet hit me in the chest as I crossed the threshold. I fumbled and it fell. As I bent down to pick it up, I saw Lily seated on the floor, back against the wall, studying her hands, studiously not watching me.

"I'm feeling a little bad about taking my dollar back," Lily said, still not looking up. Then she rubbed her hands together and put them flat on the floor beside her. "Why do you carry that wallet anyway? There's almost nothing in it. Somebody jump you a block before?"

"I just got here, I guess," I said, my mind spooning out words almost at random, since the whole of me was preoccupied with the situation: *I am in a room, all by myself, with a woman, with a Japanese woman, and we are at war with Japan, and I am an American soldier, and I've never slept with a woman, from Japan or anywhere else, and—*

"'Just got here'?" Lily said. "C'mon, sit down. Either your brain isn't hooked up to your mouth, or you don't have a brain, or you're just not telling the truth. Let's find out." She patted the floor next to her. I didn't move. "'Palm reader,' right?" she asked. "This is what you came about?"

I finally spoke up. "Listen, I've got some questions, okay? I mean, up front?"

"That's what this all about, sailor," Lily said.

"Soldier," I said.

"Well, we'll see about that," Lily said, patting the floor beside her again. "Sit, young man." She was smiling once more.

"What?" I said. But it was useless. I was already starting to sit.

Doing so was a bit painful, but not as much as I'd expected. Either my bruises were fading rapidly, or my mind was too occupied with Lily to register pain.

Lily wiped her palms on her knees. "Let's start with names. What's yours?"

I paused. "Harry," I said. "Harry . . . Crosby." I couldn't give her my real name.

She looked at me, waited, and then said, "And how *is* Bing?" She smiled. "With a brother that famous, I can see why you go under a secret name like 'Belk.'" She pointed to the name strip on my pocket. I closed my eyes. "Just what are you so nervous about, Soldier Belk?" she asked softly.

"You know why," I said. "It's that you're—you're—you know."

"Taller?" she asked. "Than you? Worried I could toss you out the window? Worried I will?"

"No," I said, imagining being heaved out the window, and then lingering on the scene as I thought about how she'd have to grab hold of me, hug me, probably, wrestle me over there, her arms wrapped around me, our faces inches apart. "You're not taller," I said, surfacing. "You're—*Japanese.*" I whispered the word like it was a secret she'd asked me to keep.

Her eyes went wide with honest, and then exaggerated, alarm. "Oh dear," she said. "You can read my every secret, can't you? Maybe the wrong person's running this palm-reading business." She held out a hand to me. "Here, let's see what else you know. Read *my* palm. Tell me my future." I still knew I had to leave, but I was hardly going to leave *now*, now that I had a chance to hold a woman's—this woman's—hand. I took it gingerly, cradled it with the same care I'd use on some new piece of ordnance that I was encountering for the first time.

But I defy you—or would have defied anyone—to read that hand. As soon as I saw her palm, I almost jumped as if she'd surprised me with another "boo." Her hand was a welter of lines, as though it had been shattered and then reassembled, piece by piece. I looked at my own hands in vain for some reference point. I looked at her other hand, compared them—but they weren't alike, at least in no way that I could tell.

Stranger still, and what I remember even more clearly, is how soft her hands were.

"Here's a little advice," Lily said. "If you decide to go into this profession after the war—and I don't think you should, because you're not doing so hot, so far—but if you do, it helps if you talk to the customer."

"Sorry," I said.

"And when you talk, don't use that word," Lily said. "It scares them. Also: *sick, death, troubling, mother*, and *price*."

I exhaled quickly and squinted, as if focusing would help me read her palms better. "Well, there goes my whole speech."

She smiled, took her hands away. "That's not a surprise," she said. "But you making a funny—that's a surprise. A nice one."

But I wasn't listening to her. I was just watching those hands disappear out of mine; the loss of that touch was almost painful. "Please" was all I could say, and something about my pathetic appearance— combined with the fact that I was harmless, just a boy to her, made her put her hands back in mine.

"Okay," she said. "But be quick. Remember, I'm here to read *your* palm. Which reminds me: How are you going to pay?"

I smiled again. "Let's take a look," I said, and studied her palm.

I decided all you really had to do was tell a story. And all I wanted was an excuse to hold her hands, so I just took any line I saw and started in: She was born in...Tokyo. An only child. Her parents were—but she stopped me, and pointed out that Tokyo was far away. How did she end up in Alaska, and speaking English? I rubbed her palm with a thumb, pretended to think on this for a moment while I savored the touch, and then settled on a ship, a great, ridiculous ship that was full of language instructors, chalkboards.

"God, that sounds boring," she said. I think now she was referring to the imaginary classroom as it bobbed across the Pacific, but I thought then that she was criticizing my imagination. Some palm reader I'd make. So I revised things; I found another line and started again. Born in Japan, on top of a mountain, a mother made of snow and a father made of fire. I didn't know where all this was coming from, but she'd fallen quiet and was listening. She spoke every language, I said, the words came to her in raindrops. Raindrops; a cloud; she'd traveled across the ocean in a giant cloud, floating this way and that, until a storm had gathered, and she'd dropped to earth in a flaming downpour—

Her hands flew away from me with a start, and just for an instant, I saw her wear another face, one she hadn't shown me before. But it passed, and then she was holding my hands. Holding them, but looking at my eyes.

"You're a very, very bad palm reader," she said. "And a creepy storyteller. I, on the other hand—I'm very good at both. You want to hear your story?"

I THINK MINE is the sort of life that almost anyone could read from a hand, or better yet, my eyes. They say those eyes never leave you, eyes that blinked awake each morning wondering if this was the day your parents would come—not some foster parents they'd found for you, but your real parents, a mom and dad, like everyone had, even Jesus. So although I find it patronizing, I long ago decided it was also true: an orphan never loses that look, those eyes.

I wasn't too surprised, then, when Lily got that part right: orphan. And I admire her for not taking the easy route and pretending she knew who my parents were, and describing these imaginary beings to me in exquisite, unknowable detail.

But maybe it would have been better for her to embroider some fiction. Because the more she talked, the more she knew, and the more scared I became. She knew about the orphanage, knew it was nothing like Dickens, knew that the Mary Star of the Sea Home for Infants and Children was south of Los Angeles, knew it was just a block from the beach, knew—and no one would ever have made this up—that the nuns treated us like the grandchildren they'd never have. She knew no family ever came for me (though if she knew why, she didn't say), and she knew that all those years saturated with sun and God's love had left me with the pure, naïve desire to be His priest.

And that's where I stopped her. Because I didn't want to know if she knew the rest, how I'd taken the train—paying the fare with money the teary-eyed nuns had given me—to San Diego. How I'd never made it to the high school seminary they were finally sending me to, because I stopped at the armed forces recruiting station first.

I didn't want to know if Lily knew I had been scared. Scared of what, I can't really say, not even now. (Maybe she could have.) All I knew was that I was a kid on a train, suddenly aware of where he was going, guessing at what he was leaving. There were soldiers on the train. And girls on the train. The world was on that train, and the world was going to war. I was going off to high school, a high school seminary, and I could see it, smell it: wax and wood and incense. The train smelled like perfume and aftershave and the ocean, which was just outside the window. By the time we got to San Diego, I was sweating and queasy because I'd realized what I would do. It wasn't that I *wanted* to lie about my age and enlist—I enlisted because I thought it the only other option God might possibly forgive.

And now, alone in a dark room in the sway of a woman who practiced magic, I finally knew He would not.

"THAT'S ENOUGH," I said. I pulled my hand away, although she hadn't really been studying it—she'd been holding it, but not reading it. For a while, she'd closed her eyes.

"A priest?" she said again, not mocking, not Gurley, just curious.

"There are worse things," I said.

She scrambled to her feet. "That's not what I meant."

"I'm—sorry," I said. "I guess it's not what I meant either." Lurking in the back of my mind had been the faint expectation that she'd make this easy; she'd just rip my clothes off, then hers, and there we'd be. I gave her another second to. And two more. Then I said I had to go.

"You'll come back?" she said, and while I knew I shouldn't, I knew I would. I wanted to know how she'd done what she'd done. And I just wanted to see her again. But reflexes preceded thought, and I found myself mumbling about the base not being far away, and sure, I'd probably get a day or two of leave every now and then. I was halfway out the door when she caught hold of my jacket. "No," she said, low and serious, "I mean, you'll come back, tonight."

Again, I felt something flit in and out of my pocket. "And bring something to eat," she said, even as the door was closing. As it clicked, I felt in my pocket. My wallet was still there. And along with it, a five-dollar bill, another message: "1."

A few paces down the street, I heard, but refused to turn and see, someone climb the steps to the Starhope, open the door, and enter.

LILY SLEPT LIKE she'd been shot. Stomach-down on the floor, limbs and blankets scattered about, mouth agape, breaths coming in as noisily as they went out.

I'd gotten sandwiches, stale ones, really just slices of bread and some cheese, but I'd not had a lot of choice when I went out. Finding a diner that was still open took some time, but not enough; I spent an hour or so wandering what there was then of Anchorage, waiting for 1 A.M. to arrive, and worrying that when it did, she would have meant one in the afternoon. There were soldiers and sailors everywhere, never in groups of less than three, which meant that walking alone, I attracted some attention—at least from those who were still sober enough to focus and speak. But eventually I navigated away from the bars and found a tiny neighborhood that looked like it had been built within the last few hours. I walked each of the streets on its grid, and was going to start on a second lap, when a man who'd spotted me earlier shouted from a porch: "Get a move on, pal. This is all families. None of those type of houses here." That's when I started to notice the signs tacked to some of the doors: "PRIVATE HOME." Somebody later explained: women were rare enough in Anchorage in those days that when you saw one enter a house followed by a man, you might reasonably assume the premises were open for business.

I wondered where Lily lived. At the Starhope? When I got back to her office and found her asleep, I thought about leaving the food and going home—back to base—myself, but I couldn't leave. So I just shut the door behind me and slid down the wall until I was sitting opposite her. I opened one of the sandwiches and ate it, anticipating a good long period of studying her, memorizing her every feature. I wanted a picture, the way other guys had a picture—or half a dozen pictures—of sweethearts, of movie stars. But I wasn't going to get one, so I'd have to make one.

But the picture kept going out of focus. She was snoring. Snoring: I'm glad I remember that detail. Sometimes, I forget it—though I don't see how that's possible. She snored like she was gargling, or choking, or drowning, or was a dog engaged in any one of those activities. I'm glad I remember her snoring, because it's real enough to reassure me that this memory actually occurred.

Otherwise, the moment seems made up of too much magic: outside, that weak, watery blue Alaskan version of midnight twilight, Lily lying there, me sitting there, she sleeping, me watching. I didn't think, then, that we could ever be closer. I'm not sure anyone can. I'm not sure there is a place closer to someone than being at their side, awake, while they're asleep.

I found it increasingly difficult to breathe myself—as if what sounded like snoring were actually her wolfing down what air remained in the room. I was watching her, but not as a voyeur—I was watching *over* her. And nothing stirs a young man's heart—particularly one so new in uniform—as the thought that his vigilance and restraint is keeping some woman safe.

But after a few minutes of listening to her snore and wheeze, my restraint failed. Something deeper stirred within me, starting as a shiver and then finishing as flat-out, coughing laughter.

The snoring stopped. Lily sat up and looked around, wide-eyed, not smiling, not frowning. I fell silent. She saw the remaining sandwich and slid it toward her, peeking inside the wax paper.

"Sorry—" I said.

Lily said nothing, just took a bite and chewed, staring ahead. "Not the worst way to wake up," she said. She took another bite and chewed for a while. "You're really—curious," she said. "You know that? Curious. Comic, soldier, priest. I'm not sure who you are."

"You did a pretty good job earlier figuring me out," I said. She yawned. "What about what happens next?"

"I'm not so good at 'next,'" Lily said. "Maybe if I was," she continued, but stopped to take another bite, "I wouldn't be here, eating this sandwich, hanging out with some sailor thinks I'm Jap." She stuffed the remaining sandwich in her mouth with the heel of her palm and smiled, cheeks bulging, as I stared at her.

"Do I look Japanese now?" she said, cheeks still huge, bits of sandwich spittling out. She took a big swallow, and then pulled on her ears, stuck out her tongue. "How about now? Martian?"

"You're not—?"

She swallowed the last of the sandwich and looked around. "You only bought one? I gave you five bucks."

"Two, but I ate one. You're not Japanese?"

"How much did it cost? That wasn't enough change. What, you think I'm Jap, you can steal from me?"

"I'm sorry, I—"

"Well, I'm not sorry. In fact, I am—" and then she said a word I didn't understand. Or was it a word? It sounded like something she'd done with her throat, her mouth. She said it again: "Yup'ik."

"What's that?"

"It's whaddyacallit, Eskimo. Or it's whatever you get when you take a Russian sailor who's far from home, and add a Native woman who's not," she said. She held up a hand for each and then slapped them together. "Boom: you get one of me. Tallest Eskimo gal for a thousand miles."

"Not Japanese?" I said, relieved, confused. Eskimos lived in igloos. That is, I knew better, but the truth is, I knew as much then about Eskimos as I did about the Japanese—or palm readers.

"Eskimo," she said. "Russian-Eskimo," she added, yawning. "Which means, that whole bit you did about fire and snow—not so far off, after all." She looked up. "And I didn't pick up language from raindrops, although I might as well have, because my father hauled my mother off when I was four or five."

"To where?"

"To Siberia," Lily said. "To Russia, Japan, the moon. Who knows? They left, and they left me."

"I'm sorry," I said again.

"I'm sorry," she parroted in a high-pitched voice. "You like saying that," she added. "I thought they tried to get rid of 'sorry' in the army."

I was about to say it again before I stopped myself.

"So you know my secret, or secrets. Now let's get one out of you." She pointed to my insignia. "What do you do?"

She waited.

"Well, it's secret," I said.

"Well, tell me," Lily said.

"Actually, it's, well, obvious," I said, looking at the patch, with its fat beet of a bomb.

"Bombs," she said. "Bomb disposal? Right. But what do *you* do? What's your assignment?" She was very serious now, which startled me as much as anything else that evening.

"Well," I said. "That—that I can't tell you. Japanese or no. Of course. I can't."

"Yup'ik," she said, and then studied me for a beat or two. "Well, that's a shame."

"Why? Why would you even ask?"

"Well, I thought you might be somebody I needed to get to know *better*." She leaned closer, imperceptibly to anyone but me, who was measuring every fraction of an inch.

"Who?"

"Somebody *useful*, soldier," she said, and waited. But I didn't say anything, and she didn't say anything. Instead, she smiled briefly, and stood.

"I got the sandwiches," I said, a little desperate. She leaned down, extended a hand.

"Thanks," she said, pulling me up. "But you run along home."

"I thought we were—" and then I think I said something tiny, like "friends."

Whatever it was, she laughed, and put her hand on the doorknob. "That's really sweet," she said. "But I got guys who pay to be friends with me. For now, near as I figure, I've been paying to be friends with you." She gave me another tight smile. "That's not good business."

All of a sudden, the doorknob jerked out of her hand. The door flapped open on two sailors, both drunk, both blond, both taller than Lily and I. Their faces were doughy, and their heavy, puffed features almost looked unfinished, infantile. It didn't occur to me then that the reason their noses appeared that way was because they'd been broken so many times. One was more drunk than the other; his name strip read "Jackson," and the way he held on to his partner, "Sanger," with a modified headlock, made his arm seem impossibly long.

Jackson tried to say something, but it fizzled into a drooling smile. Sanger lurched them both into the room.

"We're here," he said to Lily, "for a reading." He held up both hands, palms out, and doing so made Jackson slide off him and onto the floor.

Jackson looked up at Lily. "She's a *Jap!*"

"I'm closed," Lily said, her voice, eyes, shoulders all new to me, a different person, from a different place.

"You mean, busy?" Sanger said, reaching forward to grab a wrist of Lily's, which she flicked away just in time. He and Jackson looked at me. " 'Cause he don't look like he's keeping you busy."

"He's not busy," Jackson said, and wormed across the floor toward me with surprising speed. I jumped away.

"He's leaving," Lily said. "You're leaving. I'm leaving. I'm closed."

"We've come a long fucking way, lady," Sanger said, moving on her.

"All the way from the fucking moooooooon," said Jackson, and before I knew it, he had a hold of my ankle. "He don't look closed, Davey, do he?"

"Get out of here," I said, but it was useless; my voice had flown into its highest registers.

"He's a *girl*," Jackson said, pulling himself up on my knee and getting a good look at my face. "Look at this. He's a girl gotten all beat up by another *girl*."

"Poor little girl," said Sanger.

"Leave," said Lily. "Now."

"I could leave," Sanger said. "But then you'd be on your own with Jackson, here. And he don't do well on his own. Spent the whole trip here from Seattle locked in the brig for hitting an officer."

"Locked in a fucking closet," Jackson said, on his knees now, his hands on my hips, head at my stomach. "Fucking closet with two other guys."

I don't know if Jackson was fainting or attacking, but he wound up pulling me to the floor. After that, I remember his breath, his nails, his weight; I remember the way my hands wouldn't go all the way around his wrists.

Sanger, suddenly sounding sober and reasonable, broke in like a radio announcer with a product to shill. "What's the matter now, boys? We're all on the same team here. Let's not—"

I don't remember Lily leaping on Jackson, or how or when his ear started to bleed. But I remember him coming off me and then the two of them on Lily, who was writhing on the floor with such fury, it seemed she was doing more damage to herself than they ever could. It was too hard to separate out a hand, an arm, but more and more bare skin, mostly hers, became visible. I tore off my belt, and with someone else's strength, fell onto Jackson's back, looping the belt around his neck.

Lily shrieked, I yanked, Jackson bucked and would have thrown me had his buddy not fallen on top of me, his drunken logic insisting that would help. And it might have; he might have smothered me before I finished choking Jackson, but then a louder shriek entered the room, and when I twisted around, I found it was him screaming, not Lily. There was blood everywhere now, it seemed—on the floor, smeared on a wall, on Lily's palms, and most of all, on Sanger. He rolled off me; I sprang away from Jackson, leaving him coughing, using a finger to eke some breathing room out of my belt.

"Fucking Jap fuck," Sanger spat, each word weaker than the one before. "I'm going to go over to that fucking Japland and fuck and kill every one of your cousins. Your mother, your brother, your fucking father." Jackson had the belt off his neck now, and fell back, exhausted.

"Cripes, lady," Jackson said, and I suddenly realized he wasn't much older than I. It didn't seem possible that he'd really wanted to hurt me, or Lily. But a quick look at Lily made it clear that she'd wanted to hurt them. Quite improbably, I began to worry that the two would leave—and leave me alone with Lily.

"*Lady?*" Sanger said, and swore. He put a hand to the back of his head, and then brought it forward, impossibly bright with blood.

"Can't read your palm now," Lily said. "Too messy." She stepped out of the tiny office quickly. I paused for a moment. Jackson was staring toward me but not focusing. Sanger looked ready to start again. I sprang for the door and dashed down the stairs.

Lily was waiting for me outside. She started walking, and I followed, neither of us saying a word until we were some blocks away. "Like I said," she muttered then. "Sailors."

I tried to figure out a reply, anxiously shifting the duty of holding up my beltless pants from one hand to the other.

She sniffed, half a laugh, looked me up and down. Then she stepped close to me and carefully hooked a finger through a belt loop. She was holding them up now, so I let go. "Soldier," she said quietly, and then shook her head and added something Ronnie only recently had taught me how to spell: *"Yugnikek'ngaq."*

"What?" I said, matching her whisper.

"Friend," she said, even softer, and then removed her hand.

CHAPTER 7

FORT RICHARDSON HID ITS BIGGEST SECRET FROM VIEW in a flimsy, leaking, large Quonset hut, surrounded by a chain-link fence topped with rusting razor wire. A single MP was stationed at the gate to the mini-compound, right next to a little wooden placard that read "520" and nothing else.

I didn't have time to take in much more the first morning I reported for duty. Before I could finish studying the outside, the MP on duty told me to move along. I almost did, but instead, gave my name, told him my purpose, and waited while he gave me a long, exaggerated, head-to-toe inspection. Clearly, Gurley had handpicked him. He asked me to repeat my name. I did; he unlocked the gate, nodded me in, and then locked it behind me.

I had to admit: Gurley was doing a good job of intimidating me, and, I assumed, the rest of the base. Sure, everyone said they had top secret jobs, but how many worked in an outsized Quonset hut protected by fencing, razor wire, and a twenty-four-hour sentry?

A yellow bulb above a doorway directly before me seemed to indicate the building's entrance; the door itself had a small window that was blacked out. Inside, the darkness was almost total. I moved slowly; after our initial meeting in the bar, I was sure of an ambush. The door swung shut. I put up my hands to fend off the attack, but instead it came from below—a steel pipe of sorts to my shins. I staggered, cursed, and fell into a crouch, hands futilely—pathetically—around my head. "Stop!" I shouted, although that is probably me revising: I wailed.

No response. No second blow. At the far end of the Quonset hut, a door opened and light spilled out. I could now sense a vast open space. At the end of it, where the light was, an office had been carved out. The rest of the floor was devoted to all manner of war matériel, much of it unrecognizable. Giant tarps hung in odd profusion from the ceiling. Looking down, I could see that it had been some sort of a metal fitting, protruding from a cage the size of four or five milk crates, that had attacked me.

"Belk!" Gurley shouted from the office doorway. I lifted a cautious hand. "Always doing things the hard way, aren't you? That's the back door. The front door is over here." As my eyes adjusted to the gloom, I could see a door near the office at the far end of the building. But it was still too dark to see how I was supposed to get from where I was to where he was, so I started back toward the entrance I'd just come through, thinking that I'd walk around the outside. But before I'd made the door, Gurley threw some switch that illuminated the entire building. "It's an easier walk with the lights on," he called, and then stepped back into his office.

I could see, but I couldn't move.

Gurley's Quonset hut looked like the official Army Air Corps circus tent. Ropes and tackle were everywhere. Strange metal—crates, for lack of a better word—lined the walls. Piles of sandbags appeared at regular intervals. And those tarps I'd seen—with the light, I could tell they were much more than that: great fabric teardrops, upended (or balloons, once I'd thought about it), all of them limply hung from on high.

GURLEY'S OFFICE WAS an even stranger sight. Tyrannically neat, of course. Everything was gunmetal gray—the desk, the lamps, the filing cabinet, and a locker against the wall. Even the walls themselves were covered in gray metal paneling. My first impression was that the army had stuffed Gurley into a giant footlocker. I later decided that the metal fixtures and smooth walls resembled something else: I had picked my way into a bomb.

Along the back wall, a series of clocks, each labeled with a Roman numeral—up to VII, I believe. But much more interesting was the map below the clocks. It stretched across the entire rear of the office. It was a map, mostly of the North Pacific—except that it extended all the way south to Hawaii, and as far east as Michigan—and it was the only untidy thing in the room. Bright pushpins spread across the map's rinsed-out blue, brown, and green like a virulent disease, appearing singly and in clumps.

"Fifty," Gurley said.

"Looks like more than that, sir," I said, still staring at the map. The truth was, it would have been impossible to count the pins. There were dozens of them, maybe hundreds. At first I took them to be army bases, but dismissed that idea. Then I decided that Gurley had marked the map wherever he'd struck a man. White for where he'd wounded them, red for where he had killed them. There was a cluster of red just outside Anchorage.

"Fifty men," he said. Maybe I was right.

"What I am about tell you, no more than fifty men in the country now know." I started to believe him, but wondered, as he took a deep, melodramatic breath, if Gurley had not delivered this line dozens of times before. I could see him savoring the moment; he had that slight suggestion of a smile I now know steals across some actors' faces before a favorite speech. If I were mapping my own path in the war, I would stick a pin right there to mark that moment, in that office, in the light of that smile, because that's when I should have seen how helpless Gurley really was. It was as though he thought of the theaters of war as theaters, and that his role in the war was exactly that, a role.

He had paused after his "Fifty men" preamble, and now leaned forward to deliver the coveted secret. "The Japs," he intoned, "have reached North America."

I sat back: I think I was supposed to be frightened, but instead, I was confused. "The Aleutians, you mean?" A lot more than fifty people knew about that debacle.

Kiska and Attu, two brutally wet and cold islands at the end of the Aleutian chain, had been occupied by Japanese troops in 1943. The islands were of little strategic value, except in the sense that Roosevelt was enraged that the Japanese were occupying American soil. The U.S. had stumbled in its initial response; America's Army, Navy, and Air Corps all fought each other for a while before turning their attention to the Japanese. Then the weather set in. Then the Japanese dug in. Three thousand Japanese on Attu held off an American force triple their size for days. The Japanese eventually lost, but they fought to the last man, or just about. Just twenty-eight of the three thousand Japanese soldiers on Attu survived to be taken prisoner. Most of the patients in their field hospital committed suicide. Those who couldn't, or wouldn't, were killed by their doctor before he killed himself.

After the bitter slog on Attu, the U.S. brought in even more forces for the assault on Kiska, where the main Japanese garrison was located. Tens of thousands of Americans stormed ashore, guns blazing, only to discover that the Japanese had abandoned Kiska two weeks before. More than one hundred U.S. soldiers still died, all from friendly fire.

So, if the Japanese had returned—well, I couldn't speak. This is why the colonel back in California had laughed when he heard I was being taken to Alaska. The Aleutians! It was where the world ended, careers ended, lives ended. Suicides were rampant. So were courts-martial. GIs sent there weren't even told of the destination until they were safely aboard ship and through the Golden Gate, a practice Gurley himself surely approved of.

"The Aleutians?" he said. "Good God, Belk. This means you're literate—you do read, and read the papers, to boot—" He feigned awe, and then resumed. "But no. Hell no. I'm not talking about the Aleutians—the islands or the swarthy Lilliputians who populate them. I'm talking about the fucking homefront, my brother-in-arms. The watchfires of a hundred circling camps." He started tapping the map. "Washington, Oregon, Idaho, Montana." His eyes grew wider, his voice deeper. He was a prophet. A leader. The Wizard of Oz.

I should clarify: recognizing his theatricality wouldn't have immunized me against it. I think I'd have to be as unconscious as Ronnie here to have resisted Gurley's performance. But I wasn't unconscious, I was alive, and I shivered—*the enemy is here! Japs all around!*—and you know what? It was wonderful. It was wonderful the same way it's wonderful to flinch at some frightening point in a book or a movie; there's a certain dizzy pleasure that comes with knowing you've succumbed, you've been duped.

And, back then, it was a lot more than that: it was wonderful to know the war was real. You had to be young to think this; the country had to be younger, too. But that's the way it was with kids like me: it was wonderful to know that this enemy we'd read so much about was really out there, that I would finally get to fight, and that Gurley would somehow wave a magic wand, take me through a back door, and usher me right into the middle of all of it.

All of it: Japanese soldiers, hiding in trees, leaping out of mailboxes late at night. Bombs in the sky. Balloons in the clouds. A giant red rising sun on a white field, strung between the twin towers of the Golden Gate Bridge. But gradually, as Gurley rambled on, talking more to himself now than to me, my excitement began to give way to a kind of panic.

What he was talking about was preposterous. Evidence of Japanese activity in a dozen states or more? And nobody other than fifty men (fifty-one now?) knew about it? I looked around the office; I looked at Gurley as he stared at the map with red-rimmed eyes. I wondered if fifty men now knew what *I* thought I knew: here, in this lonely Alaskan outpost, Captain Thomas Gurley, U.S. Army Air Corps, had gone mad.

And he'd dreamed himself up a new front line in the process. Even as a work of insanity, it was impressive: his line stretched clear across North America—through Canada and into Michigan. He rattled on, and I marveled at the performance, and at the magnitude of the fiction. I began to wonder which would come first: my transfer away from Anchorage, or Gurley's? Who would assume his post, and its attendant, if imaginary, duties?

What a world this was, wartime Alaska. Half-naked palm readers, rampaging drunken sailors, lunatic captains raving in darkened Quonset huts, and me. If I had been older, I would have been too scared to speak.

But I was young, stupid, and, once the panic subsided, bemused, so what I finally said was "Incredible."

Gurley frowned, furious. I was not as good an actor as he. "Not enough for you," he said.

"No, no, it's—incredible. You've—you've come up with quite a, a map." I tried furrowing my brow, but it was no use—I don't even think I knew what the word *furrowing* meant back then.

Gurley would have known, though, and he knew I was mocking him. He scrambled across the desk, right over the top, growling and sputtering.

For a minute, I feared (even hoped) that I had provoked the inevitable and total breakdown. I calculated whether I could get to the door before him and raise the alarm with the MPs. I decided to jump clear. He jumped after me and then fell horribly short. I took a moment to take in the scene: he was sprawled at my feet, while the better part of his left leg was separated from him, dangling off the desk.

He extended a hand, and I hesitated, unsure what horror had just happened and what horror would now follow.

"You didn't hear a word I said, did you, you sanctimonious shit?" he hissed. He closed his eyes for a second; I could see the mask fall, instantly. But then his eyes opened, the mask was back, and it had all happened too quickly for me to see what had been revealed. He extended a hand to me, and I automatically hauled him up. He teetered back to the desk and leaned on it. On the floor behind him lay two red pins that had fallen from the map.

Gurley recovered his artificial leg and regarded it for a second. "Maybe I should just beat you with this instead of going through it all again." I stared at the leg, then at Gurley. What part of him would fly apart next? "Here's the short version: the Japs are bombing North America. Believe the map, or believe this, you insolent fuck." He hiked up the pant leg that was missing a leg below the knee and revealed a stump that looked more rock than human—angry purple and brown, mottled with scabs. He spent a moment trying to get the leg back on, and then gave up, letting it clatter to the floor. He hobbled around to the back of the desk and fell into his chair.

I slowly bent down and picked up the leg. It was heavier than I imagined, and it took two hands to place it on the desk with any care.

"Exhibit A," he said, nodding to the map. "The past." He dragged his leg back across the desk. "Exhibit B, the interminable present." Then he took out a small key, unlocked a desk drawer, and drew out a small, leather-bound book, about the size of a priest's breviary. "Exhibit C," he said, brightening again. "The future." He looked at the book for a full minute. He didn't open it. Then he looked at me.

"Let's start at the beginning," he said, and with that, began to recount the history—his history—of the balloon program to date. The first, mysterious explosions and fires. The eventual discovery of an intact balloon. The determination of the balloon's origin. The recovery of ever-growing numbers of balloon shrouds and payloads, evidence of which sat just outside the office.

"And the most recent chapter, August 1944, wherein a certain bomb disposal sergeant looks on, dumbstruck, while a balloon sets fire to a golden hillside. Said fire roasts alive several men." He sat back. "Sergeant? Am I missing anything?"

"Sir?" I asked, but even as the word was coming out of my mouth, my mind was finally making the connection. It seems odd to me now that it took that long, but of course, the balloons—as patent an impossibility as there ever was—were still new to me then.

I almost leapt from my chair: "The weather balloon! Fort Cronkhite! Sir, I—"

"Failed in your first encounter?" Gurley suggested, somehow managing a face that was half sneer, half sympathy. That wasn't what I was going to say—I had no idea what I was going to say—but his words had all the effect of his having reached over and pulled the pin from a grenade I hadn't known I was carrying.

What a cruel thing to put on a child—sure, I was a young man, a soldier in uniform, but I had the wild conscience and boundless shame of a Catholic kid, one raised by nuns, no less—and how sinister of Gurley to attempt to make the death of those soldiers on the hill my legacy, my burden.

Hours, days later, when I thought about it, I realized his gambit was only that; I knew nothing about the balloons that day in California. And if I had? I was too far away to do anything. But it didn't matter. Gurley knew what he was doing. He'd planted a seed, an irritant, deep inside me that I could smother with excuses but would still know was always there. The fact was, I had known—felt—that something was wrong, that it wasn't a weather balloon. The fact was, I'd gone running toward it. The fact was, I hadn't made it there in time.

If Gurley's aim had been to provoke in me an instant and towering resolve to avenge their deaths (while expiating my own apparent guilt), I suppose the ends would have justified his means: my commitment to the war then was naïve and relatively shallow.

But his next words made me think he had another aim altogether.

He wasn't looking to stir up some fight in me; he simply wanted to commiserate.

"That's okay, Sergeant," he said. "My first time out, I failed, too."

GURLEY EXPLAINED that he'd begun his wartime service with the Office of Strategic Services, or OSS. The OSS was the war's headquarters for Ivy Leaguers, spies, scientists, and anyone with an unusual idea for waging war. Poison cigars, exploding pens, buttonhole cameras, and worse. At the bidding of a favorite professor, Gurley had left Princeton a semester early to work in OSS research and development. He should have been a natural. Articulate, cosmopolitan, heir to a fortune (from fountain pens, of all things), he'd also spent his Princeton years studying "the men and minds of the Orient"—in particular, all things Japanese. He was even somewhat fluent. He pointed to an impressively worn Japanese-English dictionary on a shelf behind him.

Yet he'd foundered after enlisting. His ideas—fueled by "*educated* insight"—were dismissed. He watched as colleagues championed ridiculous ideas that later turned out to be quite effective, and he watched those colleagues go on to greater rank and glory. As the months wore on, Gurley was desperate to find the idea that would make him a star. A huge star: not for him invisible ink or a corncob pipe revolver.

He wanted something spectacular.

He brainstormed and came up blank, and then brainstormed with friends. Blank again. Then he found a memo in a stack of papers that had been left on his desk. A scrap of a confidential memo, actually, stamped with a security classification beyond the level Gurley possessed. He should have stopped reading immediately and reported the security breach, but (he admitted) he did not. How could he? The memo referred to a piece of intriguing, if bizarre, research: the enemy— the Japanese—considered blue foxes a bad omen. (I thought, but didn't ask: Who wouldn't?)

Gurley took up the case. His first discovery was the existence of an actual animal—"*Alopex lagopus*," he took pleasure in informing me—a type of arctic fox whose coat turned bluish-gray in winter. "But it didn't look the *least* bit frightening—or blue," Gurley said. Rather, he decided to press ahead in secret with elaborate plans for a truly blue, truly scary fox of his own design, *Vulpes livida*.

He tested and discarded the idea of air-dropping blue fox leaflets or releasing live, paint-dipped foxes (via parachute? I wondered. Torpedo tubes? Rubber rafts?), and decided on something far more spectacular: projecting a blue fox *in the sky* above enemy troops. It was bold, theatrical—terrifying. The enemy would panic and throw down their weapons in fear.

It was also impractical, silly, and foolish—but so were dozens of other ideas that the OSS researched, and many of those (including a rotating gun that attached to a railroad car's wheel) had gone forward.

"The fated day came," Gurley said. "I was to present to the full committee. Now, word had spread of all the hours I had put in. And while most didn't know the details, everyone knew that I was hoping to make my reputation. Some might have uncharitably said, *repair* my reputation." Gurley looked at the ceiling a moment, as though he were being fed lines from above. I had a slight urge to look up myself.

"Project Hannibal," he continued. "Foxtrot—the obvious, and therefore fatuous, choice. Hannibal: Sergeant?"

"Sir?"

"Why 'Hannibal'?"

I had no idea. It rhymed with *cannibal*, which seemed a bit gruesome, even for Gurley. Then I remembered that Mark Twain had grown up in Hannibal, Missouri. I mentioned this.

"Who?" Gurley said. "No, Sergeant. This is a *war*. Not bedtime stories. Hannibal, the Carthaginian general. Takes his elephants over the Alps. Hannibal: the perfect code name for the deployment of an unusual animal to seek a military victory." He studied my reaction. "No, no one got it. But I pressed on."

He took his audience through the background first: why this would frighten the soldiers, why it would, in fact, be more deadly than any conventional weapons. American bombs were certainly decimating Japanese ranks—but it was hard to claim that they had caused *fear*. Indeed, the Japanese fought more tenaciously the more casualties they suffered.

"And I was winning, Belk. I guarantee you. One man at a time. I could see, I could look around the room and watch as their smiles faded into a kind of—not awe, no, not that, but a kind of respect. Maybe that's even too strong a word. Interest, then. I saw them grow curious, despite themselves, one face at a time. I don't think I've ever seen anything lovelier."

Gurley said that he finished his presentation and sat. He wanted to look around the room—he could hear the murmurs of interest and appreciation on all sides—but kept his eyes on the colonel who had been chairing the meeting. The colonel should have been his staunch ally, Gurley said: they were both Princeton men; the colonel had graduated some ten years before. But the colonel had rarely deigned to speak with him, nor even meet his eyes, and he did neither now.

Instead, the colonel looked around the room and smiled. "What's Bob Hope say?" he asked. Gurley's stomach began to turn, slowly. Everyone's faces began to warm into smiles—not, Gurley was sure, in anticipation of the joke, but of his demise. Gurley held his breath. The colonel waited before going on. He was enjoying himself. Worse: he was playing to the crowd.

Quoting Bob Hope? What Gurley needed was a minute or two alone with the colonel. Man to man. One Princetonian to another. Some setting where the colonel wouldn't feel a need to appeal to the base instincts of a base crowd.

Gurley paused his recounting now, as well. At first I thought it was for theatrical effect, an attempt to wring whatever more suspense he could out of his story, but he looked down at his hands for a moment—only for a moment—and I saw something else. He'd left his little stage. He'd been kicked off the stage, in fact, at that meeting, and try as he might, had never quite found his way back on, at least not before audiences larger than, say, a solitary, teenaged sergeant. When he started speaking again, his volume had dropped by half or more, and I would have sworn he was crying. But he wasn't; I checked, his face was clear.

The colonel continued, Gurley said.

"What's the most dangerous thing in war?" the colonel asked. The room was already laughing. Gurley wasn't breathing. "A second lieutenant," the colonel answered, "with a plan."

With a map, Gurley told me now, seething. The colonel even screwed up the punch line, Gurley said. And everyone had to know it. Hope must have trotted that joke out every USO tour he ever made.

But if everyone knew it, they didn't care. In fact, they acted like the colonel's version was funnier. And you wouldn't even have said they were acting, Gurley said. They were enjoying themselves. As much as the colonel, who looked—and Gurley worked at finding the right word—a bit *relieved* at all the laughter. Relieved that his joke had gone over, and even more relieved that he wasn't alone in thinking Gurley's plan was poppycock.

"Dismissed, Lieutenant," the colonel said. Gurley rose and left the room while the laughter rose and followed him, and then shut the door behind him.

A friend—or someone who wanted to twist the knife a little deeper—told him how the rest of the meeting went. Gurley was almost flattered to learn he remained the subject of the meeting for several more minutes. The colonel said that Gurley had fallen into a clever trap, set by OSS internal security to catch people who had taken to reading materials that they didn't have the proper classification for. A fictionalized, highly classified memo, designed to be outlandish enough to catch a wayward eye's interest, had been introduced into the office's paper stream. It was only a matter of time before the blue fox nabbed its prey, the colonel said, and he congratulated all those remaining in the room on their now-validated discretion.

"It was a trap?" I asked Gurley.

"A lie," he said. "To be more precise. An elaborate and admittedly impressive spur-of-the-moment lie by the colonel himself." The actor was returning. "For this self-proclaimed 'friend' of mine could not help but tell me something else. Something he found so funny, and cruel, he could hardly bear not to share it. How could I not have known, he asked, that the blue fox was, in fact, quite real?" Gurley paused and looked at me. "My 'friend' went on: 'Blue Fox' was the nickname of the colonel's mistress." Gurley closed his eyes and leaned back.

"Sir," I said.

"Silence, Belk. Let us both agree that there is absolutely nothing adequate that you could say at this point, other than 'Captain, shall I fetch you a thermos of coffee?' " He nodded toward the door.

"I'm sorry, sir," I said, because I had to. He was pitiful.

"As I said, Belk: absolutely nothing adequate. Now try again: 'Captain, shall I fetch you...' "

"Sir, it's just that—"

"Sergeant, 'it's just that' ... I haven't even *gotten* to the sorry part yet. Be gone."

WHEN I RETURNED with the thermos, Gurley smiled and brought out a bottle. The label, faded, said "vodka," but the liquid inside was brown. He asked with raised eyebrows if I wanted any, and when I declined, poured himself some in a chipped mug. He topped off the mug with coffee, and then raised it.

"A toast, then, to the Blue Fox. For it was due to her that I was assigned the crackpot casebook, the file containing letters from every asylum escapee who mails the OSS some deranged idea about how to wage war or defend our homeland." Gurley rose and studied the map. "Dozens of these letters, Belk. And we read them all. Because buried in every hundredth, every thousandth, letter was something useful. A grandmother in Chicago uncovers a Nazi sympathizer. A lobsterman in Maine hauls up a trap full of codebooks and sabotage plans. And the lone inhabitant of a dot-sized Bering Sea island off the coast of Alaska, an Orthodox hermit with the unspellable name of Father Ioasaph, sends word of Armageddon. After a period of intense fasting and prayer, the good Father—whose isolation has driven him quite mad—witnesses the advance guard of the heavenly host descending in flames to his island. Or so he writes."

Gurley took a sip from the mug and put it down. Then he walked around the desk and sat on the edge, before me. I think the object was to position his left leg for better viewing. "Some people can lose a limb quickly and efficiently, close by, perhaps in a traffic accident right around the corner," he said. "I had to travel to the end of the earth."

Gurley decided to go investigate Father Ioasaph's letter, for a variety of reasons, the most important of which was that it got him far, far away from the office, where he remained the subject of open ridicule. More important, an odd detail in the island hermit's account of Armageddon intrigued Gurley and made him wonder if, just maybe, the flaming angel that Father Ioasaph had reported might have brought redemption as well. For Father Ioasaph wrote that there was a particular, and curious, reason he was sharing this glorious news with Gurley's office: *"... it would appear, dear sirs, that God's angels speak Japanese...."*

"I KEPT THE LETTER to myself," Gurley said, rising from his perch to pace. "I took leave. I didn't want to be mocked once again for pursuing folly, and, should anything come of the hermit's claims, I didn't want anyone barging in to steal credit. It took more than a week to get there. Or, rather, to get close. I found myself in a tiny Native village at the mouth of the Kuskokwim River." Gurley went to the map to show me. "Look, Father Ioasaph's island isn't even on this map." He studied the spot for a moment. "I don't think it was on anyone's map. But Father

Ioasaph was well known in the area. The Russians had set up missions throughout this part of Alaska in the days of the Russian American Trading Company. And Father Ioasaph occasionally journeyed to the mainland to say Mass. In return, the villagers supplied his meager needs. It took some doing to find someone who would take me out to him—they were fiercely protective of their local loon—but I finally prevailed. I paid a generous fare, and promised even more should the boatman return promptly the following day to collect me."

Ioasaph's island was barren and wet. His hermitage was wedged into the rear of a small ravine and looked as though it had been constructed by an animal. And what with his beard and hair forming a wild corona around his face, he might well have been an animal. He welcomed Gurley gravely, and took him on a five-minute scramble across the island to where God's messenger had landed.

Even someone not in the throes of religious devotion might have ascribed a divine nature to the scene, Gurley said. The earth was scorched; a circle of blackened grass and trees perhaps twenty feet in diameter marked the spot where the "angel" had alighted.

There was a small chance Father Ioasaph had lit this fire himself in a desperate ploy to attract a visitor, Gurley thought, but that seemed unlikely. The devastation was too complete. Gurley pressed him: What do you mean, "angel"? A man with wings? Really now.

Father Ioasaph sighed as though Gurley were hopelessly simpleminded. "No, sir," he said. "The ways of God are mysterious to us, and this time, his messenger arrived by *balloon*."

"Balloon?" Gurley asked. Father Ioasaph described a giant balloon, as big as his hermitage, dirty white in color, plummeting from the sky.

"And the angel was in the balloon? A man, you saw a man—a soldier—in the balloon?" This was the crucial question, Gurley said, and he watched as Father Ioasaph considered his answer.

"No," Father Ioasaph said. "Not a man like men we know." He went on to describe what would soon become a familiar sight to Gurley: the multilayered payload, the rings of cylinders and the tangle of wires. But Gurley had never heard of such a thing then, and thus could offer little to counter Father Ioasaph's assertion that this was the being's strange skeleton; whatever corporeal elements might have existed would have been consumed in the fire.

"But you said it *spoke* Japanese," Gurley said. Father Ioasaph nodded and led Gurley around a small rise.

Here lay the being's skeleton, or what remained of it, twisted and charred. For all the damage the payload had done, Gurley said, it was surprisingly intact. Dangerously intact, but he didn't know that. Father Ioasaph drew him close and pointed to various elements in the wreckage. Indeed, to judge from the markings, the being did "speak" Japanese.

A sense of wonder, and then, an even greater sense of greed, consumed Gurley. He had found his prize, his ticket back into the OSS's front ranks. Not even Bob Hope could dismiss this discovery.

Father Ioasaph had a hand at his elbow. "I do not know what this means," Father Ioasaph said. "Through prayer, I hope to come to know, and I will let you know when I do. But now, we must leave it be."

"Yes, Father," Gurley said. "Leave it be. Leave it to me." Father Ioasaph looked confused.

Gurley said he barked at the man: *Leave*. And the change in Gurley's demeanor must have been so sudden, so sharp, that the priest did immediately as he was told. Gurley had frightened him. Still, Father Ioasaph pleaded with him even as he moved away. "Pray with me," he said. "We must leave to God what is His and His alone...."

But Gurley did not. He turned his back on Father Ioasaph, smiled, and began to lift a piece of the wreckage with his foot. "Speak to me, O Lord," he muttered.

Whereupon, Gurley said, He did.

The blast was not deafening, not blinding. But it was sudden. One moment his lower left leg and foot were there, the next moment they were not. One moment Gurley was there, on Father Ioasaph's island, the next moment he was not.

He was, instead, lying down, in a hospital, eyes closed, listening to two men talk about him.

Incredible he survived.

That priest saved his life.

Not his leg.

Nothing to save, I'd imagine. Unless you wanted a souvenir.

How many days did it take to get him here?

Three.

A miracle, indeed. He should thank that priest.

Convert.

Then Gurley felt a surge of pain in his left foot. Pain, and then an equal surge of relief. He hadn't lost the foot, the leg. They were talking about someone else. He opened his eyes. The two men, doctors, it seemed, were standing beside him.

"He's awake," one said.

The other turned to Gurley. "You made it," he said. "Welcome back to the land of the living." Gurley said nothing, just looked at him. "How do you feel?"

Gurley told me it took him a moment to decide he was awake and not dreaming. Then he answered the doctor's question, as truthfully as he could. He told the man he felt okay. Weak, but okay.

Then, without looking anywhere except into the doctor's eyes, he said, accurately, "My left foot's a little sore, though. Really sore, kind of a sharp, shooting sore." The two doctors looked at each other, then they looked at his left foot, or where it should have been. Then Gurley looked as well.

"That'll happen," said the doctor who'd first spoken to him. "Usually it's an itch, and your brain is telling you it's there. But, in your case, it's not. Nor much of anything below the knee. Now, your brain's also going to tell you the other leg hurts, and it'll be right about that.

Kind of unbelievable it's still there. Or that you're here. But you are. And you'll walk, eventually. Couple weeks, they'll be by to fit a prosthetic. Two, three weeks. They've been busy, of course."

Gurley finished his story, looked at me. " 'Busy,' " he repeated. "It took three months." He looked down at his leg and shook it gently. "Then again, it took more than a quarter century to grow the one I'd had."

GURLEY RETREATED behind the desk. "Let's finish." He dropped into his chair, pulled forward, and then folded his hands over the small book that he'd pulled out when I'd first arrived.

"Exhibit C," Gurley said. He opened the book, riffled through its pages, closed it, and then slid it across the desk to me with both hands. I didn't pick it up. He took it back.

The leather cover had been dyed a dark green and was well worn. There were brown smudges in several places.

"Blood," he said. I just looked at him. "Old blood," he added, and smiled. He flipped it over. On the back was more blood, and you could almost see, or imagine, where a bloody hand had raked across it. If Gurley hadn't said anything, though, I would have taken it for mud or grease. But that was one of his talents: to make everything sinister.

"That's what I'm told, anyway, and I choose to believe it. It makes for more of a fair trade. A bloodied book for a bloodied leg." He considered this and then continued. "I was convalescing when this book was—acquired, let us say, by my former colleagues. As you'll see once you open it, it is a kind of atlas. A book of maps and drawings. And like Father Ioasaph's avenging angel, the book also 'speaks' Japanese. Certainly not *Chinese*, as the imbeciles who first showed it to me insisted." He opened it, found a page. "Japanese." Another page. "Japanese." He looked at me. "Seven semesters of Japanese at Princeton, I know Japanese. I am, as they say, something of an Orientalist."

He handed it to me, and I took it gingerly, trying not to touch the bloodstains. The pages were beautiful—it wasn't a book, really, as much as it was some man's private journal. The Japanese calligraphy was done in a tight, neat hand in the corners or margins of each page; in the center was usually a map or illustration, done with black ink and colored with watercolor paints or a light gray wash. The fire balloons appeared on a number of pages; sometimes in flight, sometimes lying in a wreck on the ground. The pages themselves were unusual; the paper felt brittle and had a slight sheen.

Gurley thought the book's final pages were its most curious. First, several seemed to be missing, which he found troubling. And the pages that remained—well, they looked blank. But when you looked closer you could see evidence of some color—a faint gray wash, nothing more. After a minute or two, I decided that summed up the book: pretty, but useless. I made the mistake of saying so.

"On the contrary, Belk," Gurley said. "It is extremely useful, in fact, albeit to a small number of people." He counted them off with his hand, starting with his thumb. "First it is useful to the spy, or spies, who created it. Should we find them and—secure—their assistance, then the book becomes useful indeed. Second, it is, and has been, useful to me. I was able to convince my former colleagues that the book, and by extension, the balloon campaign, was worthy of my personal and total focus. I admit the colonel was uncertain, initially, but I explained that I would be happy to brief his wife on all that I had discovered about the Blue Fox. He turned a shade of red that was indeed close to blue." Gurley smiled. "He was only too happy to send me back to Alaska."

Gurley looked at his row of clocks and stood. "It's time to go." I started to stand as well, and Gurley pointed me back down. "This book, lastly, will prove useful, I hope, to you. I have read it, studied it, translated it, but have yet to find a balloon with it, or predict, precisely, where one will land." I looked up. "Yes, we're quite good at finding them *after* they've landed. But by then it's too late: a fire has started, or worse, rumors have started among the local populace." Gurley paused until I looked at him. "So please, Sergeant, find us our next balloon, before some lumberjack does. Find me my *spy*. Find the next bomb in that book, on paper, before I find it in the field, with my one remaining foot."

He limped quite slowly around the desk to the door. I twisted around to see him go. "I'll not be back today, Sergeant. Business in town." He smiled, broadly. "But I look forward to hearing the fruits of your labors. Tomorrow, 0700, at the airfield. Do not be late. Nor empty-handed."

"I don't know what I can do by then, sir. That's not nearly enough time to—"

Gurley cut me off. "Sergeant," he said, teeth bared in his favorite apparent smile. "You've seen this weapon in flight. You've seen it land. You've seen what happens when you don't move fast enough." He spun and kicked the door with a violence that no other man who wanted to spare his foot injury could have matched. Which, when I saw his face, I realized was precisely his point.

"*Boom,*" he said, just the one word, quiet and slow, and then he left.

CHAPTER 8

I HAD NO IDEA WHERE GURLEY AND I WERE FLYING, SO I packed everything I could think of into a large duffel and hauled it down to the airfield the next morning. I got there an hour early, just to be safe. After a flight left for Juneau and points south at 0630, I had the terminal to myself, with the exception of a surly master sergeant who appeared to be in charge of everyone's comings and goings. I went outside to wait.

At 7:10, the sergeant poked his head outside the door and asked if I'd seen a Captain Gurley. I said no, and he ducked back inside before I could say anything more.

At 7:30, the sergeant poked his head outside again, saw me, frowned, and then disappeared once more.

At 7:55, Gurley bounced up in the back of a jeep driven by two sailors. None of the three looked like they had bathed, changed, or slept since the day before. Gurley climbed out of the back carefully, but quickly, exchanged a laugh with the driver, and then turned to face me. The jeep lurched away.

"Who's late, Belk? You or me?" He looked at his watch, and then caught sight of my bag. "What's this?" he asked, kicking it. "You packed me a lunch?"

"No, sir," I said. "I—well, I wasn't sure where we were going, so I packed everything I—" Gurley looked completely confused, so I tried something shorter: "That's my gear, sir."

"Lovely, Belk, but why—oh dear," he said. "You assumed—but of course you did, what with your feeble brain and eager youth. You thought you were going *with* me. That's charming."

Gurley walked us away from the building—he was concerned about eavesdropping; I was concerned about a fight—and then turned me around, put his hands on my shoulders, and said, "Before we begin, Sergeant, let us be absolutely clear on one point. What you learned yesterday is extremely secret. You are to tell no one. If you do—" Now, it would have been clear enough for Gurley to draw a finger across his own throat. But, as always, he'd devised better. Whether it was improvised or practiced, I can't say, but this is what he did: he put a thumb to my neck, just to the left of my carotid artery. And then he slowly drew his thumbnail across—carotid, esophagus, jugular— before lifting it, before I quite knew how to react, before I'd started breathing once more. He smiled. "There, now," he said. "It might just be better to pretend—and this may not be too difficult to do—that you learned nothing, not a single thing."

He was right. That would not be difficult at all, because this was Alaska.

During the war, the entirety of Alaska was declared of strategic importance. Press censorship was so tight, soldiers returning Outside sometimes weakly joked that their whole horrific Alaskan experience may have taken place in their imaginations. They'd been to this strange and wild place, after all; many of them never saw the enemy (nor the sun). Once they were home, they discovered that no one had heard or read a single word about what they'd done. Daily dispatches from the South Pacific appeared in the press, but the Alaska news blackout was almost total. Maybe nothing had happened there at all.

And if Americans thought that, if the enemy thought that, it was fine with Gurley. He fought his war on two fronts, as he now explained. On one side were the Japanese, their balloons, and the prevailing winds. On the other side, the American press and public, whom he feared and loathed even more. The greatest danger these balloons posed, Gurley insisted repeatedly, was not that they would kill a few civilians or set ablaze a few acres, but rather that they would be discovered by the wrong sort of people—in particular, members of the press, who would inevitably sensationalize the issue. And why not? Japanese bombs were raining down on North America almost daily now, and not many Americans—though surely more than Gurley's supposed fifty—knew what was happening.

Although there had been a few brief mentions of the balloons in the *New York Times* and elsewhere early on in the campaign, very little was known about the balloons at the time, and officials had quickly moved to smother any further coverage. Gurley told me his superiors had initially proposed sending out a general bulletin to editors nationwide, alerting them to the story, and then demanding that they not cover the story. Report any information they uncovered to the Army, but publish nothing.

As it happens, just such a blanket agreement was later struck. But when I told Gurley that this sounded like a sensible plan, his reply was quick.

"The best way to keep a secret is to tell as many people as possible?" Gurley said. I tensed for a fist or foot to come flying. "Tell as many *journalists*?" he pressed. "We all have a job," he said. "Our job is to beat the enemy to a bloody pulp. Their job is to sell papers." I stared at the ground. "So newsmen can choose. They can either be on our side or the enemy's." Gurley had concocted his own response plan for balloon sightings. Get a recovery team there as quickly as possible and collect or destroy any piece of evidence that the balloon had arrived. If the initial spotters or witnesses were military, the follow-up was easy. Gurley ordered their silence and made job-specific threats to ensure it.

If the witnesses were civilian, the job became a little more involved.

Depending on what they had seen—or *thought* they had seen—Gurley would either order their silence (and call on them to consider that silence a patriotic duty) or, more often, he would tell them the balloon was a U.S. Army weather balloon that had gone awry. He wouldn't go into details, or make the balloon's mission seem secret at all, figuring that the more he downplayed its importance, the less likely the witness would be to spread the news.

But now, Gurley's plan—indeed, his whole mission—was in jeopardy. He had been summoned to San Francisco by his superiors to discuss the progress of balloon interdiction efforts. Or rather, the decline of such efforts. Early on, the numbers of balloons spotted had climbed steadily, week after week. Then they had stabilized, and recently, had begun to decline. The question now was whether to scale back American efforts to track and recover balloons. After all, resources were needed elsewhere, especially as U.S. forces drew ever closer to Japan. Instead of soldiers, the U.S. would now rely on local authorities and private citizens to find and report balloons. The press ban would be lifted; a general alert would be issued.

Gurley, of course, disagreed.

"It's not just about me, Sergeant," he said. "It's not just that I sense dark forces are, yet again, trying to sweep me into some forgotten corner of the war. I have America's interests at heart." He looked at me. "This campaign has only begun. These first balloons, what have they carried? Piddly little incendiary or antipersonnel bombs? You don't develop an entire program like this to start a few brush fires. Think, Sergeant."

I did, but all I could think of was how Gurley really was taking this personally.

"There's worse coming, Belk. That must be evident, even to you." He looked at me and waited. "A *man,* Sergeant. Manned balloons. An invasion force. Saboteurs. *Spies.* Silently dropped behind enemy lines." He looked back toward the terminal, as if to make sure no one had overheard him. "Angels, indeed."

"Where?" I asked, or stammered, honestly frightened—though more of Gurley than of what his imagination had produced.

"Well, I doubt they're in goddamn San Francisco with my so-called superiors." He turned around, waved broadly at the mountains that formed a backdrop to the base. "Here, Belk. Alaska. In the vast, concealing wilderness. Our backyard, Belk. We have to find them. And damn soon, before we get shut down. So you shall be busy while I'm gone."

"Yes, sir," I said, looking up to the mountains, their crowns still scabbed with snow.

Gurley followed my gaze. "Not up there, you ninny. Or who knows, maybe. But we're not going to go hiking around aimlessly— I'm certainly not going to go hiking around anywhere—no, start your search here. Back at 520. Start with the book. I trust you came up with nothing?"

"No sir," I said. "Nothing yet." I'd stayed in the office until midnight, staring at the book until the watercolor maps seemed to animate, its rivers flow and grasses glisten after a rain. Which seemed like more than a book could or should do, so I had closed it and crept back to the barracks for sleep.

Gurley shook his head. "Well, of course I didn't expect a child prodigy. Just someone to put in the tedious work of comparing the book's maps to ours, quadrant by quadrant, feature by feature. Tedious work—you can see why I thought of you."

I opened my mouth to protest, but didn't utter a sound when I saw Gurley's face harden into the one he assumed before delivering a blow. "Sergeant Belk," he said, low and even. "One balloon, one explosion, one leg. I almost had my war taken from me." He straightened up. "I barely held on to my commission. I had to fight to even get posted to this godforsaken place. They'd rather have me in a bathrobe and wheelchair in Princeton. If we fail to find more balloons, or worse still, find one and handle it injudiciously—if I lose the second leg—or a hand, or an arm, or an eye, or the skin off my fucking face—it won't matter how much I yell. I'll be shipped home before the blood's even soaked through the bandages." He took a deep breath. "Do you understand?"

"Yes, sir," I said.

"I shall close by letting you in on a final secret," Gurley said. "A trifle compared to all that I have told you so far, but still, a secret, and an important one nonetheless."

"Sir?"

"Right, then: I know almost nothing about defusing bombs."

He paused.

"And thus, I shall leave those details...to you."

I could only stare at him. He wore the same bomb disposal insignia I did. I'd assumed that when he'd gotten himself assigned to this mission he had picked up the bomb disposal training that went with it. Of course he would have. He'd learned, hadn't he, the price explosives exacted from the ignorant?

"Sir," I began, searching for the best way to phrase this. He was an officer, I was the sergeant. The way things worked—

"You're incapable of this?" Gurley asked. "I was told you were the best in your class. Now that I have had some time to observe you, I can see that it was not much of a class, but still, I had certain expectations."

"Sir," I began, thinking back to Manzanar, the pit, Sergeant Redes, and the "rare" fuze pocket that had simply fallen out of the bomb. *Damnedest thing.* I tried again. "Our training was—I mean, didn't you—well—there was always, you know, an officer who actually did the, well, the last part. That's procedure, proper procedure and all."

"So I understand," said Gurley. "And so it was here, until recently. But, as I believe I've said, they've been trying to shut me down. Starve me. I used to have a full detail, including a young lieutenant, planning to read history at Oxford when this was all done." Gurley's actor's mask fell for a moment, and then he resumed. "I must admit, I took a certain shine to him, although he was given to a younger man's ways. And, of course, he was no good at his job, or I assume as much, because he blew himself right up on the team's second mission."

"I'm sorry to hear that, sir," I said, though I was barely listening. All I could think of was: *It's up to me—I'm defusing the bombs.* And then: *"Your Nazis, they build a good bomb...."*

"Well, I was pretty damn sorry as well. Not just because he was a good sort, but—an officer. That's when it struck me, this little swipe of genius: *this* is the work of an enlisted man. Talented, capable, yes, but enlisted. No need to waste officers on such. Surely you agree?"

"Sir, I'm not sure that, well, in training, they—"

"Yes, of course, they're always behind in training. No, no, Sergeant, I'm quite pleased with my proposal, and expect you to be as well. Or...I can...reassign you, if you like." He looked back toward the terminal. "I'm frequently told that young and able men are needed to clear out caves and bunkers on treeless islands throughout the Pacific. North or south, your choice." He waited.

"No, sir," I said quietly.

"No to the north, or south? Aleutians or Philippines?"

"I'm your man, Captain," I said. "For this mission." Gurley said nothing for a full minute, and I could feel him staring at me the whole time.

"Sergeant," he finally said, "I believe that you shall never again find a mission as intriguing—or easy. You are used to digging out half-ton bombs that have plummeted from great heights deep into the earth; these bombs flitter and float to earth via *balloons.* Thirty-some pounds, tops. Carting one off is like carrying groceries, and about as dangerous."

We began walking back to the terminal. I wondered what Sergeant Redes would have had to say about Gurley's dangerous-as-groceries bombs. *"Your Jap bombmaker...he's ready to lose a man here and there...."*

"And if it weren't all obvious enough," Gurley said, "there is even a *film.* A training film. Didn't sit through all of it myself, but it looks helpful enough."

We'd reached the door of the terminal, and he paused. "One more thing, Sergeant. Examine your heart while I'm gone. Examine your hands, for that matter. If you feel you're not up to this task—if you're not up to tackling alone what bombs we do find, tell me when I get back. Because I don't want to face another scene like I did with that Harvard man. He didn't die immediately, you know. Lasted long enough to ask me to put a bullet in him. Put him out of his misery." Gurley grimaced. "Can you imagine such a thing? Good Lord, there was hardly enough left of him to shoot."

With that, he opened the door and stepped inside.

THERE IS PLENTY of Ronnie left to shoot.

But they don't allow guns in the hospice. It doesn't matter; I have an equally efficient weapon in my hand. Ronnie's Comfort One bracelet. It is pretty, in its way. A heavy gold chain with a green and gold charm featuring the program's curious logo: the two words, plus two restroom-sign–style humanoids, a gold person standing behind a white one. Is the white one the patient, and the gold the comforter? Or is the white the soul, the gold the body? Unfortunately, what it resembles most to me is a mugging, the gold man about to pounce his hapless white counterpart.

It cost twenty dollars, as predicted, but I know it's worth much more than that. They are precious things to those who have them, and I find that more of the elderly and dying I visit in the hospital or hospice these days do. They're meant to spare patients pain and everyone else second-guessing. Ailing parishioners usually try to hide the existence of Do Not Resuscitate orders from me; they know the Church stands against euthanasia and worry that their DNRs might run afoul of such beliefs. As it happens, they need not be concerned, but that doesn't keep the patients who have DNRs from prizing them.

I marvel at some of those I visit here, so desperate to die. I think of those Japanese soldiers on Kiska, surrounded by the enemy, with no hope of survival. I think of their wounded, the Japanese soldiers in their field hospital, committing suicide. The doctor doled out grenades, gently laying one on each man's chest. Those who could, pulled their own pins. He pulled the pin for those who could not. Three hundred died this way; the doctor wrote as much in his diary. Then he put down the pen, closed the book, and picked up the grenade he'd reserved for himself.

I'm surprised Ronnie ordered the bracelet. It means he had to get the paperwork, have a doctor sign it, and send it off. It suggests planning and foresight that he never seemed capable of nor interested in. More to the point, it suggests he's going to die, and that he knows this. It makes me realize that I may be the only person who doesn't think he's going to die. Or, for that matter, the only one who doesn't want him to die. Not now. Not yet.

Which is why I'm keeping the bracelet, for the time being, in my pocket. I'm keeping it safe—I've tucked it inside a pyx. I'm sure the bishop would be horrified; the pyx is for carrying communion to the sick and homebound. But I shudder to think what Ronnie would do if I presented him with the Host. Better to let the bracelet rest in the pyx for now, where God can keep an eye on it.

Bad idea? We'll see. It's not like I had the best of models for hospital ministry.

"KILL ANYONE YET, Sergeant?" Father Pabich surprised me with a clap on my back. I jumped; his hand had hit a bruise I hadn't known was there. He'd found me walking back from the airfield terminal.

I wanted to tell him about the morning's conversation with Gurley, but didn't dare. After that first encounter with Gurley in the bar, I'd done a bit of whimpering to Father Pabich. It didn't go over well. This was an army for fighters, not whiners, Father Pabich had told me, and urged me to shoot someone as soon as I could, preferably Japanese.

Thus his question: Had I killed anyone?

But before I could answer, Father Pabich wheeled me around so I was walking in his direction. "I've not seen you at Mass for a few mornings running, and I was putting two and two together. You've been out, on a mission? What's the good word?"

"No, Father."

"Sergeant Belk," Father Pabich said. "This won't do. The meek are gonna inherit the earth, God willing, but not until men like you and me take care of a little business."

I nodded.

"Kill some Japs," Father Pabich said. I nodded again. Father Pabich coughed and looked at me. "What's the matter, son? Shouldn't you be at work, defusing some bomb, blowing something up?"

"Got dismissed early, sir," I said.

"*Father,*" Father Pabich reminded me, and I repeated the word. "And I can see why you were dismissed early," he said. "You're drunk?" He leaned in so close I thought I could smell alcohol on him. "Hungover?"

"I almost killed someone," I said quietly, thinking of the glass I'd shot out of Gurley's hand—and the belt I'd tightened around the neck of that sailor at Lily's.

"Well, *almost* ain't going to do anyone any damn good—" Father Pabich started, and then stopped walking to study me a moment. "We're not talking about a Jap, are we?" He picked up my hands, which bore some evidence of the scuffle with the sailors. "Bar fight," he said, making a sour face. I hesitated, and then nodded because it was easier, and almost true. "Come with me, son," he said. He didn't say another word until we'd reached the base hospital.

Once there, he told me to wait outside while he made his rounds, but then changed his mind and ushered me in by the elbow. The hospital was fairly new, but it was already showing signs of overuse. One or two soldiers were lying in cots in the hallway. One ward had spaces for twenty beds, but two were missing, their places taken by a tarp and buckets that were trying to do the job of the roof that had failed above.

Father Pabich visited with each man. He shared a joke with ones who could talk, and mumbled prayers over the ones who were sleeping, including one man whose chart indicated that he was Jewish. When Father Pabich finished making the sign of the cross over him, a man in a neighboring bed said, "He's, uh, not that way, Father," and Father Pabich blessed him, too. "*Baptist,* that one," Father Pabich whispered to me as we walked away.

I thought we'd seen the whole of the hospital, but then he eased open a door that led into a small vestibule and paused.

"You still feeling okay, Sergeant?" he asked.

I nodded.

"Say yes, son, so I know you're not just pressing your lips together to keep from puking."

I said yes.

"Right. Now, be a good man in this next room. No staring, but no looking away, and no being sick. These are good men." And then we went in.

In this room, there were only eyes.

Five of the six beds were occupied; the nurses were changing the sheets on the sixth. And from each of those five beds, two eyes watched Father Pabich and me enter. The rest of their bodies were swathed almost entirely in bandages or covered with sheets. I'd been told not to stare, so I couldn't confirm what my mind kept insisting—things were missing. Arms, legs, hands. Sheets lay flat in impossible places. Some of the eyes peered out of unbandaged faces that were a dirty pink, skin rubbed raw but somehow still flecked with black.

I couldn't breathe. Father Pabich told me they were burn patients, but I knew that. And I knew who they were. I knew they'd been on that hillside above Fort Cronkhite. I knew that flames had leapt up around them because I hadn't called to them, run to them in time.

And I further knew that this was impossible, that those men had died, there, on that hill, and that even if they had lived, they would never have been transported to Alaska. Sure, I knew that. It didn't matter who they were, really, because Gurley had made all such men mine: *Didn't move fast enough?*

Father Pabich went to the nurses who were changing the bed and seemed to ask them something. When they shook their heads, he straightened up and then began working his way around the room. He spoke quietly to each man; none spoke in return. Before moving on to the next man, he would murmur a short prayer and close with a slight, but slow and solemn, bow. He didn't rush. The eyes had all been open when we entered the room, and had followed our every move. But now I saw the man in the last bed close his eyes before we reached him. Father Pabich didn't notice until he was at the foot of the man's bed, and then breathed a deep sigh. We spent a longer time at that bed than anyone else's. Father Pabich slowly lowered himself to kneeling, and then pulled me down as well. I listened to the man breathe. I watched and waited for him to open his eyes.

AS SOON AS WE got outside, Father Pabich dug around for a cigarette. A breeze had picked up, and he had some trouble with his match. When he finally got the cigarette lit, he started walking away without a word. I caught up, but he wouldn't look at me. "The man in the sixth bed, the empty one—gone this morning," he said. "I should have been there. They couldn't find me." He looked at his watch, then at me. "Scared?"

I thought about telling him about Fort Cronkhite, about the explosion there, the men, how I wasn't able to or didn't help.

"You can admit to being a little scared," he said. "That's no sin. A little fear can help a man." He took a long drag on the cigarette, then another, and then, even though it wasn't nearly done, dropped it on the ground and toed it out. "I don't know what happened. They were part of a special team, gone more often than they were here. Then one night, they were all brought in from who knows where. Badly burned.

Limbs missing. Some kind of accident, I would have guessed, but— God doesn't permit accidents like that." He zipped up his coat. "No one will tell me what happened exactly, and I suppose I don't want to know now. Some things you don't want to know are possible. Coming out here, I knew I'd see men who were hurt, men who'd died, but I didn't think I'd see that—men who'd died, but are still alive, somehow, with eyes like that, like ghosts." Father Pabich looked at me. "I don't want to know how it happened. And I don't want you to tell me."

"I won't," I said. "I mean, how could I? How would I know?" But what I really wanted to say was, how could he know?

Father Pabich took a moment considering his next words. "I guess there're things you and your captain haven't talked about yet."

"Like what?"

"Like those men, Sergeant," Father Pabich said. "They're your— they're your detail. Or they worked with your captain there, once. Nobody ever knew quite what they did, what he does. What you do." He stared at me until I met his gaze. "I just hope you do it well. Or better."

"Father, I—"

"Whatever he's asking you to do, do it," Father Pabich said. "If it's going to keep those beds empty, do it." I nodded. He picked up my hands. "No more bar brawls. Next time you put your hand on the door of a bar, you think of these men. You think about where you're needed." He dropped my hands, and thumped my chest with two fingers: "You think about who needs you."

BUT TRY AS I MIGHT, it wasn't those men, but Lily, who came to mind at those words and who stayed there the entire day. I went back to the Quonset hut, I watched the training film, I stared at the little book until, once again, the artwork seemed to shift and flow and change before my eyes. What's more, I kept seeing, imagining, Lily's face, in a cloud, in waves, connecting the points of a map. I finally gave in and started for downtown.

I told myself I was going because Lily was going to help me find some of these mysterious floating bombs, help me save lives. She'd said she wasn't as good at the future as she was at the past, but she could tell me something.

THE FIRST THING she wanted to tell me was goodbye.

"Hey, friend," Lily said. She'd emerged from the entrance of the Starhope as I approached. "You came back to see me off."

I looked at her, and then looked around, in search of something to say.

"I'm going home," she said, checking to make sure I understood.

I didn't, but told her I'd be happy to walk her home. I thought I was being quite gallant; a lot of guys back then wouldn't have wanted to walk anywhere near a woman who looked like Lily. Well—maybe they'd *want* to, beautiful as she was, but they wouldn't want to be seen doing it, given who she was.

She looked down at my feet. "You don't have the right shoes," she said. "And it's a long, wet walk."

"How long?" I asked. "I don't have to be back in my barracks till midnight."

"About four hundred miles," Lily said.

I stared at her. "You're leaving," I said. "Really leaving."

"Yeah," she said. "That's the idea. I'm still working on how—travel's not as easy with this war you all got cooked up. But I've got something to do anyway, before I go."

"What's that?"

"Have dinner with a friend." She smiled and put out an arm.

LILY WALKED ME THROUGH the darkening streets to a part of town I hadn't discovered yet. There were fewer soldiers and sailors here, and more—people. White faces, Asian faces, women, men, children, and very few uniforms. I drew more stares than Lily as she threaded our way through narrower, older streets to a diner.

There were no menus; Lily said they just brought you whatever was on the stove. That night, it was a stew of Thanksgiving leftovers.

We didn't say anything while we waited for the food. I was tongue-tied—she was *leaving?*—and Lily was tired. She leaned her head against the back of the booth and closed her eyes.

I wouldn't have had words then to describe what I saw; I'm not sure I do now. Why did her hair make black seem the brightest color? Why did her breathing through slightly parted lips, her tongue flitting once to moisten them, seem risqué? How could her bare neck, all smooth curves and shadows, suggest that the loose clothes she wore weren't there at all? I suppose the chemicals that flood a boy at that time in his life are partly to blame, but give Lily and the God who made her some credit.

"Don't stare," she said, not opening her eyes.

I mumbled something about how I wasn't, and she opened her eyes in time to see that I was. The food arrived and she immediately started in.

"You were, just a moment ago, when I had my eyes closed," she said.

"I wasn't staring," I said. "I was trying to figure out what I was going to do without you."

She stopped eating, and laughed. "That's silly." She took another bite, and before she swallowed, added, "And very sweet."

"No, I had—I had a question for you." And I did, a hundred, mostly about her. But I had another question, the one I'd spend the war asking.

"I don't think those two thugs are coming back, if that's your question," Lily said. "That's what I like about sailors. Or liked. They sail away on their little ships. They don't come back."

"It's about something else." I looked at my hand, then held it up and showed her my palm.

Lily shook her head. "You know—the palm reading—I don't really read palms."

"But you know things. You knew things about me."

Lily put down her spoon; she spent a moment carefully aligning it with the plate. "What do you need to know?"

I offered her my hand, but she kept her hands at her sides and shook her head. "Not here." She looked around. "I'm not going to do that here."

"Then how can you tell me—?"

"Just talk," she said, and as she did, I could feel her feet entangle mine. "Just talk," she repeated, more softly.

By now, of course, I could hardly breathe. It took me a moment to remember what I wanted to ask. "I need to know where this—thing—will—" I stopped. "I need to know where something's going to be."

But that wasn't good enough for her. She shook her head, again and again, no matter how I phrased the question, until she finally said, "I need a place to start. A detail. Without that, it's just dreaming." I thought of all the things I could tell her: places where we knew balloons had landed and exploded; the map in Gurley's office; the eyes of those men in that private ward. Or I could just tell her my secret— Gurley's secret, our country's secret, or Japan's—I could tell her that high above the Pacific, even now, clearly visible if you only knew where to look, floated balloons laced with powdered fire. All you had to do to catch them was give up a hand, an arm, a face, a leg—or find out first where they were landing and when.

"*Are* you dreaming?" she asked.

"I'm trying to think where to start," I said.

"Here's an easy detail," she said. "What's your name, Sergeant Belk?"

I blinked.

"Your first name, brother of Bing."

"Louis," I said, relieved I could give up such an easy secret.

"Louis," she said. "See, I'm not good at this at all. 'Louis' I never would have guessed. Okay, what do you want to know, Louis?"

I looked around the room. No one was looking at us, but it seemed as though everyone was listening to us. Intently. I said nothing. Her feet left mine.

"Next time, then," she said. "Your wallet have anything in it tonight?"

"Please don't leave," I said.

"Louis, I told you my secret," she said. "I'm not a palm reader."

"But you didn't tell me how you—why you—know things."

"What *do* you do?" she asked. "Or what don't you do? Me, I don't read palms."

"I don't read palms, either," I said. She looked at me, waited. "And I don't read feet," I added. She smiled and clamped her feet back around mine. "And I don't..."

I went through a whole litany of jobs, both military and civilian, that I didn't do. This was much easier than lying, this circling, joking. She seemed to enjoy it, too, protesting every now and then that some task I said I didn't do—blow reveille on a bugle each morning—I actually did do. Slowly, invisible to everyone but me, her hands crept closer to mine, until they were almost touching, then they were touching, and then resting on top of mine, contented and relieved.

By then, the whole of me was humming. Maybe she wasn't a palm reader, maybe she had no special powers at all, but she could do this: tap something inside of me—more than hormones, perhaps blood—and seize it, take charge of it. Change the direction of its flow, or arrest the circulation altogether. Part of me believed I was allowing this to happen, part of me thought I was powerless, but most of me didn't care. I wanted to sit there, be held, touched, like that, and never move. I would have done anything to stay.

"What do you do, Louis?" she said quietly.

"Bombs," I said, the word out before I even realized it.

"Yes," she said. "But what kind?" she asked, leaning closer, the shade of a new look in her eyes, but not enough of a new look to spook me, not yet.

"Bal-loons," I said, my mind rising in alarm with the second syllable, but by then it was too late. Gurley's thumbnail slid down, and across, and up my neck.

Lily closed her eyes, slowly. And then her shoulders sank, her head sank, my blood began its nervous flow again, and my heart pounded at the secret it had just disclosed.

"I didn't say anything," I said, looking down to find my hands uncovered.

"Not a thing," Lily said, expectant.

"I have to go," I said.

"So soon?" she said. She waited a moment, and then appeared to make up her mind.

"Lily, you can't tell *any*one," I said. "You have to swear."

She waited a moment, then smiled.

"You came in with a question," she said. "Now, I have an answer."

She leaned over, put her lips to my ear. I swear she kissed me. I felt the brush of a touch, a breath, and when I looked up, she was standing by me, smiling, and then leaving.

It was a fine way to deliver a secret, because I heard nothing, not then. Oh, she'd whispered the name of the place—Shuyak—but I didn't realize that, not until later. At that moment, I was consumed with the way her breath found my ear, the way her face grazed my hair, the way her lips were moving—*Shu-yak*—so that it felt like (it must have looked like) a kiss. Even now, when I say the name of that place—*Shu-yak*—when I'm lonely or nostalgic or some unrelenting, everlasting Alaskan summer twilight has me pinned, sleepless, to the sheets, I can give myself chills when that first syllable, that *sh*, draws my lips forward, just so, like lips set to kiss.

When I came to, she was gone, the counterman was gone. All that remained was the bill, which I paid, and the whispered word, which started echoing in my head, louder and louder, as I made my way back to base.

The boy would have survived had Lily been with us. I knew that the morning of the second day, which would be our last with adequate food, water, and fuel. The day before, we'd picked our way west through the delta in dense fog. I had no idea we'd made the Bering Sea until I realized I couldn't smell the tundra's mud and grass, just water and salt. I turned north. I had a map; it showed a tiny Red Cross symbol near a mission settlement just up the coast. I had a map, but Lily would have known a better, mapless route. She would have gotten us where we needed to go.

And she could have told me more about the boy. I wanted to know his name, his real name. I wanted to know what chain of events had left him in my care. When he was awake, he looked at me with fear and barely spoke. When he was asleep—and he seemed to sleep, or slip from consciousness, more and more—he would often shout and screech, delirious. Sometimes it sounded like words, sometimes notes of music, high and thin.

If he lay silent for too long, I noticed that the seabirds—they looked more eagle than gull—would float down closer to us. If they got too close, I would bark and yell. Sometimes that was enough to get the boy raving again. But it was never enough to get him to open his eyes, fix them on me, and tell his story.

CHAPTER 9

THURSDAY. RONNIE HAS SURVIVED FOR AN ENTIRE DAY, and so have I. Maybe it's not right to compare our conditions? But in some ways mine is more dire: he's only dying, whereas I'm being asked to live out my days Outside, divorced from my Alaskan life.

Having been through extended hospital stays a half dozen times before with Ronnie, though, I can tell you what the second day is like: busy, hopeful, anxious. There is still some carryover of that day-one–type relief—*he got here in time!*—that's usually counterbalanced by day-two anxiety: *what's* really *wrong?* There are other milestones, like day six, when you realize, it's only a night away from an entire *week*; surely that's not a good sign. And then, of course, there's the Last Day, which is always a surprise.

But today's surprise arrived shortly after breakfast. Ronnie awoke. Or, as he put it, returned.

His eyes opened, slowly, and he scanned the room. Then he found me. We watched each other silently for a full minute, maybe more.

"They thought you were in a coma," I said at last. "Not a 'classic coma,' mind you." Ronnie considered this a moment; he was still coming to. Then he rolled his eyes, coughed, and declared he was hungry.

I handed over several items I'd gotten from the vending machines for my breakfast, and he devoured them as he explained where he'd been.

"Not a coma," he said, shaking his head. "The ocean," he declared, and then asked for my coffee. I handed him the cup. "I've been to the bottom of the ocean. Here and there. I went to where the seals live, the whales."

"They send their best?" I asked. This wasn't the first time that Ronnie had told me he'd "traveled." While the rest of the world thought he'd passed out in a bar or fallen into a semi-coma in a hospital, Ronnie would later claim that he had been swimming to the depths of the sea, or summiting the sky, en route to the moon. Shamans were known for such journeys; and indeed, they resembled comas. Long ago, the *angalkuq* would gather everyone in the *qasgiq*, a village's largest building, which served as both the men's quarters and communal hall. He (not always, but usually a he) would lie in the center of the floor, often bound. Sometimes the light would be extinguished, and witnesses would be left to deduce what was happening from the sounds they heard. Loud grunts, a struggle, then quieter and quieter as the *angalkuq* flew farther away, then loud again once he'd returned, perhaps with a crash or thump. Sometimes the *angalkuq* would narrate the journey, other times detail it upon his return.

Ronnie only ever spoke upon his return, and his accounts were so fanciful I ascribed them to spirits more alcoholic than otherworldly. One time, I was sure Ronnie was plagiarizing the plot of a Disney movie that had recently played at the library. (We'd all seen it, every one of us: it was an actual, first-run *movie,* after all.) But then, I'd fallen asleep halfway through the movie myself. I was no more judge of what was real than Ronnie.

This time, though, was different. He ignored my crack about the seals sending greetings and instead spoke rapidly: "I saw the boy," he said. "I saw him." He looked both excited and nervous. "Not the mother. Did you see her? There's a mother in the story. I can't remember. I can't remember if she's there." He raised the cup I'd given him. "It's the coffee. Caffeine. This is a drug. I am telling you this."

"I'd blame alcohol, Ronnie," I said. "Demon rum."

But he had already handed the cup back to me. "Wait here," he said. "I'll be right back. Tell you what I find." He lay back, closed his eyes, and then jerked awake. "The wolf, Louis—you'll watch for him." He extended a hand toward me—hard to imagine, Ronnie actually reaching for help, for me—but as he fell back, I slipped out of his grasp.

I didn't move to pick his hand back up. Because maybe he was traveling. I didn't want to hold him back. I didn't want to be dragged any further out of my world, away from my God. Maybe that's it. Or maybe it's just that I didn't want to feel the wolf's teeth sinking into my hand.

What's the difference, anyway, between what Ronnie is doing—slipping in and out of consciousness, traveling from one world to another—and my falling asleep? My dreaming of flight, and then recounting my banal dream after I awake? I don't know. I don't dream of flying. I did it once, really did it, just me and my arms and legs and the air, and I've never wanted to do it again.

IT WAS LATE WHEN I got back on base after my dinner with Lily. Something—or everything—about my "goodbye" dinner with Lily made me desperate to talk with someone, even Father Pabich, though he would probably have treated the whole matter as something worthy of confession.

I couldn't find anyone to talk to, but I couldn't see myself going to sleep, either. I went over to Gurley's Quonset hut. The sentry said nothing; he didn't even look surprised. He let me in through what Gurley persisted in calling the "back door" and then locked everything behind me. I banged my way across the floor in the dark to the small office in the rear. I had been granted access to the building in Gurley's absence, but not the office. He had, however, given me a small desk outside. I sat down and felt around for the desk lamp.

Suddenly, the hut's massive overhead lights clunked on.

"Belk!" Gurley shouted as the door shut behind him. "Working in the dark? Or sleeping?" By the time he reached me, I had some paper out and was pretending to take notes. "If there's one thing I hate more than incompetence, Belk, it's incompe*tents* trying to suck up." He clapped a hand on my back. "You've been studying?" He wasn't entirely angry. "You'll be forgiven for this shameless display—working all night, it would seem—if you actually came up with something."

Came up with something: maybe I'm guessing at the rest of the dialogue, but I know he said this. And "came up with something," meant just that: invented. This was Alaska, after all, where chaplains swore like stevedores and Eskimo women could tease your entire past from your hand. It was all imaginary, all true. I thought about dinner with Lily. I thought about what Gurley wanted to hear. And then I said what I knew.

"I know where the next balloon will land."

Gurley's presence changed the acoustics of a conversation; his being there could make your voice sound terribly small, or terribly ominous. Or in my case, both.

He didn't reply. I breathed deeply enough to get the memory of what Lily had whispered echoing in my ear once again. "Shu-yak," I said.

"What?" he asked.

"Shuyak," I repeated, working out the pronunciation and realizing as I did what Lily had said.

Gurley had been yawning and inattentive, but now he focused: "Along the Aleutians, isn't it?" I nodded, though I had no idea. I wasn't even sure it was a real place: perhaps Shuyak was the imaginary province of Yup'ik seers. Maybe it was simply Yup'ik for *goodbye*. I felt ill. "Easy enough to see why you guessed there," Gurley said. But he was appreciative, not scolding. "I've guessed at that, too. Let's look."

He unlocked his office and went over to the wall map. I entered and sat. "Truth is, Aleutians don't matter to many people other than the Aleutians. Who, as it happens, are no longer there, poor dears." He pointed to southeast Alaska. "That's why the Navy has thoughtfully relocated them here." He frowned, pointed to a spot on the mainland. "No, here. Somewhere. There's plenty of Aleuts to go around. Apparently, the Japs took some, too, in fact. Probably carted them off to some zoo in Tokyo." He studied his lip with his tongue as he drew his finger along to the end of the Aleutian chain. "Anyway, there's nobody left out there, save some poor Jap soldiers, perhaps, hiding in caves out on Kiska." He sat down and began studying his palms. I wondered if Lily had ever read his life through his hands, and if she had, what she made of the jagged scars that Gurley's pushpin doodles left behind. "It's American soil, but frozen, barren soil, so who cares?" Gurley continued. "I hope all their balloons land there. In any case, I can't find it. Any other ideas?"

"No," I said, studying the map. Why had I given myself over to Lily like that? Here I was, spouting some nonsense she'd purred.

"No?" Gurley said, turning away. "Such was my supposition."

I sat up. "Listen—Shuyak—that's where the next balloon will land," I said, my insistence stemming more from an automatic desire to counter Gurley than anything else.

"My word, dear Sergeant. When I told you to search out incoming balloons, I was just—well, not joking, no, not joking at all, this is deadly serious—but I don't expect you, or anyone, to really know where each individual balloon is going to land. It's touching, of course, that you stayed up all night in an effort to obey my somewhat facetious order—*facetious,* Belk? Another word for your list—and if that atlas tells you something about the balloons' design or construction that we don't already know, or if you pick up something that leads you to believe you know what general areas they're targeting, or what they might be planning, okay."

"Shuyak," I said. *Was* that what Lily had said? Every time I tried to replay the memory, the sound of what she said changed. But my mouth was still working, words kept coming out. "Oh-seven-hundred Alaskan War Time tomorrow morning." Now Gurley looked at me sharply. "North-northwest corner of the island."

"The corner?" he asked slowly. "You're making this up." I was.

"Corner—quadrant—whatever. The northwest part of the island," I said. It was exhilarating, lying. I felt more specifics arriving—wind speed, temperature, type of blast—but what reason remained in me held my imagination in check.

He looked up at the map again. "Closer in, maybe." He ran his hand back along the Aleutian Chain, up onto the Alaska Peninsula and over to Kodiak. "Eureka," he said. "Shuyak? Just north of Kodiak, right?" I nodded. He tapped the map. "That's not so far from here." He thought about this, and then asked, "Oh-seven-hundred?" I nodded. He stared at me for a long moment. "The problem is, Belk," he said, and stopped. He started again. "The problem is, Belk, you have to be right. You know what they told me in San Francisco? They want to press ahead with their foolish plan. Blow this all wide open. Remove the censorship directive. Let every last American know about these bombs, set the masses all to looking for them. Which is a stupid idea, but that doesn't matter, Belk. We'd be out of a job, or we'd wind up with a job similar in stature and function to the clowns who sweep up elephant dung at the rear of a circus parade." He cupped his chin and regarded Shuyak. When he turned around, he was in the midst of trading masks— Wronged Captain for Effete Ivy Leaguer, or perhaps the Brusque C.O.—or else he had forgone one altogether. His voice was softer, too. Normal, pitched well below the range at which he usually delivered his lines. "But if you're right, Belk—think what this means."

"We'll save lives," I said, caught up in Gurley's growing excitement.

"We'll save our jobs," he said, "and our secrets, at least for a little while longer. I asked for a month; they gave me two weeks to prove there was a compelling reason not to lift the press ban. *This* could be a reason. If I can tell them we've cooked up a way to predict arrivals, landings, well—that really changes matters. I'd be offering them a chance to stay one step ahead, of the enemy, and the public."

He stopped and thought about this. All the while he'd been talking, I'd been trying to work up the courage to interrupt him and better rein in his expectations. But I couldn't then and I couldn't now, and so when he said, "You'll go, then," I simply nodded and stood. Before I left, he had one more thing to add: "You'll go alone, of course. If it turns out you're wrong, it's best you fail alone." He picked up the phone. "I'm sure you understand."

GURLEY HAD LIMITED (and diminishing) authority over a special Army Air Corps crew that was stationed at Elmendorf Field. They had all been nominally trained in the spotting and destruction, though not recovery, of balloon bombs. More important, they had all been sworn to secrecy, to such a degree that none of the men would even talk to me when I got out to the field at first light, around 4 A.M. I wasn't sure what Gurley had told them, other than our destination and my name.

We were to take a floatplane out to Shuyak, a modified PBY Catalina that looked about as ungainly and makeshift as the balloons. It had the hull of a boat but the snout of a plane; its wings extended heavily from the top of the fuselage, like the arms of a lumbering giant. Pilots called it a two-fisted airplane; once in the air, you wrestled it more than steered it.

A young airman outfitted me with gear, including a chest-pack parachute.

"What's this for?" I asked.

"First flight over enemy territory?" he answered, not looking at me.

"We're just heading to Shuyak," I said. "That's well behind the front lines."

He corrected my pronunciation and said again, "Like I was saying, this your first flight?"

"I don't understand," I said. "I thought only the two outermost

Aleutian islands were ever occupied by the Japanese. And they're long gone."

"Right," the airman said. "But who's going out there to check on them these days? Thing is, the Japs have been sneaking on and off all those islands out there for a long time now." He raked down a strap. "Thing is, a hundred miles out of Anchorage, you don't know whose side you're on."

"You could be anywhere," I said.

"You could be following some idiot's hunch to go to Shuyak," the airman said, stepping back.

I climbed aboard.

THE PLANE BUFFETED along through a constantly changing sky that seemed to have leaked from the pages of Gurley's captured atlas. The sunrise chased us as we flew south and slightly west, the sky going from sooty gray to a strange, soupy green, and then improbably into pink. One of the PBY's stranger features was a pair of bubble windows, or "blisters," that bulged out just forward of the tail. Each was manned with a spotter, neither of whom seemed much interested in spotting anything. I offered to take over for one of them and soon found myself staring slack-jawed at the celestial show while the rest of the crew snoozed or snickered.

By the time we reached Shuyak, it was just before six. During the last forty-five minutes of the flight, I had come to my senses; that is to say, I had realized that I had endangered my life and the lives of a brave, if surly, crew because I had a—what? A hunch? Based on a woman's whisper? Or a hand's promise?

From Anchorage, we'd flown southwest over the waters of Cook Inlet, skirting the coast of the Kenai Peninsula. Looking out the right side of the aircraft, I watched a series of volcanic peaks stretch along the coast. Snowy and distant, they looked like mountains you might visit in a dream. I wondered if Lily's island lay beneath them.

A crew member elbowed me and then handed over his headset. As I fumbled to put it on, he shouted something above the plane's roar that I did not understand.

The sudden arrival of voices via the headset brought on a flash of recognition. Voices in my head: now, *this* was madness. "We're here, Sergeant," the pilot said. "Now, just where on Shuyak is this balloon going to land?" I had, of course, assumed that Shuyak was an island as big, and featureless, as a soccer field, and that it would reveal its secrets to us in a single flyby.

It did not. Shuyak was not an island but a wild, tiny continent. It was, in fact, flat as a soccer field—flatter than any other scrap of land in sight—but its surface was a dense paisley of Sitka spruce and pot-hole lakes. A half dozen balloons could land here and never be found.

Suddenly short of breath, I pulled my head out of the blister, only to see the entire crew staring at me, expectant. I crouched in the narrow space and, so I wouldn't have to look at them, pretended to be studying some emergency ditching instructions printed on the cabin wall.

Before I could respond to the pilot, I heard another voice on the radio: "Whaddya know, balloon, two o'clock." Everyone darted for one of the blisters; I managed to wedge my head in alongside another man's.

I stared at my balloon.

The pilot brought the plane into a wide swoop, and we all watched, transfixed, as if we'd just entered the orbit of the moon. This balloon looked precisely like the one that had crashed into that California hillside, and for a moment, my mind insisted it *was* that balloon, resurrected and airborne once more.

I wanted it.

"Not too close now," I muttered, and then realized I was speaking into the headset's microphone. "They're armed with explosives," I said, speaking up. "There's no telling what sets them off."

"Trees," said a sarcastic voice.

"Rocks," said another.

"Bomb disposal sergeants," said a third.

"Remember, Sergeant, we've been on this patrol for a few months now. We know what kind of animal this is."

"Which explains why you've had such success figuring out where and when they're going to land," I thought, and without thinking further, said.

"Okay, folks, let's take her down," the pilot said. I looked around to see where we might touch down, but saw nothing. One of the crew tapped me on the shoulder and nodded to a small canvas sling seat that folded down from the wall. Once we were seated, I asked him via hand gestures—he didn't have a headset—just how we would land. I understood the concept of floatplanes, but the island's coast didn't look hospitable to us bobbing alongside and hopping out.

My seatmate shook his head, and then pretended to shoot me with his thumb and index finger. Boom. The balloon exploded between his hands.

"We need to save it!" I shouted. Part of me wanted a scalp to bring back to Gurley; part of me was curious what magic had wrought: an island, a balloon. This was Lily's prize as much as it was mine.

The pilot came back on. "Thanks, Sergeant, we'll take it from here."

"We have standing orders, don't we, to recover all we can?"

"I have standing orders to preserve the lives of my crew," he replied.

"But this is a big chance for us—it's in excellent condition." The pilot didn't reply, and then I heard a burst of gunfire. The entire plane shook, and for a moment, I thought we had been hit.

"Bad news, Sergeant," the pilot said. "It's in lousy condition." I went to the blister. The balloon had already dropped from sight; a surprisingly thin plume of smoke was all that remained.

"Did you hit the basket or the balloon?" I asked. There was still a chance we might recover something.

"It's not that big a target," said the pilot. He banked so I could see the balloon, which had plummeted into lighter-green waters just off the island's coast. "I can't really say we were aiming for one or the other." The plane pulled up. We were heading home.

"We can't leave," I said quickly. "It's in shallow water. What if someone finds it, what if one of the bombs attached hasn't exploded? What if it went off and killed them?"

"I can drop you off, Sergeant." The pilot laughed. "Answer all your questions." I heard him radioing coded results of our mission back to base. I was feverish not to return. The balloon I'd seen—it wasn't just a balloon, it *was* magic, or more. Not just my magic. The magic of an entire nation—Japan had managed to send a bomb several thousand miles, from their shores to ours—and the magic of a palm reader in Anchorage, the magic of a whisper, a touch. I did want to see that balloon, and desperately. Not because I wanted evidence for Gurley, but because—because it was somehow the gateway to another world, a world I had invented, or that Lily had invented for me. And if I could grasp some piece of that world—that balloon—I'd make the dream real. I would prove to myself that all the rest of this awful dream— Alaska, Gurley, war—was controllable by me as well.

Or I would die in the attempt, which struck me as both noble and expedient. At least God wouldn't take me for a coward, which I was sure was what He thought when I ducked the seminary. (Don't smirk—He watched my every move in those days.) I cinched tight the parachute I'd been issued.

I had never leapt out of a plane before. Parachuting had been offered as part of our training, but few men took the course who were not required to. "Why jump out of a perfectly good airplane?" I heard a flight surgeon once ask. And the PBY didn't make the task easy—it was built to float, after all, and so holes in the fuselage were few. If I wanted out, it looked like I'd have to wriggle out the blister.

But I was invincible now, full of faith and magic. I could escape the PBY, and I could master the art of jumping after exiting the plane. I ducked quickly to read the emergency instructions I'd seen before and then reached up to open the blister.

The crewman at my right pulled at me. I elbowed him away. Another man came from the left. I kicked.

The pilot started shouting in my headset. "Don't go batty on me, Sergeant. You're not going anywhere. For starters, I can't afford to lose that headset you're wearing." I handed it off. I heaved myself up into the blister opening. The harness caught on something. The wind tore at me. The air was freezing. The men behind me were grabbing at my feet, my legs. I lost a boot to one of them and then the other.

One or two bruising kicks later, the wind snatched me away. The last thing I heard was "Head!" I looked up to see the tail assembly flash past my nose. And then I was flying, as free and fast as a shaman.

WHEN HE LATER HEARD about it, Gurley could not believe that I had jumped out of the plane. Neither could I, nor had I, technically speaking. I had kicked myself halfway out, but the wind had ripped me the rest of the way. It could as easily have been Lily's hand pulling me earthward, as surely as she had pulled me toward Shuyak when she whispered in my ear.

And some spirit was with me that day. As chance would have it, the plane was flying slowly enough for someone who knew how to jump, to jump. And parachutes are not so complicated that a man of great faith cannot come to a decision as to which toggle to pull and deploy his parachute. Had I known a little more, however, I might have been able to actually land myself on the slip of rocky shore. Instead, I plunged into the ocean. Just fifty or so yards offshore—swimmable, were I in the summertime waters of my childhood Pacific Ocean, but here, the ocean was December cold and patrolled by what looked like, at first glance, miniature enemy submarines (they were, in fact, sea lions).

The pilot later told Gurley—who told me—that, all in all, it was a good thing I landed in the water. For one, I had deployed my chute late; I would have broken bones on land. And two, he likely would not have turned back to collect me had I landed on the island. Rather, he would have dropped supplies and called for a rescue mission. Any idiot—here Gurley must have smiled—could survive for a night or two.

But no man could survive in that ocean for more than a few minutes, certainly not one with a chute weighing him down, and so the pilot circled back, landed—a rather skillful, brave act, he insisted to all concerned, and it must have been, because he earned the Navy Cross for doing so, or for saving me. He motored as close as he could and then sent two profane crew members out in an inflatable to collect me, still conscious.

He had turned around to rescue me promptly, but the approach and landing still took time. I know now that I was only minutes from death. I didn't know that then. I didn't know the water was so cold that sailors who went overboard in Alaskan waters frequently died, especially farther north—even if the alarm had been sounded immediately, even if rescuers worked as fast as they were able. The water was always faster. But I wasn't thinking about death. I was thinking about three things, all at once: the knifing cold in my fingers and ears and feet, the way the water tasted nothing like the ocean in Southern California, and most of all: the balloon.

Almost too numb to form the words, I pleaded with my rescuers to collect the balloon as well. I could see the quick calculus cross their faces: *brave or stupid, he's earned at least one favor from us.* Plus, there was the added benefit of knowing I would suffer, cold and wet, while they collected what they could.

"Just one problem with that plan, Sarge," one of them said. "Who takes care of the bombs? They don't pay any of us to do that. And you don't look in any shape to do it."

"Just—they're probably missing," I twisted around to look. "They would have gone off by now." It was right about the point I saw them silently reach a mutual "What the hell?" that I decided to go myself. "Stay here," I said. "Better yet, move back a ways."

We'd landed at a thin gravel beach at the edge of a broad bay. The balloon itself had washed ashore, but the control frame had sunk in the shallow water where it fell. I missed my boots, but I also realized they probably would have dragged me straight to the bottom. I tried wading in after the frame—it was just two or three feet of water—but the shock of the cold water once more was so painful and absolute that I had to retreat. I went over to the balloon and pulled. I could feel everyone watching—the landing crew, the guys aboard the boat—but it was Sergeant Redes I was worried about. I was hoping he couldn't see me from wherever he was, because he would never have condoned something so foolish. A bomb on the shore of a deserted island was not a bomb you risked your life for.

More to the point, you certainly didn't tug on it. I felt a thud in my chest and saw the water suddenly boil, and a plume of water shoot up about twelve feet behind the control frame. I was still so taken with the magic of the balloon's appearance that my first thought was not bombs, but *sea monsters!*—and then I got back to work.

Once the water settled, I looked at the control frame carefully. One of the bombs—the last remaining bomb, it appeared—had fallen off. I hauled what remained up onto the gravel and righted it.

I'd seen one from afar at Fort Cronkhite, and up close in Gurley's Quonset hut, and in the training film he had yet to sit through. But this one seemed extraordinary. Not just because Lily had led me here, but because I *was* here. I had found it. Mine. It was, as Gurley might have said, a beautiful specimen, largely intact. Fresh from the ocean, still dangling fuses and ropes, it looked like a giant mechanical jellyfish, less a product of war than of some mad Victorian scientist.

I waved the guys over; they hesitated. I frowned, I was freezing. I'd found my prize and wanted to go. I turned back to the control frame and thought about how it resembled the one I'd seen in the film. Mine looked nicer, I thought. I could see the expressionless, silent man in the film point out different features of the device while an invisible narrator droned on. The silent man onscreen never showed a trace of emotion, but I remembered how the narrator's voice had speeded up just once: *A good location to look for booby traps is under the*—I looked up. The crew was walking toward me now. I shouted at them to stop.

I carefully took hold of the control frame, noticed my hands were almost completely without sensation, and slowly tilted the apparatus on its side. And there it was. Not a booby trap, but the demolition block. A small tin box, about six inches long and two wide—I've got a breast-pocket Bible not much bigger now. Inside would be a paper-wrapped two-pound picric acid charge, enough to destroy any evidence of the balloon. A fire would start in a forest, and no one would ever know how. Or a benumbed bomb disposal sergeant would blow himself up on a rocky shore, and no one would care how. I cut the fuse and removed the block. Then I carefully set it down at the other end of the beach. We could have safely transported it home, and Gurley would have wanted it for evidence, but I knew there was no way I could bring it on board—not after everyone had seen me take such care. Or rather, not after everyone had seen me almost forget to take care of it.

It took a bit of convincing to get the crew to finally come over, but they did. We hauled the control frame into the boat, and then onto the plane.

Within minutes, I was in dry clothes and growing warmer, though the cold I felt remains to this day. Ask anyone who has been rescued from icy waters. One's bones, cells, never forget; they need only the barest reminder of a raw, wet day, even the sight of one onscreen, and the sea's chill comes surging back.

My swim, as the crew called it, was significant not because of what we collected—a souvenir; I believe the control frame now sits in a collection of wartime artifacts in a museum in Canada—but because of that deep, cold water. I functioned differently after that. If I knew anything about biology, maybe I could tell you how—but I know everything about me felt changed. My skin, the way I moved, the insides of my eyelids, even. I'd get these flashing headaches when I sneezed, and

I swear my blood flowed in reverse, or at least in some direction that allowed me to feel it. Really. Sitting there, I could feel all those molecules and cells and whatever other sludge blood ferries about inside us.

This would have made no sense to Gurley, nor even the doctors at the hospital back at Fort Richardson. (The army had a large, if dwindling, corps of veterinarians, holdovers from the days of a mounted cavalry and mule trains—and since everything else about the military in Alaska was jury-rigged, we just assumed they'd been redeployed to work on humans.) So I didn't tell them. But my heart had suffered some damage, and it was to my benefit. It made me more reckless, more eager for danger.

As for what happened to the other, less physical aspect of my heart, it's obvious it froze as well. In time, one led to the other—the physical death to the death of a spirit—and I found myself willingly executing Gurley's most every demand. In time, I did worse than that—I came to anticipating his demands before he would issue them. This is not to say that I became him, that he had molded me in his image. Hardly. But the truth was far worse.

"HOW DID YOU KNOW?"

This is what Gurley asked me when I returned.

It's also what I asked Father Pabich when he found me in the hospital only minutes after I was installed there. (Who had told him I'd arrived?)

And it's what Father Pabich asked Lily when she later joined me at my bedside.

When Gurley asked his question, I didn't answer, pretending to be even more groggy than I was. And when I asked Father Pabich, he didn't answer.

But when Father Pabich asked Lily how she knew what she knew about Shuyak—and how she knew me—not answering was not an option.

After his initial visit to the hospital, I didn't see Gurley for a day or two. He'd promised as much; he said he was being summoned to yet another meeting, this time in Juneau. Might be gone for a week. He didn't look pleased. I mentioned how Shuyak at least gave him something to crow about, and he shook his head. "Something's up, Belk. Not good." And with that, he was gone.

Father Pabich, on the other hand, checked back in on me several times. At first, I was touched—tough Father Pabich was actually a tender man. But when he returned again and again, and then once more right after dinner, I realized that what I was witnessing wasn't so much tenderness but curiosity. The man wanted to know what I had done and where I had done it.

Fat chance. The more callow the secret keeper, the more tenaciously kept the secret. The Army had told me to keep quiet. Gurley had told me to keep quiet. I wasn't going to tell Father Pabich, though the more he pressed, the more I realized I'd have to tell him something. Then an idea came to me, a fabulous one: I'd ask him to hear my confession. No priest could reveal anything told under the seal of confession. I didn't know much, but I knew that.

So I asked to confess, and instead of saying yes, Father Pabich looked at me strangely. He knew something was afoot, and when he turned to look around the room, he thought he knew what, or who: Lily had appeared in the doorway.

As horrible as that moment was—Father Pabich assuming I'd hurriedly asked for confession because I'd caught sight of my illicit lover—that picture of Lily in the doorway is one of my favorites. I carry it around in my head as if a photograph actually existed. The lighting is poor, but she's clear enough, and beautiful.

She had changed: she was wearing a long, dark coat (cashmere?), the collar trimmed with fur, a matching hat, long black gloves—but pretty, Park Avenue gloves that must have been useless against the cold. She was wearing equally pretty but useless boots, and was carrying a tiny black purse.

It's her face I remember best. She wasn't smiling. No, much better, she was worried. Thinking back on it now, I suppose she had plenty to be worried about—she was a woman, alone, on base, and her Eskimo features would have only made her the subject of increased attention and prejudice. But all I was thinking about then was that she was worried about me.

All the relative splendor that had caught my eye had caught Father Pabich's as well. Her appearance and my sudden desire for confession combined to convince him of one thing: she was a prostitute. He didn't say this, but he didn't have to. Lily wore all that finery and no wedding ring, and that was proof enough for him. As corroboration, a semiconscious guy a few beds down gave a low whistle. Father Pabich shot him a look and Lily ignored them both. She took off her hat, peered into the room. She saw me, took a step, saw Father Pabich, hesitated, but only a second, and then came over to the bed.

She nodded to Father Pabich first. "Father," she said quietly, and already, he was won over, just a little bit.

"Louis?" she said next, looking toward me.

I looked her up and down and grinned. "Who in the world are *you*?"

She grinned back, but then Father Pabich said, "Indeed."

"Oh, gosh, it's okay, Father, I'm just joking," I said, not quite yet realizing how much trouble I was in, or that we all would soon be in. "I know her. This is Lily," I said, and then made things worse. "I'm just not used to seeing her, you know, dressed—this way."

Lily pursed her lips. The whistler whistled. Father Pabich spoke: "Not another note, whistling soldier—or I tell the lady here, and the whole damn ward, just where it was you got operated on." The man blanched and tried to roll over. "Perhaps a chair for your guest?" Father Pabich asked me. For a second, I thought he meant me to get up and fetch it for her. Perhaps he did, but I didn't move, and he turned and dragged one from beside an empty bed.

"I'm not staying long," Lily said.

"No," Father Pabich said, and then, after a perfectly timed pause, added, "I imagine that gets expensive."

It got really quiet then, except for over at the whistler's bed, where two tiny words floated up: "Jesus Christ."

"F-F-F-ather," I whispered.

Father Pabich and Lily stared at each other, neither giving quarter. I saw Lily decide to smack him and then decide to back off. I saw Father Pabich determine to add further insult and then decide to remain quiet. Then Lily spoke, a short string of something I didn't understand. She'd said it so softly, and in such a rush, that I took whatever she was saying to be in Yup'ik. Profane Yup'ik.

Father Pabich stared at her, flabbergasted. I did as well. I was embarrassed how she was reinforcing the fact that she wasn't white—and I was embarrassed that she was cursing him in some Eskimo language that only she understood.

"I'm sorry, Father," I broke in. "She's—she's Yup'ik, and that's her"—I glared at Lily, but she didn't look at me—"and that's just her way of saying—"

"That I'm an ass," Father Pabich said.

"Well, no," I said.

"As are you," he said. "Yup'ik," he added, and shook his head. *"Qui sine peccato est vestrum primus in illam lapidem mittat,"* he said to me. "That's what she said. That sound like Eskimo?"

I shook my head. "What part of the Mass is that from?"

"It's from the Bible, dipsh—," he said, and caught himself. "Can you translate it for him?" Father Pabich asked Lily. She said nothing. "Of course you can," he added, lowering his eyes, involuntarily deferential. "What she said was 'Let him who is without sin among you be the first to throw a stone at her.' An odd verse to memorize in Latin, but there you are: John, chapter seven."

Finally, Lily smiled. "Eight," she said.

"Somewhere, a nun is smiling," Father Pabich said.

"Not in my experience," Lily replied. "I'll come back," she said to me, and then extended her hand to Father Pabich. "It was nice meeting you, Father." Father Pabich let the hand dangle there a moment, and then he shook it, cautiously.

As she left, I thought back to Father Pabich's initial question: *How did you know?* "That's how," I said, watching the tail of her coat disappear through the door.

"What?" Father Pabich had been staring after her, too. When he turned back to face me, though, I was feigning sleep.

"HOW *DID* YOU KNOW?"

I was walking with Lily downtown the night after I'd been discharged from the hospital. It was late, the streets were almost empty, and I was due back on base.

Lily answered my question with one of her own. "You really saw one? You saw a balloon."

"Proof is back at the base."

"I was right," Lily said, more to herself, and we walked on in silence for a block.

I'd never had a girlfriend—it wasn't something the nuns facilitated at the orphanage, and the Army hadn't given me an awful lot of options—and so I wasn't in much of a position to judge whether I had one then. But walking along like that, down a quiet street late at night, not even touching, but always just about to: it had to be something like this, I thought. I knew nothing of the world then, maybe I know less now, but I knew that much. I knew I was in love, or its teenage equivalent, and I knew Lily loved—well, I didn't know if she loved me, but I knew she noticed me. She'd come to the hospital to see me, she'd braved Father Pabich, and she was walking alongside me now. We weren't holding hands, but we were walking close enough to, and it felt like we could if we wanted to, and if I could ever feel that way again, just connect with another human, even my desiccated shaman friend Ronnie lying here—God forgive me, but I'd sell my soul for half price.

Lily finally broke the silence. "You believe in ghosts, right?"

I did, but in a storybook, Halloween kind of way that has nothing, really, to do with the true world of ghosts. But back then, I'd never seen a ghost. Nowadays—well, some winters you'd be hard-pressed at the end of the month to do an honest accounting of whom or what you'd seen. And I'm not talking about the Blessed Mother (who, you'll note, more frequently reveals herself to the faithful in warmer climes—like Mexico or France).

So I told Lily no. And when she looked at me, disappointed, I tried, "Well, the Holy Ghost."

"What are you going to tell Gurley when he asks you how you knew about Shuyak?" Lily asked.

"He already did ask, and I didn't tell him anything."

"He'll ask again."

"Maybe. What makes you so sure?"

"Because he will. That's the way he is."

"And you know him so well," I said, the words out so quickly, I didn't realize what I said until I saw her coming at me. Her face stopped just short of mine, and two minutes before, I would have closed my eyes and waited for the kiss. Now I blinked and swallowed and held my breath.

"I do know him," she said, and the way she said it, I would have preferred that she had slapped me or kneed me or put a gun to my chest. She stepped back. "Better than you do, better than either of you know me."

We'd stopped walking now. We were a couple blocks shy of the main road out to Fort Richardson.

"I told you I was Yup'ik—"

"Lily, I'm sorry if I—"

"And Russian—"

I tried a smile: " 'Boom.' I remember."

Lily tried to smile, too. "Well, this doesn't come from the Russian part, that's for sure."

"What doesn't?" I asked, but Lily ignored me. She was staring down the block ahead of us, talking.

"In fact, I'm sure the Russian blood just lessens my ability to— understand things. Because every generation of Yup'ik Eskimos has— people who—see. It's just that it's hard, and getting harder to see things here. In Anchorage. That's why I'm going home."

"I understand," I said.

"You don't," Lily said. "That's why I asked you about ghosts."

"Shuyak was real. The balloon was real. The ocean was very real."

"But those were things you *saw,* and felt. What about late at night? When you're all alone? You hear a noise, you close the book you were reading, and look up, your finger marking the page you were on. What do you think?"

I tried to think of something funny to say, and then something serious, and finally came up with nothing at all.

"You think, for a split second, of ghosts, spirits. You *do.* It's possible. And the feeling passes, sure, and the next morning the sun comes up, you've lost your place in the book, and everything real is real once again, but still, for that moment, it was possible."

"For that moment," I said. It really was time to go.

"It's *that* moment," Lily said. "Right now."

"Right," I said, frightened to discover I was frightened.

"Look where you are," Lily said, walking around me, whispering. (She and Gurley shared a sense of drama, or else one had infected the other.) "There's no one here. You're in Alaska. In December. Even the sun is too scared to come around for more than a few hours each day."

The street really had taken on a different cast. There were no other pedestrians, no other sounds.

"Ghosts," I said absently, almost without meaning to.

"Not ghosts," Lily said, "but possibilities. In Alaska, it's all possible.

Maybe elsewhere you need things like ghosts to explain what's on the horizon of what's real. But here, you're already past that line. And on this side, the whole world is creaking." Something, somewhere, made a tiny clink, on cue. "We're all ghosts." She came around to face me. "We all carry, inside us, people who came before us."

"Sure," I said. "Your mother's brown eyes. Your father's height."

Lily shook her head. "Stop thinking like a *kass'aq*. At home, my home, someone dies, and a child takes up the name. Feed and clothe the child, and the deceased—they are fed and clothed in the land of the dead."

"Land of the dead? Lily—"

"It's true," said Lily. She'd stopped acting: her voice was now urgent, emphatic, and didn't quite match her eyes, which looked almost full of tears. "The dead who return, they come wearing things given to their namesake. One elder arrived wearing a dozen parkas. Years of gifts, layered one atop the other."

"You've seen this?" I asked.

"I know this to be true," she said angrily. I started to say something, but she continued: "I have heard the stories. Any elder will tell you."

"Tell me a story," I said, stalling so that I could quickly scan our surroundings. Something was wrong. A lot was wrong. I'd thought this walk might lead to a kiss—even if it was just a goodbye kiss—and instead we'd found our way to wherever we were. I wondered whether there was a chance the conversation would teeter back toward intimacy while she spoke.

But when I turned back to face her, she was crying. "Louis," she said. "Please, if I tell you this—"

"Of course," I said, distracted. "Lily—"

And then I found myself beset by ghosts. One I heard behind me— a quiet footfall, like someone barefoot or wearing moccasins, followed by a slow exhale. I turned, saw nothing and didn't really expect to— my imagination had plenty to work with by then.

But I hadn't been imagining Lily. I couldn't have been. We'd talked,

walked, had dinner together. So I turned back around, sheepish smile
in place and ready to admit that, okay, perhaps she was right about
spirits, because I swore I had just heard something behind me and—

She wasn't there.

Not there, not down the block, not anywhere. I spent a minute looking, but only a minute, before starting back toward base, anxious now
to hitch a ride home through the dark. But the only vehicle I saw was
a jeep going the wrong direction—into town—and I ducked into the
shadows in case they were MPs enforcing curfew.

There was just a single man in the jeep, and though I caught only a
dim glimpse as he sped past me into town, I could tell it wasn't an MP,
but Gurley.

CHAPTER 10

RONNIE RETURNED EARLY AS WELL. AND WHEN HE AWOKE, he was angry and scared and breathless. This was a couple hours ago—not long, actually, after he'd finished explaining how an *angalkuq* traveled the tundra. He'd closed his eyes, his breathing deepened and slowed, and I assumed he was reentering his trance—or his coma—or simply falling asleep, exhausted from the actual or imagined journeys he was making in and out of consciousness.

And I felt guilty. Here was a poor man trying to get some rest and here I had been rattling away at his bedside, taking grateful advantage of a confessor deaf and dumb with sleep. I stopped talking. My decades-only stories, secrets, and sins could wait.

But Ronnie could not. I had been silent for a minute, perhaps not even that, when his eyes blinked wide. His hands, which had been lying quietly at his side, sprang open as well. Perhaps he'd met his fearful wolf, I thought, and the nightmare had awakened him.

"Lou-is," he said, and though his voice was barely louder than the whisper it had been, it was enough change in volume to make it seem like he was shouting. I jumped. "You stopped," he said. I started to ask what he meant, but he cut me off. "Talking. You stopped talking. You

must not stop talking. I have told you this. I have told you the story of
the boy and his mother. You must not stop talking."

"Ronnie," I said. "I was just trying to let you sleep."

He glared. "Not sleep. I have told you this. I have told you of my
journeys. I have told you the story of the boy and his mother."

Now I interrupted him. "You didn't," I said, forcing a patient smile
as guilt turned to anger—at Ronnie, and myself. Ronnie was a friend,
but not a believer. How could I justify sitting here, by his side, around
the clock, when others—the faithful—needed me, as they surely did?
Ronnie had not asked me to pray with him. He'd not asked me for
much of anything, in fact, other than twenty dollars and a promise to
help him die. What should have followed, then, was not an endless
vigil of two old men exchanging stories, but rather a priest administering what sacraments he could—baptism, if the man was interested,
confession, communion, and the anointing of the sick. At which point,
the talking should stop, and the priest should leave, and the dying man
should do his best to die.

I prepared to ask Ronnie if, as the hour of his death grew near, he
wanted to be baptized with the waters of everlasting life, in the name of
Our Lord Jesus Christ. I prepared to be rejected. I prepared to stand,
say a short, defiant prayer, give a curt nod, and leave.

But none of this happened, because I hadn't prepared for what
Ronnie was about to tell me.

"You must not stop talking," Ronnie said again. "You may speak
softly, but your voice must be clear to me. Your voice, your human,
kass'aq, priest-voice, it worries the wolf. This *tuunraq,* he circles me, he
circles you, but he is afraid to move closer while you are here. This is
good. I am not ready for him yet. You must keep speaking." He took a
deep breath and let his head rest back on the pillow. "Not just because
of the *tuunraq,* but also because that is how I find my way home. Hearing you. I have to travel far this time, to where the dead live. I was not
sure I had to go." He looked at me and shrugged, as though we were
discussing an unexpected need to visit Anchorage, or the grocery

store. He settled back again. "But this is what I think. This is why I told you the story of the mother and the boy."

"Ronnie," I interrupted once more, no longer hiding my anger.

His face was completely open, as though he were indulging me and not the other way around. "Then I tell it again. This was not long ago. This was when the *kass'at* brought the great sickness to our land." I wanted to stand, then, and leave, rather than be excoriated—as I'd been a dozen times before—for being of that tribe, that world, that introduced smallpox and tuberculosis and worse to the Yup'ik Eskimo. Disease: the Outsiders' invisible, potent weapon. Within years, we had killed thousands. One out of every three died from TB. More babies died than lived. It didn't matter that we later stormed the tundra with nurses, doctors, and drugs. It was too late. "And this was a mother with a new child. A boy. He was very small, this boy. A baby. He rushed out of his mother too early, and into the sickness. The other wives all scooped him up and held him close and waited for him to die. But he surprised them. He lived. It was the mother who died. The baby had come too soon. She was too tired." Ronnie took a long breath, tired himself. "They took the mother to be buried. The baby, too. No one wanted this boy who had killed his mother. Into the grave he went, placed beside his silent mother, wailing all the while." He paused, took another long breath, and I realized he was about to reproduce the baby's cry. But the sound that came out—it was unbearable, a terribly thin and eerie wail. If I had never known Ronnie until that minute, if I had simply walked into the room and encountered him there, that sound spewing out of him, I would have said without reservation that this was a man who spoke with spirits. This sound came from far, far beneath him. He caught his breath and continued. "He would not stop crying. He sobbed. This is what babies do. But he cried on and on, and his voice carried, through the dirt, through the grass, through the walls of their homes, through their skulls. He cried so long and so loud that his mother awoke. He had distracted her on her journey to the land of the dead. She heard him, as any mother would, and she knew the villagers had abandoned him. She arose and walked to the village. The people begged her to leave. The shamans begged her. But the mother was confused. She had risen for the baby, but he had fallen silent. What was she to do? She was angry. Why had she died? Why had they buried her boy? She broke things. Stole things. She told the animals to stay away. The hunters could not hunt. She would not leave. Where was her husband? Why had he allowed this? She looked for him, but he hid," Ronnie finished abruptly. "This is what they say."

Then his tone changed, from storyteller to teacher. "This is why you must never cry at a funeral," he said. "You must be quiet when death is near, or the dead will not complete their journey. And this is why you must speak to me. Because I do not want to lose my way in the land of the dead. Keep talking. Your voice will call me back."

He smiled before adding one more thing. "It is nice that it is an annoying voice. Easier to follow." But I missed the joke: the story had stunned me.

Gone were baptism and communion and the anointing of the sick. Gone was the Holy Roman Catholic Church. Gone even the hospital. There was only that room, that shaman and this priest and legions upon legions of dead pressing ever nearer.

I knew this because I knew Ronnie's story. I had heard it before, once before, years before.

It has haunted me ever since, both because of the circumstances of the telling and of what happened to the storyteller. Ronnie's version was slightly different, and I wanted to ask him why. But I was so scared or disoriented by what he said that I focused on what I—me, a man of God—now truly believed was the immediate danger: "But if I speak," I whispered, "if my voice follows you on your journey—what if others hear it? What if others have their journey disrupted? Will they return, too?"

But Ronnie was done talking. He hardly glanced at me before shutting his eyes and mouthing just the one word: *speak*.

* * *

I LEFT MY BARRACKS for the Quonset hut at 7:30 A.M., half an hour, at least, after the time Gurley usually expected me. But since I'd seen him driving into town so late, I didn't expect him to arrive for an hour or more. Surely—I tried to block the thought, but it arrived, pounding, all the same—he and Lily would have busied themselves throughout the predawn hours.

There was a jeep idling outside the Quonset hut when I walked up. I didn't pay much attention; I was busy rehearsing an answer to the question Gurley would ask first: just how had I known about Shuyak Island?

Suddenly, he was right in front of me.

"Kirby-fucking-Wyoming," he said, clanging out of the compound gate. "Was that your next guess?" He bumped past me and into the jeep. As it drove away, he turned around and shouted, "Walking to Kirby?" I stared after him. "Run, you sot!" Gurley bellowed. I looked at the sentry, who refused to look at me. At the sound of a gunshot, I turned back around to find Gurley firing into the air. I ran. Gurley had the driver slow down enough to keep me close, but not close enough. After a half a mile or so, the jeep stopped and I climbed aboard.

"Why didn't you just get in the jeep back at the hut?" Gurley said, shaking his head, and then dug into a briefcase between his legs. "We have problems, Sergeant," he said.

"But we've got two weeks," I said.

Gurley looked up with a blank face. "Until what?"

"Two weeks, you said. We have two weeks to prove ourselves."

"Oh hell," Gurley said. "It'd be nice to return to that fairyland, when all our problems were so simple." He burrowed back into the briefcase, then bumped his head against the dash when the driver stopped at an intersection. "Fuck!" he shouted, and then pulled out his gun, which he put to the driver's head. "This is an emergency, not traffic school. You stop at any more traffic signs, and—"

The jeep launched forward with such force, Gurley almost landed in the backseat with me. When he'd resettled, I had to ask: "What's the problem, Captain?"

"The problem, Sergeant, is a downed balloon."

"In Wyoming?" I said.

"Correct," he said, and burrowed into his briefcase.

"So?" I tried to sound like an old hand. "Who found it?"

Gurley appeared to find his paper and sat up. "That," Gurley said, "is part of the problem." He pointed to the page before me. "Kirby, Wyoming. Balloon found intact. By the Associated Press."

I read the transcription as we pulled up to the terminal.

MYSTERY BALLOON FOUND NEAR KIRBY

KIRBY, WY (AP) — A mysterious aircraft crashed just outside Kirby Tuesday. Local resident Gertrude Cleary, 68, said she saw what looked like the remains of a large helium balloon tangled in a line of trees at the far border of the town park, and reported it immediately to police. Police and civil defense officials refused to comment on the balloon, prompting much speculation and concern among the local citizenry. Cleary and others believe the balloon is from a nearby POW camp. Said Cleary: "So some Nazi is on the loose now, and nobody's talking. You got a lot of scared people here."

"So word is out," I said, though it didn't seem that bad. Who read the Cheyenne paper outside of Wyoming?

Gurley had the driver circle around the terminal and deposit us directly before the plane. "Things are actually a bit more fucked up than that, Sergeant," he said, anxiously scanning the tarmac. "A lot more."

The plane's propellers were already lazily spinning, but Gurley didn't board. I hung back as well, wondering if this was another invitation-only flight. Gurley asked a crewman nearby if a particular crate of gear had been loaded. The man looked confused; Gurley started yelling. Nothing would be fast enough today. The man left in a trot for the passenger terminal. Gurley followed him at his slower pace, and the two met beside a waist-high box. I was too far away to hear what they were saying, but I could see—anyone could see—that the box was labeled with skull and crossbones. While the crewman loaded the box, Gurley returned. I asked him what was inside. He shook his head and then frowned. The sincere, sympathetic look that followed it was alarming, both for its rarity and for the speed with which it had completely replaced the raw red fury of moments before.

"Sergeant," he said, and stopped. "I—yes. I have to ask you a question." He looked nervous, even scared, and he didn't look like he was acting at all. Then he gave a little smile, which made things even worse. He tried again. "And here we are," he said. "Now then, I have to ask you a question, but it's not really a fair one. The thing is, Sergeant, our war has changed. It may change for everyone, soon, but today, it starts with us. And it starts with me asking if you will *volunteer* to join me on this flight to Wyoming."

"Of course," I interrupted. I couldn't bear Gurley, human. It was disorienting, and oddly frightening. If wild, towering, vengeful Gurley could be spooked, then there could be little hope for the rest of us.

"Hear me out, Sergeant," Gurley said curtly, almost relieved to be back in the position of scold. "I've been told to formally ask if you will volunteer for this mission because of the hazards involved—"

"A balloon is a balloon, sir," I said, and then stopped speaking when I saw Gurley's face.

"Inside the crate are gas masks and suits," Gurley said. "We have word—too damn late word, if you ask me, but no one ever does—that one, or a dozen, or all of the balloons now approaching the United States may carry a new kind of bomb. Not incendiaries. Not antipersonnel. Bacteriological. Germs."

And I really didn't know what he was talking about. *Germ* wasn't that scary a word to me then. Germs gave you colds. That's why people covered their noses when they sneezed. I would eventually learn just how naïve I was, but before Gurley explained anything else, he first had to get me aboard the plane.

"This information is so new that—we—well, they're not sure if the gear we have is really, you know, up to the task. We just don't know. So I'm supposed to ask if, knowing the risks, which you really don't, you'll volunteer to go. And I'm supposed to let you stay behind if you want." He took a step toward the plane. "But I can't really do that, Belk, you know why?"

The officer defuses the bomb. I looked at him a moment. "Because you need help with—? Because I will, sir," I said. "Even though I didn't really train for—"

Gurley smiled. "Yes, Belk," he said. "I need you for that. But I also need you for the simple reason that, when the question was asked of the NCOs present at the meeting I flew to yesterday—well, there were no volunteers."

"Sir," I began.

"Good man," Gurley said, his actor's smile and flourish returning as he swung himself aboard.

GURLEY GAVE ME MORE background on the flight. The supposedly weeklong meeting he'd been summoned to in Juneau during my Shuyak convalescence had been cut short when word of the Wyoming balloon arrived.

At first, he tried to summarize the briefing he'd received, but I interrupted him with so many questions that he finally gave up and handed his top secret briefing packet to me. He put a finger to his lips, as if to say "shh," and then raised his thumb. He didn't have to draw it across my throat, or his. I began reading.

Evidence of Japan's germ weapons program was arriving from an increasing number of credible sources, the report said, even as the information relayed was becoming increasingly incredible. A highly specialized and extremely secretive Japanese army medical corps named Unit 731 had set up shop—factories, really—in Manchuria, where they were conducting horrifying experiments on local peasants, as well as whomever else they might come upon—White Russians, Koreans,

Gypsies, missionaries. Men's chests were split open and their organs removed while they were still alive. Limbs of men, women, even infants were frozen, then beaten or thawed and refrozen to examine the process of frostbite.

The authors of Gurley's report, however, were not worried about frostbite.

There had been reports from a Chinese informer that Unit 731 was experimenting with germ warfare. Typhoid, cholera, plague, syphilis, and anthrax were injected into patients and the results examined: depending on the disease, body parts might turn black, hands fall off. The informer swore he had seen this. And more: prisoners had been taken to a remote area and staked to the ground in a great circle. A specially modified tank had driven to the middle of the circle and begun...spraying.

There was also an active breeding program of rats and fleas; the fleas were infected with disease, the rats infested with the fleas. It was thought that these fleas, or possibly gnats and even mosquitoes, were candidates for balloon travel, to be sent aloft in special porcelain canisters that—

"Did you get to the part about the fleas?" Gurley shouted at me. I nodded. "Fleas!" he repeated.

"Rats," I said, for lack of a better response.

"Yes, well, *rats,*" Gurley said. "Now, there's a troublesome threat," he added. He grabbed the papers back from me. "It's bad enough I get saddled with balloons, while other men are off battling warships or rockets or desert armies. But now I find I am enlisted to fight fleas."

"This unit—sir—dissecting men alive? Babies?" I stared at the papers in his lap.

"If they airdrop lunatic doctors," Gurley said, "then yes, we will have something to fear. Even more than we would have to fear from our own medical staff—"

"Sir, I—" I was surprised to find myself interrupting; I usually let Gurley babble on. But I really was afraid now, a different kind of fear than I had ever felt in bomb disposal school or ever since. I'd always seen my death as a bright, sudden event—an explosion—but what Gurley's briefing papers promised was something much more slow and gruesome.

"Yes?" Gurley asked, less annoyed than I thought he might be.

But I didn't really have anything to say. I had just wanted him to shut up; I had wanted him to let me sit and think through everything I'd just read; I had wanted him to ask me where I'd been the night before, so I could tell him *With Lily, before you*, even if it was just for dinner and talk of ghosts. I wondered now: Had Lily told him, too, that she was leaving?

I didn't answer Gurley. I stared down at my hands, rubbed my palms together, imagined first the one and then the other swelling, rotting, turning black and falling away.

Gurley watched me for a moment before he spoke. "You have a question." I must have looked surprised, because he added, "I know—it's this gift I have. I'm a mind reader. Otherwise, I don't know how I'd figure out what lay behind that impenetrable countenance of yours."

"Sir," I began again, having missed most of what Gurley had just said. His using words over two syllables was usually a clear cue to tune out. But the term *mind reader* had stuck. And Gurley saw it. I don't know how much he saw, whether he saw Lily and me, last night's meeting or the nights before, saw us almost holding hands, saw her smiling only for me (I was sure), but he saw Lily inside me clearly enough. I panicked, and stayed panicked, even when he started smiling.

"Ah," Gurley said. "How soon I forget. We have a mind reader in common, do we not?" He feigned being interrupted by a private and quite enjoyable memory, or perhaps actually had one. Then he focused on me again. "Is this our boy-becomes-a-man talk? I should have known. A lad goes off to war, and—did your father sit you down before you left, young Sergeant?"

"Sir, I—"

"Oh, yes, yes—no father, no mother, a bastard raised by nuns. Delightful. Though *they* couldn't be counted on to—well, now, could they? Mmm...*there's* a thought." He must have seen my impenetrable face opening to anger, because he stopped. "So," he said. "Lily: What's your question?"

I waited, too long, before I spoke. "That's not my question," I said, and it hadn't been, though now I wasn't sure. I tried pushing Lily out of my head. She wouldn't go, but I pressed on. "I wanted to know why we're flying all the way to Wyoming. Why not some guys out of Denver? Or San Francisco?"

"Or perhaps Paris—or Cairo," Gurley said. "Why not just sit back and let the other boys do our job? Steal our medals. Win our war." He drew himself up as best he could in the seat restraints. "Because, Belk. That's why. Because, one, as I told you, volunteers were few and far between at the meeting yesterday. While they fret over what to do, we've got the chance to leap ahead and seize the initiative in what may turn out to be the most important campaign of the war. I make fun of their fleas, but make no mistake, if that report is even ten percent right, it won't matter who wins in the Pacific—all those GIs will return home to stinking corpses strewn across the prairie." I turned away, and he elbowed me so I'd turn back. "Because, two, there's already been a story published, so the potential for further fuckups is pretty high. With bacteria-encrusted bombs on the way, there's no question now of disposing with the ban. This must be kept secret." Now he sank back. "And because, three, any chance to leave our fucking frozen Xanadu for warmer locales, even late winter Wyoming, is a chance we *take*." He closed his eyes. "Really, Belk."

I sat back, too, and thought about making a mistake when I handled our next bomb. Our next normal one. It wasn't the first time I'd thought this, but the reason for the mistake was changing. Early on in Alaska, I'd spent some long, lonely days daydreaming about—well, blowing myself up. Maybe doing it in such a way that I'd only be injured—lose a foot maybe, a finger or two. But you couldn't count on that. It was a safer bet to try to kill yourself outright.

But lately, I'd begun to think about Gurley.

"About the mind reader, though," Gurley said after a few minutes, eyes still closed, and then added, "Lily is a lovely girl." He waited. "Mmm?" I nodded, realized he couldn't see me nodding, and then grunted in agreement. I wasn't sure what would come out if I opened my mouth. "But you do realize," he said, opening his eyes to catch mine, and then closing them again, "that she's a—that she's a busy woman. A businesswoman, in point of fact."

"Yes," I said. I wiped my palms on my knees.

"I'm just saying, don't grow too attached. Not that you have. It may seem like they're only six girls in all Anchorage, but there's more coming, all the time."

Now I closed my eyes and leaned back. Not to go to sleep, but just to escape, somehow: the conversation, the plane, the mission, Gurley. I opened them when Gurley tapped me on the chest. I found him leaning as close to me as he could. "I guess what I'm saying is, just between you and me, I have a unique fondness for our mutual friend. And I'm thinking of—how shall I put it?—taking her off the market. For the duration, at least. Not sure I can see her back East, let alone Princeton, but then, I'm not sure I can see myself there anymore, either."

"You're going to get...married?" I asked.

He looked at me. "In a gold carriage pulled by four white horses. You'll be a ringbearer, or flower girl." He rubbed his forehead. "Jesus, Belk. If you were about ten years older and a hundred years more mature, we could manage a conversation on this topic. As it is, I don't know what's going to happen. And I don't want this to get around—but, yes, I have a soft spot for the girl. I *care* for her, and would like to take care *of* her." He looked up toward the cockpit. "Which is why I want to take care of this mess, as quickly as possible."

"Have you told her this?" I asked, probably sounding a bit too desperate. Why hadn't she told me this? Or was this why she was leaving Anchorage? To escape Gurley? Or elope with him?

"Yes," he said, and thought for a moment. "Yes, I have. Which is the war's biggest surprise so far, Belk, if you're keeping track—bigger than Pearl Harbor, bigger than balloons and bigger than fleas. If you'd have told me before I enlisted that I'd return from the war with an Eskimo bride, tall enough to look me in the eye and—have you ever noticed, Belk? She has the most remarkable eyes. Jet black, almost. You look in those eyes, you're liable to forget your name, the date. And legs like—well, suffice to say, she's not the type you meet over punch at the Vassar mixer." He pulled himself up. "Of course, I understand your meetings don't give you the opportunity to learn such details. She tells me you just consult her for palm readings." He delivered this as both statement and question.

But I was thunderstruck that Lily had told him about me. She and I were the only ones with secrets. "She told you?"

"Don't be embarrassed, Belk," Gurley said. "Or do be—I'm sure the nuns back home would be horrified. I, for one, find your interest in astrology or whatever it is... affecting. A trifle immature, but harmless." I heard in that *harmless* a word of warning, and one look at his face told me I'd heard right. Then he broke into an almost giddy smile and dove into his satchel of papers again. I tensed for what terror would emerge this time: perhaps blue foxes gone rabid. Maybe Lily herself.

"All right, all right," he said, needlessly looking around to see if anyone was watching, and then handed a torn piece of newsprint to me. "Now, I'd always fancied myself the kind of suitor who'd stride down Fifth Avenue to Tiffany's for the robin's-egg-blue box, but—" He stopped. "You have no idea what I'm talking about." I didn't, but I wasn't listening, either: he'd handed me an ad for an engagement ring. "I went by, you know. You'd think it's just a little small-town glitter shop, but the man's an old pro. Gets his gold from right here in Alaska, diamonds from wholesalers back East. Once he realized I wasn't the same sort of army rube he's used to getting, he took me in back—you know, the pieces reserved for *special* customers." The ad showed a gaudy diamond ring on a hand with long, delicate fingers that looked nothing like Lily's.

"Will she—" *marry you?* is what I wanted to ask, but only the first two words come out.

Gurley took the clipping back. "Wear it? I know what you're thinking. Not that type of girl. Not for her, china and lace. But here's a secret, Belk: they all like pretty things. Hell, the Indians sold Manhattan for a bag of beads. And the rings *I'm* considering. Well." He returned the ad to his satchel, paused a moment, and then drew out a single sheet of paper. "That's not the problem. But Alaska—Alaska is. I'm not sure she'd leave. I have the loveliest spot picked out, too. Some land, north of San Francisco. Hillside, overlooking the ocean. Found it when I did a brief tour at the Presidio. But Alaska has this hold on her." He looked absently at the sheet he'd pulled out. I couldn't read what was on it. "And I don't know—I don't know if I could make it here. After the war." He tapped his leg. "They've civilized Anchorage, Juneau, Fairbanks, a few other spots, but she's no city girl. She'd want to be out—in the bush, on the tundra. I don't know, Belk." He finally handed the paper to me, but I didn't look at it immediately—I was fascinated with his face. Gurley, who ruled all, was betraying an honest sense of longing. Even regret.

I was sure I knew why. It wasn't Lily he'd miss. No, he'd stay in Alaska, in the bush, but forever be isolated from his old world. His Princeton classmates. Their clubs. A night at the theater. The opera. Museums. He was displaying a prissy softness, and I looked down, embarrassed for him. The sheet he'd handed me was titled "Germ Warfare Balloon Protocol." But I was so surprised by what he said next that I looked back up at him.

"It's not safe, Belk. When the war's over and the shooting stops, the world, most of it, will be safe. Safer. That's what we're fighting for, right? All of us? But Alaska, after the war? It will be as dangerous as it always was. And if you lived here, you'd be fighting along, alone, you versus the weather, wildlife, the wild. Fights you can't win. Not with one leg. Not with two hands trained for banking or books." He rubbed his face and then stared straight ahead, an old man of twenty-five. "It's just so easy to die up there."

GERM WARFARE BALLOON PROTOCOL
Fourth Air Force
The Presidio
San Francisco

To summarize, intelligence reports received now indicate the likelihood if not certainty that future Japanese Army balloon bombs will carry bacteriological warfare payloads. Until the first such payload is identified and more is learned, these procedures must be followed:

1. The media blackout must remain total. The mere suggestion of alien germs breaching the nation's borders could cause panic, causing civilians to overwhelm civil and medical authorities.

2. Emergency mass quarantine plans should be reviewed and updated, and should include protocols for the use of deadly force, particularly in areas of military significance. Significant transportation throughpoints, such as highways, bridges, and train stations, should be evaluated for purposes of securing them, or, as a last, but not implausible resort, their destruction.

3. State and county agricultural agents <u>nationwide</u> should monitor livestock and crops for trends and vulnerabilities. A separate, detailed bulletin is being prepared for veterinary authorities.

4. *<u>Previous orders to shoot down balloons on sight are hereby rescinded. Destruction, even at sea, could result in uncontrolled release of germ warfare agents. All future sightings must be reported immediately, and the balloons then tracked and recovered with extreme care.</u>*

* * *

WHAT REMAINED OF the Kirby balloon was heaped in a corner of a truck bed.

It was dirty and gray, with stiff folds, and had all the appearance—to me, as I think of it now—of a roadside heap of late winter snow. Along with the balloon was a pie-sized piece of metal that I recognized as the balloon's gas relief valve. Also present was the control frame, seemingly intact. The incendiary and antipersonnel bombs were gone (over the Pacific, one hoped, and not in some farmer's field—or the cab of the truck), and the demolition block was nowhere to be seen. But these all seemed like ancient and simpleminded fears now. So a bomb explodes. So someone loses a limb or dies. Show me the canister where the rats live. Show me the fleas that have carried the plague thousands of miles, across the ocean from Japan and across the centuries from the Middle Ages.

We'd landed on an empty road leading into town and had taxied into a field adjoining a small farmhouse. Within minutes, everyone was there: the widow from the farmhouse, the man whose truck now held the balloon—Will McDermott, the apparent sheriff—and lastly, via bicycle, the AP stringer, Samuel Leavit. Gurley dismissed the widow, scowled at Leavit, and finally settled on McDermott.

McDermott had raised his right hand in greeting, but it was his left arm that had caught my eye. A gentle breeze had picked up his empty left sleeve, causing it to flap momentarily back to life. I had seen Gurley take note and relax. A man he could do business with.

"That's an entrance," McDermott said, nodding to the plane.

"Wasn't my choice of landing spots," Gurley said. "But you know—pilots."

The man's face darkened a bit. "I do. I am one. Was one."

"I'm sorry," I blurted out.

Gurley winced and then turned to McDermott. "You're the sheriff?"

"Sheriff's somewhere in the Pacific," McDermott said. "I'm the man with the sheriff's truck. But I've got what you need."

This is the point when he'd led us around to the back of the truck. Gurley and I had exchanged a quick glance. We'd left the germ warfare gear in the plane, assuming that we'd be led to the balloon after meeting with the local authorities. Instead, we'd had it delivered. We watched the sheriff and stringer wander back around. There was nothing we could do but follow. Gurley went first, and I watched the back of his head as he walked. The officer defuses the bomb.

"Now this," McDermott said, reaching for the control frame, "this I don't get at all."

"Don't!" I shouted. Gurley looked at me, furious one moment and anxious the next.

McDermott toppled back like he'd been shot, and then relaxed, straightened up. "Easy on me, Sergeant," he said. "I don't take too well to sudden noises nowadays, not that I ever did."

He looked carefully at both of us, and read too much in our faces. "This isn't a weather balloon."

"Yeah," said Leavit. "Why's the Army need to know the weather in Wyoming?"

"Back off, AP," Gurley growled.

"What's going on?" Leavit asked. "This is big."

It was, especially for me. My first performance in front of Gurley. And civilians. And germs. Now that I make my living as a priest, it would be nice to look back on moments such as this and remember how a sudden burst of prayer powered me through. But it didn't happen that way. Nothing happened. I simply took a deep breath, and then held it, suddenly worried I'd already breathed in some deadly germ. I twitched the tiniest bit when Lily's face flashed in my mind, but then it was gone, and I swung up into the truck bed. I could take care of this. Somehow.

"Careful, Sergeant," Gurley said, and with that, I knew he was willing to play along. Probably because the primary risk so far was me blowing some part of my body off.

"Should I get the—" I looked at Gurley and nodded toward the plane. Gurley looked back at me, struggling to keep a perfectly blank look on his face, but still making his response perfectly clear: we'll *not* be hauling out a giant crate marked with a skull and crossbones, and then donning gas masks and suits in front of a reporter.

"The what?" said Leavit.

"Cookies and milk," Gurley said. "We so like to entertain our civilian guests. Please, gentlemen, let us step away while the sergeant makes his inspection." Nobody moved. Gurley looked around, and then shrugged.

I had to believe that any live animal or insect would have bounced out and off the truck on the drive over. Or died on the flight over. But still, I kept an eye out for them, or anything else odd as I worked through my standard procedures.

First: check to see that none of the fuses is smoking. (If they are, run. They were always in such a tangle, you never had enough time to figure out which one to cut.) The truck bed was dusty, but I didn't think I saw any smoke. Now for the demolition block, which was probably hiding in its usual spot. I was tilting the frame onto its side and had just spotted the demo block when Gurley stopped me.

"Sergeant!" I watched his face as he worked out a new strategy, one that began with a rather sick smile. "Step down for a moment, Sergeant, if you would, please."

"There's a story here," Leavit replied, staring at Gurley, who was worth staring at right then. The captain was running his hands all over the truck, ducking underneath, around, like he'd forgotten something. "What're you up to, Captain?" Leavit said. I wasn't sure either, but I could see Gurley picking a day like today to detonate himself. He suddenly swatted the side of the truck bed so forcefully that even McDermott jumped. And unlike me, McDermott didn't know that hidden in the mess in his truck was that demo block, a little two-pound brick of picric acid. Just above the gas tank, from the looks of it. And who knows what else.

A cat sidled up behind the truck and sat, expectant.

"Hop up," Gurley said to Leavit. I wanted to back away, but I couldn't without attracting attention. I watched as the reporter examined the balloon's black powder–laced carcass. I suppose part of me knew there was no way the contraption could go off, not without a lit fuse, not if it had already crossed an ocean, crashed, been kicked around, and then manhandled into the back of a truck—but still, you don't watch someone get that close to explosives and not hold your breath. We had McDermott right there, after all. The man was missing an arm. Gurley, a leg. I still had the memory of Gottschalk's hand in mine. And Gurley and I both had our newfound fears.

"I'd join you, but..." Gurley said, stepping back, and then leaning over, rapping the wooden part of his leg with his knuckles. He completed his performance with a shrug, but Leavit missed it; he was just fascinated with what he'd found. What I saw in his eyes reminded me of the first time I'd seen a balloon, back on that hillside in California. Your face just went blank; the mind couldn't be bothered with fixing an expression while it hungrily swallowed up everything it saw.

Gurley let Leavit have all the time he needed, hoping, I'm sure, that the reporter would get around to kicking or poking it, and then that would be that. Boom. For a moment, I wondered why Gurley didn't realize that a reporter getting injured or killed would make our mysterious balloon an even bigger story. But then I saw the way Gurley was taking in the scene with almost leering delight, and I realized it didn't matter how big the story got, or whether the blast killed all of us and sent the old woman's house tumbling end-over-end onto the south lawn of the White House. To have an irritant, an enemy, obliterated: the pleasure was worth any amount of resulting pain.

Leavit looked up with half a smile on his face, the same kind of smile I'd worn when I'd spotted that balloon at Shuyak, or better yet, the same kind of smile I had when I was, what, nine? and first opened a ship model kit someone had donated to the nuns for an orphan's Christmas. All of those pieces in there, all tiny and perfect and important, all of them adding up to something if you only had time and patience to put it all together just right. These balloons were something like that. They had that look. They didn't look machine made; they looked handmade—little irregularities caught the eye here and there, a bolt that was a fraction too long, a piece of metal that stuck up in a funny way, the way a seam was joined. Sergeant Redes would have muttered something about the shoddy workmanship of Japanese bombmakers, but I was struck by something else. It looked like something you could make—and what really made you stop and stare was the realization that someone *had* made it. Just like I'd always wanted that ship model to come to life and really float, or heck, blast a horn and steam away from my hand in the bathtub, or just like Leavit probably wanted some kit plane he'd once worked on to really take off and fly, someone had wanted this balloon to fly.

And it had. That was the most amazing part, and Leavit didn't even know that yet. Someone had built it, and it had really flown—all the way across the ocean, from the shores of some island far across the Pacific to a place in Wyoming that probably none of those Japanese folks who had made it had ever heard about. Didn't matter. It was all part of a dream anyway.

Now Leavit was crouching a little lower to look at the contraption, and I awoke, incredulous that I'd let things go this long. He was a few inches from being maimed or killed, and taking a few of us with him. I scanned frantically from where I stood for an oddly shaped or colored canister, crafted of that supposedly telltale porcelain, probably with air holes, or mesh—

"It's a remarkable device," Gurley said, his face flushed.

"I'll say," Leavit said. "It's Jap, isn't it?"

"Well," Gurley said slowly, rolling his eyes at McDermott, like they were two old friends who knew better. McDermott did know better. So did I. I hurried around to the other side of the truck, took a deep breath, regretted it, and climbed back up over the side.

"It's a hell of a thing, is what it is," I said as enthusiastically as I could. I finished scanning. It was clear. Looked just like all the others had. Except—

"Can I quote you on that?" Leavit said, not even looking up. "Need your name, rank, age, and hometown."

Now Gurley stepped closer, and when he spoke, I could tell from the tone of his voice that he was upset I'd screwed up his plan to have Leavit explode. I suppose I was a little touched; Gurley's being upset must have meant that he didn't want to see me blown up, and that was some kind of progress for us. "I'm afraid you *can't* quote him on that," Gurley said, rather seriously, and now I was the only one who could tell he was still acting. He turned around to include McDermott. Leavit looked up, and Gurley offered him a hand down from the truck. His other hand was a fist. Leavit took one last look at the device, then at me, and then climbed down. "You can't quote him, or me, really, because this is very, very, secret," Gurley said. He looked around and then announced that this was an "experimental targeting device" of the Canadian Expedition Force. McDermott's eyes went a little wider, and mine did as well. That he'd made it Canadian was the kind of useless flourish Gurley adored.

"But I'm telling you *none of this*. If word gets out about what the Canadians are doing..." He looked skyward.

"There's a story here, Captain, I'm sorry," Leavit answered.

"There is," Gurley said, drawing himself up, and turning Leavit by the elbow toward the plane. "But frankly, it's not to be found in the back of this truck." He turned to me. "Sergeant, log the serial number off it and then do whatever you like with it—box it up or burn it. But let's go. *Quickly*." I needed another second or two of Gurley's gaze to understand what he was up to, but I didn't get it. Certainly he didn't want me to burn anything. I checked his shoulders, his posture, to see if he was going back into that stance; perhaps he was going to take Leavit off and pummel the memory out of him. He still had the one hand clenched in a fist.

With them safely out of earshot, McDermott turned to me. "Your captain's a funny man, Sergeant."

"He has a way of doing things, sir," I said briskly.

"I never knew a man like him in my army," McDermott said.

"There isn't one, sir," I said, climbing into the truck bed one more time, trying to figure out what struck me as different about this balloon. It was the control frame. The top tier. It looked different. Had it been damaged? There was an oily stain. From the demo block? Something else? I'd seen the demo block, hadn't I, when I'd examined it the first time? Only the demo block? I looked for Gurley, saw him loading Leavit into the plane, panicked, and then tilted the control frame away from me, holding my breath.

I was never so relieved to see two pounds of picric acid in all my life. Nothing else, just the block. My old fears returned in a rush. The picric acid was extremely explosive, too explosive to leave where it was as we transported the control frame. As I pried it off, the two pounds felt like two hundred. There are objects like that. Ronnie's Comfort One bracelet, for one. The Host, for another, when I elevate it during Mass. I intone, "the Body of Christ," and some days, I'm certain, I'm hoisting all 170-odd pounds of him.

I stepped out of the truck bed, carefully, and looked over what I'd left behind. It could travel. The demo block could travel, too, but I didn't want it to. I wanted to leave it right here in Kirby. But the rule was to recover everything now. McDermott drove it all over to the plane, with me in the passenger seat, demo block on my lap. He helped me crate the control frame, and watched suspiciously as I did all I could to render the demo block safe. Then I thanked him and climbed aboard.

McDermott stopped me. "What was that?" he asked, looking at the crate we'd just loaded.

I looked, too. If there had been any rats aboard, they'd left before we'd gotten there. Maybe they'd never gotten on.

"A relief," I said, and shut the door.

* * *

WE SPENT AN HOUR flying Leavit around Wyoming. Gurley had told him that the Army was investigating the region for a whole new network of "intracontinental defense bases." He pointed out one imaginary site after another. He was in full performance mode, charming and arch, though I knew he was tense—he kept that one fist clenched the entire time, at his side, or behind his back. But Leavit didn't notice, he was too delighted with his scoop. The story he later wrote caused a bit of consternation among Gurley's higher-ups and Wyoming's congressional delegation, but the matter was soon forgotten.

Not forgotten, at least by me, is the exchange Gurley and I had after we'd deposited Leavit in Cheyenne and taken off for home.

"Dodged one there, sir," I said, flush with the success of duping Leavit, disarming the balloon single-handedly, and, most important, discovering a germ-free balloon. I assumed we'd formed a new kind of camaraderie on the way down, and thought I'd take advantage of it by needling him. "Course, sir, when you slapped the side of the truck there," I said, "I thought that might just have been enough to get that little demo block to go—"

Gurley slowly raised his fist. I'd been mistaken about our friendship. I noticed it was the same fist he'd kept clenched all this time. But he hadn't swung at Leavit, and he didn't swing at me. Instead, he turned his hand over and slowly opened it. I stared down. Ribbing me for my supposed love of palm reading?

But you didn't need to be Lily to read the story there. A smear of dried blood and two black specks, crushed carcasses of the tiny flying insects he killed. I shook my head, I held my breath. If he spoke, I didn't hear him. I just watched him, hollow-eyed, as he fished the jewelry store clipping out of his bag and numbly scraped the fleas' remains onto the paper.

CHAPTER 11

OH, RAPTURE.

An aging priest, I fear this most, this rapture. Evangelical Christians claimed rapture—sorry, Rapture—from Revelations, promising that the good would be sucked skyward When The Time Came. The truth is, the good disappear even earlier than that—lovely, ordinary Catholics are sucked out of my church and into the arms of these new, fresh-faced teetotaling missionaries. The young are thunderstruck, the old relieved; what a glorious, dramatic, prospect this Rapture is.

But they've not seen previous Raptures. I remember when brave and good Alaskans began disappearing before. The Japanese immigrants were the first to go; overnight, it seemed, they began disappearing from storefronts and sidewalks in Anchorage, shipped well south to California. Native Alaskans vanished, too. As Gurley had said, Aleuts had been relocated by the military, but in a most disorienting fashion: they were taken from their weatherworn, mostly treeless islands and deposited in the hush and dark of a thick southeastern Alaska forest.

And they were the lucky ones: other Aleuts, farther out on the Chain, were dragged from their homes by Japanese soldiers and taken back to Japan, where they spent the remainder of the war. Close to half died there.

That was rapture; that was when governments presumed to play God and did so with requisite carelessness. Anything in Alaska could be done if required by the war (or whim, the two terms so close, it seems now). Homes, buildings, towns, and airports were taken up and dropped elsewhere.

That was when the end of the world was nigh, not now as penny-ante preachers would have us believe. I believed then, I most definitely did. Thunderous hellfire. The dead blanketing the earth. Plague and pestilence: upon our return to Anchorage, Gurley and I waited anxiously for test results—his own, mine, and of the two fleas Gurley had "captured."

Those were the days of Armageddon, when one horror slipped into the next, from the threat of your skin erupting with pox to that of a spy approaching from behind and slipping a wire around your throat.

It was this last threat Gurley and I returned to. As nervous as we were about finding ourselves on the front lines of the germ war, a small part of us—a very small part—had also been pleased that we would be back in the spotlight.

But our hopes were dashed, as the Army unfailingly would do. Gurley was greeted with new bulletins announcing that the germ warfare threat was now believed to be traveling our way by both balloon and *human* means: saboteurs might even now be in our midst, ready to release animals and insects ridden with disease, or perhaps, in the manner of kamikaze pilots, they had been infected themselves, their only goal to ensure they did not die alone.

Alaska was thought to be a likely point of entry, its vastness a perfect cloak for the solitary spy. It sounds mad now, doesn't it? But there we were, with those bulletins, with word of captured Japanese documents and messages describing one- and two-man submarines, paratroopers dropped from impossible altitudes, frogmen leaping from the surf.

And, of course, those balloons: that soldiers (however small) would someday arrive in them seemed inevitable. We had done experiments: the balloons would have to be larger; the soldier aboard would need additional gear, but they had the technology, rudimentary as it was. They had the balloons. They had men willing to pledge their lives. It was absolutely possible, as possible as shipping fleas.

Alaska was not unfamiliar territory to the Japanese. Even before the landings on Attu and Kiska, even before the war, there had been reports from Alaska's southwestern coast of repeated visits by Japanese "fishermen" who seemed more interested in touring and photographing than fishing. Were Japanese spies here now? No one would say.

But I discovered a second, trusted source who could.

LOVERS. I SAY Lily and I were lovers because we had secrets, but other men who knew her wore the title more accurately than I. Gurley, for one. She did not speak as freely of him as he did of her. But I knew, through his innuendos and her silences, that he still visited. In the hopes of avoiding him, and perhaps disrupting their plans, I always tried to get Lily out of her "office" whenever I went to see her. She liked leaving less and less, though, what with the recent rapture of those other Asiatic faces from the sidewalks.

Gurley and I entered a quiet period when we returned from Kirby, a kind of self-imposed quarantine as winter devolved into a wet and muddy spring.

Then the results arrived, and relief and disappointment with them: Gurley had killed two all-American fruit flies. They were clear; no sign of plague. But still we kept to Anchorage. I felt fine—I knew I was fine, with a certainty that seems altogether foreign to me now. But Gurley was convinced they'd made a mistake with the tests—he worked his way through a variety of symptoms, and produced a fairly convincing rash on his torso. He sulked in the office and waited for calls from the hospital.

The balloons weren't venturing out much either, it seemed. We'd had no new reports of sightings or groundings. This was evidence, Gurley said (and I agreed), that the Japanese were pausing while they changed over to the new, germ-carrying balloons. The new wave would arrive soon.

Until then, we would wait. And while we did, I wandered. Downtown, as often as I could, where I cultivated a growing hatred of Gurley.

Now, consider the sailors Lily and I had battled in her office. I hadn't seen or heard them since we'd left the two bleeding on the second floor of the Starhope. But Gurley I saw every day. And the more I got to know him, and the more I got to know Lily, the more I despised my captain. In a way, I was glad of his connection to Lily; it made his iniquity total and freed me from worrying that I was overlooking some part of him that was worthy of respect or charity.

As the object of my fascination, as the only friend I had in Alaska, Lily was beyond reproach, but as time wore on, her relationship with Gurley wore on me. I became increasingly indignant. Sometimes my thoughts restricted their wandering to the moral high ground—I had defended her against those evil sailors; surely I should defend her against Gurley as well.

Other times, I wandered lower.

I teased her, or rather, I was past the point of teasing; I taunted. I wanted to know her as these other men had, but she showed little interest, and I, less courage. In the meantime, I derived what bitter enjoyment I could from making her feel bad about her "relationships," even though I could see she loathed her employment as much as I did. She no longer talked of leaving town, though I knew she still wanted to. I almost wanted her to, as well. I knew I would ache at the loss, but I'd still draw some pleasure knowing she was out of Gurley's arms.

"Your boyfriend's been in a bad mood recently," I said one afternoon. Gurley had been even more insufferable than usual, his hypochondria, theatricality, and temper combining demonically. I slid down to the floor in her darkened office, having arrived with sandwiches in the wake of the night's last customer. The sandwiches, always stale bread and cheese, always wrapped awkwardly in wax paper, had become a tradition.

She cursed at me, but without much spark, and gestured toward the door. "Definitely *not* my boyfriend," she said. She took a giant bite of the sandwich I'd given her and sank back, relieved. "This is my boyfriend," she said, patting the sandwich and closing her eyes.

"No, your *real* boyfriend," I said. After a minute, she opened her eyes and studied me. It was because of the way she looked, on this occasion and previous ones, that I assumed Gurley was, in fact, that "real" man: "Good old Captain Gurley," I said. I smiled, though any humor, even dark humor, had faded by now.

"You're jealous of *Gurley*?" she asked.

I thought of the ring, the jeweler, the clipped ad that had disappeared with the suspect fleas. Instead, I said, "Of him and every other guy who comes in here, not even with sandwiches, and gets more— out of you—than I ever—"

"Gets what?" she asked.

"I don't know," I said, and then added, too quickly: "I'm guessing some men up here feel like they spend enough time with their own palms. Maybe there's other stuff of theirs they want to get read. Maybe—"

But I didn't finish. Lily stood—

No, I need to describe this carefully. Lily, standing there, me on the floor, the two of us lit only by the lights from the street, until she went and pulled the blackout shade. Then it was completely dark, only breathing and steps.

Click. The light went on. And while I blinked, she stepped around in front of me and stopped, just out of reach. It's inappropriate for me to say what her face looked like then, because it was a private thing, a horrible thing, a mix of fear and hate; it was her true face, the one she wore beneath whatever smile she presented to the men who visited her.

I couldn't look, but she stared at me until I did. She was wearing some old fatigues, unlaced workboots. She looked like a recruit about to wash out of basic or a civilian who'd lost her home to a fire and had had to go begging for clothes. The name strip on the shirt was gone, the color worn out of the pants.

Once I'd finished this inventory, I looked back to her face. As soon as I'd met her gaze, she hooked her thumbs into two belt loops and pushed down, first right, then left. Once free of her hips, the pants fell to her knees and she bent, pushing them down farther till they gathered at her ankles. I saw the legs I remembered from the first night, except the knees looked older, the deep brown bruises and scrapes more plentiful across her shins and across what parts of her thighs that weren't covered by the oversized shirt.

I followed the trail of buttons back up to her face, but before I got there I saw her hands descending, undoing each button, one at a time, like a doctor snipping stitches from a scar. When she was done, a narrow, dark ribbon of skin had been revealed. I turned away, and when that wasn't enough, closed my eyes, pulled in my legs.

"Look," she said. And because, for one syllable, the voice sounded like the old Lily, my friend Lily, the one who helped me find balloons, the one who shared sandwiches with me, talked with me, preserved me, I did.

But it was a trick; the old voice came from this new, horrible face, now set grimly above a body not naked but stripped, everything visible except the feet and ankles, which were hidden in the pile of sloughed-off uniform.

"You read maps," she said, and ran her hands painfully down her front, palms flat to her skin, fingers rigidly splayed. Then she brought her arms out before her and examined them. She found a bruise on her right forearm. "I got this in Anchorage," she said, looking up. She lifted her left arm and found a patch of mottled brown-white skin; it looked like a burn. "Bethel," she said. She tilted her head back, felt her neck: "Dillingham," she said, her fingertips fondling a thin, small scar where her shoulder began. She pushed her hands down across her breasts, which were slight enough to disappear beneath her palms. She revealed her chest again, studied it, and seemed about to say something, but gave a thin smile instead and continued. Now her left hand drifted to the base of her stomach while her right searched out something just above where her pelvis jutted out. There. An appendix scar. "Memorial Hospital, Fairbanks," she said. She brought her hands together, and lower, covering her sex as if now shy.

I looked away, and then up at her, but she shook her head and nodded down. I looked away again; she stepped closer, and took my hand, my right, in hers, and slowly ran it flat across her stomach. I could feel each little hair. Back and forth, up and down, until she said, so quietly that she did little more than move her lips, "Feel that scar?" I shook my head; I didn't breathe. She took my hand by the wrist, lowered it, and slowly began to run it up the inside of her thigh. I tried pulling my wrist away, forcefully at first and then desperately, but she held on. "Some of my scars, you can only touch," she said. "Even I can't see them. They're too far away."

"I don't want to," I said. "Lily, I'm sorry."

"Why are you sorry, Louis?" she said. "You didn't make the scars." I said nothing. "Or maybe that's why you're sorry—you think? Jealous there's no scar on me you can claim?"

Lily waited another moment, then moved to the other side of the room and dressed slowly. When she was done, she came back to my side of the room. She turned off the light, and then, back against the wall, slowly slid to the floor until she was sitting beside me in the perfect dark. We sat that way for a while until she got up and opened the blackout shade. The light in the room rose to a gray glow.

I missed the dark. I couldn't look at her. I looked at my hands, at the door, at the grain of the hardwood floor. When I finally turned to face Lily, I was surprised to find her looking relieved, even pleased. She gave me a nudge and sat back. I inched away.

"Louis," she said, and shifted closer. "I'm sorry," she said.

"No, no—Lily, I'm sorry, I—should I leave?"

"No," she said, and nodded toward the middle of the room. "It's your turn." Then she laughed, so loudly and so briefly it sounded like a cough, and asked for my coat. When I hesitated, she laughed again, softer this time, and said, "Don't worry—that's all I'll ask you to take off." I looked at her. "I'm *cold,*" she said.

I took the coat off; she put it on and shivered once.

"Louis," she said, settling back, her eyes closed. "If I tell you this story, the whole story, will you promise not to believe a word of it?"

"I promise," I said.

"Think about that first," she said. "You promised too quickly."

"I won't believe it," I said.

"You will," she said. "That's what you do. You believe—believe *in*— everything. Don't you? You believe in your country, you believe your country is going to win this war, you believe in your God." She sat up now, looked me in the eye. "You believed that I was Japanese, that I was a palm reader."

I nodded.

"Well, you're wrong about all of that. Your country is going to lose. Your God is a fake, and so is your—"

"And so are you," I said.

She took a deep breath. "Good," she said. "That's a start."

LILY CAME FROM Bethel, Alaska. Describe Bethel today—tiny homes, riverfront warehouses, a lot of sodden earth in the process of freezing or thawing, a horizon whose limits seem more lunar than earthly—and you would more or less capture Lily's Bethel of decades ago. It's more crowded now, more stores, more houses, more whites, more government people and programs, but it's still the same place, a permanent splotch on the tundra.

But nothing about it was permanent for Lily—half Russian, half Yup'ik, missing both parents, Bethel didn't have much to hold her. It did, however, have plenty of missionaries—Moravian, Catholic, Methodist, Orthodox, and more—and Lily convinced one of them to get her a place at a special girls' boarding school in Fairbanks. It was supposed to be just for the smartest girls—which Lily, without a wink, told me she was—but Lily was a compelling candidate in another way. An orphan, she was a more attractive prospect than many other Yup'ik children, who had to be pried away from wary parents before being sent off to distant schools where they would learn the ways of a white world.

What no one could tell her in Fairbanks, however, was why going there had made her so keenly aware of yet another world—a world just like this one, but a world in which she was privy to the secrets of people, places, and things. She had sensed this world back in Bethel, but it was only a sense, and seemed as much imagination as anything. But in Fairbanks, she knew differently—she knew, for example, the life stories of girls she had just met, before they had said a word. She knew when the weather was bad back in Bethel, whether the seal hunt was going well, even the date of breakup—the day the Kuskokwim River finally thawed.

Before she knew better, she talked about such things with the other girls, and they in turn talked to their families about her whenever they returned home on breaks. Lily always stayed in Fairbanks. But then, one break, one of her classmates said that her father wanted to meet Lily, and so Lily made the long trip back to Bethel.

Her classmate's father was known as Peter to the white community, a capable, if grumpy, boatbuilder. But the entire Yup'ik community knew him as one of the last shamans.

"Among every generation of Yup'ik," Lily told me, "there are those who are granted special sight, and special powers." If you were sick, if you were worried about the presence or absence of fish or game, you went to the shaman. When to move to fish camp, when to return to town—all these things the shaman knew. But, she added, "the missionaries hated shamans. They told the people that the shamans were just magicians—people who got in the way of God."

Peter had gotten in the way of God for a long time and had suffered for it, suffered physically, he told people, as though God were throwing an elbow every time they passed. Old and hurting and lonely, Peter was looking for someone to take his place.

But Lily? Could it be possible that the magic should have survived in this girl? Lily's long-gone father was a *kass'aq*; she was being educated far from home; she was female. But after a day of observing her and another day speaking with her, Peter decided that Lily was, in fact, gifted.

Or rather, able to receive the gift: it really wasn't for him to choose; they'd have to go out, deep into the tundra, to see for sure.

He wouldn't tell her where they were going, he wouldn't let anyone else come with them. They traveled downriver for several miles, until they came to a bend where the river had worn much of the bank away, exposing a small bluff that looked as though it were built of layered chocolate. He found a place to beach the boat, and had her climb up the bank with him. Then they went walking. Do not be afraid, he said, but this is a place for—

"Ircenrrat." Lily knew this. Little people. Sprites. They could be friendly or not, Lily told me, depending on how you behaved. There beside Peter, Lily was worried. Walking along that eroded stretch of riverbank was not good behavior. Growing up, she'd always been told to avoid this place.

"Let's look for mouse food," Peter said. Lily just wanted to leave, but Peter insisted. Tundra lemmings foraging for the winter would often build up little subterranean caches of roots and stems that Yup'ik men and women would later seek out. (Dried fish or cracker crumbs might be left by way of thanks.) It took a practiced eye to spot and follow the little pathways the lemmings wove through the tundra, and a practiced hand to find the soft or spongy areas that signaled a likely spot. Lily was surprised to see that she was having more success than Peter.

She was looking over at him at one point, wondering what he was up to, as she sunk her hands into the tundra moss and cottongrass. Then she felt something odd—warm and slick. When she looked down, she saw that she'd uncovered a roiling cache of insects—worms, beetles, ants, all slithering through her fingers. She yelped and tried to leap up, but somehow, Peter had made it to her side. He held her down.

"*Melquripsaq*: the worms, the insects! You have found them," he said, smiling and breathless. "The *ircenrrat* have let you find their magic."

"Let go of me!" said Lily, about to scream. Several of the insects—bigger and stranger than ones she'd ever seen—had begun to trail over her wrists, up her forearms.

"Wait," Peter said. "Let it come to you."

"No!" Lily shrieked. She could feel them swarming now, prickling up past her elbows.

"Wait!" Peter shouted. "You'll see! You must do this!"

"No!" Lily yelled, and broke free. She swung her arms wildly, clapped her hands together, scraped at her scalp.

Peter fell to his knees and searched the grass. "Too soon," he cried.

Lily looked down. Her arms were clear. She looked around. No trace of insects. She walked back to the cache. Empty.

Peter stood and walked back to the boat. "I cannot say what will happen to you now," Peter said once she'd joined him. Lily later left for Fairbanks without his having said another word to her. His daughter did not return to school.

Lily told no one about her trip out on the tundra with Peter. But back at school, if the other girls ever started talking about shamans, about the stories the elders used to tell, Lily would listen carefully. That's how she learned that her experience was not unique; many shamans before her had sought and received their powers the same way. One or two of the other girls said they had uncovered bug-infested caches as well, but none had ever plunged their hands in, frightened either by the bugs themselves or because they knew magic was at work.

And something was at work in Lily. A strange thing had happened after she'd left the tundra with Peter. Her previous abilities had dimmed. Where once she could look at a girl, even from a distance, and know her village, what her father was like, whether she'd been kissed, or smell the air midwinter and know if the summer would be wet or dry, now she needed to touch something to know anything about it at all. Even then, the knowledge she gained was shot through with static, sometimes to the point of incoherence.

She tested herself and found she did better with people than with objects. She might sit at a desk or hold a book and get a sense of who had done so before her, but these stirrings were faint. But if she shook a hand, received a hug, that contact might grant her visibility into the other person's past or, more rarely, future. Sometimes she'd feel a strange sensation in her hands and forearms—*qungvagvuk*—as though the insects she'd uncovered were skittering along her skin once more.

She returned to Bethel at the end of the school year, but it was a bitter homecoming. Peter had died, his family moved away. Before he'd died, though, he must have told others about the trip he and Lily had taken, because everyone knew what had happened. No one approved.

Those who had rejected traditional beliefs and become enthusiastic converts to Christianity rejected Lily for seeking to indulge in "the black arts," as one missionary termed it. But Lily received even sharper censure from those elders who still had an admiration for, if not faith in, older Yup'ik traditions. A gift had been presented to Lily, and she had refused it. On the tundra, rejecting a gift freely given—whether the gift was shamanic powers or the season's first seal—was unconscionable.

But then, what do you expect, people said. She's a girl. A girl whose mother disappeared with a Russian sailor. This girl, half Yup'ik, a shaman? Peter had made a mistake. The *ircenrrat* had made a mistake.

Lily tried to explain, she hadn't sought the job, she didn't want the job, but that only made matters worse.

In time, Lily realized that it wasn't just her who was making the Yup'ik community mad. It was the world, its missionaries, its *kass'at*, all flooding the tundra with new ways, food, language, ideas. Even if one no longer needed the services of a shaman to heal a sick child or predict weather, you still wanted one around, as a link to that other, older world they'd all once known. And with Peter dead, and Lily ducking the job, there really wasn't anyone around. Now, there was a young man from Lower Kalskag, a good distance upriver, who came to town occasionally. There were those who said *he* was a shaman, said they'd even seen him fly. But others said he only flew when he drank, and the only way you'd see him fly is if you drank, too—a lot.

Townspeople pressured Lily to leave. Go to your parents, they said. Go to Russia, they said. Go live with the other *kass'at*. Leave us alone. Lily weathered a winter of this and then decided to do as she was told. She'd go to Anchorage. And from there, maybe Russia. Maybe anywhere.

She waited through the spring, and just as the summer began and she was getting ready to leave, she found a reason to stay.

He was Japanese.

HER REASON HAD BEEN living, temporarily, in the back stockroom of Sam's Universal Supply. The Supply was Bethel's second, and lesser, general store, and Lily worked there as a cashier.

Saburo spoke English fairly well, a little better than Sam, in fact, who had been born an unknown number of years ago to Japanese immigrant parents in Southern California. How Sam had made his way to Bethel, and whether he had done so on purpose, was never clear. But he'd done well once he'd arrived. He was kind, honest, fair to a fault, and extremely generous. Until the war with Japan began, his being Japanese attracted little attention—Bethel had a small but persistent collection of people who were neither white nor Yup'ik, and as a result, little discussed.

Saburo's arrival was only mysterious if you thought about it: one week he wasn't there, the next week he was. And people didn't think about it, not even Lily, at first. People were always passing through Sam's employ, particularly those, like Lily, who didn't quite fit in anywhere else.

She took Saburo at his word when he said he was a relative of Sam's; she didn't realize differently until they were a few days into a fishing trip together. Sam had suggested that Lily "show Saburo Alaska"; she had thought he was making fun. But then, it *was* summer; almost all of the Yupiit and many of the whites had already left town, journeying south and west to fish camps across the vast, marshy delta that surfaced each year beneath the lingering sun.

And there was the article she'd read in a two-week-old copy of the *Fairbanks Daily News-Miner*. Persons of Japanese ancestry were being relocated to special camps throughout the American West, "for their safety." Two days later, Sam received a large white envelope emblazoned with a government eagle. Before he even opened it, he suggested the trip to Lily again. The next day, Lily and Saburo were off, down the Kuskokwim River in a haphazardly packed outboard.

Lily had assumed she would serve as the guide; as a child, she'd often joined friends for the annual summer trip into the delta. But half an hour south of town, with Lily in the stern, piloting, Saburo pulled out a map—a journal, really, filled with page after page of drawings, charts and notes. After a few minutes' study, he looked up and pointed right.

Lily shrugged; if you weren't aiming for a favorite spot, it really didn't matter which waterway you chose once you left the broad expanse of the Kuskokwim River. Depending on the thaw and the previous week's weather, there were hundreds, even thousands, of sloughs to follow. And if a slough ever proved to be a dead end, all you usually had to do was turn around or drag your boat through the mud and grass and reindeer moss for a few minutes before another waterway appeared.

But Saburo's decisions that first day led them to one portage after another. By evening, they'd found themselves on a small, reasonably dry patch of tundra. Lily was exhausted. Saburo wanted to go on; it was still light, after all.

Lily shook her head. Saburo pursed his lips, looked down in his book.

"I did not need you to come," Saburo said.

Lily looked at him and then back toward Bethel. "I didn't need *you* to come," she said. "It was your uncle's idea, anyway. He thought you'd get lost out here, and after what we've been through today, seems like he was right."

"Not uncle," said Saburo after a pause.

Lily started unpacking some cooking gear and then changed her mind. She didn't want to cook—and she definitely did not want to cook *for* him. They'd eat some of the canned fish and dried blubber Sam had urged them to take.

"I can come back, pick you up," said Saburo.

"That's sweet," Lily said. Saburo glared, but Lily said nothing, just sat and chewed for a while. She offered a piece of blubber to Saburo. "How would you find me?" Lily asked. "That book of yours?" When he refused to answer or eat, she wiped her mouth with her forearm and reached for his journal.

He snatched it away. He started to stalk off, but there was no place to go; the tuft of dry tundra they'd found for themselves wasn't much larger than Sam's store. Venture too close to any edge and your footprints started filling with water; a step or two later, you were knee-deep.

Lily finished eating. She swallowed, and then asked him, very quietly, "May I see your book?"

"Not a book. It's in Japanese. Hard to understand."

"I'm good at understanding things," Lily said, wiping her hands on her pants.

"You know Japanese?" he asked.

Lily shook her head. "You know your way back?"

He frowned, checked the height of the sun, and then handed her the journal. Smiling at him, Lily held it closed on her lap until he turned away, took a few steps north, and started scouting the route they'd take next.

He was scouting the wrong way. Lily knew it instantly; she didn't even have to open the book. Just holding it there, on her lap, she knew what he was looking for, though not why, and where the object was, though not how it got there. She started to call for him, but hesitated. She didn't trust herself. Her powers, such as they were, had been waning after all, especially with things like books. And besides, what she was seeing didn't make sense: a black bit of earth, smoking, like the remains of a giant campfire. There was some wreckage—something had crashed—but it wasn't a truck or a plane—maybe books? Books didn't seem likely, but that was what she felt, could almost smell: paper, burning, grass, burning, and all of it just to the south.

With Lily as guide, they reached the spot an hour and two portages later. Lily was surprised, even disappointed, that the fire she'd imagined seemed to have burned itself out some time ago. All that remained were some charred, bent metal strips—some kind of a crate?—and a few dozen square feet of earth that looked as if it had been seared by a giant, fiery thumbprint. Saburo took out his book and started writing.

He didn't tell her the whole story the first night, and even after two months together, crisscrossing the tundra, she was never sure he had told her everything, even when she took up his hand and held it tight. But he had told her enough: he was Japanese, a soldier, a spy, sent behind enemy lines to see if early tests of a frightening new device were having any success. They were called *fu-go* weapons, bombs carried across the Pacific by large, gas-filled balloons. Hundreds had been launched, but so far, little news of their impact had made its way back to Japan. Scouts were sent behind enemy lines to see what they could learn. Saburo had been given southern Alaska, another scout had been given British Columbia, and a third who had already been living in San Francisco got the northwest coast of the United States. Each had too much territory to cover completely, but they were armed with maps and projections of where the balloons were likeliest to land, given the trade winds and the design of the balloons themselves.

The *enemy,* I remember asking Lily: Weren't you afraid? Weren't you alarmed? Weren't you worried how you would get word to the authorities? You, an American citizen, I said, *alone* with a Japanese soldier. I didn't know what to say. I think the farther from the enemy you remained—and I'd spend the entire war on American soil—the more you believed that should you ever actually *meet* your foe, violence would be automatic, instant.

"I was never scared," Lily said.

"Wasn't he scared of you?" I asked. "Here you were, an American—"

"I don't usually get taken for American," Lily said. "Not even by me."

"Lily."

"Louis," she said. Smiling a mother's smile, she lifted both my hands in hers, glancing at my palms. "Louis," she said again, looking up. "This man—had *extraordinary* hands."

"Hands?" I looked down as she held my hands, and then watched as she traced a line on my palm.

"And he believed me," she said, just like that, in a very small voice. "He didn't ask how I knew what I knew, or why I could sometimes tell where we'd find the next crash site. He just listened." She folded my hands together and then folded hers on her lap.

I suppose I should have hated him more, this Saburo. He was the real boyfriend. Not Gurley, not any of the other men who visited Lily at the Starhope. She never said as much, but just to hear her talk—to *see* how she talked—you could see what a fierce, tender, protective love she reserved for him—still. And if that weren't upsetting enough for me, there was also the fact that he was Japanese. Not just the enemy, but *my* enemy: he was tied to the lethal balloons Gurley and I had been risking our lives to chase and smother.

My next decision seems easy, doesn't it? We were in Anchorage. Fort Richardson and the easily stirred Gurley were just a few miles away. Local and military police could be notified; Lily arrested, interrogated. Who knows what we'd learn. How many balloons we might stop. How many germs. How many lives we'd save.

Such simple equations. Here, you do the calculation, Ronnie: what if you could look into her eyes, as I did, and find there the two things I saw?

One, she really loved him, but she *trusted* me, and that's enough like love to make a boy like I was swoon all the same.

Two, she'd told me quite a few secrets, but it was clear there was something else she wasn't telling me, not yet. Betray her now, and lose the larger story?

"Some days, we didn't find anything," Lily said. "Nothing ever came to me as strongly as did the image of that first day's crash site. But it didn't matter. Louis—it was a beautiful summer. Warm, clear days, cool nights, whole weeks without rain." Weather like the tundra had never seen. And those hands: Lily was fascinated by them. Late one night—actually, the next morning, when night had finally fallen—they compared names for the stars and constellations. Lily eagerly pointed out several, but then fell silent, eager to see Saburo's hands, instead, flutter there in the air above them, more beautiful than the stars beyond, and so much closer.

The hands also turned the book of notes and maps into a beautiful journal, a work of art. Each day ended with Saburo re-creating the preceding hours on paper—first, a sketch lightly done in pencil, brought to life by watercolors, detail added with pen and ink. Lily asked what he wrote and drew on the days they found no evidence of balloons. He said that he wrote about her, about them, about the beautiful summer.

Here the story stopped. Lily looked at me.

"You know this book," Lily said, and of course I did. From her descriptions and the way my heart was trying to thump its way out of my chest, run into the street, and call the police itself, I knew that this book was the strange journal or homemade atlas Gurley had had me study in his office. "I—I need it," Lily said.

"Lily."

"Louis, he's gone."

"Where?"

"I want it, just to have some piece of—some piece of him, that time." She was watching for my reaction. "That makes sense, doesn't it? That a girl would want that? You're a boy."

"Yes."

"It's at Fort Rich. His journal," Lily said, looking down now. "I know it's there."

I suppose I could have lied, but I didn't. "It is," I said, and decided to go a step further. "I've seen it."

Lily feigned surprise, so badly that she immediately confessed. "I—thought so."

I told Lily that I'd prefer her pretending to be surprised than confessing that she had just been using me all this time to get some keepsake of a summer romance—with an enemy soldier, no less. Was this why she'd advertised herself as "careful and correct," so as to better lure a bomb disposal man, someone who might be more *useful* to her than the average soldier?

Very quietly, very slowly, Lily said two words. It was the first time I'd heard a woman say them: *fuck, you.*

She stood up, opened the door. "*He* is not the enemy, not mine. It's not—a *keepsake*," she said. "And I was never *using* you," she said. "You came and found me, remember? A very *average* soldier, looking for help." She closed the door slightly and lowered her voice to a hiss. "I have been trying to use your captain, but he's been better at using me."

The door opened again, wide.

CHAPTER 12

WHEN GURLEY SAUNTERED INTO THE QUONSET HUT THE morning of June 13, 1945, he was two hours late and missing an eye. Well, missing a normal one. There was an eye peering out of his left socket, but it looked like something he'd stolen off some particularly nasty page in the atlas. He had a shiner, to start with, but the blackened periphery was nothing, a frame, really, for the eyeball, which was crazed with red veins and weeping almost constantly. I'd never seen an eye like that, which surprised me until I remembered this was Gurley; any other man who'd gotten his eye in a way like this would have done the decent thing—for himself and others—and slipped on a patch.

"Good morning, Sergeant," Gurley said, bright and loud. He was dying for me to ask, so I did. He held up both hands in weak protest, and tried to do his usual fluttering of eyelids, but the pain of doing so caught him up short. That he wanted me to join him in his office was clear; either the story was long enough that it required seats for both of us, or he was about to collapse. Either way, he needed a chair.

I'd learned over my months with Gurley that he picked fights with whomever he could, just to prove he wasn't who everybody thought he was—some effete Ivy League snot who'd been sent to the war's most distant margins because he was hardly worthy of any critical post—though this was all true.

And he was waging war with Alaska, of course. You were either man enough to survive here, or you weren't. You alone knew, in the end. And Gurley must have found himself wanting, because he entered one scrap after another to prove he could take it, whatever it was.

It didn't help that his official foe, the Japanese, their balloons, weren't coming out to fight. March had been busy, true: we'd logged 114 balloons, more than all the previous months combined, and we'd learned of the germ warfare threat. But then, of course, had come the drop-off, the one Gurley and I attributed to their needing time to ready the balloons for the coming bacteriological assault. But the months passed, and the assault wouldn't come. Forty balloons in April, no sign of germs. Hardly more than a dozen balloons in May, and all of them as conventionally armed as could be.

Since trouble was steadily avoiding us, Gurley went looking for it himself, usually in downtown bars, before or after visiting Lily. He was still seeing her; I was not. I'd been too angry, and then too ashamed after that night she'd confronted me about the atlas. But we were going to patch things up eventually, I was certain. A bit like Gurley's quest, it was just a matter of me going downtown to prove my courage. Instead of pretending to be "just walking by" her window—which I "just" did a lot—I'd have to walk on up. Knock on the door. Say I'm sorry. Hand over the book. Flowers. Book first? Was she a girl who liked flowers? Well. Maybe Gurley did have it easier when it came to testing his mettle.

But one look at him today reminded me he'd chosen the more physically painful path. He'd picked a fight, again, with someone he shouldn't have, again. Nevertheless, he seemed satisfied with the result. He held up a fist. The knuckles were scabbed and the back of his hand had a freshly crusted scar.

"I mounted a vigorous defense, Sergeant. You would be proud."

"I'm not so sure, Captain. You don't look so good."

"I took a tooth off the blackguard, Belk," he said, and extended the fist closer to me. Then he smiled a broad smile. "And retained all of mine."

"But your eye," I said, wincing without meaning to.

"A tooth, Belk," he said, and fished around in his pocket. I had no idea what he was doing until it was sitting there before me, a little ivory chip, the tooth, right there in the middle of the blotter of his desk. "I may have it mounted," he said. He tried to smile, and then explained that he'd gone another round in what he'd proudly called his "Franklin bouts." They were named for the nation's thirty-second president, Franklin D. Roosevelt, whom Gurley loathed.

I'd heard all about the first bout two months ago, the morning of April 13. The day before, despite the nonstop clamor of church bells, despite the people openly weeping and clutching each other on the sidewalks, Gurley had managed to avoid learning that Roosevelt had died. It wasn't until he wandered into a bar, ordered a drink, and asked the bartender just what everyone's problem was that he heard.

"Thank fucking *God,*" Gurley said, a remark that efficiently set him against anyone who admired Roosevelt as well as those who didn't like their God prefixed so. Gurley used the silence that followed to try to clarify—no, really, he thought Roosevelt a complete *ass*—and round one began.

A month later, May 12, he was telling me that "just by coincidence," he'd found himself back in the same bar. Again, the bar was hushed and somber. Again, Gurley asked—an honest question, he assured me, and such tactlessness was certainly not beyond him—what was going on. It had been a month to the day of Roosevelt's death, he was told.

"Good God, people!" Gurley shouted. "Even the worms have had their fill of him now!" Round two.

And last night, round three. Delighted to discover that the monthly mourning was occurring as scheduled, Gurley had surreptitiously ordered a drink. Then he smiled a huge smile, raised a glass, and shouted, "The king is dead! Long live the king!" Which no one seemed to quite understand, though their faces all made one thing clear. This would be the third and final round.

A woman began "screeching" at him, Gurley said, about being a "traitor" to his own commander in chief. Gurley took offense and sought to correct her. "I just wanted a word with her," Gurley said. But he got much more: fists, a stein of beer, part of a chair, and from the woman herself, the heel of a shoe. It was this last blow, he added quietly, that had caused the most damage to the eye. "Ironic," he said, "but heroic all the same, don't you think?"

I didn't answer, distracted by the discovery that the glee had gone out of Gurley's voice. He was no longer enjoying his story. I assumed that pain had now overtaken him and he was regretting this last fight, and probably the fights before. But that wasn't it at all.

"Do you know that our current military force in Alaska is less than half what it was a year ago?" he asked. "It's a month since the Germans surrendered. Almost two months since we landed on Okinawa. We're running out of time, Sergeant." He slowly raised a hand to his eye, but he seemed unable to stomach anything more than his fingertips grazing his eyebrow.

"Let's get that looked at, sir," I said, sitting forward. I was worried—and it wasn't as irrational as it sounds—that his eyeball was going to pop out in a spray of blood and land on the desk.

"The war is not over, Belk," he said. "I doubt this Truman knows that. I wonder if FDR knew that. Europe is won. But the war in the Pacific, Sergeant. The ocean will run red for years to come." He took a breath and closed his eyes with a wince. "We can only hope," he said.

MY LAST BAR FIGHT was in Fairbanks, just a few years ago. It was my fault, for the most part. I'd flown into town to do some business with the diocese, and Ronnie had invited himself along, as he'd done before. On such occasions, I referred to Ronnie as a deacon or president of the parish Holy Name Society—certainly not as a shaman. We'd only just started our "alternative health care" visits at the hospice, and word had yet to spread.

On this particular flight, however, Ronnie was not doing well at playing the role of a devout Christian. He kept opening and closing a small pouch that appeared to be full of various talismans and other tiny, carved figures. And he kept talking about murder.

As much as he took responsibility for his own drinking, he also faulted those who'd served alcohol to him. This may sound curious to those who don't live in our community, but given the rapid, ruthless way alcohol takes hold of Native Alaskans—well, Ronnie had a point.

Ronnie had accompanied me on a previous trip to Fairbanks years before. This was when he was still wrestling with alcoholic demons; this was when I still thought I could help him do so all by myself. I'd asked him along almost as an experiment. I thought he might do better if he were removed from the familiar temptations (and hidden stashes) back home. I had some business at the chancery, so I left him in God's care before a side altar in the cathedral.

I never got it straight from God what transpired next, nor from Ronnie when I later visited him in the hospital. He'd found a bar, the Bear 'n' Moose, he'd run up a tab, he hadn't (probably couldn't have) paid, he'd hurled some insults, gotten some back—I suppose God might have been involved in the end, because it's inconceivable otherwise that anyone had enough charity in their heart when it was all done to call an ambulance.

So Ronnie was now going to go back and set things right. He assured me he wouldn't go into the bar—that he wouldn't, in fact, even have to go near the place. He patted his pouch and told me he'd simply go into a shamanic trance in the cathedral (while previous bishops spun in their graves in the crypt below), fly over to the bar, invisible, and invoke a curse or two.

My miscalculation was assuming that he would simply fall asleep in the course of his trance—he'd done so more than once before, usually when he was boasting to me of his long-departed powers—and I'd discover him contentedly snoring in a pew near the statue of Joseph. But my meeting ran long, and when I returned, Ronnie was gone.

I went straight over to the Bear 'n' Moose.

I walked in right after Ronnie had fallen off the bar. He'd apparently been dancing a complicated dance that was intended—or so he'd been shouting—to render everyone within earshot impotent. That made his listeners angry enough, and his falling into their laps and spilling their drinks made them angrier. A stout older fellow who looked a lot like Santa had Ronnie in a choke hold while his companion, also old and fat, but less Santa-like, poured drink after drink from the bar over Ronnie's head.

Ronnie screamed and kicked. I hollered at the bartender to make them stop, but he only rolled his eyes. I shouted at the two Santas, which distracted them long enough for Ronnie to kick one of them where he shouldn't have, and then it was all fists and feet. The bartender began to come around the bar—slowly—while I dove into the middle of the fight. I tried to tug Ronnie free, and then somebody—it could even have been Ronnie—clouted me behind the ear. I retreated. We were all much too old.

Fortunately, or unfortunately, the Bear 'n' Moose was decorated as you might expect, giving an angry priest bent on smiting an array of options. I chose an incongruous harpoon. Ronnie, delighted, began ululating wildly (something he's always been quite good at). But it was a mistake. As I advanced, the Santas dropped Ronnie, knocking him out.

Police, ambulance, hospital, and the next morning, Ronnie awaking with a wide smile. "Bear 'n' Moose," he said, uncovering the meal the nurse had brought. He stuffed a piece of toast in his mouth and looked around for a clock. "When does it open?"

* * *

IF THE BEAR 'N' MOOSE were open back when Gurley and I visited Fairbanks—if the business had even been established—we never got a chance to find out. We only went there once, and only stayed four hours.

Gurley's lamentation for his war, and his eye, had been interrupted by a phone call. Gurley answered with a "yes," and then held the phone to his ear, saying nothing else. At first, I thought the line had gone dead, and that he was simply too tired (and too eager to show how tired he was) to hang up. But as his second minute of silence began, I watched his face change, his remaining eye squint and then widen with equal parts glare and alarm. He waved his free arm at me, then started scrabbling for a pen. Finally he shouted, "Yes! Yes, sir! Yes!" and dropped the handset without even hanging it up.

He was around the desk and dragging me out the door before I'd even had time to ask what had happened. "Ladd Field, Sergeant," he said, as we staggered through the Quonset hut to the exit. He looked at his watch. "If we can make it to the airfield in three minutes, we'll catch the noon transport, be at Ladd Field in Fairbanks in time for the briefing."

"What's happened?" I said. "Balloon?"

Gurley shook his head no, then yes, and then grabbed me by the shoulders. "Belk," he said. *"They're here."*

"THEY" WERE LAID out on two long metal tables, side by side in a makeshift morgue. I didn't get a very good view; Gurley and the other officers had closed in a relatively tight cordon around the two bodies, one of which was covered, the other not.

The major who'd been briefing us in an adjoining room resumed his account from behind a surgical mask. "Two males, Japanese, mid-thirties, our best guess. Age isn't particularly important, except to note that they're not kids; that is, they're not cannon fodder, so deduce what you will about the importance or sophistication of their apparent mission. No rank or insignia on their uniforms. And the ship's report says they weren't really in uniform anyway, perhaps better to carry off the ruse that they were simply fishermen." He raised his eyebrows behind his mask. "In any case, you'll have to take my word on their clothing—it's gone now; we had it burned, of course." Some of the officers looked at each other and shuffled back from the bodies an inch or two. Gurley remained where he was, riveted. He looked like Frankenstein. He'd acquired an eye patch after his arrival in Fairbanks, but his Franklin Bout wound had wept through the gauze and dried. Plus the straps of his surgical mask had snapped, so he was holding it to his face.

"Men are working on decoding the notebook they had with them. Early report is that it's not a code they've been using; seems altogether unique. Could take a while. But we can tell a lot of the tale just by… reading their bodies, if you will. We'll start with Subject One, and leave number two covered for a moment, for reasons which will become obvious."

"Whole damn thing is pretty obvious," said a red-haired officer whom I'd heard someone call Swift. "I'm no doctor, but look at those hands. Look at those damn fingers. Look like pieces of charcoal. These boys were working on a bomb, went off too soon, boom, fire, burn, ow, ow, dead."

At the mention of *bomb,* I moved a little closer. But I couldn't see those charred fingers. Just the feet, or the toes, really, which were also black. Sergeant Redes had never taught us how to defuse anything with our toes.

"Well," said the major, scanning the crowd for a sympathetic face, and finding Gurley's. Only Gurley appreciated the art of performance, and how much the oafish Swift was screwing up this one. We all waited for the major to speak again, but I think Gurley and I were the only ones who saw the major give up: *what the hell, out with it,* his slumping shoulders said. But Swift interrupted yet again.

"Look, if you don't know, you don't know," said Swift, and while he looked around the room to collect smiles, I watched the major prepare to let him have it. He spun around, and I actually flinched, so familiar was I with Gurley's theatrical roundhouse punch.

But instead of swinging at Swift, the major swept the sheet off the second subject.

I could see this body much better, which was much worse.

He was lying on his stomach. His fingers and the whole of his toes were a shiny, brittle black. And black, too—unlike a burn, unlike paint, unlike anything human—was the giant lesion that covered much of his back. What wasn't black was purple.

"I *know*," the major thundered, and I would have smiled at how the drama had so quickly resumed, with such hysterics, except, like everyone else, I felt nauseous. "I know what *Justinian* knew. I know what medieval *Europe* knew. I know what a dozen spies and intercepted cables know is *true*." He turned to the inhuman corpse and then back to Gurley, who did something inexcusable: Gurley stole his line, the best line. But he did it with the panache of a fellow professional, and the major could not help but smile.

"The Black Death," Gurley said softly, "is among us once more."

As we onlookers slowly recovered, or simply found other places to look, the major found ways to draw our eyes back to the cadavers, pointing out various telltale signs of the disease. It was when he'd gotten to the men's almost egg-sized lymph nodes that Swift decided to strike again. The major was giving us the Latin etymology behind the technical term for the swollen nodes—buboes, *bubo* meaning groin, meaning swelling, hence the Black Death's actual name, bubonic plague....

"Squirrels get bubonic plague," said Swift. "Rats, I think. Maybe deer. Hell, when I hunt, I—"

"And humans," said the major.

"Maybe civilians," said Swift, businesslike and dismissive. "But I got vaccinated. We all got a plague vaccine. Standard army issue." He looked at the major. "Maybe you're too far back from the front lines, I don't know—"

"I have been vaccinated," said the major. "And what's more, one imagines these men, given the nature of their mission, were vaccinated, too. Which means we may have reason for concern."

Not a sound in the room. Everyone had stopped talking; most, like me, had stopped breathing as well.

But Swift was undeterred. "Or that you got your diagnosis wrong."

The major didn't answer. He looked at Swift, he looked at Gurley, and then he looked down, studying with great interest the fingers of his own right hand, which were rosy and pink.

THE TWO "FISHERMEN" had been discovered adrift two hundred miles west-southwest of Nome, Alaska. Their fishing trawler was small, barely big enough for ocean travel. But it was big enough to hold the both of them—one lying on the floor of the bridge, the other slumped over the tiny galley table belowdecks—and their gear, which included almost nothing for fishing.

Instead, there were four wire cages, the size of milk crates—all empty. Two porcelain canisters the size of flour jars; both empty, both broken. Two large cylinders of hydrogen. And a long, bulky roll of material that the sailors who'd first found it mistook for a sail.

It was, rather, a balloon.

After we'd gratefully moved back into the conference room, there was a brief period of debate as to whether the fishermen had launched any other balloons before succumbing. But it was difficult to reach any conclusions; unfortunately, the fishing vessel had sunk not long after the boarding party had retrieved the bodies, books, and a few other items. Already waterlogged when it was discovered, the ship had given little notice before slipping completely beneath the waves.

"There is a possibility," the major said, "that this was *not* some dastardly plot, that plague-carrying rats just happened to be aboard their vessel already—this, after all, is how the plague has traveled the world for years—and that they were merely bitten by the infected fleas the rats hosted." The major shook his head. "We'll know more once we've opened them up; secondary pneumonia is supposedly a sign of... manufactured plague, if you want to call it that." He drew himself up. "But frankly, gentlemen, with the way the war is going, with the desperate, bizarre reports we are hearing from Okinawa, with the sickening intelligence that continues to come in about this Unit 731's medical 'experiments' in Manchuria—"

"Yeah, sure," said Swift, undeterred. "Experiments are one thing. Figuring out how to bomb people with it is another. Which, given the experience of those two"—he couldn't help but pause—"doesn't look like they've figured out yet."

"Nineteen forty," said the major crisply. "October. China. Chekiang Province, Jap plane flies over city of Ningpo dropping rice, some paper. Two days later, first plague cases ever to appear in that city."

"But—" Swift began again, but he was already ceding the point.

"Nineteen forty-one, Hunan province. Plane flies over Changteh—"

"All right," said Swift.

"Believe what you want," said the major. "I believe it was Doubting Thomas who needed to probe Christ's wounds with his own hand before he'd believe. You're welcome to stick a finger in...."

Swift waved a hand in surrender.

"Gentlemen," the major said, obviously satisfied he'd managed to salvage some of his theater, "I don't need much more evidence to know what I believe."

Neither did Gurley: the cages had been for the rats, the rats had been for the balloons, the balloons had been for Alaska, for America, for him, and he could hardly contain himself. He stole looks at me the entire meeting—*Pay attention! How about that? Isn't this something? Isn't this wonderful? I was right! I told you so!*—looks that I found hard to bear, not because of their content, but because his eye had started bleeding again. I pointed to it, and he dabbed at it with a handkerchief, annoyed.

The meeting broke up with plans to reconvene in five days. Gurley was incredulous at the hiatus and said so, but he was brushed aside. It would take at least that long, if not longer, to decode the materials found on board. And as much as the major had enjoyed the little bit of fear-mongering that he'd done, he was clearheaded enough to know that, in the near term, there was relatively little they could do. The Navy ship that had made the discovery had been quarantined and sprayed with insecticide. The crew, all of whom had been vaccinated previously, were being monitored; nothing yet.

Moreover, it had simply been a stroke of luck that the vessel had drifted so far north. There was almost no chance the plague would somehow have found its way from the boat to the mainland, and even if it had, it would have encountered one of America's most unpopulated regions—the western coast of Alaska. The suspect fishermen presumably had been making for much farther south—Vancouver, or Seattle, possibly San Francisco—when something had gone wrong.

So, then: five days. Authorities across the region would be notified, discreetly, and told to keep watch—for mysterious illnesses or deaths among animals or people, and, of course, for spies. And at the end of those five days, if all agreed it was necessary, a search of the region would be mounted. Though the arrangements for this, too, would take time; the Army had few resources in the area and knowledge of the terrain was scant.

"We do have a base in Nome, and another at Bethel, primarily occupied with lend-lease planes," the major said in closing. "And ATG— Alaska Territorial Guard—volunteer Eskimo units in a number of remote locations. I suppose we could call on them." The officers, all white, hardly even registered the comment. "But given the sensitivity of the task and what's at stake, well—five days, gentlemen?" Heads nodded, save Gurley's: five days.

The meeting broke up and the men dispersed. I saw Swift look toward Gurley and mutter something to a companion on the way out. But Gurley didn't catch it. He was busy buttonholing the major, asking for a final favor before heading back to Anchorage. I kept a discreet distance while they spoke. I could see that, while the major was reluctant, Gurley had earned his respect, even gratitude for his performance at the postmortem.

Sure enough, when the room was clear and it was just three of us, the major gave Gurley a quick nod and ducked through the door. Gurley waved me over.

"What time's the flight back?" he asked.

"Wheels up at 1600," I said, looking at my watch. "Less than ten minutes."

Gurley looked at the door the major went through. "Well, I told him we'd only look at it for a minute."

"At what?" My stomach started to turn; I was sure Gurley had asked to see some even viler piece of evidence, like a flyblown rat.

"Their little book," Gurley said. "A 'unique code,' I'm sure," he said. "Ninety percent of these Nobel laureates think the Japanese language is a unique code."

The major reappeared. He gave me a suspicious look, but Gurley reassured him with a quick nod of his head. The major produced the book. He didn't allow Gurley to touch it, but he flipped through a few pages, slowly. The major was right; Gurley was wrong: even I could tell that it was a strange code, it wasn't Japanese.

But Gurley was right about something else, something he didn't tell the major, something he didn't have to tell me. The little journal, with its distinctive paper and soft, scuffed green leather cover, was a relative—perhaps the twin—of another book, a beautiful book, one we kept in a safe, back in Anchorage.

WE MADE THE 4 P.M. flight, but were diverted to a lonely airstrip down the Kenai Peninsula due to weather. It was hours before we were airborne again, and by the time Gurley and I arrived back in Anchorage, it was close to midnight. He was spent. Adrenaline had powered him through much of the day, I realized, and excited as he was, he'd have to turn in. I was relieved; I'd imagined he'd drag me into the office for an all-night session poring over our little map book with new-found intensity.

I'd been studying his eye as well. There were no new signs of bleeding, but he looked extremely pale, and had difficulty making it off the plane.

Once on the tarmac, he just stood there and looked around. I stood with him and watched the ground crew attend to its duties.

After a minute or two, he looked at me. "Sergeant?" he asked. "Are we to stand here all night?"

"No, sir," I said. "If you don't need me, I'll be heading off to—"

"Of course I need you, Sergeant. Do you think I'm going to drive myself downtown? Find us a damn jeep."

"It's close to midnight, sir," I said. "Standing orders are—unofficial traffic is restricted to—"

"A jeep, Sergeant. *That* is an order."

On the pretext of speeding Gurley to medical care, I commandeered a jeep. I actually did drive toward the base hospital, but as soon as Gurley realized what I was doing, he redirected me toward the main gate. He waved off the gate sentry and then we were bouncing along the road downtown, headlights out, with only the stars and half a moon to light the way.

Without my asking or his saying, we drove straight to the Starhope. I pulled up and turned off the engine. I tried not to look up, but couldn't help it. Lily's office window was dark; I couldn't even see a sliver of light that might indicate she merely had the blackout shade pulled.

"Oh my God." She'd materialized beside Gurley while I'd been staring up at the window. After all this time, it seemed fitting that the first time we'd see each other would be like this: a sudden apparition. I gripped the steering wheel, worried now that I'd be the one to black out, not Gurley. She gave me half a look that wasn't angry or accusatory or even wistful, just concerned. Then she turned to Gurley, and I saw what I'd missed all these weeks.

They'd fallen in love. Maybe Gurley had cared for her before—cared enough to shop for that ring—maybe she had cared for Gurley. But something had happened. I checked her hand: no ring, but there was a married familiarity to their movements (or so it appeared to this wise teen).

I watched, in awe, aghast, as she put a hand to his cheek, while Gurley feebly attempted to stop her. I watched as he relented, sank back in his seat, and closed his eyes. And then I watched her hands move lightly around his face, his hair, his head, examining, comforting—and maybe, healing. I knew, or remembered, that magic.

I had to look away. But I kept turning back, mystified, horrified. I might as well have been watching them make love. She was too beautiful, her hands too gentle, and Gurley impossibly peaceful.

She helped him from the car. Gurley hadn't said a word since we'd left the base, and now he only grunted a bit, sucked in a rapid breath or two. It finally occurred to me that it couldn't just have been his eye; his uniform was likely concealing a dozen more injuries. I sat and watched her walk him to the entrance. Then she stopped, turned around. I looked up: yes, yes? She carefully lowered Gurley until he was seated on the stoop, and then walked back to me.

Later, I let myself think. I tried to send the words to her, invisibly, from my forehead to hers: *I'll come back later, okay?*

But Lily said, "What happened?"

I sighed and said I didn't know; Gurley had said something about a fight last night in a bar. "You know, the Franklin bouts," I said, but she shook her head.

She looked back at Gurley, and then back at me. "Where were you?"

"Today? In Fairbanks," I said, excited just to be talking to her. And a day like today: this was the kind of day I missed her most, when such strange things had happened, and I had no one to tell them to. Secrets? I just needed another chance.

"No, last night, when he got hurt? Why weren't you there? You know he's not—he can't—you know he needs looking after."

I was too taken aback to speak.

Then Gurley called for her, quietly, a kind of moan.

Lily glared at me. "Please," Lily said. "From now on? Louis?"

My mouth was open to say something, but the best I could do was nod.

"Okay, okay," Lily said, distracted. She walked back to Gurley and helped him inside. I watched and waited. The light in her office came on; I could see now that the window was open. She came to it, looked out, looked down, saw me, looked like she was about to say something, and then pulled the shade.

I sat there, staring up, watching as the thinnest line of light appeared and disappeared whenever the shade fluttered gently. I kept staring, long after the window went dark and remained dark, and the only light there was came from the sky. The moon had set and I had to use the stars to help me home.

CHAPTER 13

GURLEY DIDN'T COME IN THE NEXT MORNING. I DIDN'T expect him to. I almost went looking for him in the vain hope that I would not find him where I knew he was. But I stayed put. He was Lily's, for now. And she could have him. She could use Gurley, leech whatever secrets she might from him. That's what she wanted, all she wanted.

Alone in the Quonset hut, I spun open the safe, removed the atlas, and set it on my desk.

But I didn't open it, not at first. To do so would have been to stumble into another tryst. Lily and Saburo's romantic summer scrapbook. The most I could console myself with was that here, at least, lay evidence that Gurley had competition, too.

I laid my hand flat on the cover. How big was Saburo's hand? Was it callused? Soft? Smooth? Creased? What did it look like, when it was clenched as a fist or with fingers splayed, cupped or about to caress? Had it ever unlocked a cage, delicately removed a rat? Swatted a flea?

I wiped my hands on my pants, despite myself, felt foolish, and then opened the book again.

The problem was, our book—Gurley's and mine, Lily and

Saburo's—was too beautiful. It might have looked like the other atlas on the outside—and the more I looked, the more certain I was that they came from the same source—but on the inside, it was completely different. What little I'd seen of the other book had revealed only writing, a scribbled diagram here and there, hasty notes, that strange code. No pictures. No watercolor sketches.

But this book—

I leafed through the drawings, the written passages alongside. Much of the book was given over to weather observations, with notes of wind direction and speed. The balloons were mentioned repeatedly, and predictions were made as to where they would land in North America, Alaska in particular. Some of these locations were plotted on maps. Beyond that, however, little was clear. The book was "maddeningly poetic," Gurley had said; the descriptions grew more lyrical and opaque as the book progressed. The maps were rich in topographic detail, but none bore place names. And they were done on a microscopic scale; no pages depicted the whole of Alaska, say, or the entire Pacific Northwest. Instead there were detailed coastlines of indeterminate islands. Stretches of riverbank. Tempting paths plotted across lush but vague landscapes.

I tried to imagine Saburo's hand at the end of a day, cradling a pencil or brush, dabbing at the page while Lily stoked a small fire for dinner. I tried to tease figures of Lily out of the watercolor sketches. That vertical brushstroke, there, the way it intersected with that thin line: *that* was Lily.

Saburo and I shared this, at least: only we knew that she was everywhere in this book of balloons and bombs, hidden within the stroke of a pen or a brush. There was no trace of her if you didn't know how or where to look. Once I decided I did, I found her everywhere, even in the little maps that were inked in here and there. One seemed to trace a path clear into a sun—clear across the Pacific, most likely, the route Saburo wanted to use to spirit Lily home.

I know what you're hiding, Saburo. Where you're hiding. Right— *here*.

But it was no use. Trace the drawings as I might, rub at the maps with my thumb until the page began to smudge, nothing emerged, nothing of Saburo, of Lily. Gurley had thought bombs were hidden here, and I suppose there were, if Lily had been telling the truth. But I hadn't seen them, not balloons, not bombs, and certainly not buboes, swollen with disease. I found myself wanting to exonerate Saburo, at least from this last, most heinous crime. Well, Lily was alive and healthy, that was evidence enough, wasn't it? He couldn't have been handling dangerous germs, not without risking her life, let alone his own—

He's gone, Louis.

Oh, Lily, no—

I stood to leave. I had to find her, ask her. Even if Gurley was still with her. I looked at the clock: 1900 hours.

I was about to put my hand on the door when it banged open in front of me.

THE EYE PATCH WAS GONE, a red-stained, black-rimmed eye in its place. His color was better, though, and from his first words, I knew he had recovered, as much as he ever would, anyway.

"Sergeant...Belk," he said, with enough space between the words to make me wish I'd left long before. "And where are you going? Please join me, in my office. We have much to discuss. So much."

"Sir?"

"In—my—office."

I followed him in, sat down. He went to the map and studied it for a while, running his finger along Alaska's western coast and then on to Russia. He examined some spot in the Bering Sea. Then he removed a pushpin to play with, and sat down.

"Sergeant Belk," he said. "First of all, I must thank you."

Better to just sit there than respond.

"No, really. I shouldn't have gone to Fairbanks—delightful as it was, as it always is to see two dead enemy soldiers, stretched out before you. And you? A stalwart. Standing there, the soul of discretion, restraint. Didn't even turn green. You've earned my admiration. For getting through Fairbanks, and getting me home. And getting me downtown last night." He'd been playing with the pin, but now looked up. "And for so much more, I understand."

This time, he waited for an answer. "Sir?" I asked.

"My companion—our, what? mutual *friend*—tells me that you both have been, well—*looking out* for me. This is touching."

"Sir, Lily and I haven't—not for—"

"Not fond of sentences that start that way, Sergeant, if we can get right to the point. I'm not fond of learning that I'm being *looked out* for, either, as though I were some doddering *uncle,* as though I were some amputee *invalid* unable to wipe his own *ass*—but no, what troubles me more is this 'Lily and I' business."

"Captain, I'm not sure what—"

"Neither am I. I thought we had a rather clear, specific discussion about this topic on the plane to Wyoming so long ago. Christ, Belk, I showed you an ad for a ring. What did you think I was up to? I thought we had an understanding. I trusted you. And Lily. I told you that she was... unavailable. And now I learn you availed yourself of her quite consistently."

"That was way back, sir," I said, before realizing that made it sound like something *had* happened. "It's been weeks, sir. Months, since—" Worse. "Nothing ever happened. Or will. I swear. I promise." What had Lily told him? I watched his hands, surveyed the desk, wondering which way he'd come for me, what he would hit me with.

"Sadly—for you—I almost believe that, Belk. But you're what? Fourteen? What *could* happen? No, the lovely Lily offered no insight into matters carnal between you. Rather, it was left to me to review all that she said—the number of times she used your name, or included you in a 'we,' or spoke tenderly of how you both would *conspire* to take care of me—and determine for myself exactly what you had or had not done."

And that was his error, or hers, or mine: that he'd said she'd repeatedly mentioned my name; or that she had, even after all these months; or that learning this so thrilled and alarmed me that I turned the guiltiest shade of red a man can manage.

"Nothing happened, sir," I stammered.

"Nothing, indeed. Without trust, there is nothing."

"Surely Lily told you—"

"Oh, that woman," Gurley said. "As painful as it was for me to hear her say *your* name, I find it even more grating to hear hers come from you. Silence."

And so we sat there. Gurley stared at me for a while, as though I might break under the pressure and confess to—I don't know what. Had she told him we'd never shared more than a meal? Had she told him about that last evening we'd had together, about the map of her body that she'd undressed to show me?

I was too scared to speak, or move, or even look away. I sat there, swallowing his look, unable to muster anything for him in return. He finally swung around in his chair and looked at the map again.

"You know how I hate a spy, Sergeant," he said, looking at me over his shoulder. "And by spy, I mean traitor. Do you know what I mean, Sergeant?"

"Yes, sir."

"You know that I would still be serving in the main of the OSS, serving in *Paris,* most likely. Or Rome. Or Casablanca. Some part of the war where there was as much sun as wine as women..."

"Yes, sir."

He came around the desk, finally, and towered over me. "I'd still have two fucking legs to stand on, Belk, had it not been for a *spy,* for lack of a better word, for whoever betrayed me, got me kicked out of headquarters and into this maliciously absurd duty. Chasing balloons. With a boy sergeant. And an Eskimo—oh, what? Whore."

He didn't hit me. He lost something with the mention of Lily, and after a moment, retreated back behind the desk.

"That's why this upsets me. More than wondering if you and Lily did ... anything, that you discussed, plotted to—"

"I told her, sir," though of course I hadn't, "you didn't need taking care of. I didn't know why she was talking about it. I could have cared less. I don't care," I added, a second before realizing how far I had gone.

Gurley drew a deep breath and smiled. "That, too, is touching, Sergeant," he said. "No better way to extricate yourself from a tight spot than by shooting yourself in the foot and then taking aim at your captor." He smiled, and then pulled open a file drawer and rummaged through it. Out came the bottle. Then two glasses.

"We met over a whisky, Sergeant," he said, unscrewing the bottle, smelling it, and then pouring a measure in each glass. "Let us part the same way."

I stood so rapidly that I knocked over my own chair. I really thought he was going to kill me. Had he been wearing his holster? The way he was sitting, I couldn't tell.

"Sit, dear boy," he said. I backed a step away. He rolled his eyes. "And to think—I had such hopes. A young, tractable mind. A mind to fill with knowledge—wisdom." He pointed to a spot on the wall to the left of the map. "Greece," he said. "Right about there. What did the ancient Greeks do to traitors, brave Belk?" He took a sip. "Good Lord, son, sit. It tires me so to see you devote feeble resources to both standing *and* thinking." He drank down the rest, and then poured himself another shot. "We're sharing a drink, Sergeant. Appreciate this for the outlandishly generous gesture that it is—the sentry might burst in and charge me with fraternization, surely—and so sit down, and take, up, your, glass."

I righted the chair, and moved around into it. What had Lily told him to make him this mad? It was jealousy, but it was more than that. It might have been his leg. Betrayal.

He raised his glass. I raised mine. *"Salut,"* he said, and watched me. "Now is when you drink." I drank. He closed his eyes in pleasure. He pointed to Greece's spot on the wall again. "You were killed, of course," he said. "That goes without saying. Still true today. Spies are hanged. But—the ancient Greeks did us one better, as is true in so many things. The goods of a spy were seized. Their houses—razed. Their progeny treated as outlaws. And their bodies, Belk? Not buried, but cast out in some wild, desolate place." He sipped at his drink. "Not as good as what I paid for it, but better than I've had of late. What think you?" I nodded.

Gurley turned back to the map. "So shall be your sentence, Sergeant." I froze, but Gurley waved his glass at me when he saw I had. "No, no. I've had all day to think about this. You have no goods to seize, no house to raze, save that orphanage, I suppose, and I have no interest in immolating nuns."

"Sir, I just want to apologize," I said, only sure that was where to start.

"Accepted," Gurley said. "Now, then. As I was saying, circumstances being what they are, my options are limited. The Greeks would have executed you, yes, perhaps, but they didn't have our modern legal system to worry about. So execution is tempting, yes, but... messy, for so many reasons. This leaves me with one option."

"Sir, I don't understand how—if—I'll never go downtown again, sir."

"No, Sergeant," he said, putting his glass down. "You shan't." He stood and went to the map. "Downtown, Anchorage, the Starhope— the lovely Miss Lily—will all be very, very far away." He turned back to me. "For while I cannot kill you—though I do reserve the right to— I shall still cast your body out into a wild, desolate space. I'm having you transferred, Belk. To...Little—where are you?" He searched the map. "Yes. Diomede."

"Where?" I stood now, too, squinting after him at the map. Was that near Russia? In Russia?

"Goodness, Belk, I'm not sure exactly *where*," he said. "We'll leave finding it to the plane or boat that deposits you there. La Petite Diomede. An island in the Bering Sea. Wild and desolate, and—"

"Captain," I said, still unable to spot my specific destination on the wall. "Little Dio-what? Diomede? I don't understand. It looks—it looks like it's too far north. It's nowhere near the flight path of these balloons. I'm not going to find anything there."

"Exactly, Sergeant. I should hope you don't find anything. That might complicate things considerably." He found his chair and sat, though he kept his eyes on the map. "I did consider the South Pacific, of course, the front. Trench foot, land mines, snipers, tenacious enemy soldiers who insist on being killed, and killing, one by one by one. Surely death would find you there." Now he turned back to me. "But you see how that would be disappointing, your suffering liable to end so quickly. No, I much prefer this island I've found. I understand it's a mostly treeless rock. Some Natives, some soldiers—rampant suicide, homicide, but I trust you'll hold your own." He lifted his glass, saw it was empty, and put it back down. "See, Belk, I can be generous. Even to a traitor."

Bravery, alcohol, the delight in escaping the front-line tropics— something inserted a thin line of steel within me, and I spoke. "Not generous," I said quietly. "The South Pacific? Lily would never forgive you—for doing that to me."

I saw him tense. I saw his hands curl into fists, and I saw the thoughts progress in his mind. This didn't happen quickly, but slowly and deliberately, as he considered each image before him. Heaving his chair at me. His desk. Leaping across the desk for my throat. Lowering his hand to his hip, removing his gun, raising it, aiming, pulling the trigger.

Instead, he slowly drew the book across the desk toward him, star- ing at me all the while. "Before we part, Belk," he said. "There was al- ways something I had meant to show you. Something that will demonstrate to you why I might have predicted these balloons would, literally, come to ill in due time. Here is my point, Belk," he said. "You must never underestimate the *nefariousness* of the Oriental mind."

He sounded like Gurley the actor, but he no longer looked like him. He was no longer playing a part; he'd been consumed by it. One hears the term *wild-eyed,* and thinks of what? A raving drunk? A rabid dog or raccoon? Not nearly: this was wild-eyed. If I'd been nearer, he would have nipped at me, teeth flashing, and it wouldn't have mattered if I myself were a foaming pit bull or lion, or—take note, Ronnie—wolf: he would have bitten my nearest limb clean through.

His voice skittered high and low, the words tumbling out with manic speed.

"You admired the art in the book," he said, flipping through it to the back, to those mysterious empty gray pages. He looked up, I nodded numbly. He smiled and produced a pocketknife. I leapt up; he clucked. "Shh, Sergeant. Down, boy, down. As though I'd sully my quarters with your foul blood." He unfolded a blade and then added an after-thought: "Besides—who knows what disease lurks dormant in you?"

I sat, slowly. He sliced out a page, with difficulty, which shocked me almost as much as anything else: our precious book! Lily's book! It felt like he was peeling away an expanse of skin.

"As I said, you've admired the book, but your appreciation has been superficial, as it could only be." He poured the glass before him almost full, and then folded the blank page and poked it in until it was sub-merged. "The paper, Belk. The paper, Sergeant, is most remarkable."

I could be out the door in two steps, maybe one. Or the phone: it was within reach. But the knife, still open, was within his reach and much closer.

"The paper for the balloons is made of, what did we determine? Something like the mulberry bush." He sang a little to himself while he poked at the paper. "Round and round the mulberry bush, the mon-key chased the weasel...." Then he looked up, head lolling as though he were drunk. "Quite similar, in fact, to the paper in this book, which, my *yeeeeaaaars* of education inform me is *washi* paper. Some of the balloons, in fact, appear to feature a few panels which are this very *same* paper." I looked on, genuinely distracted with surprise. "Didn't that always strike you as odd? A mission this daring, this important, and they entrust it to *paper?*" I nodded, caught up, despite myself. "Indeed. Well, as it happens, as no one else in this grossly undereducated army seems to know, this paper has precisely the pedigree for the job. It's very strong, for one, curiously strong—so strong that—well, let me show you." He drew the now-sodden paper out of the glass.

"Tradition holds that assassins—not radio show adventure heroes—made use of such paper. Say you wanted to kill someone," he said, his voice sinking. "Say you wanted to kill someone and have no one find out. You wait until your quarry is sleeping. You take a billet-doux–sized sheet of *washi* paper and wet it"—he held up the dripping page—"don't worry, it won't disintegrate. Your prey lets out a great exhale—and you set upon him!" Gurley started, and I jumped, involuntarily, as he intended. "He awakes; he cannot breathe. He is startled, confused, he struggles, but you hold him *down*," Gurley said through gritted teeth. "You hold that paper right where it is. And he sucks and gasps, but all he's doing is pulling that paper tighter and tighter and tighter." I looked away; it was too sickening, as though one of those plague-infected ulcers were spreading across his brain.

But he started speaking again, and when I looked at him once more, I saw that instead of his usual hideous smile, his face was slack and his eyes full of what had to be tears. "Why couldn't they have just done that, Belk? Why couldn't they have just—why couldn't Father Ioasaph's angel been a real angel? Why couldn't he have leapt from his smoking basket beneath the balloon and set upon me?" He was talking solely to the paper now. "I asked them how long the pain would last, and one doctor said, 'What do you mean?' and the other doctor said, 'Forever.' I ask Lily to move with me south—the medical discharge is there, whenever I want it, a free ticket home, a check every month— and she says one thing and then another but never yes. She talks about how this is her home, but she never talks about the real reason. A god-damn leg that won't—"

What happened next is ridiculous, except that it really happened, in just this way. Gurley took the sheet he'd so carefully prepared, and slapped it to his face. And sure enough, it settled there, a second skin, each gasp further sealing it with an additional suture. He turned red, fell to the floor, and spasmed. The paper held absolutely fast. Maybe a minute passed, maybe two, and then I remembered that I wasn't Gurley, that I didn't have the stomach to stand by while someone killed himself, and that, however hard he'd tried to convince me other-wise, my first loyalty was to Lily, and she had said: *take care of him.*

I fell to the floor, reached to peel the paper away from his face, but lost my balance as he thrashed.

That's when he made his move.

And then the paper was on me. It smelled of whisky and spit and Gurley and something else—rice, I suppose, strange as that sounds. He couldn't get it to adhere, not as well as it had on him, but he didn't need it to; he was on top of me, pressing me down, his hands making up for anything the paper failed to do.

"And you hold him down, Sergeant. He sucks in, he gasps for air, but he is only making it worse."

If I'd have taken a breath first, if I'd been prepared, I would have had no difficulties. I would have had the air to slither out from under him. But I hadn't taken that breath, and now, instead of fighting, I was panicking. I watched him, watched for him to watch me. *Look at me,* I willed him. *Look at me.* Wouldn't this make it harder to kill me? Even for Gurley?

I don't know. It would have made it harder for me. But for whatever the reason, he did look, and maybe he saw me, or maybe he saw Lily, or maybe he saw himself. He tore the paper away, rolled off, and stared at me while I panted there.

I slid away from him, but only a short distance; I was surprised by how tired I was. I looked back at him; he was tired, too. Sitting on the floor, back against the wall, he even looked a bit like the old Gurley, comically instead of criminally mad.

We sat like that for a while. I think it was only a minute, but if someone measured it as an hour, I wouldn't argue.

"I'm sorry," he finally said. He waved an arm so that his apology included the whole office, the whole war, perhaps. "I'm—listen," he said. "Help me up."

I laughed. Well, I didn't laugh. I puffed. I rolled my head to look at him, and then rolled it back to stare straight up. His left foot was cockeyed; the leg had detached.

"Louis," he said: my first name. I don't know why; I wish he hadn't. "I still think—I mean, we can see, but—given everything. Maybe you should go anyway to—maybe it's best." He stopped.

"Sergeant," he said, the old voice. Not angry, but the officer once more.

"I'll go," I said.

"You might be able to help from there," he said. "Truly. That fishing boat—it wasn't so far south of there. It's just that, with Lily and all—"

"I'll go," I said, and slowly got to my feet. "First thing," I said. "First flight I can get going anywhere. Anywhere north."

"Good boy," said Gurley. "Good man. I'm sorry, Sergeant—"

"Good night, sir," I said, going to the door.

Gurley put on what he must have thought was a brave face: he wasn't going to ask, again, for help getting up. Which was good, because I wasn't going to.

"Louis," he said, which was again so strange that I turned back to look at him, even though I was through the door.

But he was still slumped against the wall, and the half-closed door obscured his face. I could only see his legs, and hands, and the sheet of paper, drying on the floor.

And I could hear him softly calling after me: "Sleep well!"

CHAPTER 14

I HAD THOUGHT ABOUT SPENDING THE REST OF THE NIGHT on base, maybe even seeking out Father Pabich to help set me straight or simply to say goodbye, but I found myself skirting the pickup baseball and football games behind the barracks, making for the main gate and downtown.

It was a Monday. Lily charged less on Mondays to read palms than any other day of the week. I'd asked her once if it was to drum up business, but she shook her head: she said she was tired on Mondays, and didn't feel she did as good a job. Whatever the reason, Mondays were a slow night, and the building was deserted when I entered. I climbed up to her office and found it dark, the door ajar. I waited a moment while my eyes adjusted to the light, just so that I could be sure she wasn't hiding in the shadows. Then I went back downstairs and outside, where low and heavy clouds were bringing the evening to an early close.

I had just started to walk back up the street when I heard Lily's voice behind me, delighted. "Louis!" But when I turned around, her face fell. "What happened?" she asked. "What did he say?" She shoved her hands in her pockets and stared at her fists through the fabric. For the briefest moment, she looked like a little girl. I felt like a little boy, the two of us on our way back to Mary Star of the Sea. Then she looked up. "I'm sorry if I made things awkward. It's just that—but he's not a man who likes being babied, even if he needs it."

"Then why try?"

"Let's go inside," she said.

"I can't stay," I said. "Something happened. If he came now—"

"You mean Gurley," she said. "He has a jealous side, doesn't he? Which is strange. But you don't need to worry."

"Lily," I said. "I'm leaving. Tomorrow morning. First thing." My voice grew quieter with every word.

"Where this time?" she asked, forcing cheer. "You two have such adventures. I'd have signed up for the army if I knew—"

"Leaving," I said. "I don't know what you said to him, but I'm *leaving.* He's sending me to Russia or damn close—Little Diomede. A rock in the ocean. He's getting rid of me. He almost tried to get rid of me tonight. He thinks I was trying to steal you away from him," I said. And then, mostly because she was still trying to smile this all away, I added, "Guess I was."

Lily stopped breathing then. Her mouth was open, but it stayed open, no air coming in or out. And she made one wrong face after another—concern, dismay, horror—until I turned away and did what kids do when they get upset, which is turn red and wait to cry.

"Louis," she said. But she didn't put her hand to my face. She didn't take my palm in hers. She let me stand there, my only comfort being that the tone of her voice sounded exactly like I wanted it to, heart-broken. I wanted to hear her say my name again, just that way, so I didn't turn around. I waited. "Louis," she said, and then came a hand to my elbow, and I turned.

The clouds had descended almost to the ground. The street was empty. Just Lily, crying, and me, watching, and some man, two blocks down, walking toward us in the mist, the whole of him indistinct save his slightly irregular gait. Step . . . step. Step . . . step.

"Louis," Lily said once more.

"Gurley," I whispered. "Down the street. Coming this way. He'll see us." And he did, or whoever it was did, because he picked up speed: step, step; step, step.

Lily spun.

Then Lily's name came tumbling down the street, half shout, half moan, and she began to run. Gurley did, too, or at least lurched into the odd gallop he used those few times he did run. I stood my ground, long enough for him to see me clearly, and long enough for me to see that he hadn't expected me. Then I ran, too.

GURLEY KEPT US IN SIGHT far longer than I thought he would. I began to tire, but Lily kept streaming through the city, passing all sorts of places I thought might be good to hide or disappear into—an empty building, or a busy bar.

Eventually, Anchorage began to run out of streets and buildings. Lily kept running, until the street became a dirt road, and then a trail, and then we were in the woods. I stopped, exhausted, but also anxious to see if Gurley was still following us. I heard nothing, only the sound of Lily's footsteps ahead of me, growing fainter. I turned back to the trail and continued into the forest.

TEN, TWENTY YEARS AGO, I went back to that trail. The area is parkland today, popular with joggers in summer and cross-country skiers in winter and wildlife any time of year. It all looks as it did fifty-odd years ago when Lily and I walked into it, except it wasn't called a park then. It was just the place where Anchorage gave up and the rest of Alaska began, and it would have seemed silly to put a sign up and call it a park. Keep walking into that forest, deeper and deeper, and four hundred miles later, you'd cross the Arctic Circle. Another three hundred miles or so beyond that, Point Barrow, the ice cap, the North Pole, the place where all the longitude lines on the map begin, a place where, certain times of year, the sky seems low enough and the stars thick enough that you'd only need to be a bit taller to reach one down for yourself.

There were no stars visible; the clouds were lifting, but it was too early for stars. And the farther we walked into the forest, the more of the sky that was obscured, the damper the air and earth became. I remember how nothing was as strange or exotic to me as the smell of that forest, then; it wasn't anything like the sage or chaparral smell of Southern California wilderness, which made you think of dust and sun and sometimes smoke. This forest smelled wet, green, and cool, and the scent stuck to you like you'd dipped your face in a stream.

I caught sight of Lily within a few hundred yards; she'd started walking. She didn't stop, though, when she saw me. She wanted me to keep up, but not catch up, not yet.

We kept climbing through the forest, ever more thick, well past the point I would have ever ventured alone. Even in the short time I'd been in Alaska, I'd heard stories of guys wandering off for a weekend of camping and drinking and encountering all sorts of animals and trouble. Favorite stories involved run-ins with bears. I don't think every guy who had a bear story had actually seen one, or if they had, that they were as large as described. The way you knew they were telling the truth? They didn't talk about teeth or eyes or the sound of a roar—they talked about smell. And the more they talked about that horrible smell, the closer you knew they'd come. That detail had to be true; you didn't make up a story about stink to impress people. So while I heard bears all around me—cracking branches, and in the distance every now and then, something like a bark—I only smelled the wet and decaying forest, and knew we were safe.

Eventually, the mist grew thick enough that Lily seemed to be only a glow whenever I looked up the trail toward her. If I chanced to look away and then back, she faded away even more dramatically.

We had been tracking along the banks of a stream, knee-high ferns deepening from green to black as the light faded. We'd been walking toward a sound, it seemed, one that started out like wind, high in the trees—but the closer we got, it emerged as rushing water, perhaps rapids. I lost Lily for a moment then. She was just twenty yards ahead of me, maybe more, and she'd disappeared. I kept moving forward in the direction I'd last seen her and then there she was, standing on what looked briefly like a cloud. Maybe she could have done just that if she had wanted to, but this wasn't a cloud, just a large flat outcropping of rock overlooking a waterfall. I let Lily stand alone for a moment. Then she looked back toward me and I stepped forward.

"You walk slow," Lily said, looking down at my feet. We'd been walking for two hours or more and I could feel precisely each of the warm, stinging spots on my feet where blisters were forming.

"I wasn't sure I was supposed to follow you," I said.

"You're too polite, Louis," she said. "You must make a lousy soldier."

"I do," I said.

She sat down, cross-legged, and I sat stiffly beside her. I looked down the trail. "He was with us for a while, but I haven't heard him in a long time."

"He's not coming," Lily said, looking in the direction of the waterfall. "He's heading back to Fort Rich. Probably already there."

I tried to get her to look at me. "Is this you speaking as a shaman?" I asked. I'd earned at least that, I thought. Some teasing.

"No, as his lover," she said, turning to me to confirm she'd landed a blow. "I know him. So do you."

"Did you know he'd send me away?" I asked, after swallowing. "This something you cooked up together?"

She shook her head and looked at the dirt beneath us.

"That's it, Louis. That's just how it happened. He asked me, 'Do you have any really good friends? Guys who don't use you for sex? Guys you can trust? Guys you can always talk to, count on to stick up for you, like a brother? Because I'd like to give that guy a free plane ticket to the end of the earth. What do you say there, Miss Lily?'" She wiped her nose with the back of her hand. "It's all going just like we damn planned."

"I'm sorry."

"You're always sorry, Louis. Let's try this: Did you at least bring a going-away present? Did you bring the map book? The journal?"

"Lily," I said.

Lily gave me a long look, time to give a different answer. And when I didn't, she let out a long breath, not a sigh. "You're sorry. I know."

We sat. There were no sounds of bears, or Gurley, just the water rushing by below us. Alaska's summer sun doesn't so much set as sink, exhausted, but we still had an hour or two of light left. Some summer nights—that night—I swear I can feel the light stretch, as though one part of it had been pinned to sunrise and the rest pulled all day to that faraway sunset. Then the light breaks, and you definitely feel *that,* a band of rubber snapping against your skin, and everything finally goes dim.

Lily's touch felt just the same, and maybe that's what I feel those summer evenings when I'm up too late, that endless sun abetting an old man's insomnia. Maybe it's not the snap of the light I feel, but the memory of Lily, that night, as she extended a hand to me, slid it across the surface of the rock until it reached mine. I didn't move then, and neither did she. She let our two hands stay there, as if mere proximity had brought them together. And then she took my hand in hers, and I would have given her anything. Ten maps. Every codebook we had. A balloon.

But I had nothing.

"Did you ask Gurley for it?" I finally said. "I mean, obviously—that seems so easy."

She frowned, and for a moment, I thought she was going to let go of my hand, but she didn't. She just shook her head. "You know Gurley. Or maybe you don't. I could have asked for a dozen roses—a lot damn harder to get in Anchorage than that journal—and I would have had them, that day, and every day after until I begged him to stop. But not the journal. Asking would have spooked him. I just hoped we'd find ourselves in a . . . situation . . . at some point where the journal would be nearby, and I could somehow sneak it away, without his ever knowing."

"So you never told him about your summer, about Saburo?"

But Lily didn't look at me. She just said, "No."

If I believed in that sort of thing, and I suppose I do now, I would have said Saburo was there with us, then. I didn't hear him say anything, and I didn't hear Lily say anything to him, but I felt him. For a moment, he was as real as Lily was beside me, and then he was gone.

I couldn't say if Lily saw him, but she relaxed. Her frown left. She let go of my hand, rubbed her face, and stretched.

"Plan on finding a lot of balloons on Diomede?" she asked. "When do you go?"

"I'm not going to be able to find another damn balloon, not on Diomede, not anywhere. Not without a new palm reader, anyway."

"Shuyak," she said after a pause. "That was a neat trick, wasn't it?"

"Impressed me," I said.

"Hard to do *that*," she replied. She leaned to one side, slipping a hand into some hidden pocket. She pulled out a little sheaf of several tightly folded pages. "At least *I* brought a going-away gift," she said. She smoothed the pages out on the ground and then handed them to me. "Everything I know about palm reading, and finding balloons."

I looked at the pages. Though they were creased and dirty, I could tell immediately what they were—or rather, where they had come from. Faint watercolor sketches, diagrams in pencil, notes in black ink, in Japanese. And on the reverse of one page, a half-dozen tiny portraits. Some were more finished than others, but it took no imagination to see Lily in all of them.

"Before he left, I told Saburo I wanted him to leave behind a sketch of himself. He said he would, but when he finally got ready to go, he gave me these pages."

"This is you," I said, looking up at her to compare.

"He said every face he tried to draw came out as me. I told him he should have tried harder, but he said if I looked at these sketches long enough, I'd see all of him I needed to see."

"That's romantic," I said, not even teasing.

"Doesn't look like him or me," she said. She reached toward me and turned one of the pages over, revealing a more familiar terrain of sketches and maps and charts. "I saw him here, though." She traced her finger slowly down the slope of what looked like a cloud. "And here. And here." She sat back. "I look at these pages and I see all of him. I remember him hunched over, making these charts, explaining as he went."

I sifted through the papers a little more, and then came back to the page with her portraits. "So how's this going to help me become a better palm reader? Just stare at you long enough—?"

Lily took the pages. She shuffled back and forth through them until she found what she was looking for, and then held it out to me. A column of Japanese characters ran down the left-hand side of the page. In the middle was a gray-green blob, with a crosshairs in the lower right. Tiny numbers were written in each of the crosshairs' four quadrants, and at the bottom of the page, a single word in English characters, which I read aloud: "Shuyak."

When I looked up, Lily's eyes were full of tears. "Any drunken soldier who walked into that building and actually wanted his palm read, I could tell him anything. But you—once I knew you actually did work related to what Saburo was doing—that you might have access to that journal—" She stopped. "Like I said that night I first told you about Saburo—I wanted to be useful to you."

"Useful?" I was discovering what it was like to be Gurley; I could feel rage uncoiling inside me, seeking out a fist or arm. "And Gurley?" I said, to stall.

"Yes—or no. I mean, I knew he was involved, but eventually I realized he wouldn't help. Couldn't. And then it was too late. Things with Gurley—I don't know."

"You tricked us?"

"Louis," she said. "I wanted you to need me. I needed you to."

"Gurley, too?" I asked, but she didn't say anything. I felt her hand inching closer to mine again, but I didn't move. I tried very hard to stare at the page before me and nothing else. "You were helpful," I finally said. "Or, I guess Saburo was. But how did he know about Shuyak? Portage around the Katmai volcanoes? Kayak across the Shelikof Strait?"

Relieved, I think, to submerge into detail, Lily began speaking rapidly. "Shuyak was an old crash site, one he'd heard about before he'd come to Bethel. I sent you there thinking you'd find an old balloon, not another one, a new one."

I quickly scanned the other pages with new eyes and saw rivers, peninsulas, mountains, even towns emerge. One page looked particularly interesting. Green to the left and then a series of arrows to the right. Had Saburo known about plans for germ bombs? Had he told her? I wanted to ask her, but I couldn't. I was so angry and sad and defeated, I didn't want to know. More than that, I didn't want to see her lie, not to me.

She saw me studying the page. "I don't know what that means," she volunteered. "We were going to go through the whole book, him explaining, me figuring out, translating names, but we didn't get any farther than Shuyak." I didn't want her to say another word.

"So you lied about being a palm reader," I said, the anger in my voice surprising me more than her. "You lied about—or didn't let on why you thought I'd be so useful. Did you also lie about your supposed 'powers'? You hold something, and you know its story? How the hell did you know about me? About who I was? My childhood?" She snatched the papers away and crumpled them, tighter and tighter. "Did—did Gurley tell you? Was that a trick, too?"

"No, Louis," Lily said.

"So what am I thinking now?" I said. "Read my thoughts. Prove it." But there was nothing to read. I can't tell you what I was thinking. I was angry, but it was a boy's anger, fiery and violent and insensible, and even if you'd cracked my skull open to look inside, you would have seen nothing, only red.

I don't know what Lily saw. She said she saw nothing anymore.

"That's part of the reason I came all the way out here." She held the ball of paper to her nose and mouth and breathed in. "In the city, in Anchorage, the longer I've been here, the harder it's been, the more everything—everything I know—is fading." She took the papers away from her face and put them in her lap, absently smoothing them out. "I see Saburo now, but I don't know if that's the paper or just memory. And even those memories—I'm losing those, too." She dropped the papers, found a crevice in the rock and wedged her fingers there, closed her eyes. After a minute, she'd stopped crying and was breathing deeply.

"There is a story, Louis," she began. "About a boy, a baby boy, and his mother, that's been told for many years..."

I stopped her. I couldn't hear it. I wonder now what would have been different if I'd let her tell the story, the whole story, then, if I'd just been patient enough to hear her out. But I wasn't. I didn't say a word, I just raised a hand, and she stopped. She didn't argue, but just looked at me, disappointed and resigned.

"You really believed," she finally said.

I nodded and sighed and slipped the papers back toward me. I studied them for a few minutes until she spoke again. Then she said, "Look."

I turned, slowly, and saw nothing. But as I turned back, something above us distracted me, and I looked up to see something like clouds, or thinner than that, mist, twisting and undulating, changing colors as it did.

It would have done no good to tell me that I was seeing the aurora borealis for the first time and nothing more. This deep in the woods, this deep in the war, this far along with Lily: nothing was real anymore, at least nothing that I could not see, right at that moment.

And the lights above me, these I could see. I slowly leaned back until I was lying there, staring, looking up and watching the display, wondering if this was magic, or if the book had been, or the balloons, or if Lily was a magician, or Saburo, or Gurley.

"Lily," I finally whispered, worried the lights above were too fragile for me to speak any louder. Lily made no reply. I called her name, and when there was still no reply, I craned my neck to see if she was still there. She wasn't. Then I surprised myself. Instead of leaping to my feet and running off the rock to find her, I lay there, staring up. I suppose the word is *hypnotized,* but that doesn't give me enough credit. I was entranced, but I wasn't in a trance. It was like it always was with Lily: a debilitating fascination. So I lay there, and after a while, I heard her voice. She wasn't far away.

"I had seen the northern lights growing up in Bethel, but in Fairbanks, it seemed like we could see them almost all the time." I kept staring at the sky, now pulsing. "Are you scared?" she asked.

I shook my head. I wasn't scared, just surprised. Minutes ago, I had wanted to scream. I had wanted to hit someone. Lily. And now here I was, lying on the ground, looking at the sky. If it wasn't Lily's magic, then it was Alaska's, made present by the northern lights.

"Some people get scared. Of course, in Fairbanks, nobody was. The lights were as familiar as rain. But one March, far earlier in the evening than was usual, a tremendous red cloud of light appeared, just to the north. The lights had only just gone out in the dormitory, and as soon as they had, the cloud became instantly visible to all of us inside. We rushed to the window and watched it fold and wave, first one way, then the next. And then suddenly—" Lily slapped her hands together, and the light show above me disappeared. I blinked, squinted, and then blinked again.

"Lily?" I sat up on my elbows, and when she didn't reply, stood up.

When she first touched my hand, I flinched, but then she reached out with her other hand and touched me gently on the chest. I relaxed, and let her take my right hand back in hers.

"People who have lived here their whole lives—white, Yup'ik,

Inuit—will tell you the northern lights never make a sound. They did that night. They made a crack, just like that, and they were gone."

"What happened just now?"

"One of the teachers tried to tell us what the lights *really were* the next day, like it had something to do with science. But we all knew what the lights really were. Really are: the souls of women who die in childbirth. Suicides. Those who have been murdered. That's who you see."

Lily fell silent, and when I looked over a moment later, she was crying. "Who do you see?" I asked.

She didn't answer. Then she said, "When I first came to Anchorage, there were things I could see, I could hear, there were things I *knew,* but the longer I've been here—it's flowing away from me. I can *feel* it." She ran her hands along her arms. "Here—here."

"Lily," I said. "I know why you want the journal. You want to find him." Lily kept rubbing her forearms. "You want to find Saburo."

"Saburo," Lily said. "He's gone. He's died," she whispered. "I know it, or knew it. What I want to find is—"

"Whatever you need," I said. "I'll help you."

Lily looked at me.

"I'll talk to Gurley, when he's calmed down. I'll get this transfer canceled or postponed, and I'll go with you. I'll help."

"Tonight," she said. "We have to leave tonight."

"Lily."

She stepped away. "Come with me," Lily said. "I'd go alone—I should have already gone alone. But I don't want to. He left something for me, out on the tundra. Something I need to find, to see. Something that's going to be very hard for me to see. I want a friend with me. I want you, Louis."

"I want to be there, Lily. It's just that—"

"Jesus, Louis. If you won't listen to the real reason, how about this one, since it's the one you'd believe anyway. I need to *use* you. I can't get out of Anchorage, can't get to Bethel, can't get into the bush, can't go anywhere, without permission from the military. The whole state is restricted. You know what it's like to be a civilian here? A *half-breed* civilian? Wasn't so long ago the goddamn officers' club was off-limits to any girl who wasn't white."

She just wanted to use me. I'd fallen, again, for that fiction about friendship and trust and whatever simulacrum of love that offered, and then she'd come out with it. Why she really needed me, then, there. The worst part—for her—was that I couldn't help. A kid sergeant like myself? Like I'd be allowed to escort a civilian—a "half-breed"—into restricted areas.

Years later, with the benefit, or burden, of knowing all that would happen next, I see that she was right, of course—about everything. About what Saburo left her. About the need to leave that night. About how Anchorage was sapping her. About how she thought of me, first, as a friend, and about how she knew I'd never think that was enough.

What I want now is another chance, just one more chance to live this life over. To make the right choice back when I stepped off that train in San Diego, or all the way back, when I left my mother's womb for someone else's arms. To answer the right way when Lily asked a final time, *Tonight?*, to not hear myself say, *I can't*, to not hear her say quietly, *I know you can, or knew.*

Instead I'm just left with the memory of her drawing close a final time, and picking up my hand, my left. She held it to her mouth, I could feel her breaths, tiny and rapid. She drew her lips along the back of my hand. I leaned forward. But she was already backing away. In two paces, she was gone into the dark, and for a horrible moment, I thought she'd leapt off the rock into the rapids, but then I heard someone, something, beating through the brush.

I followed her, the sound of her, for as long as I could hear her. An hour, longer. I had the right answer for her now.

But by the time the sky had gone light again, I had nothing left to follow. No sound, no sign. The forest floor was a trackless carpet of pine needles. I stopped, looked around. Overhead, I heard the first morning planes in and out of Elmendorf Field. I was about to turn and head back the way I had come when I saw something hanging on a tree. It was a tiny mask of weathered gray wood, no bigger than my palm. The face was simple—two eyes, a nose, a mouth set in a line. A small feather dangled from the chin. I took down the mask and turned it over. Then I lifted it to my face, peered through one of the eyeholes, and saw—another feather? I lowered the mask. Sure enough, not twenty yards away. Not far away, I found another feather, and not far from that, another. They were tiny, and easy to miss, but what they led me to was not. A clearing with a giant boulder in the center like a bull's-eye.

The balloon had missed its target, though. It dangled from a tall tree nearby, explosive payload intact, the whole mess swaying and creaking with each gust of wind.

The first day, it was still possible. The hospital was just a few hours away, I was sure. I could see it plainly on the map: on the coast of the Bering Sea, just below the mouth of the Yukon. We would make it there in time, the boy would live. We'd used up most of the morphine, but I administered what was left in order to keep him comfortable, especially as we'd soon be in open water. He didn't like the needle, but he was too tired to cry.

I left most of the gear behind. I hadn't wanted to waste time packing, and thought the trip ahead would be brief. I avoided portages. I ran the throttle wide open whenever I could and tried to let all that was invisible guide me. I listened; I tried to remember how to concentrate. I prayed. But all that came to me was the roar of the motor and, occasionally, the crying and raving of the boy.

Then the clouds came, at first soft and high above us, then lower and thicker until they surrounded the boat and it was no longer clear which way to go. I looked at the map; it was useless. It showed the land and sea: we needed one for clouds.

We spent a day in those clouds, and then another. And when the mission infirmary materialized around noon that third day, I was more angry than relieved. Never finding it would have meant absolution, that I'd gone in search of something that wasn't there.

CHAPTER 15

I DID NOT SLEEP HERE LAST NIGHT—I HAD PREPARATIONS to attend to—but it seems as though I missed little. Ronnie is still unconscious.

I thought this morning, when I entered and shouted, "Good morning!" that Ronnie flinched, or raised an eyebrow, but the nurse who was already there saw nothing. I sat with him awhile, and then checked the ward for Friday's new arrivals.

I eventually returned, greeted Ronnie again—nothing—and sat. I opened my breviary and tried to read, but could not. Ronnie wasn't flinching, but I was, every time the high hum of another plane finally grew loud enough to reach my hearing. Thursday's weather had cleared, and long-delayed planes were pouring into Bethel. The bishop, or his emissaries, weren't due in until late this afternoon, but perhaps they'd decided to play it safe and catch an early flight. Perhaps they'd decided not to come at all.

Could they really take me away from all this? Kidnapping is what it would be. Murder. I can't breathe Outside. Some attic apartment in a Seattle rectory? A room, way at the end of the hall of some Gonzaga dormitory, in Spokane? No weather or shamans or wilderness to battle? I'd suffocate.

I imagine these men landing, the plane's door popping open, and them peering out. I imagine them clambering down the steps and crossing the tarmac to the terminal. Inside, they'd look around for me with false but energetic smiles. (As though I would go to meet them, even if Ronnie didn't need me at his side!) There was a pay phone there that sometimes worked; maybe they'd use it to call the church. Maybe they'd ask around. Maybe they would sit, and as the waiting area emptied, discuss what they planned to do.

I tried not to worry. I'd been gone for the night; Ronnie had gone without the sound of my voice. (But how far?) I studied him carefully, and then, after ducking into the hallway to make sure no one was around, went back to the bed and raised the sheet. I wasn't sure what I would find, whether I'd be pleased or frightened to discover that another limb had fallen prey to something as invisible as it was ravenous.

THE AIRPORT TERMINAL at Bethel today is a sturdy, modern building, where the signs are all bilingual—"EXIT/ANYARAO"—and the atmosphere is informal. The male and female restrooms ("ANARVIK") share the same bank of sinks, and those sinks are located in an alcove that's wide open to the waiting room. Look in the mirror, and you can see everyone in the waiting room looking back.

Back at Elmendorf, back in the war, the airfield terminal was even more intimate, if that's the right word. The building had but one window, and that was almost always covered with a giant chalkboard listing the day's flights.

I remember searching the chalkboard the morning after Gurley had ordered me to the post on Little Diomede. To attract as little attention as possible to my supposedly top secret mission, I was to travel as far as I could on regularly scheduled flights. That meant I had to make my way first to Nome, and then determine the most efficient and least attention-getting means—sea or air—of continuing on to Little Diomede.

I'd already missed the 0600 flight to Nome. I'd not made it out of the forest until about eight-thirty. I'd spent some time looking for Lily, time I should have spent lowering the balloon to the ground and rendering its payload safe. Instead, when I found my way back to the mysterious crash site she'd led me to, I found it ablaze. The incendiary bombs had fallen to the forest floor and ignited. The balloon itself, still trapped in the tree, had caught fire as well, and as I stood watching, the tree sloughed it off to the ground, a fiery scab. I thought the incendiaries meant it was unlikely germ weapons had been aboard—and if they had, they'd likely been incinerated.

Even so, I held my breath as much as I could as I ran for the river, expecting the fire or a belated blast to take me down before I'd made twenty yards. But twenty, fifty, one hundred yards went by, and I was still upright and running, ricocheting through the spruce down to the river. If anything exploded, the noise was lost to the rapids, which I followed back down to the trail, and then the trail into Anchorage. Instead of dissipating, the smell of smoke had only grown stronger the farther I had run. And once I was running along the city streets, I could see why—a great column of smoke now rose from the forest.

I didn't stop running until a hungover soldier, sprawled on the sidewalk, called out to me, "Didn't have enough money to pay 'er?" Then I realized I'd attract less attention on the nearly empty streets if I walked, and so I did, straight to the Starhope. Lily had to have escaped the forest before me. But the front door was locked. Lily's window was dark, and no one came to it when I called, not even Gurley.

EVEN THOUGH IT WAS almost 10 A.M. when I got to base, I had decided to follow through on Gurley's orders. To be honest, part of me wanted to escape Gurley and the growing mess—which now included a balloon crashing in our backyard, not to mention a forest fire—and part of me thought I might be better positioned to help Lily. Little Diomede might be a barren rock in the Bering Sea, but it was well out of Gurley's sight. I'd discover a way to sneak off and find Lily—and Gurley would never know.

But Father Pabich would.

"My favorite sergeant!" he said when I walked into the terminal.

"Father," I said, quietly.

Either Father Pabich didn't detect my anxiety or didn't care. He got up from the crate he was sitting on and came over to crush my hand.

"You look like twice-baked dogshit, Sergeant," he said. "I'll take that as evidence you've been working hard." I thought he might take silence as evidence I agreed, but when I didn't answer, he said, "Sergeant? Haven't seen you around, haven't seen you at Mass. Only one good excuse, and you better have it."

I took a deep breath, trying to reacclimate myself to the real world: the war, Elmendorf, Father Pabich. I tried to smile. "I've been saying the rosary?" I said.

"Goddammit, son. Learn that joke from your little Protestant friends? Just for that, let's have you say the rosary, three times, each day this week."

"Sir," I said.

"I warned you," said Father Pabich.

"Father?"

"And pray a special devotion to our Blessed Mother," he said. "Now then—"

Two other soldiers walked in, and Father Pabich smiled and shouted at them as well. I was relieved to be out of the spotlight, and maybe sad that I no longer warranted it. He brought the two men over, introduced me—two Polish boys from Chicago. Good boys. They were shipping out to the Aleutians, and he was going with them. They'd be there for six months; Father Pabich, two weeks. Laughter. Some of the soldiers out there hadn't seen a priest for a year, he said. Any longer and we might lose them to a wandering Russian Orthodox missionary. Laughter. The two Polish guys looked younger than I, and even more embarrassed. We all smiled, though, and sincerely, because this was our priest. One of us. For us. And here he was, in Alaska, the abrupt edge of the world, tending to the likes of us—when we all knew none of us had souls worth tending. We were boys, after all, about to leave our teens, and we were being sent out to kill people.

Though Father Pabich had been out to the Aleutian Chain just last month, he was going again—all the other chaplains, of every faith, had been called elsewhere. Not that anyone begged for the duty. The conditions were too harsh, the men beyond saving: those who didn't kill themselves or each other were often done in by the weather. Father Pabich had almost been stranded on Kiska during his last trip.

"I was supposed to be on Kiska for only an hour," he said, settling back. "I was spending my time on Attu, but they flew me out to Kiska, said the men would like a visit—said they had more than twelve Catholics there, and that's my rule: when you outnumber the apostles, you get a priest. So I went." He patted his pockets for a cigarette, but one of the Chicago boys leapt in with his own pack. Father Pabich removed one, winked, and pocketed the pack. "Williwaws? You know what I'm talking about? Those Aleutian storms when the rain falls up as much as it does down? I'm in a PBY—Navy's flying me—goddamn pilot is flying like he's an atheist. Like he's not going to have God to deal with if he crashes that goddamn bird into the side of goddamn Kiska. Excuse me." Puff. The other Chicago boy wanted a cigarette. He pointed to the pack in Father Pabich's pocket, but Father Pabich waved him off. "So we land. I almost drown getting to shore, but I get ashore. The pilot's said I've got an hour. Maybe forty-five minutes. Storm coming in and then nobody's taking off. So I get inside. First of all, there aren't twelve Catholics. There's six guys, tops. And one of them's a Jew. Tells me he is. *Tells* me he is. But he says they're all going to die. The island's haunted with ghosts from the Battle of Kiska, storms a-coming, wild dogs—and I don't know what. Scared. Wants to go to Mass. What am I supposed to do?" Shrug. "Like the Holy Father's gonna know." Puff. "But I've been using up precious time talking to this one. So it's on to Mass. 'Oh, no, Father,' this other one, red hair, now says to me. 'I got to go to confession. I can't receive communion if I'm not in a state of grace.' Jesus *Christ,* is what I tell him. We're all going to be in a state of death, son. But—right, what does the Bible say? This might be Jesus Himself talking to me. So I sit down, send the other boys out, start with the confession. In the name of the Father. Now—of course you don't reveal what's said under the seal of confession, but mind you, he's not saying *anything* of interest. He's been on Kiska, for Christ's sake. The world has been sinning against *him.* But he's going on and on. Talks about his Friday fast. Says he's been eating things on Friday. Like what? I say. 'Like meat, Father,' this one says. Meat! When he'd been lucky to get a goddamn ration of meat out there. No time now. It's going to be a twenty-minute Mass at this point. No Litany of the Saints—like I can afford to piss *them* off. Hurry up, lad, I tell him. What other sins you got? Let's go. You ate meat, now what else, what else?"

Father Pabich leaned back, took a long drag, grinned ear to ear. I remember thinking, here's a man about to risk his life flying into the world's worst weather, and he couldn't be happier if he were the pope himself.

"You know what he says?" Father Pabich leaned forward, and then bellowed, " 'PEAS'! Oh, sweet Jesus, 'What else, son?' *'Peas, Father.'* Oh my Lord." We laughed. Everyone in the terminal laughed, but no one laughed harder than Father Pabich, who roared until he coughed and teared up and accidentally lit a small fire when his cigarette fell from his fingers into a nearby wastebasket.

I suppose that's how Gurley was able to enter without anyone noticing.

I was helping the Polish guys put out the fire when I heard my name. I straightened up, but didn't turn around—I wasn't nearly ready. They called Father Pabich's plane. He picked up his bags, smiled, and punched me the best he could with his elbow. "Be a good boy, now," he said. "Fight us a good war." I'd like to say that I ran after him, told him an elbow wasn't good enough, that I wanted to shake his hand before we parted, receive his blessing, but I didn't. Gurley was already coming toward me then, so I blame him, not the Japanese soldier who, a month or so later, overran Father Pabich's position as he was giving last rites to a Marine on Okinawa. The Japanese soldier bayonetted them both.

"Sergeant," Gurley said, grinning for some reason. "I greet you with the very best of news." I studied the exits, decided which would be easier to reach. But I didn't move.

First, Gurley said, he was not going to charge me for disobeying orders—though I had clearly done so since I was still in the terminal instead of on a flight to Little Diomede. But the better news was that he no longer wanted me to go. He had found a far more important and interesting task, much closer at hand. He couldn't tell me this in the terminal, however, and so ushered me outside, hand at my elbow.

"Sir," I said, "I thought we agreed. I thought it was clear that I should go. That this would be best."

"Would have *been* best, Sergeant," Gurley said. "But things have changed. This is what happens in war. We must let bygones be bygones, we must put our differences aside, and we must—"

"Sir," I said. "Last night, the office—the paper?"

Gurley's theatrical glee momentarily waned. "Yes, Sergeant?" he said. "And who have you told about that?" I looked away. "No one, I take it?" He waited until I met his gaze. He looked around to see if anyone was close to us, and then threw an arm around my shoulders, hissing into my ear as we walked. "You may think your captain mad, but what have you done about it? Nothing at all, it would seem."

"Maybe I will do something," I said. "Sir."

He hustled me farther from the building before he spoke again. "Maybe you will, Sergeant. But you haven't yet, and I daresay you won't. Because your case is thin, because as scared as you are, you're even more curious, and because..." He let the word hang there while he looked at me, as though waiting for me to finish the sentence. But I couldn't, so he did, speaking slowly and evenly: "...you know that *lives,* the lives of certain people, depend on the actions you take." Did I know whom he was referring to? This is what his gaze now asked. I lowered my own eyes; this was my answer.

"Good," he said, smiling once more. We started to walk. "I admit, we have had our difficulties. But I promise, dear Sergeant, that all that will be forgotten in the excitement of the days ahead." He darted a quick look behind us, and then replaced his arm around my shoulders. "What did those fools say up at Ladd? Five days? We'd wait five days before searching the tundra for signs of sabotage, or saboteurs?"

I nodded. "Three now, I suppose."

"Three days," Gurley said. "Seventy-two hours to beat that major, that galoot Swift, and the rest of the Army to the waning war's greatest prize."

"Sir," I started.

"Belk," Gurley said, but I persisted.

"Sir, the major was right. They probably never got to launch their balloon. And even if they did, they probably did nothing more than make some moose sick. Maybe some mice, or ravens. And that's assuming the infected fleas were able to fight their way through the tundra winds long enough to—"

Gurley put one hand to his lips, another lightly to my chest, and shut his eyes. "Sergeant Belk," he said, and then opened his eyes. "We are no longer chasing fleas. Your captain's snare may have finally caught a *spy.*"

GURLEY CONTINUED speaking, with very few interruptions, for the next two hours. At least, I remember it that way. I remember him meeting me at the terminal late that morning, and I remember him dismissing me from the Quonset hut that afternoon, and I remember him talking the entire time.

I don't remember much of what he said, however. Because I learned one important piece of information early on, and after that, found it hard to focus on much of anything else he said.

Lily had told him about Saburo.

Not much, not everything, but enough. Enough to convince Gurley to venture out into the tundra in search of Saburo, and enough to insist Lily accompany him as a guide. I would come along, too, of course—one could never imagine what sort of menial or distasteful tasks might arise. In fact, Gurley wanted me to precede him and Lily to Bethel. He needed a bit of extra time to finagle Lily's passage, but I could make the most of the delay by securing supplies in Bethel and "doing a bit of sleuthing" around town to see if I could come up with any information about Saburo on my own. Gurley and Lily would follow in a day or two. Depending on the weather—and Lily—we would disappear into the bush shortly thereafter.

Replaying these memories, it seems unmistakable now to me how completely mad he was. And I don't mean madness like the kind that doctors like to cure nowadays with dollops of prettily colored pills. I mean old-fashioned, Edgar Allan Poe–type madness, incurable but for a gun placed at the temple. The words fast and steady, the volume rising and falling, the eyes darting this way and that.

Yes, that's precisely how it looks now—insanity—but to have seen it through my eyes then, you would never have thought him so sane. Missing were the theatrics, the powder-keg rage—that way he had of flushing red and trembling like he was his own private earthquake, every extremity poised to fly off in pursuit of the leg that was already gone. In its place was this calm, constant, reasoned stream of language, punctuated every so often with words that almost set me to trembling: *Lily, Saburo, Lily.*

She had told Gurley about Saburo. She had told him his name. She had told him that he was Japanese, a soldier, a spy. She had told him almost everything that she had told me, except—and I listened carefully—that they were lovers.

The longer he went without mentioning this most important (only to me?) fact, the more rattled I became. How could she not have told him? Saburo: her first love, that golden summer, those perfect hands? As Gurley rambled on, however, I had time to think about it, and came to realize that she had every reason to lie to him. Her one desire was to make it out into the bush in search of—well, I'd never let her spell it out that night, but I knew she was searching for Saburo's body. But she couldn't get to Bethel without a military escort—that's why she had wanted me to come. I'd failed her, so she'd gone to Gurley. Riskier, but also better—he would have access to better resources. He could operate with more autonomy. He was an officer, after all, unlike me. He was her lover.

But I got to Lily first that afternoon. I'm sure Gurley expected me to go directly to the airfield without even stopping at my barracks, but instead, I went directly downtown, where I found Lily, peering out her window, as if she was expecting me, or someone. She smiled and gave me a little wave. I ran up to the second floor, a new question popping up on each stair—*Did we really see the northern lights? Did I really see a balloon? Did we really run into the forest, the two of us, together, last night?*—but when I reached her, what came out first was Gurley's decision to go to Bethel.

She looked both delighted and scared. "We're going to go?" she asked. "You're sure? Me, too? He said all of us?"

"He didn't tell you? It seemed like things were pretty well decided."

"Last night—" Lily began, "or I guess it was this morning, after I made it back into town, I came back down here, I found him wandering the street."

"Was he angry?" I asked. "He must have asked why you ran. Did he see me? I was sure he saw me."

"What did he tell you?" Lily asked carefully.

"About last night?" I said. "Nothing. Just that you'd had this conversation." I waited for her to augment this, but she didn't, so I went on. "About a 'spy.'" I paused again. "Lily, what were you thinking?

Look what's happened—he's carting us all off to the bush, and God knows what he'll do there, where he won't have to worry about anyone other than us witnessing him completely cracking up. He's dangerous, Lily. He's ready to kill. Starting with me."

Lily went to the window and checked the street. "That's why I told him," she said, and then turned to me. "To spare you."

LILY'S ACCOUNT OF the early morning hours differed from Gurley's. Gurley hadn't mentioned to me that he'd seen Lily or anyone else on the misty streets; and he'd heavily edited his conversation with Lily. He left out, for example, what Lily said was the first thing he'd asked her—*Was that you and Louis I saw in the street?*—and he'd left out her reply.

"Yes, it was me," she told him. "But not Louis. You've scared him half to death. I'll be lucky if I ever see him again."

"I'll be luckier if you don't," Gurley had said. I wondered how he'd looked when he'd said that. With me, it would have been behind a sneer, or preceding a fist. But it had to be different with her.

"He's just a boy," she told him, and didn't even smile at me as she repeated the line now.

"Well," Gurley said. Lily said he kept looking around, like I might still be lurking in the shadows. "Who was it, then? It *was* someone. It was someone. I know I saw someone with you. A man. Not a 'customer'? I thought we had an agreement. I thought I'd taken care of that for you. You should have enough now, enough to get by without—God, Lily, we've talked about this. You know what I've said, what I'm planning for you, for us—"

"Not a customer," Lily said. She told me now that she had been stalling, frantically trying to come up with a plausible scenario. He'd been watching her grow upset, and suddenly decided he knew what had happened.

"No, Lily—you—you were attacked," Gurley said, grabbing her

arm. "My God. My God: he hurt you. And me, limping along after you, your helpless defender. Did he—did he—my God, Lily, did he—rape—?"

Lily said she started crying: she could see no way out. He'd taken over her story—now rape was involved; should she admit to that, peg it on some random thug? One of those brawling sailors, unexpectedly returned? Lost and distraught, she blurted out—because it was true—"He was a friend."

She gasped, destroyed now because she'd thought she'd revealed once and for all that it was me.

But I was apparently gone from Gurley's mind, and he pressed in on this new quarry: "*Was*'?" he asked. "Who was he? A friend? Why would you cry if it was a friend? What kind of friend is that?"

And that was all Lily needed. Because when he asked the question, the obvious answer, the real answer, came to mind, immediately. What friend had she cried over, again and again?

Saburo.

She started telling Gurley before she'd even planned it all out, but the longer she talked, and the more fascinated she saw him become, the more she realized how it could all work, how well it could work. Saburo was the man who'd accosted her in the street, not Louis. Saburo was the reason she'd run from Gurley, not to him: she told Gurley that she couldn't admit, not then, that she knew—that, long before she'd met Gurley, she'd befriended—a Japanese soldier, a spy.

And there it was: Saburo was the reason Gurley needed to take her to Bethel. Saburo had run off after her, into the dark, had begged her to leave with him, that night, told her he was going back to Japan, that he would take her with him, if only she would come, right then. "Someone sympathetic to the cause" had a floatplane waiting, would fly them west, as far west as he could. Then there would be a ship, or a submarine...

I was awestruck. First, by the facility of Lily's storytelling, and second, by the slow realization that this story might have been, must have been, at one time, true. There had never been a midnight race through Anchorage with Saburo, but there had been promises of an airplane, of a ship, of a home across the ocean.

"More than a friend" is how Gurley answered all this, both mollified and roused, and Lily nodded, as though he had broken her, and because he had.

"More than a friend," Lily repeated to Gurley. "That's what he thought," she said, and then fell to Gurley's chest. She didn't have to say it: *the spy asked and I did not go.* "I don't know what he thinks now," she told Gurley then.

"I do," I told Lily now.

IT DID NOT LOOK LIKE its nickname—"Paris of the Tundra"—not from the air, not from the river, which I had to cross to get from the airfield to the town, not from my walk up its main street, nor the walk I took back down that same street, having quickly run out of road. But Bethel must have looked like Paris to the communities that dotted the tundra around it. If a clock hand began its circumnavigation of Alaska at Anchorage—about five o'clock—it would find little to interrupt its sweep west and then north to Nome, at nine o'clock. Little, except Bethel.

Bethel sits at around seven or eight on that clock face, smack on the banks of the Kuskokwim River. The Kuskokwim shares the duty of draining western Alaska with the Yukon. The two rivers conspire each summer to turn the tundra into a vast delta so soggy and remote that, even as tourism booms elsewhere in Alaska today, it sometimes seems there are fewer humans in this corner of the continent now than there were during the war.

When I first arrived in Bethel, however, it wasn't bustling, even then. There weren't many people around, almost no cars, just a few jeeps. I later learned that vehicles were something of an extravagance—you couldn't drive *to* Bethel from anywhere; you could only drive around in

Bethel, or, when the weather was right, around the wide unbroken tundra that surrounded the town. In the winter, you could drive down the frozen river when they plowed it. In Anchorage or Fairbanks, if you ever get a hankering and the road's open, you can drive right out of Alaska, into Canada, and hell, on to Miami. But in Bethel, you always have to turn around eventually and come back.

The flight from Anchorage had lasted long enough for me to work out a plan, or as I think of it now, a kind of essential theology. Gurley represented evil, a powerful, but not unbeatable, foe. Lily was Eve, of course. Lovely, and susceptible. Did that make me Adam, or did Saburo have more claim to that title? Maybe I was Adam after he'd eaten the apple. Maybe I was the snake.

DEALING WITH THE LOCAL military authorities was easier than I had expected. The same frenzied culture of secrecy permeated Bethel as it did Anchorage; the soldiers I met at Bethel's Todd Field were so interested in keeping their mission a secret that they were scarcely interested in mine.

But Lily had kept another secret from just about everyone, as I was soon to discover.

I was standing on the long, low porch in front of the optimistically named Bethel Emporium of Everything, sleuthing. After a short walk around town, I'd been unable to find Lily's old store, Sam's Universal Supply, and was starting to wonder if she'd told me the truth—about that, or about anything.

Four men were on the porch. One heavyset white fellow, standing, and three men I took to be Yup'ik, all sitting, all watching the white man like they were waiting for him to leave.

"Jap Sam, sure," the white man said. "Good fella," he said. "Never went there much, but heard he was a good fella." He looked to the others on the porch, and so did I. "Mind you, the man had products of *inferior* quality."

"Good prices," one of the Yup'ik men said to the empty street. "Good man," another said.

"'Good prices,'" the white man repeated. "Not if you're buying junk. Mind you, that's what I thought at first, when I saw them come up in the jeep and take him off: I thought, there you go, he's getting *arrested* for selling *inferior* products. But no, wasn't that at all." He looked again at the Yup'ik men, all of whom stared at me.

"Where'd you take him?" one of the Yup'ik men said.

"I don't know," I tried, taking a moment to figure out what he was asking. "Some soldiers took him?" My questioner turned away.

"Now, boys," the white man said. "Not every soldier knows every other soldier. See here, he's not from that kind of a unit." Instead of pointing to my bomb disposal insignia, he pointed to my sergeant's stripes. "No, the government took Jap Sam down to California, I hear, for his capital-S *safety*. Mind you, he was Japanese, and I'm sure we're all safer, too, knowing all them Japanese are safe in that camp."

"No one's never heard from Sam," one of the Yup'ik men said. "Never since."

"Mind you, boys," the white man said. "There's a war on." He looked out into the street. "Good day, Captain," the man said to me, and left.

I stood there a minute, trying to decide what to do next, growing tense under the collective stare of the men. "What you want Jap Sam for, anyway?" said the one who'd spoken up earlier.

"Met a friend of his down in Anchorage," I said.

"Jap friend?" the man said.

"No," I said. "She's Yup'ik." Glances were exchanged; I must have gotten the pronunciation close. "Well, Yup'ik and Russian."

"Lily!" one of the other guys said with a shout and smile. Suddenly, they were all talking. "How's our Lily?" "How's that girl?" "She still tall and pretty as anything?" Then one guy gushed, "Wasn't there a kid? How's he doin'?" and the other two frowned and fell silent.

No one said anything for a moment, and if you'd asked me, in that very instant, if I'd ever be able to speak again, I'm not sure if I'd have said yes. I'd been asked to believe a lot of things over the course of the war—that bombs could float through the air for thousands of miles, that teenagers could be given guns after a few weeks of training and be called soldiers, that the frozen-solid emptiness of Alaska was of strategic importance—but now I was being asked to believe that Lily had once been pregnant, had had a child.

The Yup'ik man who'd first questioned me looked up. "You're going to want to see Auntie Bella," he said. "She's going to want to know about Lily, what she's doing and all." He gave me directions, and when he finished speaking, it was clear I was to leave, immediately, without asking another thing.

BELLA: THAT NAME PROMISED someone huge, and round, and, I assumed, Yup'ik. But Bella was as thin and worn and white as the wooden posts that held up the porch outside her small boardinghouse.

Before I could say anything, she told me she had no vacancies, but when I told her I had news of Lily, she reluctantly let me in. Bella asked a lot of questions, mostly about Lily's health. Whenever I tried to ask a question, she interrupted with another one, asking questions about me when she'd run out of ones about Lily.

A noise outside distracted her and I jumped in. "One of the men I met, he said something about a kid—Lily has a child? Here?"

Bella gave me a hard look. "If she didn't tell you, don't imagine she wanted you to know," Bella said, and we sat in silence for a bit.

Finally, Bella spoke up. "Wasn't no *kid*," she said. We sat a while longer. "I'm thinking about telling you a story," she said. "But if I do, it's only because I want you to feel bad for having asked."

"I already do," I said. She snorted, and then got up and left the room. When she returned, she had a single, steaming mug of something, which she put on the table. After a moment, she picked it up and took a sip.

"I'm down to the one decent mug these days," she said. "So I don't mind if I do." Another sip. "Now, from all that you said, you sound like you're a friend."

"I am," I said.

"Boyfriend?" she asked, and I was so taken aback, I said nothing.

"Didn't think so," she said, and shifted in her chair. "Well, you'll still feel bad," she said. "But you'll probably also want to help her. And that's reason enough, I suppose." She put the mug back down. "Feel free," she said, nodding to it. But once she started talking, I couldn't move, and lost myself to the story.

LILY HAD RETURNED from her summer trip alone. People took some notice, but not much; few had seen her leave on her trip weeks back with Saburo, and in the meantime, the person who probably knew the most about Saburo, Sam, had been taken off to California, interned at Tule Lake.

And as the months passed, few people even noticed Lily had returned from her summer pregnant. Winter clothing concealed her secret from most everyone, except Bella, of course, who'd given Lily a room in the back.

Bella said you'd never seen a woman so happy who had so little reason to be. Here Lily was, alone, and with child. Sam, the man who'd taken care of her for so long in Bethel, had been hauled away and imprisoned. Saburo, the man she'd loved, had vanished—Lily wouldn't say where or how, but Bella assumed Saburo was attempting to return to Japan.

"Lily says he's dead," I blurted out.

"Dead," Bella said. "Not sure how she would know, but—then, I'm not sure how she knows half of what she does. Or how she could be so fool stupid, too." Bella counted off the degrees of foolishness on her fingers: no money, no family, no husband.

"But she had you," I said, and Bella nodded, puckered her lips.

"What we needed, in the end, was a doctor," Bella said. Bethel shared its doctor with several towns up and down the Kuskokwim. One evening, Lily told Bella that dinner hadn't gone down well; a few hours later, Bella said, it was clear it wasn't dinner but the baby who was making problems.

"Now here we were, seven months in, I'd say, though she never knew when exactly she got in the family way, of course. Or wouldn't tell." Bella exhaled. "And no doctor—he's two villages up, and bad weather's keeping him there. But this baby—this baby is *coming*. I got some of the other aunties in town over here double-quick, but all of us just knew wasn't going to be nothing we could do once that child come out."

Bella sent word over to the airfield, to see if their doctor was around. He was, the report came back, but he couldn't work on civilians. "Couldn't work on Eskimos is what they meant," said Bella. "Couldn't then, couldn't now. Couldn't or wouldn't? Well, you tell me, soldier boy, why we got problems with the soldiers in this town, drunk or sober?"

Lily read the panic in the eyes all around her, and grew panicked herself. She knew as well as they did that the baby was coming. She sent them all away and then called them all back in; she screamed for Saburo, she screamed for her mother. And then, twelve hours after dinner, two months too early, she delivered. A baby boy. Perfect in every way, but one: he was dead.

"Not a mark on that child," Bella said. "Just the biggest head of black, black hair you've ever seen." It looked like Bella was crying, but I couldn't be sure; the light was dim and nothing else had changed in her face or voice. "Tiny. Tiny, tiny thing. And here's where we disagree, the other women and me. I think—I know—that little boy took a breath, a single breath"—she gave a little gasp—"and that was all. Lily said so, too." She reached for her mug and saw there was nothing in it. "No matter. Nothing any of us could do but sit there and cry with her a spell."

But the hardest part came later, Bella said. Lily wouldn't give the baby up. The ladies let Lily have the day with the child, but when they came for him that night, she wouldn't move. "Saburo has to see him," Lily said, though she wouldn't answer any questions about where Saburo was or how he would know what had happened.

"She wasn't making a whole lot of sense," Bella said. "Said we needed to send for help—and I'm thinking, 'A doctor? It's too late for a doctor'—and she's saying no, someone much better, much smarter than that." Bella stopped. "Well. If this Saburo had been so smart, I don't think she would have found herself in this predicament in the first place. Course, I didn't tell her *that.*"

Bella looked in her mug once more. "Imagine they're expecting you back about now," she said, but she didn't make a move herself.

"What happened?" I asked.

"Baby died," Bella said. "Was dead. Told you that."

"But who did you—"

"Aw," Bella said, "this part of the story ain't worth the telling. What you might call a medicine man, a shaman: that's what she wanted. Hell of a bad idea, turns out. Oh, we got this man—young man— down visiting from Lower Kalskag. He comes in—drunk as a fart— I'm ready to turn him out. But Lily, she was beyond hollering by then, just screeching, and the fact is, none of the other aunties wanted to be in there. I didn't want to be in there. I don't think this shaman much did, either. But we left, he went in, and—" Bella thought about this for a moment, and then drew herself up before going on. "The next morning, it's just Lily lying there, wrecked, like something'd exploded. And she won't talk, but she don't have to. No baby. No shaman. No father. She's in there all alone."

CHAPTER 16

WHEN I GOT BACK TO TODD FIELD, THERE WAS A MESSAGE waiting from Gurley. They'd arrive late that afternoon. Continue my preparations. Tag along on a reconnaissance flight, get a better idea of the terrain.

I'd assumed Lily had all the knowledge of the "terrain" that we would need, but with all the other supplies for our expedition secured, I had nothing else to do, and so hopped on a flight the next morning.

To my surprise, the crew hardly protested at my joining them—the flights were so boring, they said, they'd love someone like me along. When I asked what that meant, I was greeted with some mumbles and laughs, and I realized they knew about Shuyak and the infamous sergeant who jumped out of planes.

I disappointed them. I got up to look out the window once we were in flight, but I didn't jump. And the landscape disappointed me. Or rather, shocked me. It was the first time in my life that I have ever seen that much nothing. No balloons. No bombs. No soldiers. No smoke, no villages, no people, not even animals, at least animals visible from the air. And you couldn't see fleas from this high up.

We flew for hours over the same terrain—grasses, a clump of scrub alder here and there, mountains in the distance, and everywhere, water puddling and flooding, curling and spilling from one spot to another via waterways fat or thin. If the angle was wrong, or right, the water's surface would catch fire with the reflection of the sun, and if you didn't look away in time, that burst of sun would stay with you, even after you'd blinked. It glowed behind your eyelids, and then reappeared in some other portion of the sky—sometimes looking briefly like a balloon, if that's what you were looking for, or a second sun, which, if you thought about it (and we didn't), was no less impossible to believe.

WHAT RONNIE HAS always found difficult to believe is that Alaska's mosquitoes bother him more than me. Maybe it was the alcohol, maybe it was the departure of his *tuunraq,* but Ronnie has always been impotent when it comes to Alaska's unofficial state bird. Mosquitoes have driven him crazy every summer, especially during what became our annual expedition into the delta. As soon as we were clear of the city limits, the mosquitoes would descend on Ronnie, masses of them, until any remaining patch of exposed skin bore at least one or two drops of blood. Honestly, they never found as much interest in me, a fact I attributed to the primacy of the Roman Catholic Church's path to salvation, and one that Ronnie attributed to my love of sour-cream-and-onion potato chips.

We'd go for a month or more. Originally, the trips were designed to get me out and around to some of the smaller villages and seasonal camps that would emerge each summer over the delta. But in recent years, Ronnie and I had done a kind of joint revival wherever we stop; I said Mass in the morning, he told stories and attended to shamanic requests at night.

Our pairing was both fun and funny, and surprisingly collegial. Even before he'd gotten wind of what we were up to at the hospice, my bishop frowned on such professional camaraderie. He'd liked things better, it seemed, when Ronnie had been more serious about trying to do me in. Try to pin my boss down on the issue, and the good bishop would always laugh and say, "Now, I'm not about to tell you we need to go back to the days when missionaries outlawed dancing and we shipped the kids off to boarding school, but—"

"Then don't," I'd say, and things between the bishop and me would be set for another six months or so.

I see now, of course, how it was all adding up.

One thing I never told anyone was how I liked the traveling part of the trips best. Once we'd *arrived* somewhere, I was Father Louis, and in demand for a steady stream of confessions, baptisms, Masses, a calming word solicited here, a scolding one requested there. But *traveling* from one spot to another—in a beat-up old skiff that Ronnie had helped me find and repair—I was no one again, just a man out enjoying the widest skies on earth.

Ronnie stayed up most nights. More often than not, I did, too. Because whatever skills Ronnie lacked as a shaman, he more than had as an amateur astronomer, or meteorologist, or skywatcher. It wasn't that he knew scientific names, or that he had a talent for predicting the weather (although he was fairly good). He simply had a way of using the sky as a canvas at night, using it as a means of telling a story. He'd analyze the way the winds were pushing a cloud, point out how the sun this far north was always fighting to keep from sinking below the horizon. In time I learned that you could get at least half the story from watching his hands alone, the way they moved a cloud or poked a hole in the blue and let a star shine down.

It sounds funny, I know, to be so fascinated with another man, let alone his hands, but it has something to do with being a priest. No, not in *that* sense, thank you, but more of a professional interest. A good priest is sensitive to his hands the way a pianist might be to his. They are essential to his work—praying, celebrating the sacrifice of the Mass, offering communion, the sign of peace. It's well known, at least among missionaries, certainly among Jesuits, how Isaac Jogues, Jesuit missionary to Canada in the 1600s, had to later receive special dispensation from the Vatican to say Mass. His hands had been mutilated during his tenure in North America, fingers frozen or eaten, and without the pope's express permission, he would have been considered unfit to serve at the altar. (Jogues's later plea to return to Canada was reluctantly granted, but his arrival coincided with sickness and blight. The Mohawks took this as evidence of sorcery and cut off his head.)

I think the real reason I admired Ronnie, or those hands of his, was that he clearly had never used his hands the way I had mine. He was a drunk, a failure, a grifter, but the earth was no worse for his being on it. If Saint Isaac Jogues had ever descended from the sky during one of those trips in the bush, he would have reached for Ronnie's hand first, and Ronnie would have taken it, whatever condition Saint Isaac's hand was in, and shook it firmly. Ronnie had a grudge against missionaries but admired men who, like him, had survived.

More to the point, if Jogues ever dropped down, Ronnie would have been the first to see him. Ronnie was always looking up, especially in summer, especially out in the delta. He had a theory that if you sat in one spot long enough, stared at the sky carefully and remembered all you'd seen, you would be the wisest man in the world. All the knowledge of the world was contained in the skies, he said. He was going to write it all down one day, he swore, a book of *amirlut,* an atlas of clouds, and it would sell better than any bible. I asked him how he'd ever manage to chart on paper something that was always changing. He shook his head at my stupidity. "Not a map of where things are now," he said. "No: where they will be."

I WONDER IF RONNIE'S right, though. That staring at the sky will give you a better sense of what's to come. After the morning reconnaissance flight, for example, I was back out at Todd Field, searching the skies for some sign of the C-47 Gurley said he'd be on. And when

I finally caught sight of one, I followed it all the way down to the ground, half thinking that, if I concentrated hard enough, I'd be able to see if Lily was inside.

But Gurley could have had Saint Isaac or Saint Nicholas aboard; staring revealed nothing. It wasn't until I saw them emerge that I knew.

They'd taxied to a stop some distance from the terminal, and a pair of jeeps raced out to meet them. I couldn't make out faces, but the first man at the opened door was certainly Gurley, whose preening I could have spotted from the moon.

And the second person: no hat, no uniform. Just long black hair, black trousers, and a knee-length, Native-style shirtdress I've since learned is called a *kuspuk*. Though I could see well enough that I saw her turn to face my direction briefly before continuing down the stairs, I could not see her features. I couldn't be sure, but I was. Military men are trained, after all, to recognize the silhouettes of aircraft and ships, friendly and foreign. And Lily had trained me to believe in what I knew, what I knew because I was certain of it, not because I had evidence.

So it was Lily. Gurley hadn't sent me to Bethel just to get rid of me; the three of us really were going to journey into the bush. But then something happened that shook my faith a bit. Gurley and Lily exchanged words, it seemed, and then Gurley stepped back. The MPs took Lily by both arms, placed her in the jeep, and sped off toward some buildings at the other end of the field.

Gurley watched them go, then turned and began to walk toward me.

GURLEY HAD A NEW name for Lily: Sacagawea. We were discussing their arrival in an office he'd commandeered. I interrupted to ask him where she was. He said she'd been taken to Todd Field's "VIP quarters," and then pressed on with his monologue.

"I introduced her this way, as 'our very own Miss Sacagawea,' thinking that a rather clever shorthand introduction—to wit, our Native

companion and guide—when, to my slowly building horror and delight, I realized that the good men of this forgotten outpost were assuming that that was her actual *name*. Sacagawea. Tell me, Sergeant, of
the many subjects no longer taught in school—is American history
among them?"

Gurley seemed hurt when I did not reply.

His eyes were sunken and dark and he looked even more skeletal
than usual. His hands were covered with fine scratches, as though his
Franklin bouts had devolved to his fighting stray cats. But then I remembered the wall map, the pushpins, and the trails he'd trace across
his skin.

"Dear Sergeant," he said. "You're rather glum. This is a lonely outpost, and I imagine quiet duty, but look here: you have been given a re-
prieve, and your friends have come to join you. Where flees your
smile? Think of what lies ahead: to catch a *spy*."

For a moment, my mind had seized on *fleas*. I'd been out of Gurley's
company for so long, I'd lost some of my ear for his strange language.
As a result, it took an extra beat for the words to come out of my
already-open mouth. "Sir, I'm not sure that—"

"Splendid, dear Belk. You are still among the living. You are sentient
and curious and apparently sober. And so you have your questions.
But more important, do you have my spy? Or will we, in fact, have to
set out after him?" The words sped from his mouth, faster and faster.
He smiled, as if he noticed this, too, and thought it delightful. "Forgive
my eager possessiveness: but yes, before we speak of the devil we
know—fair Sacagawea, dear Lily—let us speak of the devil we don't.
Mmm?"

Mmm. I told Gurley about my wandering around town. I told him
about the Emporium of Everything, and about Jap Sam. Maybe Lily
wasn't worried if Gurley didn't find anything—anyone—but I was. So
I tried to describe the now-interned Sam in such a way that Gurley
might take *him* for our missing quarry. That would mean we could just
pack up and leave Bethel—ruining Gurley's fun and Lily's quest, but

giving us all, I thought, a better chance of finishing out the war alive. You didn't need Lily's kind of magic to sense the evil that was looming. Or maybe you did, and that magic had attached itself to me: here in Bethel, far from the numbing, civilizing influences of Anchorage, the spiritual world hummed that much closer to everyone.

Gurley wasn't the least bit interested in Jap Sam. He wanted Saburo. Lily's Saburo. The enemy's Saburo. *His* Saburo.

"No sign of him, sir," I said. "I didn't go house to house, of course. But you'd think—in a town this small—he'd attract attention, too much attention to hide." I made another attempt to derail the search. "If you want to know what I think, sir—"

"Always a dangerous preface, Sergeant."

"Yes, sir. But I think he died. I think he's dead. Captured, and we don't know about it, maybe, but I bet he"—I tried to call on a little magic for inspiration—"drowned. There's a lot of water around here," I added, not hearing how foolish that sounded until I saw Gurley's face.

"There is *that*," Gurley said. "I assume you're joking?" he added, suddenly brusque. He patted his pockets for cigarettes that weren't there, and stood. "Perhaps you forgot we *saw* him. Lily and I, both. In the mist. In Anchorage. Perhaps you—" He started to pace. "I'm afraid I—I'm afraid I didn't tell you everything about the other night, about what Lily told me." He was scanning the room as he spoke, not looking at me. If he had, he would have seen me turning red with alarm: What now? "She swore me to secrecy," he said, talking more to himself now. "And what could I say? I shouldn't tell you, but I will, because it's relevant to what we have to do. To our mission. To our *quest*. But I tell you this in the strictest of confidence because—because—no woman, no girl, no girl even with a past as—as—weathered as Lily's deserved to have happen to her what happened—Louis!" He spun on me, with such force I almost burst out, *I'm sorry, I know I shouldn't have gone to see her!* He knew! He had to; he was just toying with me, but before I could speak he said something even more bizarre: "He *raped* her, Belk. The filthy, yellow—when we find him, Belk, no quarter. Lily. Lily."

My heart was still pounding at the news he'd just delivered, and it was a moment or two before I was able to remind myself that he'd made this up—that the shadowy figure in the mist with Lily had only been me, that Saburo's presence had been Lily's invention, just as this rape was now Gurley's. But was it? Had she told him something else? Had Saburo been there, in the forest, farther on, in the dark, Lily running toward him, his having just arrived by balloon? No: Lily had lied to Gurley. She'd told the truth to me. She always did. But—maybe— just not—Lily, what about the baby? Why hadn't you ever told me—

"So it was wrong to grow attached," Gurley said, his eyes full of tears, but not full enough to cry. I wondered now if it mattered whether Gurley had invented the rape; he clearly believed there had been one, just as Lily believed there had been a Saburo. He wiped his nose with the heel of his hand, and then held his face for a moment. "A ring. There was a ring, Belk."

"There was," I said, automatically.

"He was always there," he said. "Even before . . . this. I knew him before she told me of him, I could see him, sense him, somewhere back behind her eyes, whenever she and I kissed. Made love." He sat in his chair, somewhat calmer now, and found a handkerchief, which he un- folded and then twisted between his hands. "I could never have all of her. I knew she wanted me to have as much as I would, but some- where, back in there, deep inside her, this fiend held on—it's like he holds some piece of her *soul.* Holds it so tight that he is able to pull her all the way out here."

I'm right here, sir: I wanted Gurley to look up, see me. I wanted to tell Gurley that *I* was this other person, but more than that, I wanted it to be true.

But when he did look up, all he saw was Saburo. "We have, what? Two days now, less maybe, before that major in Fairbanks sends his dogs out across the tundra in search of plague or spies. I've said I wanted to find the prize before him, and I do. But the reason is not so much for glory but revenge. If the major catches him, this spy becomes a prisoner of war, a resource. If I catch him—and we will, whether it takes forty hours or months—I will finish it. I will find him, remove him, and release Lily, to me."

And what would happen when we didn't find him? Lily said he was gone. But Gurley was determined to find him—he'd have to find, and kill, someone. Lily hadn't thought through this part of her plan. But then, it hadn't really been a plan.

"Sir," I said, making one last attempt. "I'm just not sure we will find anyone. It's more than a needle in a haystack, sir, it's—"

"It's a needle in a haystack for the major," said Gurley. "But we have Lily." He smiled. "We have you." He rose.

"I'm just not sure, sir, what we'll find. What if he's dead?"

The color slowly returned to Gurley's cheeks. It was his fury rising in him, but in a way, it was a relief to witness—I'd had plenty of experience dealing with Gurley furious, and could steel myself against it. I'd been frightened, on the other hand, to find myself vulnerable to feeling sympathy when faced with Gurley despondent and broken-hearted.

That danger had passed.

He walked toward me, closer and closer, until he'd backed me up half across the room. "You wish him dead. Fair enough. So do I. But you wish him dead because you wish to be done with this mission, this war, me. You are scared, Sergeant. Both understandable and unattractive." And closer. "This man is a *spy,*" Gurley continued. "A spy for the enemy. The enemy whose one interest is slaughter. Have you heard what's happening in the South Pacific, Sergeant? Of the bodies of men and women, men like you, missing eyes and hands and whatever they had between their legs, stuffed into their *mouths*?" Gurley's mouth was now quite close to mine. "This—Saburo—*raped* a woman that I love, that I hope to spend the rest of a very, very long life caring for. If you need more reasons, God knows they're offering us plenty—from fires to plague to who knows what next—go ahead and do this for your country. But you know what? Our country's got more than ten million in uniform fighting for it." He stared at me hard. "Lily's only got me."

I'M NOT SURE IF it was a product of our conversation or his simmering madness or his fear of the major on our heels, but two minutes after he'd left, he returned and declared that we would leave at midnight. We may not have agreed on much about Saburo, but he didn't think Saburo was hiding in town, either. I thought Gurley would sneak off to Lily's "VIP quarters" before our departure, but he had me walk him down to the riverbank, doling out additional instructions all the while. He confirmed the time with me, and then I watched him hire a boat to take him across the Kuskokwim to town, in search of a drink or worse.

I figured I had at least an hour, maybe more.

I walked quickly back to the headquarters building, in search of Lily. When I asked the duty officer about her whereabouts, he gave me a blank look. He was putting on a front, of course; Lily had to be the only woman on the base—perhaps the only woman on the base in six months or more. Finally, he leaned back and said, "Oh, you mean the *prisoner.*"

Now it was my turn to put on a front, and mask my alarm with a knowing nod. The prisoner. The man said he'd been left instructions that she was not to be disturbed, but I countered that I was under orders from Gurley, and the man accepted my bluff. Gurley had obviously made his usual terrifying impression.

They didn't have cells on the base, so they had put Lily in a signal shed by the airfield with a guard stationed out front "for her protection." When I entered and the guard closed the door behind me, Lily was sitting perfectly still in the middle of the room, on the only thing in the room, a chair.

Neither of us said anything; we just looked at each other. I'm not sure what my face looked like, but Lily kept hers completely blank. I could have been Gurley, I could have been Tojo, I could have been a six-foot raven. She stared.

I looked at her hands; they were cuffed. What had Gurley done?

I knelt beside her and tried to take one hand of hers in mine, but she moved away. "I'm okay," she said.

"Lily, I'm so sorry," I said. "Who did this? I'm going to get you out of here. No, I promise. I think—I think Gurley's finally lost it. I mean, completely. I think he's gone, or going. I don't think it will be long now, not at all. Jesus—he wants to leave at midnight. And he's got you locked in a closet. In handcuffs."

She shook her head, and rolled her eyes—the first I had seen so far of the old Lily. "He has me here for my *safety,*" she said and smiled. "He told them I was a prisoner of war, someone with information. He told them that so they wouldn't bother me. So no one would wonder why a captain flew an Eskimo girl out to the bush." She smiled, and I couldn't decide what to do. Was Gurley this crazy? Was she?

I felt bad for her, but now I also felt angry. Part of it was the old anger, jealousy—Gurley held her completely in sway. The new anger was that this growing debacle was all her doing. She'd told Gurley some story about Saburo in order to get herself back to Bethel, and now here she was, cuffed, and here I was, suddenly party to the whole rotten plan. "Why are you doing this?" I asked, but I got up as I said it, and ended up delivering the words more to the room than her.

But she still heard me. "Louis," she said. "I'm so close now. I'm almost there."

I turned to look at her and realized that Gurley was with us—or rather, within me. Standing there, eyes cast down at her, chin pointing up, disdain on my face. I was becoming him or had become him. And I couldn't shake it off. Maybe Gurley was a wizard, too. He'd obviously possessed Lily somehow, even though she was a shaman in her own right. Who was I to think I could resist? And when I spoke, it was his words, his tone.

"A rapist?" I said, and everything about her changed. Her face, her hands, her body, flushed and strained against the cuffs. "You told him Saburo was a rapist? To get yourself out here?"

"What?"

"He told me Saburo *raped* you. Lily, what does he really know about Saburo?" She clasped her hands together until the knuckles went white. "You told him he was Japanese, a spy, but did you tell him everything about that summer, Lily? Did you tell him everything that he'd find out if he'd gone walking around town today, like me?"

I was ready for her to scream, but what came out was more of a groan—"No." Then she said, "Louis, don't do this."

"What was the baby's name?" I said.

She looked at me for a long, silent moment, waiting for me to unsay the words, or maybe for history itself to unravel back past the point that there had ever been a war, a Saburo, a long summer under open skies full of light. Then she cried. I closed my eyes, and kept them closed when she finally began to speak.

"He didn't have a name," she said. Then nothing. When her voice returned, she went on. "I knew it was going to be a girl. I was going to name her Samantha—Sam, for Jap Sam, who'd been so good to me all that time until he was taken away. Introduced me to Saburo." She stopped. I could feel her looking at me, waiting for me to open my eyes, but I didn't. I was too frightened of what I'd done or started. "But it wasn't a girl. I should have known then! What woman with the kind of sight I supposedly had wouldn't know what lay inside her, a boy or a girl? Wouldn't know he was dying?" She stopped again, and it was a minute or two before she started once more. "That little boy, inside me, dying, drowning like I'd thrown him into the sea. And then—" Lily stopped, caught her breath and tried again. "And then, he was in my arms, dead. Bella and the other aunties wanted a doctor or a priest." I could feel her staring at me. "Keep your eyes closed, then," she said. "That's what I want. What I wanted. No doctor, no priest, nobody. Nobody to come say, 'Lily, the half-breed girl, whose parents ran away!' 'Lily, who went away last summer with that Jap and came back pregnant!' 'Lily, who thought she could have a baby on her own, and it came out dead! Look at her! Ha!'" She sniffed and coughed.

"How much did Bella tell you? Did she tell you the story she told me? Bella, so smart. All the aunties, so smart. That's what they thought. Them and all the elders before them and before them, all of them. And now, they said, don't cry. Don't cry."

And now: the *angalkuq*. I waited for Lily to tell me about the shaman, but she did something more curious. She told me the story Bella told her, the story she'd wanted to tell me in the forest, the story that Ronnie so startled me with when he retold it yesterday.

There was a boy, a baby boy, and his mother.

But in Lily's version, in Bella's version, it is the baby who dies and the mother who weeps. Don't cry, Bella told Lily, and Lily told me, crying. Don't cry, or the baby will wake. Don't cry, or the baby will wake and lose his way to the land of the dead. And then you will have him with you always. Always a baby, always needing you to carry him, soothe him, always making you cry. Mind the story of the mother whose baby died and could not stop crying. The village begged her. Shamans begged her. Her husband begged her. But she would not stop, and the baby awoke, and he never left. Eventually, they all moved away. The other families, the whole village, even her husband. She was left all alone with the baby. You see her tears every summer when the snow thaws and the delta floods.

Lily looked at Bella, still crying, unable to speak. Then what did it mean that her summer with Saburo had been so dry? Bella surprised her: Ever go hunting for mouse food? Lily held her breath, felt the prickling along her arms. Reach down sometimes, and what do you find? Mouse food? The little gnawed roots, shaped like teardrops? Little teardrops. Whose tears do you think those are?

Bella reached over then, Lily said, and tried to take the baby from her. No, Lily said, and then repeated the word, with a hiss. Bella recoiled, shocked and hurt.

Remember the story, Bella said. Remember what happens. The mother's left all alone. Everyone leaves her.

"It's just a story," Lily shrieked.

"Then where's *your* husband?" Bella said, and left the room.

THERE WAS NO SHAMAN, no *angalkuq* from Lower Kalskag in Lily's story. There was only Saburo, her lover from Japan, who came, and disappeared, later that night. Lily said she had called to him, had sent animal spirits sprinting out across the tundra in search of him, and then there he was. Proof of magic, or love. And those hands: she had loved him for those beautiful hands, and now she knew why. The way they moved the hair from her face, the way they pulled away the bloody sheets, the blankets, slowly, gently, and laid bare the boy. She had not let anyone else hold the baby, and now it seemed obvious why: no one else had hands fit for the task, to hold something that tiny, that fragile, that hopeless. She told him the story Bella had told her, and she loved him all the more for his reaction: he cried. They cried together, and while they were crying, whispered and planned.

Saburo would take the boy away, bury him in a special place in the bush, build him a tiny shrine as he would have done were they in Japan. Lily begged to come with him, but he insisted she rest. He would come back for her, bring some token from the shrine, and then—he would spirit her back to Japan. He didn't say how.

Days passed. A week, then two. "I was worried, but not scared," Lily went on. "I thought I had powers, and I thought they were strong, despite everything that happened: something had made him appear, after all. But nothing was making him come back. I went outside one night and listened for him, finally. After a while, I was sure I heard him, very faintly, very far away. In Anchorage. So I went."

But Anchorage was too "noisy," Lily said. Once she got there, she couldn't find Saburo anywhere. In time, she needed money, just to survive, and, once she'd saved up enough, to get back home. Another

Yup'ik woman told her about fortune-telling. She didn't tell her, though, what the men really came to find out—whether you would have sex with them. If you did, they paid you more. And as scared as she was of losing Saburo, as scared as she might have been for what he thought of what she was doing, she kept doing it, because something told her that she was getting closer.

She was: Gurley arrived one night, and she knew immediately that she'd found a link to Saburo. Lily didn't know what the link was, not at first, but she knew she had to cultivate a relationship with Gurley. When she did, and various details slowly surfaced about his work, such as the balloons (Gurley! Master of secrets!), she knew she'd done right. Eventually, he'd lead her to Saburo.

But after her initial excitement about Gurley's connection to Saburo, the notion that he would lead her to him began to fade. Not because it seemed impractical or implausible, but because—well, it will sound preposterous coming out of my mouth, so I'll just quote what Lily said:

"There is an old tradition, from generations ago, that the night after a hunt, the women of the less successful hunters would seek out the men who had been successful, and have sex with them. It was thought they might then pass on some of that power to their own less fortunate husbands. It had nothing to do with love or even sex. It was about do-ing all you could to make sure your husband, your lover, would bring honor to your family. Gurley was successful."

I think Lily asked me then, "Does that make sense?" I don't re-member answering. But I do remember what she said next.

"We stayed on and on in Anchorage, Gurley and I. We didn't leave. And any idea I had about finding Saburo faded, and faded, until I could no longer see his face anymore. And then his face started to be replaced with another. I studied it each night in my dreams, and each night it came closer and closer, until one night I saw who it was. I woke up and saw him there beside me: Gurley."

By now, I had opened my eyes, but I wish I hadn't. Then I could have imagined some look of disgust on her face when she said the name *Gurley,* but instead I had to watch her as tears came to her eyes, and listen as she went on: "You see why I have to tell it to you this way? Why I can't simply say that I fell in love with him? Because I had loved another man. And we'd had a baby, a boy, and we'd lost him, and then I lost Saburo, and then there was this other man, so strong and proud, and he was going to help me."

It wasn't love, she said. That's not wishful revising, at least not on my part: that's what she said. She said it wasn't anything she could really even put into words. But whatever the connection was, she needed it, she needed him. All the while, she told herself that the need sprang from her need to find Saburo, but eventually she began to wonder if that was true.

Gurley had begun to talk about life after the war, together. About some property he'd bought while posted in California, north of San Francisco. It was near the ocean, part of an old ranch. There was a hill you could stand on and see—well, everything. That's where the house would go. Big and broad with a long porch that would ramble around the whole of the first floor. From there, you'd be able to see the land unfurling all the way down to the water, where the ocean would carry the eye on to the horizon and the clouds above. Such clouds, Gurley had told her, such a sun: the pleasures of the sky there were so vast. How like Gurley, I thought, to think that some small panorama he'd purchased might sell a girl who'd grown up beneath the world's biggest sky. Still, I could hear him: "Such a sky as would befit a century's worth of painters! Imagine, heaven's cloak..." And what is there to say, really, against that, or against him? Decades on, I'm not sure I can tell you precisely what the sky looked like above Mary Star of the Sea, or what the walk from the orphanage to the ocean looked like. But I can remember that imaginary house of Gurley's. I can see them both there; I can see every blade of grass, every window, every flower, every cloud above.

I told Lily it sounded beautiful, and she shook her head quickly.

"That's why I was so glad you came, Louis. I was falling for him, I had fallen for him—so much of me still has."

My heart swelled, is that the word? I was precisely the knight I had taken myself for.

"When you came, you were so different. So young." We smiled. "And so, so frightened. So unlike anyone else who'd ever come to that dingy little office. I felt it immediately. And you frightened me. You'd been sent, I knew that right away. Not like Gurley. You'd been sent to remind me."

"To what?"

"To—to—rescue me. To shame me. To remind me to—stop crying. To go home, to find my son, his father. Saburo."

Things were going horribly wrong. I'd been sent to rescue her, but for myself. I tried to protest: "Lily, I—no one sent me."

"No one you knew, but you *knew*, somehow, didn't you?" she said.

Lily, I loved you: but I didn't say it. The words were there, but all I could do was cough. "You *knew*," she went on, "that I didn't need a lover, that I needed a friend."

If I coughed again, if I even opened my mouth to speak, I knew I might lose whatever was in my stomach.

"You understand," said Lily, relieved.

I pointed to the door.

"Gurley doesn't, but you do. *I* don't even understand. I don't even understand what I feel about Gurley—that's why I came here, out here, where I was born, where I can understand things better." I knocked on the door for the guard to let me out. "The sooner we go, Louis, the better!" she called after me. The guard smirked. I wanted to slap him, but could barely manage to nod as I stumbled down the corridor.

I kept walking until I reached the riverbank. I found our boat, a long, broad skiff, equipped with five days' worth of food, gallons of gas and water, tents, and for appearance's sake, a crate of bomb disposal equipment—tools, plastic explosives, blasting wire, and a little ten-cap hell box. There was one other small item, too, one that I'd secreted from Gurley's office and now kept hidden in a knapsack. I wouldn't fail Lily this time: I'd brought Saburo's map.

I looked it all over and then I sat, the good friend. I stared across the river and listened for some sign of Gurley—the whine of a boat, the crack of a gunshot.

CHAPTER 17

I'VE SEEN RONNIE FIRE A GUN ONLY ONCE, BUT IT WAS TO great effect.

A couple had lost their child. A tiny child. A baby girl, who, like Lily's child, was stillborn. But the baby was terribly early, terribly small, and the whole thing so horrifying that when the couple was asked immediately afterward if they'd like the hospital to "take care of things," they numbly agreed without knowing what they were agreeing to.

The hospital cremated the body.

They found this out a few days later, when the husband returned to claim the body. He was told it had been cremated; shocked, he asked for the remains; alarmed, the hospital told him there weren't any. Our bodies are mostly water, the man was told, and tiny babies like yours—they sometimes simply evaporate. There's nothing left.

The man returned to his wife, and then, beyond grief, even past rage, the two found me. I did what I could—I arranged a memorial service for their child, I offered to secure an empty burial plot where they could at least place a marker. But they wanted more.

So I summoned Ronnie. He talked with me, and then with the couple, and then he told them to meet him outside the hospital in two days' time, at 5 P.M.

Though it was July, the sky had gone dark early, black with threatening clouds. The first drops landed on my windshield as I parked. I found Ronnie and the couple in the small play yard outside the hospital, and watched as he threw a handful of ashes north, then south, then east and west. The couple looked on, stupefied.

This sounds like a myth. It is not; I was there. (Though saying so makes it sound all the more mythic, I know.)

Ronnie dusted his hands of the ashes and reached into a small pouch. I expected him to remove some amulet or tiny mask; instead, he removed an old, rusted .38. (It may have been mine; the parishioners had given one to me "for my safety," but I'd hidden or lost it and it had been missing for years.)

The wife looked terrified and grabbed her husband. The husband maintained a kind of crumbling defiance: shoot me, his face said. Shoot us both. We no longer want to live.

But Ronnie shot at God instead. He raised the gun over his head, shouted angrily, and fired. It's hard to describe how perfect an act this was, but the evidence was on the couple's faces, first the husband's, then the wife's: here was the angry retort they'd wanted to send to heaven, futile as an oath, but so completely satisfying.

Ronnie wasn't finished, though. Or heaven wasn't.

The rain began. Slowly, and then heavier and heavier. The couple started to move toward shelter, but Ronnie told them to stay. They looked puzzled, sad, depleted. Ronnie held his face to the sky, soaking it. Then, looking at the couple, he slowly wiped his face and presented them his hands, water pooling in the creases of his palms.

It was pouring now, so I couldn't hear what he said then, but I could just about make out his lips. *She's here.*

They were too stunned to move at first. Then the mother and father raised their faces to the flood and wept, as the clouds returned their daughter.

* * *

MIDNIGHT CAME, and there was no sign of Gurley. Above, a tumble of clouds arrived, and with them, an early twilight. I was still studying the sky when the jeep pulled up behind me. I turned to see: Gurley and an MP were in front, Lily in back. Somehow, Gurley had made it back across the river from town, silent and invisible.

"Everything ready?" Gurley said, and then repeated himself as he looked everything over. I nodded, and started to ask a question, but by then, he was already moving back to the jeep, where the MP was unlocking Lily's cuffs. Gurley then walked Lily toward the boat, one hand of hers in two of his. Every so often, he would whisper to her, and she would smile. Beyond, I could see the MP taking great pains to appear professionally disinterested in all that was taking place.

"Thugs," Gurley said to me when they reached the boat. "Imagine: handcuffs." He took one of Lily's hands to help her aboard. "I'm only sorry I didn't come to your aid sooner, dearest. You must forgive me. Thugs." He followed Lily into the boat, and turned to me. "Handcuffs? Can you imagine? Find out his name, and when we get back, make sure that he is severely dealt with," Gurley said. I turned to look back up at the MP, who was now getting into his jeep. "Too late," Gurley said quickly. "Fair enough, just get in, get in. Cast off, skipper, or whatever you do." Lily was staring across the river at the town, which was disappearing into a haze of cooling fog. "Mademoiselle," Gurley said. "I insist you choose the seat of preference."

Lily gave him a quiet smile, nodded to me, and went to the bow. I started the motor in one pull, cast off, and pointed us out into the middle of the river. The man who'd issued me the boat said I was crazy to be setting out so late; we were likely to run aground before we'd gotten five hundred yards. I studied the surface of the water for any clues. Gurley looked back at the town. And then Lily turned, leaned so I could see her face behind Gurley's back, and gave me a smile. Bigger than the one she'd given Gurley—I was sure of it. "Louis," she said, just mouthing the word. And then she half extended a hand, and mouthed two more words: "Follow me."

* * *

WITHIN AN HOUR, the clouds had gone, but the sun was done with us anyway. The thin tundra twilight had finally dimmed into a kind of night, more blue than black. We would have to land soon and make camp, but Gurley showed no signs of stopping. He sat in the middle of the boat, between Lily and me, and scanned the horizon. I suppose he might have been searching for Saburo, but his look was so vacant and the light so poor, I wasn't sure what he was doing or thinking.

Lily, on the other hand, watched the water before us intently. She had had me slow down, and whenever she thought I needed to adjust my course, she would point one way or the other, and yip. It was eerie, that sound—I would not have thought a single, clipped syllable would be enough to convey that she was speaking a different language, but it was. It completed the scene, really: wartime Alaska had always been a strange place, but we were streaming into something altogether different, a kind of dreamscape, where every reference point had been replaced with a not-quite-identical twin. The sky was a blanket, the water was ink, and there, in the bow of the boat, a woman I once knew was speaking a language I did not. Not English, not even Yup'ik. I could feel the blue dark slither up my skin.

Gurley barely managed to break the spell when he finally called for us to stop. I could hardly see Lily now, but it seemed as though she nodded her head without looking back at him. A few seconds went by, and then all of a sudden, I could see her face floating in the gloom. Though it sounded as though she were whispering, I could hear her clearly: we weren't far from the shore of a small island; I was to slow down and gradually steer us to the right. I still don't know whether she saw the island or if she sensed it; whatever her method, we made land smoothly enough. The grass scraping beneath the boat sounded like static as Lily climbed over the side and then waded through the water to pull us ashore. Gurley seemed uncomfortable that he wasn't doing any work, but then appeared to decide something and settled back.

I had asked for three tents but now discovered that I had only been issued two. I set up one while Gurley watched. Lily had walked off soon after we'd all come ashore. Gurley had started to follow her, but she'd turned him back with a silent look—not a threatening look, just a look—and Gurley had straightened up, checked to see if I had been watching (I had), and then peppered me with instructions about setting up camp.

Lily had not returned by the time I had finished the first tent. Unsure if setting up the second tent would prompt or prevent a discussion about sleeping arrangements, I paused for a moment, and then tore into the second bag.

I hadn't made much progress when Gurley stopped me.

"So industrious, Sergeant," he said, and surveyed what I had done. "How many tents do we have?"

"Just two, sir," I said.

"You little devil," he said.

"I asked for three," I said. "They gave me two."

Gurley made no reply. He walked away and then quickly returned. "I really do care for her, Belk," he said. "About her. For her. I do. That's clear?"

"Yes, sir," I said.

"The cuffs were a mistake," he said. "*Their* mistake. That's obvious, isn't it?"

"Absolutely," I said, now sure of the opposite.

"*Sir,*" he added, for me.

"Absolutely, sir," I mumbled.

"I'll chalk up that missing *sir* to fatigue instead of insolence," he said. "You may retire."

I looked at the second tent, which lay in a crumpled heap. I hadn't even found all the poles.

"Sergeant," Gurley said. "You are kind to struggle with the tents, but you have done enough. Leave this to me."

I stared at him for a moment, giving him time to change his mind. When he didn't, I crawled into the first tent, exhausted. I rooted around in the dark for the blankets I knew I'd thrown inside at some point, and listened to Gurley softly cursing his way through the raising of the second tent. In five minutes, I was fast asleep.

At least I think that's how it happened. The truth is that there is a short period where I don't remember anything at all, and so I am chalking it up to the most innocent explanation—sleep. Or a better explanation: what happened next was so extraordinary, it has crowded out most of my other memories from that evening.

I awoke (or was awake) when the tent flaps parted. Convinced that Gurley had belatedly decided to play the gentleman and leave Lily a tent to herself, I rolled to one side of the small, two-man tent, to give him room to lie down. I kept my eyes closed, hoping that he would assume I was asleep—or at least, fiercely pretending to be. I could smell the tundra muck and wet on him as he crawled in; it wasn't unpleasant, exactly—although I knew it would be after a few hours. It smelled of water and grass and mud, a lot of it, and I realized that pitching the second tent must have proven quite a battle. I imagined he'd had trouble finding another patch of dry ground adequate enough for the tent. I was about to roll back over and apologize for leaving him to do the job alone when the voice came in my ear.

"Louis," Lily said. My every muscle came alive. I tried to twist to see her, but she whispered "no" and held my shoulder. "Just listen," she said.

"Where have you been?" I said, craning my neck. "Where's Gurley?"

"Whisper," Lily said. I started to repeat myself, and she interrupted: "You don't know how to whisper." She put a finger on my lips, which almost made me stop breathing as well as speaking.

"Louis, he's gone," she said. I tried once more to roll over and face her, and this time she let me. I was surprised to find her face right above mine. "Not Gurley," she said. "Saburo. Saburo is gone. I went and looked for him, and he's gone."

"Lily," I said.

"Please," she said. "You'll wake Gurley." I rubbed my face. Lily waited until I was looking at her before she went on. "I went looking for Saburo," she said then. "All night, as I was guiding us down the river, I could feel him growing closer and closer. And then we came here, and the sense was overwhelming. I could hardly breathe. I wasn't sure what I would do when I found him, but I knew I would find him, his body. That's why I went wandering off into the brush. There's more island here than you might think—you'll see it in daylight. But I followed him—it was almost like following a trail—and finally I came to a small clearing by some scrub alder. His campsite. That's what I had found. He had been there. And gone. He's gone now." She turned away.

"And the . . . shrine?" I said.

She shook her head.

"Lily," I said.

"I need your help now," she said.

"Lily, I brought it." She looked at me. "The map. I brought Saburo's book." Oh, such eyes—why couldn't I have done this sooner, basked in that look so much earlier?

But as soon as the book appeared, I lost her. She took it from me, held it, felt it, bit her lip and then opened it, crying her way through the pages. She asked me about the translations; unsure how she would react, I said they were Gurley's. She fingered them like delicate leaves.

Page by page she progressed, until she neared the end, when she began turning the pages two and three at a time, looking, I was sure, for Saburo's last map, the one to their baby.

"Lily—" I said, but she'd already found them. The empty, gray-washed pages.

"What did you do with them?" she cried, loud enough that she might have spooked Gurley.

"Nothing," I said. "I was going to ask you. We were—I thought, maybe secret writing, but Gurley would have made fun of me and I guess I don't—"

"There's nothing here," Lily said, shaking her head, almost unable to speak.

"Lily, I—maybe there's something earlier." I offered to take the book from her and look myself.

She shook her head.

"I guess he—maybe he didn't—I don't know, Lily," I said. "Maybe he didn't get a chance to—" and I really was going to say, *dispose of the baby's body properly,* but somehow managed to catch myself. "Maybe he didn't get a chance to make the map. He went out, he—he—got captured—escaped?"

But while I was babbling, Lily had stopped crying. She was staring before her, and, it seemed, listening. Not to me.

"Lily?"

"Louis," she said softly. "I need your help. There's something—there's something here. Nearby. It's him, or—it's someone. Near here, and moving. But too fast for the boat, too fast for feet. I need to follow him."

I looked at her for a moment, uncertain if this was the new Lily, or if some old part of her still burned inside. "How?" I said finally.

"First," she said, "some rope."

THERE IS THE OLD, familiar challenge of describing the midnight sun, the moon on the snow on a subzero night, the northern lights, the empty Kilbuck Mountains or the endless gray sea to someone who has never been here—and then there is the unique and forbidding prospect of describing what happened in that tent that night, a few weeks shy of the end of the war and my first life.

I'll start outside, since that's where I had retreated once Lily had started to undress. She hadn't asked me to leave, hadn't needed to—and I wonder, just now, if things might have been different if I had stayed. But she'd slipped off her boots and had started to shrug off her pants when I crawled out. I took a quick look at her face—our eyes didn't meet, but I could see she was in the process of putting on what I now think of as her shaman's mask—her face empty and slack, her eyes unfocused but not yet vacant. I imagine my face might have looked somewhat similar as I stood there, studying her tent and Gurley's, some twenty soggy yards away beside a clump of cotton-wood.

I moved a little closer to his tent, to make sure he really was in it. It was tough to tell in the dark. There wasn't a moon, or there was; when I looked up, all I could see was a dim and shifting murk, dimly lit. I imagine it's what divers see when they look back up to the surface, only to find the way obscured by a passing cloud. But I didn't have to see Gurley. As I drew closer, I could hear him, lightly snoring. Every so often, his breath stopped completely, and then resumed in a kind of cough.

He'd left the tent flaps undone, obviously assuming Lily would join him at some point. In the meantime, though, he was at the mercy of the mosquitoes. The tent looked as though it might collapse before morning.

Then I heard another sound—Lily's voice—and I crept back toward my tent.

"Louis," she whispered, and I could tell she was just inside the flap. I waited a moment, then took a breath and answered. "I need your help," she said quietly, and when I didn't reply, she asked, "The rope? Some rope?"

I looked around and then whispered, "Wait."

I found some tangled in the floor of the boat. Once I'd finally freed it, I decided it needed rinsing off and quietly dipped it into the water. Then I heard Lily calling me again. I shook the rope out and walked back to the tent. I squatted, poked open the flap with the coil of rope, and headed in.

First, there was a smell—or a scent—of smoke. Opposite the open-ing, a squat candle burned on one of the tin mess plates. The plate was wet and spread with leaves or mud of a sort—I'm not really sure, because I didn't pay attention to anything else once I realized Lily's clothing was all piled in a heap in the middle of the tent, and that she was curled up, completely bare, just beyond.

My eyes began to water and I coughed—pungent smoke was filling the tent; for a moment, I thought it was on fire. Then I felt Lily's hand pressing down on my shoulder. "Lower," she said. "Stay low, like this." I lowered myself, and saw her face, intent, her arms and hands, and her chest, suddenly pale and ordinary now that I could see it in full. She lowered herself, too, until she was on her side, almost bent double, and it seemed the whole of her was disappearing into the dark.

"Please don't be scared, Louis," she said. I shook my head. "Now give me the rope." She flinched when she took the rope from me and found it wet. She gave me a mock frown and then a little smile, the last of the night.

She wound the rope around her neck, and then her shoulders, then her legs and torso, folding and unfolding her body as needed. Here and there, a drop of water would trace a slow, shiny path across a smooth expanse of skin. I should not have been so saturated with desire—even at that moment, I remember thinking that something was wrong, that she'd disposed of a healthier self with her clothes and had instead assumed the body of someone fragile, terribly thin and gaunt. And maybe that's why I didn't turn away or leave the tent or simply freeze: she had been beautiful, but this new fragility made her—if not more beautiful, then somehow more desirable.

With the rope wound around her in loose coils, she looked at me carefully. "Louis, from the pouch there—I need—yes, that pouch. Just open it."

It was a small leather pouch, extremely soft, with a flap like an envelope. Inside were a variety of small objects—a feather, what looked like rocks or teeth, and some small wooden disks. It was a moment or two before my eyes adjusted and saw the carvings—faces—emerge. "These are the things I need," she said, and then added a word in

Yup'ik that I did not know. "These help me fly. The feather gives me flight, the walrus teeth strength, and the other amulets are for animals who'll help guide me back home." Unlike Ronnie, I suppose, Lily still had command of a *tuunraq* or two and did not need a human voice to lead her back.

I studied the objects in the palm of my hand, and then looked at Lily—not at her face, because I couldn't, not then, maybe not anymore, but at her body, the slope and shape of it, the way it evaded the rope in some places and strained against it in others. "I need help," she said. "I need to tie the objects to me. Spirits are powerful and will run away from you if you do not bind them tight." She lay down quietly on her back, closed her eyes. I didn't move, not for a full minute, and then she looked up. "Let each object tell you where it goes," she said, and then closed her eyes again.

It was too much to look at her like that, to be able to study her without her studying me. I was searching for an innocent patch of skin to place something, but as she lay there, nothing looked innocent, everything was charged. Charged: and I say that not as an expression but because it was true, there was a hum, electric, I could hear it, and I could feel the vibrations, and though you might peg it to something less complicated, at the time I thought it was pure magic, and still do.

The teeth I knotted near her knees, one amulet I placed at her shoulder, and then the feather floated across her chest and I let my hand follow it. I cannot tell you when that light touch became a caress, or how my hand continued its light tracing after I'd woven the feather into the rope at her stomach. And I cannot tell you that I do not remember all that happened next. It was both hands, my lips; I found places for everything, for all the amulets, all the charms, and then I lay there beside her and waited to explode.

And then she said—had it been seconds, minutes? An hour?—a most remarkable word: "Untie."

It should have happened then, just as soon as I'd worked her free of the cord and its knots and charms. I should have slipped free of my clothes and we should have lain together and fallen in love, made love. But I couldn't and didn't, because as I untied her, I watched the body I was releasing release memories, too. I saw and felt Gurley, and the summer's romance with Saburo, the phantom child they produced. I saw her growing up in Bethel, I saw her mother and father. I saw all the things she had told me about her life, but in different colors, scored with different sounds. I suppose it sounds like I was sitting there watching a movie, but it wasn't that, because I was moving through the landscape. I'd more readily compare it to what I've come to believe death is like, based on dozens of people I've seen go through their last moments here in this very hospice: for an instant, there is all the immediacy of life—all the people, sights, sounds, smells. We hear people talk about how one's life passes before one's eyes, and we think of a parade, with a beginning and an end. But it's not like that. The dying don't see their lives pass: their lives flash, complete, and vanish. It's the lifeless corpse that lingers.

I have spent a life fighting my way back to that moment with Lily, that flash. I have spent a life trying to get back to that precipice and leap off it. I've not been chasing after sex—good Lord, what a fleeting goal—but intimacy, *knowledge*. I had not gone on Lily's journey with her, but I was there when she came back. And when she asked me to untie her, she was allowing me to participate somehow in what she'd seen and done. That's why I saw the whole of her life like that. And had the moment lasted any longer, I think I would have seen the whole of mine. I really do.

Getting that moment back: That's not enough to spend a lifetime pursuing? It has been for me. I knew I could never become an *angalkuq* myself, so I marched down the closest spiritual path allowed me. Priesthood. I suppose I could have contented myself with regular churchgoing, or rigorous self-examination, or drugs. But none of that would have gotten Lily to where she went. She had been subsumed by the spiritual world; I wanted to be swallowed whole, too, and join her, so I consecrated myself to a spiritual life. I'd go off in search of God and His knowledge—and if I found Lily there in the ether, somewhere along the way, so much the better.

But I've not found her. It may be that I should have tied myself to Lily when I tied on those other charms, and made her take me with her wherever she flew. And when we returned, I would not have untied us, we would have held on, skin to skin, until Gurley found us, shot us, and let us die, our blood pooling together. Our lives would have flashed then with a brilliance only suns could match.

But Lily didn't die that night. Neither did I. After spending a moment watching me, and, I was sure, waiting for me, she quietly got dressed. When Lily was finished, she leaned close, her eyes sad, her face exhausted. Then she said, "Thank you," and gave me a kiss: yes, a kiss, her lips to mine.

It was a tender moment, or would have been (I was sad, but somehow, also satisfied) but for the fact that Gurley tore open the tent flap at precisely the moment that Lily was pulling away from me. I was able to look at him blankly enough at first, but Lily reddened with shame and stared at the ground, and then I turned away, too.

Gurley looked from one to the other of us, eyes wide and bloodshot, face taut like someone in that moment between receiving a wound and feeling pain. He finally exclaimed, "Good morning!" and then pulled his head out of the tent so fast he knocked over a pole. I struggled out first, then Lily.

"Good morning, Sergeant," Gurley said again, with that compressed smile he usually employed before hitting someone. But then Lily was taking him by the elbow and trying to lead him away. He followed her for a short distance; I watched Lily try to speak to him while he turned his head up and away from her. They kept walking, out of sight, and I set about striking camp, because it was all I could think to do. I was almost finished with the tents when Lily returned, alone.

"Where's Gurley?" I said.

"He doesn't believe me," she said quietly. "But you were there, you can tell him."

"I don't think he'll believe me, either," I said, scanning the brush for signs of him. "He looked in, he saw you kiss me, or maybe just missed it, but still, all he had to do was look at us and figure it out. Thank God he didn't see us when you were—on your journey. Without your clothes."

"Oh, I told him about that," Lily said.

"Jesus, Lily," I said. "That's why he hasn't come back. He's looking for a club. Does he have his gun?" I ran to the pile of gear and started to rummage through. Of course he had his gun; he always wore it.

"Louis!" Lily cried.

"Get in the boat!" I said, now looking in the gear for a gun of my own. I could see Lily explaining to him what had happened; I could see her trying to explain how she had called on her shamanic powers to climb into the clouds. I could see her mentioning, without being asked, that she had had to remove all her clothing. How she had had to have an assistant, well, watch her, carefully. I could see Gurley hearing all of this, understanding none of it, except for the part where his naked girlfriend lay in a darkened tent with another man.

"Listen," she said. She came over and tried to tug me free of the pile. I used one arm to keep her away and kept searching with the other. Then I felt a sharp pain in the back of my knee, and suddenly I was sitting on the ground, staring up at her. "Louis," she said. I started to get up, but she put a hand out and pointed to the knee. "Would you like it to hurt more?"

"Lily," I started, then stopped. "No," I said. I scooted away but didn't stand. "I think I have, we have, a right to be scared. He's not—Gurley's never been on an even keel, and hearing about you and me in a tent could set him off—will set him off, for sure."

"I don't care about what he thinks happened between us last night—or the last five months, for that matter."

"Then what are you worried about?" I said.

"What indeed," said Gurley, who appeared beside us with all the speed and pallor of a ghost.

I scrambled to my feet. "Sir," I said.

Gurley kept his eyes on Lily. "The lady is speaking, Mr. Belk. About something that worries her." He turned to me. "And unlike you, I want to hear what it is." I couldn't tell what the cold fire in his eyes meant: violence, certainly, but to Lily or me and when?

Lily stared at him. "I'm worried you don't believe what I saw on my journey. Or even that I went."

Gurley looked at her, then me, then her, and then turned and walked over to the pile of gear. He began packing items. "Oh, the journey part, I believe that," he said, and leered at me. "But what you saw, no—in fact, it makes me wonder if I've been in Alaska too long. At war too long. Chasing balloons too long. What have I done, Belk? Hauled an Eskimo woman out into the bush to play fortune-teller and find me balloons. Spies." He cinched tight a pack and stood. "Really, now. I should be shot."

And with that, he removed his prized Colt from his holster and began to examine it.

I stopped breathing. Lily spoke.

"We're very close to the spot," she said.

"Tingle, tingle," Gurley said, not looking up from the gun. "Can you feel it, Belk?"

"What, sir?"

"Didn't you tell him, fair Sacagawea? When you got back from your trip? Without a stitch of clothing? Or did you have other things to talk about?"

I turned to Lily.

"I didn't get a chance to," she said.

"My goodness," said Gurley, raising his eyes. "By all means tell him. See what he thinks. I *trust* Sergeant Belk's judgment implicitly." He returned the gun to his hip and then hefted a bag toward the boat. Lily looked after him and bit her lip.

"There's a very special balloon nearby," she said quietly.

I looked quickly in Gurley's direction, but he was busy stowing the bag. "Is it Saburo?" I whispered. "He's actually come for you? Is that what you saw?"

She looked at me, eyes instantly full of tears. "No," she hissed. "I told you before, he left as soon as we got out here. I could feel it; I knew it. No—this is different. Not a plane. This is a balloon." She took a step closer to me, and looked over my shoulder to Gurley and the boat. "But there's something…" She twisted her neck to look back into the interior of the island.

"Not Saburo?" I asked.

She looked around, as if searching out someone who would better understand her. "Something," she finally said to me. "You have to believe me. He has to believe me. We have to go—to follow—"

I could hear Gurley walking up behind us.

"What's this?" he asked, never more brittle. "Whisper, whisper."

"I'm not sure it's safe out here, Captain," I said, trying hard not to exchange a look with Lily.

"A hunch, Sergeant?" he said, and raised his eyebrows. "Don't tell me that you've caught the soothsaying bug, too?" He smirked. "Quite a night in the ol' tent. Sorry I missed it. Finish loading, Sergeant."

I did, and as I did, I watched Lily lead Gurley into another whispered conversation. I couldn't hear them, but I could see them. I could see Lily pointing, gesturing. I could see Gurley standing tall, and then, after a few minutes, just slightly—easing. And I thought I could see why. The tiniest part of him really did believe her—not just about her sense of where to go next, but about her need to convince him, to connect with him. That is to say, he had started to believe that she really did care for him. And the strangest thing about that to me was that I sensed he was right.

I thought about it as I finished loading the boat. I replayed the trip we'd taken in my head, and I stopped the film whenever I saw them exchange a glance, or better yet, when their eyes didn't meet; when just one of them was stealing a look at the other.

I don't know what had happened, or what was happening, but

clearly there was something working on all of us—more of Lily's magic, I suppose—and when we got back into the boat, Gurley returned Lily to the bow and me to the stern, and pointed ahead. "Onward, Belk," he said to the air, and then turned back to me. "Follow that woman in the bow wherever she tells us to go." Then he took out his handkerchief and let it rest on his knee while reaching down with his other hand to unsnap, once more, his holster.

CHAPTER 18

THE CLOUDS RETURNED, THIS TIME TO STAY. A SLOW, STEADY rain seemed to follow us down the Kuskokwim, and no arrangement of tarps and ponchos could keep us all from getting soaked through.

Occasionally, the rain would lift, but then the mosquitoes would descend. They took a particular interest in Gurley, which I enjoyed except for those times when he had his gun out. He'd been obsessively removing it, cleaning and polishing it with the handkerchief, then replacing it and starting again thirty minutes later. But whenever the mosquitoes wreathed his head, Lily and I would be treated to the terrifying display of him wildly swatting at them, gun in hand.

Gurley had put his faith in Lily to lead us through the delta, but ever since then, she had grown more hesitant and unsure. She would point us one way, then another. She let her hand drift along in the water outside the boat. She studied the skies. And with each passing hour, she grew more anxious.

When Gurley suggested we stop for lunch, she just shook her head. Gurley looked at me and rolled his eyes—a standard gesture of his, but darker, somehow, out here alone in the bush. He and I tore into some C rations that had been stowed, and we continued on.

About one o'clock, the engine sputtered, coughed out a few mouthfuls of smoke, and died. While Gurley and Lily looked on with great concern, I uncoupled the gas line from the primary tank and inserted it into the reserve. Then I started the engine again. Miraculous. My passengers turned away, satisfied. I thought to joke that we'd need Lily to use her powers of divination to find us a gas depot eventually, but it wasn't a joke—we would.

I was the first to see it. I had been following the contortions of an ever-widening waterway, wondering if we'd made it back into the main channel of the Kuskokwim. Even though it was wet, Gurley was slumped in the floor of the boat, sleeping or pretending to. Lily was looking at him, and I was trying to catch her eye when something downriver caught mine.

Of course, I thought I was hallucinating. There had been the strange appearance of that fire balloon my last night in Anchorage, but to actually see a balloon, in flight—that hadn't happened since Shuyak, and that whole episode had seemed like a kind of dream anyway. But now, here one was, drifting along, not fifty feet above the ground, bright as the moon.

It was beautiful. I mean that. I knew these balloons had killed people and that one might someday kill me. But they were spectacular all the same. They were the most gorgeous things the war produced; and again, I know that's a horrible thing to say, given their intent. But they couldn't help it, even if their makers could. Nothing else soared the way those balloons did. They even elevated the quality of that pokey training film that Gurley had made me watch. Before getting down to the dirty business of charts and diagrams and the stolid reenactment of disassembling a balloon, the film lingered over a long, sweeping shot of a balloon in morning flight along the Pacific Coast. The balloon seemed to be moving incredibly, effortlessly fast. Part of the thrill came from thinking how lucky the filmmakers must have been to actually capture one in flight, but even if they'd just reinflated one and sent it aloft for filming, it was still extraordinary. It felt like the beginning of an epic. There are films I see today that have such aspirations, but, honestly, none matches the power that film's balloon had sailing through that sunny, black-and-white landscape.

Such memories have made me biased. Balloons were mankind's first aircraft, and I do not think we have improved upon them. Planes are noisy, metal things, all angles and exhaust, that require you to tell them where to go. Balloons are a much purer kind of flight; they go where they will and leave you little say. I wondered then and wonder still what it would have been like to travel aboard one of those bomb balloons. What would the sky have looked like from up there, or the ocean, or a man on the ground like me?

If you've ever been that man on the ground, you know there is something about the silence of a balloon in flight that consumes you, that renders everything around it silent, as if the balloon's magic included not only flight but the ability to swallow sound. Accept that, if you like, as my reason for not shouting, for throttling back the engine and just drifting, watching as the balloon seemed first to come toward us, then turn away, and then float closer once more.

Lily was silent as well. But as the balloon drew closer she began to rise in the boat, steadying herself with one arm and reaching up with the other. Gurley, on the other hand, might never have awakened had the balloon not begun bleating.

It sounded like a bird and I assumed it was, but the closer we drew, the more distinct the noise became: a whistle, the kind air raid wardens frantically blew, the kind you might have mistaken for a cricket, except the sound went on too long. Still, I was ready to chalk it up to a bird or some strange way that the wind moved through the balloon's ropework, until Gurley startled awake. He saw the balloon and scrambled shakily to his feet. Without taking his eyes off the balloon, he snapped his fingers at me. "Glasses, Belk. Binoculars. My God—Lily. My God." I found the binoculars in a case beneath the seat and handed them to him.

The balloon had crossed our path, and the river's, and was now making a slow descent to the tundra. As the river carried us past, Gurley shouted at me to hold our position and then cursed, fumbling the glasses. He caught them, but when he raised them again to his eyes, he had one hand on his holster.

"Find and load your sidearm, Sergeant Belk," Gurley said. "Lily, get down. Lie down." Lily didn't move. "Bring us ashore here, Sergeant. Lily, down." Lily crouched down, but put a hand on Gurley's pant leg as she did.

"It's okay," she said. "Don't worry."

"It's landing!" Gurley said. "It's going to crash! Beach us, Belk, dammit, land!" He dropped into a crouch, and I sped to the bank. Luckily, we tangled in some grass, or I think I would have sent us all flying out of the boat in my haste to execute Gurley's order.

Gurley splashed out into knee-deep water and began pulling the boat onto the shore. With one last tug, he beached the boat, and then turned to face Lily and me with delight. "The enemy!" He looked up. The balloon seemed to be hovering with indecision about a hundred yards off, about two stories off the ground. Then a gust of wind pushed it toward us, and lower. Gurley ducked down.

"Sir?" I asked. It all seems so inevitable now, but at the time, I had not figured it out.

Gurley was checking his gun, so Lily answered for me, with bit lip. "There's a man—there's someone inside."

Gurley looked at her with some surprise. "Perhaps you possess some magic powers yet, dearest. I would have thought one needed the binoculars to know that." I stared at Gurley, unable to speak. "Belk, with me. Miss Lily, stay here." He checked his gun one more time. "Finally," he said.

Lily grabbed for him, but Gurley darted ahead, and then waved me after him. Lily caught me before I got away. "Don't let him—" she started.

"I won't," I said.

"Don't—"

Then the blast came.

My first thought was that the balloon had exploded, but when I looked up and saw it still there, I realized that the noise had come from Gurley's gun. Leave it to Gurley to shoot at something as big as a balloon and miss. He was just a few yards in front of me, holding the gun with both hands, head cocked to the side to help his aim. I came up behind him.

Once he sensed I was beside him, he lowered his gun and turned to me. The wind had picked up again and the balloon began to drift away from us. Gurley cursed, looked at me, and then raised the gun again. I put a hand on his forearm as gently as I could.

"Sir," I started.

Gurley yanked his shooting arm away. "Don't ever," he said, glowing red. Lily crept beside us and Gurley looked at her for a moment. "Get back in the boat, Lily."

"Sir," I said carefully. "Aren't standing orders now to, well, to not shoot them down? For fear of what the balloon might release?" Gurley wasn't listening. "I mean, even if it was a regular balloon—the explosives? If we fire at it from this close, we could—"

"It's not a regular balloon," Gurley said. "And I'm not about to let some little Jap fire on us at will. Give me the goddamn glasses." The balloon was still a hundred yards off, but just a few feet above the ground now, drifting slowly. A rope trailed along behind it like a tail. A rope, or perhaps that long fuse, the one that was supposed to ignite the balloon itself. But with the balloon so low to the ground, the rope or fuse kept snagging in the grass. Then the wind would pull it free, the balloon would bounce, and the rope would snag again. Finally, a clump of alderwood caught the fuse, and the balloon was trapped. Now, when the wind blew, instead of breaking free, the balloon pulled to the ground. As it did, we could see the man inside grow agitated. Gurley had the glasses, but it was still clear to Lily and me that the man was standing, peering about. Moreover, he looked drunk—or weak. As the basket pitched back and forth, he seemed unable to keep his balance. He would topple and disappear from view and then struggle up once more. Sometimes he wouldn't even stand; we'd only see his head, peering over the side like a little kid.

He should have noticed us by now, but there was no sign he had. He seemed too intent on the rope that had snagged to pay attention to anything else. "What are you going to do?" Lily whispered, angry. Gurley kept staring through the binoculars and said nothing. Every now and then, he'd shake his head, whistle low. Finally, he lowered the binoculars.

"Well, Sergeant," he said. Then he turned to Lily and nodded. "Ma'am, if you'll excuse us." He looked back to the balloon. "I'm not going to take the chance that he somehow gets that snag free and takes off again. There's no way we'd be able to keep up with him across this sodden mess. We're going to have to take him, or the balloon, or both, down. Sergeant?"

I shook my head. I wasn't sure what to do. The war had proceeded so slowly for Gurley and me. It was partly a function of our quarry: whatever the balloons were, they weren't speedy. Elsewhere, rockets flew, airplanes dove, bullets raced. But the balloons: you could watch them move. You never saw a bullet in flight, just the aftereffects of its stopping. A balloon let you see the whole progress of death, from anticipation to impact.

And though I didn't have the words to say it then, I knew Gurley was tampering with this measured, preordained pace. It was as though he'd placed the alderwood there, he'd arranged the snagged line, he'd frozen the balloon like we'd reached some crucial point in the training film that he had wanted me to study carefully. But I'd frozen along with the film.

Gurley was about to smack me back into motion when the film lurched forward of its own accord. A quick shout from Lily drew our eyes back to the balloon, where we saw the figure crane out of the basket and work at the snagged rope. Gurley shouted, too, and now the man looked up at us. I'm not sure what he saw, but it obviously frightened him enough to work at the cord more frantically.

Gurley fired a shot. The man looked up again.

Lily stood, and moved toward Gurley. As he took his second shot, she grabbed his arm. The shot went high. I saw something tug at the top of the balloon, but didn't take time to figure out if he'd actually hit it. Instead I scrambled to get myself between Gurley and Lily. But I was too late; he'd backhanded her with the gun. She fell, hands to her face, the too-red blood of a new wound leaking through her fingers.

I could have avenged Lily then; I could have finally struck Gurley myself, or better yet, found my own gun and shot him. But I did not. I suppose cowardice was part of the reason, but it wasn't the only reason. Because before I could do anything, before Gurley could even spit out an apology or added insult, another sharp report cracked across the tundra. Gurley and I dropped. Gurley cursed and muttered something about how we'd given the balloonist all the time in the world to fire upon us. But when I looked, I didn't see a gun, but rather, a tiny figure of a man dangling from the balloon by his right arm, which was caught up in the rigging. A tiny puff of smoke was already dissipating. His legs were limp and his feet dragged along the ground as the balloon continued its feeble struggle against the alderwood. I thought he was dead, but then saw his head move. I grabbed up the binoculars for myself this time and focused while Gurley continued his sputtering.

"Enough of this," Gurley said, just as I brought the glasses into focus. That's when I saw the man lift his head, that's when I saw the tears stream down his face, and that's when, finally, I saw who he was. Not Saburo. Not some other Japanese spy who'd flown here from Japan.

He was, more incredibly, a boy. A Japanese boy.

I saw his mouth open before I heard his screams, but then we all heard them, high and jagged, and then we all knew what we'd found.

"Don't shoot," cried Lily.

"Sir," I said. "It's a—it's a boy."

"Good Christ," Gurley said. "I don't care if it's an octopus. Now duck. I'm bringing this tragicomic chapter of the war to a close."

I was still staring through the binoculars, so what happened next really did have the feeling of a film, the actions before my eyes operating at some mediated remove from actual experience. And none of it made sense: a boy, dangling from a balloon, a woman, her hands bloody, running toward him, and then, lurching after them both, a U.S. Army Air Corps captain. The woman stumbled into a puddle that turned out to be as deep as a pond, and the captain tumbled in after her. They struggled for a moment until he finally heaved both of them out of the hole and into the grass. She pulled free of him, but he caught her legs. She kicked at him and then he had blood around his face. He caught her again, higher, and this time simply held her until she stopped twisting and turning, until it was finally the two of them lying beside each other like lovers, which they once were. Or always were. I lowered the glasses, and that was better, the details were gone: from a distance, there was no blood on the two lovers, no tears on the boy.

I walked toward them, picking my steps carefully at first, and then, through no decision of my own, began moving more rapidly, tripping, falling, running.

WHEN I REACHED Gurley and Lily, she was crying and he was whispering to her, brushing her hair from her face. Without taking his eyes off her, Gurley told me to go check on the boy, and secure the balloon so that it would be safe to investigate. I tried to catch Lily's gaze before moving off, but she'd shut her eyes in a grimace. Gurley told me to get moving.

I crept toward the balloon. Either one of Gurley's shots had punctured the envelope or it had torn previously, because the shroud was wheezing to the earth. The basket had dropped further, and now rested on the ground, occasionally hopping up a few inches whenever the breeze was strong enough. The boy, his arm still caught in the rigging, lay along the side of the balloon like he had leaked out of it. I could see that parts of the usual balloon payload were not present. The antipersonnel and incendiary bombs that usually dangled beneath the basket weren't there, at least not that I could see. Two cylinders that looked like incendiary devices still clung to the sides of the basket, however, and there were all the tiny charges ringing around the control frame. That last shot I thought I'd heard: it must have been one of those charges popping.

Once I got within thirty feet, I couldn't move any closer. It couldn't have been fear: I'd been faced with much more dangerous explosives than the ones before me then. There was no sign of the porcelain germ weapon containers. All in all, it looked as though it would be simple enough to render harmless.

But that wasn't it, of course. It was the boy. In fact, it took me a long minute or two to realize that I'd paused because some part of my brain was processing the boy as a new kind of bomb, one that lay far beyond the reach of my training. Perhaps he was his own bioweapon container.

He looked up, saw me, and gave a tiny groan. Then he screwed his face tight and, biting his lip, began to struggle to stand. I shouted for him to stop, and his eyes snapped open. I started speaking rapidly, explaining how he had to be careful how he moved, or else he might set off some of the charges. He frowned and replied in Japanese, and the two of us went on conversing like that for another minute, each of us oblivious to our inability to communicate.

Finally, I pantomimed an explosion, and told him, as best I could, to sit tight. He did. I studied things, walked around the balloon, decided on the best route to disarm the balloon and safely free the boy. I told the boy I would be right back, and then returned to Gurley.

He and Lily were sitting now. She was staring after the balloon, tears in her eyes, but no longer crying. Gurley was still whispering into her ear, her hands in his. I stood at a distance waiting for them to turn to me. I tried to blot Gurley out of the picture and just take in her eyes, imagine that she was looking only at me, had only ever looked at me, but I couldn't. Gurley was there, and Saburo before him, and now, somehow, this boy, too. They were all there, all claiming a piece of her.

"Too complicated?" said Gurley, looking up. He began to disentangle himself from Lily while still holding her hands.

"No, sir, I—"

"Because I thought it might be," Gurley said quickly. He gave Lily a squeeze and stood. He made a sour face and looked at the balloon. "Bastards. Can you believe—" he said, facing me, but really speaking to Lily. "Can you believe people would do this? Send children into war? Tie them to a balloon? And for what ungodly purpose? The cruelty—unspeakable. Cruel to him, but also to saps like us, called upon to witness the slaughter of a child."

"I think we can—"

"I assume it's booby-trapped, Sergeant," Gurley said, fixing his attention on me more sturdily now.

"Well, sir, it looks a bit like—"

"I mean—my word," Gurley said, more confident with the direction his performance had taken. "Is it more humane to shoot him and then detonate the balloon, or—?"

Lily gave a half-cry and rose. "There has to be a way," she said, looking at Gurley and then me. I looked at Gurley, too, unable to decode the strange signals he was sending. He wanted to do the bomb disposal job himself, for once? He wanted to impress Lily.

"Well, I think—sir, I think there is a way," I said. "Some of the worst stuff you find on these balloons—well, on this one, it looks like that's all gone already, never put on or maybe dropped in the ocean." I stopped. "As you know," I quickly added. "All that's left are a couple of firebombs, the little charges, maybe the flash bomb on the balloon, but—"

"You trust there's no booby trap, Sergeant?" Gurley said, looking at me very carefully now.

If Sergeant Redes had been quizzing me, I would have said hell no, never trust a bomb about anything, especially a Japanese one, but instead I said, "This looks as safe as safe gets." Then I looked at Lily, eager to win her favor. "And, well—the boy. Sir. It's worth a try." But Lily was staring at Gurley, waiting to hear what he would say.

"The boy," Gurley said. "Well." He looked around the tundra, as though searching for other balloons, other boys. Then he looked at me. "I wonder if you'd be so quick to dismiss a booby trap if it were *you* who were doing the disarming." He gave a tight smile, and when I started to protest that I would be happy to help—I wanted to impress Lily, too, and moreover, I didn't want Gurley to kill us all—he waved me away. "Officers' work, Sergeant," he said. "You know that," he added, pinning me with a look that I'm sure he hoped would keep me from mumbling something about all the previous times I'd done the work of an officer. He stood, hands on hips, and surveyed the balloon. "Get the kit," he said, "prepare the site." Lily looked at him with such renewed fascination I almost felt ill; in the next moment, I almost grabbed for his damn gun.

PREPPING THE SITE consisted of checking it once more for any obvious booby traps—which, Sergeant Redes forgive me, I now dearly hoped to find and keep secret. I dug a small pit not far from the balloon to place the bombs in for safe detonation. It quickly filled with water, but there seemed to be no other option, so I let it be. I said what I could to calm the boy, tried to explain that Gurley would soon come to free him, and then laid out some of the tools from the kit. I made sure not to unpack the explosives, blasting wire, or hell box, afraid of what Gurley might do with them.

I then returned to Gurley and Lily and explained what I had seen. He nodded with a practiced weariness: *yes, yes, Sergeant, you have told me all you know, which is, of course, so very little.* Then he nodded to Lily, told me to take her back a safe distance, and proceeded toward the balloon.

I don't think Lily could tell how nervous he was. She didn't know his walk the way I did; she'd probably never seen him scared like I had. But I could see, in the hunch of his shoulders, his broken gait, that he'd wished he'd dispensed with the bravado and let me do the work. Replaying the conversations from earlier, I realized now that he'd simply wanted to fire at the balloon, its bombs, and the boy from a distance and be done with it. We'd lose a tremendously valuable prize, but, *so what,* his thinking must have run, *we have other balloons.*

We saw him speak to the boy and the boy speak back.

"Gurley knows Japanese," I told Lily, as though she didn't know this and needed to. "He's a Princeton man," I added, as a kind of dig, but I had little idea what I was saying and neither did Lily. We looked back toward the two of them.

We were too far away to tell, of course, but I was sure he'd frightened the boy, and I hoped Lily could see or sense this. But she just watched in rapt silence. I found the binoculars and handed them to her, hoping that her seeing Gurley close up would expose a bit of his ersatz heroism.

It didn't. Gurley went for the boy first, taking the wire clippers to the cord that held his arm fast to the balloon. The boy shrieked as the arm fell free, all wrong, as loose and slack as a piece of rope. Even without the glasses, I could see it bend in too many places. Lily lowered the binoculars and looked at me in pain. The gun had left a jagged cut that climbed her cheek, a crease of dirt and blood.

Gurley pulled the boy free of the balloon and laid him down. He seemed to be examining the boy, then working on the arm. The boy writhed, Gurley calmed him, the boy writhed again, and finally Gurley stopped what he was doing. He scooped the boy up in his arms, an act which made the boy shrink in size even more. It was hard to believe we'd ever taken him for a man. As Gurley walked toward us, we could see him try to take on a face he felt appropriate to the act—a sympathetic warrior, the soldier with a heart. But Gurley was so consumed with perfecting his walk that he wasn't paying enough attention to how he carried the boy, who was screaming in pain, shattering whatever pacific image Gurley was trying to project. By the time they reached us, Gurley's lips were drawn tight and he was sweating. I could tell he was angry, furious, and I wasn't sure at whom: me? Lily? Probably the boy for spoiling the show. I was angry because Gurley had managed to leave the defusing task to me.

Gurley set him down gently enough. Lily's hands flew about the boy, not quite touching him, as if she didn't know where to start. Finally, she went to his face and ran two fingers along his cheek. The boy interrupted his crying to study her.

Gurley called me aside, and I tried to anticipate what he was going to say. "Shall we detonate the remaining explosives, sir?"

"What?" Gurley said, watching Lily watch the boy.

"The balloon?" I said. "Clear it?" I looked around. "Not that anyone would ever come across those bombs out here, but—still. Should I save the balloon?"

"Yes," said Gurley, still not looking at me.

"But blow the explosives?"

"Yes," Gurley said.

"Or disarm them?"

"Yes," he said again, kneeling now behind Lily, almost as if he were hiding from the boy.

"Sir?" I asked again.

Gurley twisted around. "Goddammit, Belk."

"But—sir?"

"Leave the balloon be, and get the damn medical kit out of the boat." He turned back to the boy. "Jesus. The fiends." He put a hand on Lily's back. "Lily," he said. "Fiends."

We didn't have much of a medical kit. Some bandages, antiseptic, a syringe, and a precious vial of morphine. When I returned, I saw that Gurley had broken off a thin alder branch to use as a kind of splint for the arm. He was standing now, hands on hips, surveying the scene.

"Lily," he said. "Dearest."

Gurley looked at me briefly, and then back to Lily.

"Lily," he repeated, but she wouldn't turn around, so he turned to me. Nodding to the boy, he drew a finger across his throat, trying—unsuccessfully—to appear remorseful as he did. Then he spoke up again. "I think—I think we're too late, Lily. I'd like to help, but—maybe if we'd caught him...sooner. Maybe if—maybe if they'd never launched him in that damn balloon." He looked at me, and then off at the crash site.

"Go," Lily said quietly, so quietly the word didn't seem to come from her; it was as if it had welled up from the earth or seeped out of the boy. She turned, then stood and stared at Gurley and me. "If you want to leave, leave. Both of you. Leave the kit, and leave us."

Gurley clapped a hand on my back. "Of course we won't leave you," he said. "But Lily, he's done—I mean, he's not going to make it."

Lily looked at me.

"Just a broken arm, Captain?" I said. "We can probably figure out a way to—get him back to—get him somewhere." I could tell by Lily's face that I was wrong, but I couldn't figure out why. "That splint there," I said, mostly to have something to say.

"You can splint his arm all you like, Sergeant," Gurley said. "But you can't splint what's not there." He walked over and stood above the boy, who had begun to cry again. Or rather, his face looked like he was screaming, but nothing was coming out, not really. Every now and then, a note or two of his high horrible moan would break through, but otherwise, it was just hiss and breath. I went over to the boy and knelt. Like Lily, I found my hands floating above him, unable to find a place or reason to touch him. I was no judge of kids then—I was a kid—and so I couldn't tell you his age, only that I knew he was younger than he looked. His face was chapped and creased, burned by the sun and wind. If you studied just the wrinkles around his eyes, you might have taken him for a dwarf grandparent. But if you looked at his eyes, if you looked at what soft, smooth stretches of skin remained, here and there, along his scalp, under his chin—you could tell he was a child. Eight or nine or seven: however old you have to be to find yourself in a balloon floating across the Pacific, or lying on wet ground, hurt, so far from home, and no one like your parents anywhere near.

He was wearing khaki coveralls; they'd been labeled with a number and several Japanese characters on his chest. He had on several pairs of socks, but not shoes. I looked at the arm. It was more than broken. Mangled. Maybe Gurley was right. Splinting wouldn't help. The boy suddenly broke out of his silent screaming and shouted something at me in a high voice. He lifted his head as best he could and looked down at the arm. I did, too, following the arm and his gaze all the way down to his hand, or where his hand should have been. Instead, there was a giant, bloody ball of bandages—someone's socks, perhaps a torn piece of a shirt—none of it quite adding up to the tourniquet Gurley must have intended. But even the mound of bandages couldn't hide the fact that most, or all, of the hand was missing. I turned quickly to Lily and the boy shrieked.

"He—he lost—" Lily said, and knelt beside the boy once more. She laid a hand on his good arm and he quieted.

"Blew off his damn hand when he was trying to get out, must have," Gurley said. "Probably just one of those little squibs that helps control altitude, but still—big enough. He's lost a lot of blood. He's going to lose more." Gurley broke off, looked back toward the boat. "There are other problems," he finished.

"Just leave," Lily said. "And there will be no problems."

Gurley put on a thin smile. "You make a fine nurse, dear, but no soldier. I don't want to say it, but it's true: it would have been better if he'd died when he landed. Now, it would have been even better if he'd never found his way into the balloon, but once he had, it would have been better if everything had proceeded to—the Japs' admittedly *sick*— plan. Because—here we are, he's in pain, he's dying, and even if he did live long enough for us to get him to—where? The corner hospital?"

"Bethel," Lily said.

"Bethel," Gurley repeated. "Okay, we get him to Bethel, and then what, Sergeant?"

"Transport to Anchorage?" I said.

"No, you foolish boy. Think. We bring a child into Bethel, a Japanese one, no less, one who, by all appearances, has *flown* here in a balloon, and what happens?" Gurley looked at us. Lily turned away. "All hell breaks loose. The entire United States Army descends on the tundra to find all the other Jap miscreants who've flown here in balloons."

"There aren't others," Lily said quietly, and looked at me.

"There's one other," Gurley said, "out here somewhere. Remember? Or did you lie about that, too? The rapist?"

"He's not—" Lily began. "Here. That man is not out here. I know."

"You know because of your hocus-pocus Eskimo magic, or are you just saying this so I'll give up?" Gurley said, and looked around. "Or do you want me to believe that this little boy is your Saburo? Because the lad didn't mention you. All I got was some claptrap about his parents. Apologies, regrets, sorry, sorry, and so on." He studied the boy like he was something he'd found washed up on the beach. "He's some sort of weird experiment, I figure. Who knows? In any case, he's not the point end of an invasion force. But—"

"So, bring him to Bethel," Lily said.

"I think I just explained," Gurley said to Lily, and turned to me. "Did I explain?"

"Well, sir, I'm not sure the entire army—"

"Jesus Christ, Belk."

Lily looked at the boy for a long moment and then turned to us. "Okay," she said. "We'll camp here for the evening." She looked at Gurley. "How's that?"

"That's lovely," Gurley said, waving an arm in front of his face. "It's just lovely here."

"We have light left," I said, looking at my watch. "We could probably make it a good distance of the way back—"

"He's not ready to go, Louis," Lily said quietly.

"Well, I don't know," I said. "You've got that splint on him and—"

Gurley had begun to growl after Lily spoke, and now reached a roar. "She means *me,* you idiot!" He and Lily exchanged a long, silent look. Lily finally broke away and knelt down before the boy.

"Fuck!" Gurley shrieked, and I really mean *shrieked*—a high, piercing, birdlike noise. He tottered over to the boy and stood over him. "You don't know how lucky you are, young man," he said, in English. "You've found yourself in the clutches of two—no, three—fools." Gurley struggled into a crouch. "So here is our deal: if you survive till morning, off we all go to Bethel to face God knows what repercussions." Gurley then turned to us; the boy turned his head, too. "And if he does survive, that will be evidence indeed of magic. Pretty damn strong magic."

Lily looked at me. "Stay with him," she said, and I wasn't sure if she meant the boy or Gurley. "I'm going to get some things from the boat."

"That's cheating," Gurley called after as she walked. "I want to see magic alone get him through the night." Lily raised an arm and waved off Gurley's words. It actually relieved the tension a bit; her weary wave seemed less the act of a mortal enemy than a long-suffering but indulgent spouse.

But Gurley quickly ended the respite. "It's been nice knowing you, Sergeant," he said, staring after her.

"Sir," I said, not meeting his eyes. I was busy looking for his hands, his gun.

"I know you think it heartless. Or I think you do. I know Lily does. But leaving the boy here, yes, killing him, would spare everyone a lot of misery."

"Sir," I said, not sure if he still had a mind you could reason with, or if I was better off just leaping on him, and sparing everyone a lot of misery. "Just wait. She'll surprise you. I bet he'll surprise you. Kids are—"

"He's already surprised me," said Gurley. "He flew across the fucking ocean. And that's not all. Come." Gurley went to the boy, knelt, and then roughly tore open his coveralls. The boy fought him weakly. When he started to cry out, Gurley raised a hand as if to hit him, and looked to see if Lily had heard. She hadn't. The boy went silent with fear and looked to me for help. I screwed up what courage I could and stepped next to Gurley. But before I could lay a hand on him, he spoke: "Surprise," he said.

I looked down. The boy's exposed chest and stomach were a mottled purple. The skin just above his collarbone was raw and red. I knew what Gurley was doing; he was diagnosing plague. "I saw it when I was working on the crash site," Gurley said, and stood. "I didn't look in the groin area yet, but I don't have to. You've got lymph nodes here, too," he said, fingering his neck. "You see why we have to get out of here? They sent the best germ weapon container possible: a human. A human rat. Which means he was dying anyway. Hell, he's lost enough blood he may not even survive long enough to die of plague. But we've got to get back. Get away from him. So we got a vaccine: like the major said, What if this is a new strain?"

I didn't know. I didn't know enough about plague or enough about how much Gurley knew about medicine to know if he was lying. The boy looked ill, but he'd just come across the Pacific in an open balloon. The rash on his neck could have been from the coveralls. Where were the blown lymph nodes, the buboes? I saw Gurley glance back toward the boat. Lily was walking back toward us.

"You've got to tell her, Belk," he said. "She's not listening to me right now."

"Sir, I don't think—"

"Redo the math, son," Gurley said. "You thought you were just risking the boy's life when you sided with her before. Now you're risking yours. And mine. And hers." I didn't answer. I just stared at the boy, then at Lily. When she finally reached us, she gave Gurley a look that caused him to rethink whatever he was about to say and stalk off instead. He looked back just once, and then loped away, hands flying about, swatting mosquitoes.

Lily turned to me. I hadn't had enough time to decide what to say, or how. But Lily didn't wait for me to speak. "Louis," she said, and we both looked down at our very ill charge. "Can you pick him up?"

CHAPTER 19

I TOOK A BREATH, I KNELT, I LIFTED HIM UP. AND THEN I
carried the boy back to the spot where we'd beached the boat. It was a
longer trip than we thought—I'd estimate a mile, but trudging through
the tundra was such slow going, it could have been ten. The mosquitoes clotted around his open wounds like shifting scabs.

Lily and I eventually decided the best thing was to undo the mess of
bandages Gurley had applied and apply a proper tourniquet, or as
proper a one as we could manage. We also resplinted the arm and
bound it to his side to immobilize it completely. But we only came to
these decisions gradually, after several painful false starts. The boy's
screams grew louder and louder. Several times I found myself wondering if Gurley was right: it would be better if the boy had died, or could
die, quickly.

There were moments when he seemed he would. I've seen it happen to enough others in the hospital to know he was going into shock.
The boy's red, windburned face somehow managed to lose all its
color—or rather, soak up a new color, the blank white of the endlessly
cloudy sky. At times, his color returned, but then I couldn't be sure—
perhaps it was just that the light was failing and it was no longer easy
to tell what he looked like.

Lily paid no attention to the sky or me or Gurley, whom we could now see, back at the crash site, sticking out of the horizon like the last post of some abandoned fence. Lily gave the boy water and fed him broken bits of cracker. When he shivered, she found a blanket, wrapped it around him tightly. And when night finally did come, she had me set up a tent and help her move the boy inside. Then she crawled in herself. I tried to stop her before she went into the tent.

"Lily," I said, and she twisted around to shush me.

"What?"

"Lily," I said again. I still hadn't told her about Gurley's diagnosis. The more I'd seen of the boy, the more I thought Gurley was wrong. I didn't want to tell Lily about any of this, but I didn't want her to expose herself any more than she had, either.

I said nothing.

"Louis," she said. "Will you keep watch?"

"Lily—"

"Please, Louis. I'm worried about Gurley. I'm worried about the boy. I'm worried about him and the boy, what he'll do. Just wait."

She disappeared into the tent for several minutes. I heard some whispers, tears, and then nothing at all. Finally, her face reappeared.

"Where is he?" she asked, squinting toward the crash site. But it was too dark now to see, or to tell Gurley apart from the lonely stunted trees that cropped up here and there. She climbed out and stood up.

"I don't know," I said. "I thought he was staying out there to defuse or detonate the remaining bombs, but I never heard anything." What I'd really been listening for was the sound of a single shot from Gurley's sidearm, his skull perhaps muffling the sound if he held the barrel close. But there had been nothing. Just the wind, and when it paused, the whine of mosquitoes finding an ear.

"Did Gurley find out his name?" she said.

"His name?"

"I can't read the writing on his coveralls."

I stared at the tent. "Lily, I don't know. No, if he did, he didn't say.

I—I don't know Japanese either. Didn't Saburo—your Saburo—teach you any?"

"This is my Saburo," she said. She closed her eyes, and when she opened them once more, they were full of tears. "I—I think I killed him."

"Lily, what's happened?" I moved for the tent, but she stopped me. From inside the tent, the boy gave a little moan, and Lily winced. More than winced, really—she buckled slightly, grabbing her elbows, hunching her shoulders. "Can't you hear him?" she said. "I killed him," she said softly.

I grabbed her. "Lily, the boy? You killed the boy? Right now? Jesus, Lily. What are you doing? Gurley would've—"

Another tiny moan came from the tent.

The Yup'ik say the tundra is haunted. But *haunted* is a white man's word, and it doesn't mean what the Yup'ik mean. The spirits found in the bush—animal and human, living and dead—do not haunt, they exist, as real and present as any other aspect of life: water, breath, food.

I didn't understand this for a long time. When I was a young priest, I would tell people that ghosts only haunted those who believed in them. Don't put your faith in specters, I would say, put your faith in God: *that* faith will be returned.

Only later, too late, did I learn what is really true, a truth that, in some ways, has nothing to do with God: ghosts only *haunt* those who do not believe. Someone who already believes can never be surprised to see something he knows already exists. The shadow that disappears into a corner of the community center one winter night is doubtless your cousin who drowned the year before. The creaking floor that wakens you is your husband, finally returned from the hunt. The face outside the hospital window is an *angalkuq*, pulling rain from the skies.

And the boy in the tent, the *tan'gaurluq* who dropped from a hole in the blue—

"Louis," Lily started, stopped, and then started again. "I don't know why this happened. Or how. I was so anxious to get back out here, where I thought my powers would be strong again. That's why I went on my journey the other night. To see what had changed since the last time I had been able to see that other world—that world of spirits and life and everything real. And I wanted to see Saburo, see where he had put our little boy. I didn't see anything at first—but what I saw—what I finally saw frightened me."

Lily had seen another child. At first she thought it was her own, but came to understand that it wasn't. It was a boy, a Japanese boy, who had come from beyond. And since no spirit comes into the world without another life departing it, Lily explained, she knew then that Saburo had died, and this boy had come to tell her that. The spirits—Saburo—had sent him to her, just as they had sent me. But whereas they had sent me to remind Lily that Saburo lived, they had sent this boy to let her know that Saburo was dead.

Worse, she believed she had killed him, by falling in love or into the spell that Gurley cast—whatever it was, she had lost hold of Saburo. "I let go of his memory, Louis, and when I did, I let go of him, he sank away, he died. No one should take another lover while the first still lives, while you are still in love with him. I knew this."

I know: madness. Arctic hysteria. Or half a dozen newfangled names they now have for conditions like Lily's (or Gurley's, for that matter). But we had none of those names then. We had a first-aid kit with some bandages and another kit to blow up bombs. We had a boat. A balloon. A boy.

Lily's maternal instincts already lay raw and exposed; it was easy for her—perhaps essential for her—to believe this boy from the sky had been sent by the sky. Any hope for the happy repose—and forgiveness—of the Saburo she lost now lay with this child, whatever his name was.

She was absolutely certain, and wanted me to be, too.

"He cannot die," she said. "If he dies, I will die with him, and I will join Saburo, but not in a good place. In this place, we will wander, all of us, searching for good souls to take us."

"Lily," I interrupted.

"Louis, listen to me: if the boy lives, he may go on to a life of honor, he may do the work that the spirit world requires of the living. Feeding us, sheltering us, bringing us peace until that day when he has finally done enough and we may all rest." She turned to the tent, and then to me. "Louis," she said. "I'm not—I can't do what I once could. I'm not strong enough, not against a man with a gun. But you know Gurley. You'd know how to stop him. Just don't let him take the boy. I'm afraid of what he'll do. He's just a boy. Louis? Promise me. Please. Louis. Protect him." She clasped her hands together. "Us," she said finally. "Protect us."

AND WHAT DID I say then? With Lily's eyes shining, or maybe glistening, with what faint light still held, and looking to me for help?

I said nothing. I stepped past her, around the tent, and into the brush, toward Gurley. I was afraid I would start crying—over the childish confusion and disappointment over everything, but finally, over that *us*—"protect us." She might have been talking about the boy, or Saburo, or even in some strange way, Gurley—people whom she had loved. But not me. I had been a friend, just a friend, and worse still, I was now failing at that as well.

Stumbling in and out of holes, crashing into the brush here and there, I was making enough noise to hide any sniffling, and later, enough noise to allow Gurley to walk up and take me by surprise.

"Sergeant?" he said, his voice not quite a whisper. He spoke as though we'd been planning to meet, just like this.

I squinted hard to make sure my eyes hid any trace of tears and answered him: "Sir?"

"That's a good lad," he said softly. "You had a choice to make back there, me or her, your country or your crotch, and I'm glad to see you chose your country."

It started as a punch, my right fist right to his face, but I was too angry, had been imagining this for too long, and found myself follow-ing my fist with my head, plowing into him like we were brawling in a schoolyard.

But there'd never been this much blood in the schoolyard, nor the orphanage. I'd never found myself atop a foe so quickly or easily, swinging away, had never discovered how nauseating it is to beat someone who won't beat back.

And he wouldn't. Not after blood had run into the seams between every tooth, not when his left eye had swollen into its own kind of bubo, purple and wet, not even when I—I know I didn't do this, that I couldn't have done it, but I remember it all the same—when I bit his forehead, right at the hairline, and tasted blood.

He laughed, not a sensible laugh, but an off-key cackle that I could feel—because that's where I was sitting—in his diaphragm. That's why I bit him, if I bit him. If he laughed at my fists and feet, what did I have left? My head. Those teeth. I'd learned this from Gurley, this wildness.

The bite caused his laugh to switch to a screech, but it was all part of the same wail, and when I stood, disgusted as much with myself as with him, the laugh returned. Then he felt around in the back of his mouth for something, and winced. Two crimson fingers returned with what must have been a tooth.

"Tallyho!" Gurley chortled, or gurgled. He held up the tooth to me and I looked away. I expected him to get up, but he lay back and blinked several times and looked at the sky.

I was about to walk away when he spoke. "She's still with the boy?" he asked, and I almost had to ask him who.

I finally nodded, once, and he nodded in return, and struggled to sit, and then stand. The place where he had fallen had begun to fill with water, and he bent over the puddle to study his face. When he stood again, I looked him over, embarrassed. He looked both worse and better than I thought he would, like he'd been attacked by a dog, or had snapped his head against a steering wheel.

I turned away again.

"There, there, Sergeant," he said. "I'm sorry. Very sorry. We should have gotten that over with long, long ago. Shouldn't we have? Shouldn't we?"

I left him there. I walked away—away from Gurley, away from the balloon, away from the tents and the boats. I walked toward nothing. But I didn't get far before I ran out of land. I waded in, stumbled, soaked myself, and retreated. I walked back toward Gurley, who was still talking—to me, to himself—and tried a different direction. Again I sank. I just wanted to leave, and leave all of them behind. I wanted to keep walking until I could no longer hear Gurley's voice, until I could no longer see anything. But wherever I stepped, the water rose around my feet. I wanted a balloon of my own.

I returned and stood by Gurley. He kept talking, and talking, whether or not I was looking at him. Usually I wasn't. I was embarrassed with what I'd done to him. I might as well have attacked the little Japanese boy; Gurley looked almost as pathetic and wild-eyed.

Gurley made it worse by insisting that he *forgave* me. He said this in a dozen different ways, cited anecdotes, quoted the Bible, said he understood, offered consolation, commiseration. Unfortunately, I was young enough and Christian enough to want and need, and worst of all, believe, that forgiveness. Which meant that when he finally worked his monologue back around to Lily and the boy, the two of them in the tent, it was already too late for me. The most potent tranquilizing drug would not have worked on me so quickly or so well. He was planning, and I was listening. "A little awkward, a little awkward," he concluded, "but—we'll make it work. We'll find a way. We've had bigger challenges in this war, haven't we, Sergeant?" I looked away. "And bigger yet to come. Now, let us find our way back to the boat, and I shall tell you what we—what you, in particular, have to do."

Gurley used what light the night provided to pick a way back to the boat that didn't lead us directly past the tent. There wasn't much of a moon, but somehow the tundra still managed a silver glow. I was too full of all that Lily had told me to stop him or even speak up. The only things I had to say, in fact, were about Lily, and I couldn't find a way to tell Gurley what I knew. Did he know that Lily really loved him? Actually, the word probably wasn't *love* but it was something like that. Needed him. Had found herself bound to him. Gurley, meanwhile, spoke of bombs and fuses and delays, and whether we had the equipment required to detonate something remotely. Then he stopped talking, and after a moment, I realized he was waiting for a reply.

"I think we do—I think we have all that, sir," I said, having trouble readjusting from the world we were in to the one we had left, where there were rules, a war, and bombs, and people like me who dealt with them. "You want to blow up the balloon after all?" I asked, mostly to get additional time to refocus. It took a moment: after Lily's frantic whispers, I'd forgotten that it had been a balloon that had brought the boy here, not spirits, not magic, not Lily.

Gurley stopped walking and looked at me warily. "Yes," he said. "I want to blow up—the balloon." He looked over my shoulder in the direction of the tent. "No need to save it. We certainly have enough balloon carcasses by now," he said. "But you *see* the problem, Sergeant—yes?"

Peter betrayed Jesus three times before the cock crowed at dawn. To my knowledge, the devil has asked me to be faithful just once—right there, before dawn—and I obeyed: I listened.

Gurley wanted to blow up the balloon, yes, but he also wanted to blow up the boy. A living, breathing Japanese who'd arrived by balloon was a glorious prize, but an outdated one. The war was ending. Worse yet, men like the major in Fairbanks would add the boy to the two dead "fishermen" and decide the sum equaled the start of a massive, and manned, balloon campaign. That could only mean extra months (years?) in Alaska. No: we had to dispose of the balloon and the boy, destroy any trace that they had ever existed, and we had to do it immediately. The major and the men from Ladd Field were likely just hours away from deciding to strike out across the tundra in search of germs.

The boy was dying, Gurley said, building his case. What was wanted was mercy, not agony, not for anyone. Now, he couldn't put a gun to the boy's head, Gurley explained. He wasn't a barbarian. And he couldn't ask me to do it: I wasn't enough of a soldier. (He didn't even pause to smirk.) No, things had to proceed according to the natural order of things, which was this: whoever had put the boy in that balloon ("A stowaway?" I asked, merely to have some way to counter him, but Gurley rolled his eyes) had intended for him to die in the ensuing explosion. When the balloon crashed, it should have exploded. He should have died. Our presence had upset this plan; we could give fate its due by placing the boy back at the crash site, and then detonating the balloon. This was not about the army, or war, or anything else. It was about predestination. The divine order of things. We had the equipment, which was simple enough. C3, blasting wire, a little hell box. Put the boy in position, affix the explosives, run the wire, retreat to safety, depress the plunger, and—

"Lily?" I asked.

Gurley spun around, then turned back to me, relieved. We'd reached the boat. "I thought you meant she was here."

"No," I said, taking a quick look for her myself. "But she'll hear the blast."

Gurley nodded and exhaled and said nothing for a while.

When he started speaking again, his voice had changed. Just slightly, but the effect was startling. "It's too much," he said. "It's too much to ask her, too, to die—of simple heartache," he added. "Not over *me,* of course," he said, his face tight with disdain. "But dear *Saburo.*" I stared. "Rapist and rival, and spy." He waited, clearly looking for a sign in me that I understood what he meant and did not need him to go on. But whatever he saw wasn't enough, so he continued. "As you must know, hormone-besotted as you are, Fair Belk, Miss Lily has become a . . . difficulty, yes. 'Tis true?"

"Sir," I said, and stopped. "My—my God—"

"Yes," Gurley said. "Your God. Does not smile down upon this part of the world. No, tremble not, Sergeant. As convenient as it would be if Lily, too, lay beside the boy, beside the balloon, only to disappear with the rest of the mess, it is a trifle inconvenient as well," he admitted. "Morally."

"She—loves you," I said. It was all I could think of to say. "She told me."

Gurley looked at me. First his face said: *a lie.* Then it said: *how sweet if it were true.* And then he spoke. "Well, Sergeant," he said. "You see our dilemma."

I COULD HAVE REFUSED to set the charge against the balloon. Refused to unspool the wire, refused to attach it to the hell box. I could have refused to knife the wall of the tent where the boy and Lily lay, refused to snatch the boy through the gash—his screams instant, inhuman—and sprint for the crash site while Gurley wrestled with Lily, quieting her with the force of his words and, when that didn't work, force alone. I could have refused to set the boy in the place Gurley had designated within the balloon's wreckage. I could have refused to bind the boy's arms and legs to the control frame just as Gurley insisted he would tie Lily to the boat, or to stakes in the ground, or to whatever he had to in order to keep her from following us back to the balloon.

But I did as I was told, and, with Lily's plea still echoing, a little bit more. When Gurley and I met, however—me walking back from the balloon site and him walking toward it—I realized, too late, that I could have done better.

He looked furious, on the point of weeping. He didn't break his stride nor even turn to look at me as he spoke: "Change of *plans,* Sergeant." I think my heart stopped beating. I certainly stopped walking, and turned to watch him lurch through the swampy tundra toward the balloon.

He had killed Lily. I had failed her, utterly. And now what: Was I supposed to chase after him? Leap on him, press his face into the nearest puddle and drown him? Or race to where Lily lay, apologize to whatever life of her still remained?

I ran to Lily. There'd be time enough to deal with Gurley. But Saburo, Jap Sam, the girl who died in childbirth at her boarding school—all the seeing spirits might all be drawing Lily into the clouds, even now.

I said prayers as I ran. Ones I knew by heart and others I made up. Whatever I said, though, it must have been powerful. Because when I reached the camp, I found Lily, alive and upright, packing our supplies onto the boat.

"Lily," I cried. I went to hug her, but something about the way she looked at me stopped me short.

"Where's Gurley?" she said. I was anxious to explain away my role in hustling the boy away from camp, to mention how I needed to do so in order for the rest of the plan to work, but Lily wasn't interested. "Where is he?" she asked again, nervous now.

I know what I wanted to say, but I hadn't heard the noise I'd been waiting for yet. So instead of answering her directly, I explained what I'd done. I'd *protected* them, her and the boy, and by extension, Saburo. Gurley had wanted me to wire the balloon to explode. He'd planned to place the boy in the balloon, retreat to a little tuft of tundra where I'd placed the hell box. Then he'd depress the plunger, the charge would go down the wire, and all his problems, save Lily, would disappear.

I'd placed the hell box on the small patch of dry land, as requested. I'd run the wires out to the balloon, as requested. The wires disappeared under the balloon, as though that were where they connected to the invisible charges. But they actually continued on past the balloon, hidden in the grass, and looped all the way back, still hidden, to the tuft of land where Gurley now stood.

Evil as I was, or am, I could not kill a man. I knew this even then. The granting and taking of life is best left to fate, to God, and I had left it so. I could lay the wire, attach it to charges (not a stick or two, but all we had) buried in the grass beneath the spot where Gurley would have to stand, but only God could see to it that Gurley did what he did. That is, if Gurley chose to kill the boy, he would kill himself. If he spared the boy, he would spare himself.

But Lily did not fall into my arms, sad and relieved. Instead, she cried: "What have you done?"

"Protected you," I said, quiet with shock. "Both of you."

"Didn't you see him?" she said. I nodded. "He was going out there to get the boy."

"He was going out there to kill him," I said. "He was going to—he talked about—he was going to kill you. He said, 'Change of...'—he—I thought he had."

"Louis!" she cried, and began to run.

During the past hours, we'd worn a path from our landing spot to the balloon, and for a while, Lily stayed on it. But as we grew closer, she left the path for the most direct route, sloshing through the water and brush straight to Gurley.

I stayed on the path. It would be faster.

I saw Gurley stoop and pick up the hell box. Even before crying a warning to Lily, I wanted to yell to her, *See what he's doing? He was going to kill the boy!*

The morning was just breaking, and we were close enough now to see everything—the balloon resting lightly on the soggy tundra, as though it might inflate and fly once more; Gurley, hell box in hand, surveying the scene.

"Stop! Stop!" Lily screamed.

I kept along the path, not saying a word, calculating how large the blast zone would be and when I would enter it.

Stop, stop!

She loved him.

The boy: she needed the boy.

But Gurley: she loved him.

And when Gurley looked back and saw her, I had to hope he saw this. I couldn't see, I couldn't see his eyes, I could only see him turn to face her as she staggered out of the last stretch of water. I wish I had been closer! To see Gurley, to see if he were angry, or bemused, if his cheeks were flushed or if he rolled his eyes. To see if when their eyes finally met, he realized that he had been in love, had been loved.

Or to see whether, in that moment before Gurley pressed the plunger, they touched, whether their hands met, or their lips, whether it was their lives, whole and complete, that flashed before their eyes, or whether it was merely the flash of the blast itself.

But I wasn't closer. If I had been, I might have been killed instead of merely deafened. Thrown by the blast, I was flat on my back in an inch-deep puddle that had already been there or that I had created. I may have blacked out; I'm not sure. I could feel my fingers tangled in the *ayuq,* I could feel the tundra ooze pulling at my boots, my shoulders, my scalp. I could smell and taste the salt of the far-off ocean, and for some moments I thought the water was high enough that it had entered my ears—all I could hear was a dull, muffled rustling somewhere inside my head. But when I finally stood, my ears didn't clear.

I stared at the blast site waiting for my hearing to return. It never has completely, but in a minute or two, some sounds returned. The rush of wind, a mosquito that sounded miles distant but appeared on my palm after I'd absently slapped at my ear, and after that slap, a high wail, also distant. I'd forgotten about the boy: even though I'd made sure that his spot in the balloon wreckage would be well clear of the explosion, the blast must have frightened him, and now he was crying.

But he was closer, too.

A few yards up the path, in fact, in a patch of salmonberries that were growing beneath a stunted cottonwood, where he was keening, choking, screaming, not having moved an inch from the spot where Gurley had safely placed him.

CHAPTER 20

THE SMOKE AND NOISE OF THE BLAST HAD ALREADY DISSI-pated. The sky, incredibly, was just as it had been before. The birds that must have shrieked into flight were long gone or had already returned.

And now, this boy, wailing.

This partial deafness has been a curse all my life, but I was grateful for it then. Because if I had heard Lily screaming in pain, or Gurley moaning, I know I would have gone to them. And because they would have been too wounded for me to help in any way, I would have had to simply crouch by them, endure their screams—and eyes! Eyes! How they would have looked at me!—until they finally fell silent. Who first? Gurley? Lily? Or would they fall suddenly silent together?

And if I had heard the boy screaming, full volume, I don't think I would have stooped and tended to him. I would have been too angry. Two people dead; an officer, his lover, the man I served and the woman I loved, and this boy screaming as though his were the only real pain? I wouldn't have gone near him.

But I did go to him. I didn't go to Gurley and Lily. Because I heard Lily tell me to go to the boy. It wasn't her voice, just Lily, herself, there, inside me. Perhaps *hear* isn't the right word, then—but I knew that she wanted me to take the boy to the boat, to a doctor. You could argue that I knew she wanted that before she died, before I "heard" her within me. Fair enough. But as I pushed off from shore, the boy, barely alive, in the bow, she was there, too. And after the motor had hiccuped to life and we began picking our way down through the delta to the ocean, she was still there, marking sandbars and pointing out which turns to take when. She told us where to stop the first night, and again the second.

You still don't believe me.

Then what of this:

The morning of the third day, the boy was weak, close to death. Once we were in the boat, I gave him water, broke up some of our rations into tiny bites, some of which he spat out, some of which he ate. After the food, but especially the water, he seemed to recover some of his strength, but spent almost all that strength on moaning with new fervor. I waited until we reached a wide, almost currentless stretch of water, and then throttled back, letting the boat drift while I rummaged in the medical kit for the vial of morphine. I had wanted to wait for as long as possible before administering any, to stretch out its use for as long as possible. But now I found the needle, pierced the seal, drew a small amount, and carefully moved toward him.

I thought his eyes would be fixed on the needle, but they weren't; he stared straight at me. And the closer I got, the less he moaned, the more open his face became. When I was close enough, I put a hand out to touch his good arm, and stopped. The rapid breaths that had come after the crying were slowing, and through that touch alone, I could feel the whole of him relaxing, degree by degree. This wasn't me. This couldn't have been only me.

He laid his head back and stared at the sky a moment, then at me, and then closed his eyes. I started; I thought this was the moment. I reflexively raised the needle until I realized he wouldn't need the morphine now, not if he had reached the moment of death. I eased back and watched.

But one minute passed and then another with the boat still drifting, its progress no longer measurable. He didn't die. He kept breathing, ragged breath after ragged breath, and I couldn't break away. Who was he? How had he gotten here? I should have been able to tell with that touch. Even if we couldn't speak, I could learn, as Lily could, through touch alone, through the power of a hand, what secrets lay within.

So I closed my eyes, too, and concentrated, but all I could think of was Lily, and then Gurley, and the sun coming up, and some tundra spirit seeking me out, and then Father Pabich—nothing about the boy.

What happened next seemed to be the boy's decision more than mine. Or perhaps it was Lily's. As I was sitting there, staring at my own hands, the boy, eyes closed, reached out. I put a hand in the way of his, and he caught up two or three of my fingers in a tight grasp. It reminds me, now, of what infants will sometimes do, at the hospital or after a baptism. And the parents smile and laugh: such strength, such affection!

But I didn't smile then. His hand was a boy's hand, but it was dry and cracked. I found myself checking the tips of his fingers for gangrene—some telltale sign of Gurley's black death settling in. But they were just a boy's fingers, the dirt ringed beneath his nails the only black to be found. The feel of his hand, though, that surprised me: rough, callused. I wanted to turn his hand over, examine it more closely as Lily might have, or must have. But he held on tight, and I didn't move, and a story seeped through—a small boy, who'd been pressed into service in a wartime factory because all the able-bodied men were at war. The balloons he was helping build were more wonderful than anything he'd ever made for himself, and he wanted so much to fly in one.

They were experimenting with a new, larger model. They flew it on a short tether, overnight, to test a new mixture of gases. He'd watched from outside the fence. It was so close, so tempting. He crawled under the fence, and then, before he realized what he was doing, he was climbing up the rope. Climbing up, hand over hand, just like they'd been doing in school, all of them training to be strong young warriors, ready to fight when the last stand began. And then he was inside. It was impossible that this was happening, of course, impossible to any adult in particular, impossible to anyone who was not a boy who wanted to fly. He took out a knife, a little one. This they hadn't taught in school; this was what his father gave to him before his father left on a train that took him to a ship that took him to what his mother said was a tiny island, surrounded by a wide ocean, far away, so far that the boy was still waiting for an answer to the letters he'd written his dad, telling him how careful he'd been with the knife, how skilled he'd become with it.

He cut the first tether, the rope he'd climbed up on, and the knife worked beautifully, the rope helping him, each strand shattering as he drew the blade across it. When the rope snapped free, the balloon lurched, and he almost fell out, almost dropped the knife. But he was okay now, he was okay, a little scared, maybe, but okay, and his hand—saving the knife caused him to get a little cut. Was it bad? He held it up; he couldn't see it well, it was dark. It felt moist, sticky, but it didn't hurt, not yet. He licked it, and then it started to hurt, so he made a fist and sat back for a moment. It wasn't much of a cut, but it was in the same place he'd gotten scratched by that cat. That cat! She'd cornered the mouse he'd been keeping—these men had been keeping the mice in these little cages, outside, but he'd gone and gotten one, just for himself, he'd take care of it, and then that cat. He'd like to have his little mouse with him now, he'd like to see this: look, he was cutting the second tether. There were three. Snap. The balloon lurched again, but this time he was ready, braced, the balloon now rocking, angry or excited, he couldn't tell. If he were a balloon, he'd want to fly, he wouldn't want to stay tied to the ground. Now for the last cord. His hand was bleeding again, not badly. He wiped it on his coveralls, the little worker coveralls they gave him when he started at the factory. "So grown up!" his mother had said, crying for some reason, when she saw him for the first time in the coveralls. She should have been happy: he was helping now. Helping Father. Helping Mother, who was working in the same factory. If only he had had brothers, sisters, they all could have worked, all could have helped. All of them lined up in their uniforms.

He put his knife to the last strand and paused. The ground looked funny from the balloon. Really close one minute, really far away the next. He wondered how far the balloon would fly. Would someone come after him? Would his mother be angry? Would he get hungry? Thirsty? He had a stick of gum in his pocket. How long would this take? How long before he saw his dad, down on the beach, on an island, just like this one, but smaller? The boy could see him there. Dad! Up here! I'm coming! He sawed and sawed at this last rope, but it was tougher than the others, took a while, and now he was nervous. He was late. He was expected. He worked faster. His dad was right: it was a good knife, but even with a good knife, this took time. His hand started bleeding again, the same hand that held the knife. Sawing, sawing. The knife was getting dirty, getting bloody, and he thought of his father's stern face. He stopped sawing for a moment to clean it off, and the knife fell away.

His father's knife! It took forever to fall, and when it did, he had to strain to hear it land. He could see it, glinting there in some far-off light. He checked the rope. Could he climb back down, back up? He gave it a tug. He was almost done! Dad! The knife! The rope didn't understand what was happening. The knife was gone, but the rope kept splitting, shredding, tearing, the sound just like that first day at the factory, when he'd slipped and fallen and hurt his leg, torn his uniform. The older boys around him, teasing, yelling, and then his mother there, scooping him up, shrieking at the bleeding, at the boys yelling, then setting him down, taking the cloth from her hair, and tearing it slowly—it was hard to tear—crying as she did, yelling at the boys, and then at the boss when he came, she was crying and yelling while she tied the cloth around his leg, the blood seeping through and then stopping. And then snap, the rope broke, and he was gone, the balloon vaulting up like the moon had been waiting for it, impatiently, and finally just yanked it free like a flower.

It was incredible, wonderful, more wonderful than he could have imagined. His hand didn't hurt anymore. He wasn't crying anymore. (When had he started crying? He touched his cheek, wet.) And now he was flying, really flying, just him. Not a sound. Up over the factory, over the town. Where was his house? There? He waved. Bye, Mom! He looked out over the ocean. Where was Dad? How did you steer? Oh, but these were army balloons; they would know where to go.

It grew cold. While he was looking out over the town, for that cat, his mouse, looking out over the houses of all those friends who would be so jealous, a sudden gust of wind pulled the balloon so violently, he almost fell out—again!—and when he finally caught his breath and looked out, looked down—it was all gone. The town was gone. It was somewhere back there, a dark shape, no lights, of course, but the ocean now beneath, dark, too, and invisible. It was like the sky just stretched dark in every direction, above, below, before, behind. It made it hard to breathe, just to think of it, all that dark, all that night. Was the balloon moving? Going higher? Lower? How long would this take?

In the morning, he was frozen. Couldn't move. His hands curled up tight, little fists, his hair crunchy with frost. He had some trouble opening his eyes, but he did. And he pounded his fists together, pounded and pounded, and they opened up, slowly, like they were made of metal. They hurt, his fingers were stiff, numb, but he was still there. This was wrong, though. His father had gone to an island, where Mother said it was hot. The sun all day long, the heat continuing through the night. And the boy, he was cold, freezing. He pulled his arms inside the coverall, looked around.

But what a world! The sun so bright, you had to squint wherever you looked, even at the clear blue sky. Down below, something green. An island? The island? Or ocean? It stretched for miles. He was sleepy.

He'd just woken up, but was sleepy. The sun was everywhere, crowding things out so there wasn't room for anything—no clouds, no islands, no air. It was hard to breathe, unless you took little breaths, teeny little breaths, like you were sleeping. Little breaths. Little breaths.

Now he was always hungry. Always cold. His feet felt funny—like they weren't there at all. And his eyes hurt. From the squinting? Just from the air. Just opening them hurt, and he didn't even look anymore. His father would have to see him first. If he closed his eyes, he could imagine it. His father, looking up, and him, looking down, just drifting down, like a cloud. He could see it, just like that. Eyes closed. Little breaths.

He was a cloud, a little cloud, and he was wet, always wet, and all around him was gray, other clouds, and no matter how the wind blew, he still felt wet and cold. But warmer now, somehow the wet made it warmer, and the ocean looked closer. The island! He must be getting close to his father's island. But it was so hard to see now, and all he could see was a mottled green scab on the ocean. It stretched along the horizon. And the next day, he looked down, and saw he was above the scab. Now closer and closer. And there were trees, little trees. In the middle of the ocean. And patches of grass. But where was Father? And water, of course, everywhere, a spider's web of rivers. A fire! There was a fire! And people! Where was Father? It was so hard to see. Little breaths. Father!

He dreamed he'd fallen again, was running in the factory again, his mother running after him, warning him, reminding him what had happened before, but he wasn't listening, he was running, across the roof, and then leaping, flying, until the ground rushed up at him and he'd landed with a thud.

And what had happened then? He lay there, little breaths, but now the air was thick and wet, you had to open your mouth wide to swallow any of it. And where was the balloon? He looked up. The balloon was gone. How was he flying without the balloon? He crept up the side as best he could, looked out, looked down. The green looked so close now, the ocean was right there. He looked around. The balloon lay in an exhausted heap beside him. Land! He was on land! He tried to stand up, but couldn't. His whole body was frozen. Not cold, now, but frozen. He needed to get out. He tried rolling out, but his hands wouldn't work, his feet wouldn't work. And when he finally tumbled over the side, his hand got caught in something, some of the side rigging, and there was a little flash, brighter even than the sun, and though he could feel the hand still clenched there, he couldn't see it, his hand. He screamed.

This man wasn't his father. He didn't answer when the boy said his name. Wasn't helping with the hand, just hurting him more. Carrying him to—smelled good. Food. And water, more water, it trickled down his throat and hurt, but not as much as his hand. Had the man brought his hand?

Then it was inside, dark, warm. A woman there, a man there. And bright again, the balloon again, the flash again, crying again. And here was the other man now, coming up to him, picking him up, taking him flying again, the two of them sliding through the water. He would understand. I can explain, the boy said, and began to, talking on and on until he was uncertain he was still awake or if the man was, whether he was part of the man's dream or the man was part of his.

IT WAS THEN that I opened my eyes and saw them, Gurley and Lily. I didn't see them from the boat, I just saw them, on the ground, after the blast, a vision. I didn't see how their bodies had splintered, what had been severed and what had been burned. I only saw how a tiny breeze put a ripple on the water rising around them, and how the thin morning sun slowly lit their two faces, eyes closed, Gurley's lips just parted and Lily's a silent seam. They both wore expressions not of anger or sadness, but just the mildest concern, as if they'd been sleeping in of a winter Sunday, and had stirred slightly awake to a sound from somewhere downstairs in that great big house on the hill—the kids—the youngest probably—was crying. Not the sharp cry of pain, just hungry or sad or lonely.

Then I heard the crying, too, and like them, I thought it came from somewhere distant. But they were right and I was wrong; I looked up and saw that the boy was crying again. My hearing was returning. He'd let go of my hand. The vision vanished, replaced by the sight of a dock and a shack and a radio mast flying two flags: above, the Stars and Stripes, and below, a plain red cross on a worn white field.

AND THEN what did you do?

I'm slumped asleep in a chair beside Ronnie's bed in the hospice. I'm not really asleep, though; only as much as you can be in a chair. And since I can't enter a state quite deep enough for dreaming, I seem to be passing the time by talking with Ronnie in my imagination. I tell him the rest of the story—it's easier asleep. My throat's sore, besides. I've been talking too long.

You have.

It may not, in fact, be my imagination. If I accept my experience with the boy as evidence of some—spiritual—ability, perhaps I really am speaking with Ronnie. How far is it, after all, from intuition to connection, from guessing at what someone's thinking to actually knowing? I'm a priest, besides. I should know what it's like to look into another's soul. Whatever the source of my ability, I'm good at it, I have to admit: my imagined Ronnie interrupts me in all the right places, says all the right things.

You're not imagining me.

Like that.

What happened to the boy?

(Or this.) But I should answer: he died. He died, just like he was always going to. And not of plague. I got him to the infirmary—

Where Lily had led you—

Where Lily had led me, and once I got there, he died.

And so you must lead me.

And this is where I wake up. Because I always try to wake up before these conversations go on too long; it's not healthy. Not at my age. You reach a certain point in life and you discover that the little moat that's always surrounded your mind, kept it safe, defined things—this is real, this is not—has dried up. One day you're daydreaming and the next day someone's joking about Alzheimer's, and the next day you wonder—just what day is *this*?

"The next day."

This I am not imagining. I don't think.

"Lou-is," Ronnie says, and his eyes now meet mine. "You are awake?"

I nod my head.

"The next day," says Ronnie. "What did you do then? Or was it that night?"

I can hear him, I can see him, but I need a little more time to adjust to Ronnie, still alive.

"Lou-is," Ronnie says.

"Ronnie," I say. "You came back."

"One last time. I heard your voice and followed one last time. I did not know why, but now I do. Because of what you are about to tell me. What did you do then?"

"When?"

"With the boy. Lily's boy. The boy from the sky."

The boy from the sky was as gray as the sky as the boat skidded west, out to sea, away from the infirmary where no one would help us. I had lost my mind or left it behind; I was making for Japan. The boy was Japanese. I would take him across the Pacific in my little open boat, the reserve tank almost empty, our food and medicine gone, completely gone.

I never saw Japan. A large island just off the southwestern coast of Alaska got in the way. I'd landed, a madman, only to be faced down by another: Father Leonard, a missionary, the last man on an island of women who had lost their husbands, sons, and brothers to the war effort.

Father Leonard was gaunt, bald, with a thin white beard, and no longer smiled or waved. When he saw my uniform, he said, "You're not taking any more." He paused to make sure I understood. I didn't, and he went on: "What did you think would happen? Draft all the able-bodied men, and how are the wives supposed to find food? Tell me you brought food."

I didn't answer. I presented him with the lifeless body of the boy. And Father Leonard took a deep breath, didn't ask who or why or where, just took the boy in his arms, and began working his way back up through the rocks behind the narrow beach I'd found. For a moment, I considered pushing off once more, using the thimbleful of gas I had left to set myself adrift. Then I'd wait until the time or sea or clouds were right and I'd go over the side, feel the water, feel the cold clamp my lungs, and then, feel nothing at all.

But then I looked up and saw Father Leonard struggle with the weight of the boy as his climb grew steeper, and my reaction was automatic. I scrambled up the rocks after him, offered help, was refused, insisted on at least steadying him, and then the two of us—three of us—made our way to his tiny house.

He asked some of the local women to wash and prepare the boy's body. And then there was a cemetery forested with weathered white whalebone, a short ceremony, horizontal rain, and the boy disappearing from view.

Everyone left; I stayed. I took down the tiny wooden cross Father Leonard had fashioned for the boy; I wasn't so sure the boy was ours to give to God. I waited the rest of the afternoon and into the night, afraid and hopeful that Lily would come for him.

Or perhaps for me.

I waited there for her, on Father Leonard's island, the Bering Sea island where I'd taken the boy. Father Leonard so despised the government that he was only too glad to shelter and hide an AWOL soldier. I waited for weeks; the war ended. Then weeks turned into months, into a year, and still I waited, for I knew what Jesus knew: "Watch therefore," He said, "for you know neither the day nor the hour." He was speaking of the maidens awaiting the bridegroom, who sat waiting, as I do still, late into the night. The foolish ones used up their lamp oil. The wise ones waited. And hadn't Lily told me as much? Awaiting Saburo's return, she had acted foolishly; she had taken up with Gurley. I knew I would not be so unwise. When Lily came, I would be alone, and ready.

So when, in time, Father Leonard mentioned the seminary, I stopped what I was doing and listened. He had read into my quiet, steady patience a vocation, or perhaps he had spoken with God, who reminded Father Leonard that I had been at the doorstep of the seminary not two years before and chose war instead.

But to return to the seminary now seemed fitting and just. If the ensuing deprivations proved painful, so be it: I could not live a life long enough to do adequate penance for my war's worth of sins. And truth be told, the life's promised restraint held real appeal for me, especially celibacy. I would not make Lily's mistake and fall in foolish love.

The priesthood offered something else, as well. A way to be with Lily, or tap into her world, while I waited. It would have been better to be a shaman, but I was not one and could not become one. It had been a struggle enough for Lily, and she had Yup'ik blood in her, had grown up in the bush. Becoming a priest was as close as an orphan Catholic could get. Please understand, though: I have never debased my vows. I do not pretend to pray to God while secretly seeking contact with the spirits of whales or walruses. I render unto God what is God's, but in my prayers to Him, I have always asked that He make me aware to *all* things unseen, not simply His mysteries.

But by now, if I am convinced of anything, it is God's omniscience—how else would He have seen to arrange my life as He has?—and I fear

He knows the ulterior motive of my spiritual life. Knows it, and cannot abide it, and so my half-century waiting search for Lily has been a lonely one. He has never helped.

But I didn't know that then. I only knew Father Leonard, and he always helped. Indeed, in all my time with him, he never denied me anything, never except in the very beginning, the day we buried the boy. I had become obsessed with a need to build a fire, a fire large enough to consume the boy, cremate him, and send his ashes swirling in the air. Father Leonard said no, gently, and then firmly, and even tried to reason with me: there wasn't enough fuel for such a fire, to start with—

"The balloons," I said. "I can do it. I just need one of the incendiaries from the balloons." I was so addled I didn't realize that there was a possibility—or rather, as was always the case, a probability—that no fire balloons had happened to land nearby.

Father Leonard looked at me. "Balloons," he said. "What, in God's holy name, are you talking about?"

Tell me how he died, Lou-is.

Ronnie: I glance at him; did I just hear him speak or imagine it? His eyes are closed. I take a deep breath. And then he says it again: "Tell me how he died."

This time I am sure I hear him, and this time, for the first time, I realize something else.

"You first," I say.

CHAPTER 21

SOMETIMES I DREAM I KILLED HIM. THAT I CLUBBED THE doctor who wouldn't ease his pain with morphine and went for the cabinet myself. Sometimes I find the morphine, enough to administer a compassionate, lethal dose. Sometimes the cabinet is empty. Sometimes the boy screams, and the doctor screams. Sometimes the doctor shoots him, sometimes I shoot the doctor.

And sometimes, the boy's wailing stops and his eyes close. And I move to his pillow, and I place the barrel of my revolver just two inches from his head. And then I wait. I wait for him to stop breathing, so as to render my bullet unnecessary. I wait for courage. I wait for mercy to replace rage. I wait for Lily to come into the room and open my hands and find the future there.

I wait for Ronnie to speak.

"There was a boy," Ronnie said. This was just a few hours ago. "A boy and his mother."

Would not stop crying, I could have said, but did not have to; Ronnie knew what I was thinking.

"I did not tell you this," Ronnie said. "There was a mother and her baby, a baby that had come too soon. And no one could help her, and the doctor wouldn't help her, and they sent for me."

I—

I couldn't move, or speak: Ronnie had been *there,* in that room, with—

"Lily," Ronnie said. "Yes. This was Lily," he said, and waited. I still said nothing, and he went on.

"When I was young and strong, my *tuunraq,* my wolf, he was a good spirit helper. He could go inside a sick person, tear out the sickness. He would return to me, his jaws red with blood, and I would know he had done good. I saw this. I know this. But that night, with Lily, that was when he ran away. Lily had asked me to help her, and the *tuunraq,* he ran away. When we journey, we *angalkut* tie them to us, these spirits, because this is what they do, they run, and they will run away if they can. And this wolf broke free. I could not stop him. I have searched for him ever since. I wanted to find him before he found me."

He did not so much speak as take the words and place them, one by one, behind my eyes, beneath my scalp. I can feel them there now.

Ronnie started again. "When they came for me, asked me to help Lily, I did not want to go. These were women's matters. But I came and I looked and I saw what the others had seen. The baby had come, the baby had died. I saw this. But I also saw something else, something else no one saw, something Lily had hoped I would see. I could see the child's spirit floating just above him, in the dark. You know what this looks like?"

Yes. I do. And I could see Lily's baby, just as well as I could see the boy from the balloon. I could see blood and hair and tiny hands and—

Ronnie was shaking his head. He held up a hand, palm up. "Like this," he said.

"Like what?" I asked, staring at Ronnie's face, not his hand.

"A breath," Ronnie said. "The boy was dead, maybe they thought he was born dead, but he had taken a breath, a single breath—did you know this?—and when I got there, it was still hanging in the air above him."

"Ronnie—"

"No," Ronnie said. "My wolf saw it, too, asked me if he should fetch it, take this spirit, this breath by the scruff of its neck, and plunge it back down inside the boy. The wolf looked at me. He asked me this. Lily was saying things, too. I did not hear. I just looked at the boy. The wolf looked at me. Then he lunged."

Ronnie had been staring before him as he said this. Now he turned.

"But I was too quick for him. I was younger then. Faster. With two feet. I sprang for his spirit, that breath. I jumped and I got it." Ronnie made a sudden fist and then opened his hand once more.

"Listen to me," he said. "I jumped before the wolf. Because I understood. I thought I understood what the wolf did not. This boy was not to live here. Within him ran Yup'ik blood, but also the blood of another place. And I knew that this blood would be the end of us. Just as I knew when I first saw you and the priest before you and the priest before him. Such new blood would be the end of us. The end of how the Yup'ik lived. *Yup'ik*: this means the real people. This child was not real. I saw this. I knew this. When I saw the boy, when I saw his father."

Worse than hearing this was believing it, and I tried to stop: "You were there, Ronnie? You were really there? This isn't alcohol or diabetes or—"

"You have the proof," Ronnie said.

We stared at each other.

And I almost wish it had ended that way. That each of us, in turn, would feel our eyelids droop and close, our jaws go slack, and then, slowly at first, but with ever-increasing speed, our life seep out of us and into the floor.

But it didn't.

"When the wolf left, I knew I had done wrong," Ronnie said. "I took the breath, I went to the boy—but it had been too long now, and without the wolf, I could not plunge his breath deep enough inside him. Lily only knew—Lily only knew that I tried. She saw my tears and saw my failure, but did not see all of it. Lou-is: when her lover came, this Saburo, when she asked me to help him out of town, help him deliver the baby's body into the tundra? Yes. I would never say no again.

"One of the aunties had talked—there were soldiers, police, everywhere. We almost got caught, several times. We took two kayaks; I led him an hour downriver, and from there, he insisted he go on alone. You would know the place? Where the bank is worn away? Where the *ircenrrat* gather? He said to wait there for him, that he would come back, return the map—the path Lily might take to see their son." Ronnie shook his head. "Why there?"

"I know it," I said quietly. "I know the place."

"It was not a place I could go, not then, not after my *tuunraq* had left me, run before me and set all the other spirits against me. I could feel them coming, worming through the *ayuq,* the soil, down the bank, to the water. I ran for my kayak, I started upstream."

"You left Saburo?"

"He found me," Ronnie said. "I took the map from him, but—but by the time he caught up with me, I'd almost made it back to Bethel. A boat—with a light—it saw us. I went to shore, into the cottonwood. Saburo went downriver. I heard yelling, shots, then nothing."

I waited before speaking.

"What did Lily say when she saw the map?" I asked.

"I couldn't face her, not then," Ronnie said. "Not after what I knew had happened to Saburo. I found some gin. Then more gin. I got drunk. Police came. And when I woke up in my cell, the book was gone. I at least gave Lily and Saburo this: I would not let them beat the truth out of me. I played the drunk fool, said I had no idea where the map came from, what it meant." Ronnie scrunched his face at the memory. "I was the drunk fool," he said, and looked at me, shrugged. "Proof."

I shook my head. Ronnie smiled, exhausted, and looked outside.

"The wolf, he's closer," Ronnie said. "Not close enough." The window looked the way our televisions up here used to before satellite: snow swirling against a dark screen, pressing to get in. "But you'll help him, Lou-is, won't you? Give him what he's coming for." Ronnie paused, tried to smile once more. "Tell him he's late."

"Ronnie," I said, on my feet, desperate to stop him. Or the wolf. "It's no good, Ronnie—wait. I don't believe—"

Ronnie looked at his wrist. "I need the bracelet," he said.

I slowly shook my head.

"I need it for the wolf," he said.

"Not yet," I said.

"I need it to tie him to me. I'm not going to let him escape again this time."

"Ronnie," I said.

"Lou-is," Ronnie said. "What have I asked?"

I sat silent, then reached in my pocket, took out the pyx, opened it, and removed the bracelet. I unraveled it as carefully as if it were a chain of diamonds and then affixed it to his wrist. "Let's pray," I said, not looking up.

Ronnie looked pleased, and shook his head. "I can't pray if I don't believe, Lou-is."

I couldn't answer, only taunt: "Well, I'm getting ready to go after your wolf, and I don't exactly believe in him, so—"

"It's okay," Ronnie interrupted. "He believes in you." He smiled, but to himself, and then lay back on the pillow. "Now," he said, the word coming quite clearly, "this is what you must give him—" But here his voice faltered again. He went down, deep in his chest to find his breath, to cough it out once more, but this time it did not come.

I shouted. I shook him. I ran to the hall. I called for help. I was crying, tears actually running down my face, my old man's face. I dropped the side rail. I bent over him. And then—

I breathed. Once, twice. My mouth to his. Then my hands on his chest. One, two, three, four, five. But it was no good: the bed was too soft. Sometimes there was a board beneath you could pull out for CPR. I couldn't find it. I thought about dragging him onto the floor, but there wasn't enough time. Jesus, Mary, and you, too, Joseph.

Breathe. Again to his chest. One, two, three, four—I could hear foot-steps, voices behind me.

Thank you, Lord, for this: for the help of doctors and nurses, for those who can truly bring the dead back to life. I explained between breaths, between compressions, what I was doing, how I was saving him, how I needed help. I was on the verge of saying why—of saying that I needed to save him from the wolf, or for the wolf, or that I needed to keep him alive long enough to tell me, an old priest, a be-liever, one baptized in the waters of everlasting life, just what it was that I had to give this wolf.

They pulled me away from Ronnie. I fought, but they pulled me away—and I decided: they know best. They know better than I: they are the professionals; they are younger. Let them breathe, let them save him.

They did not.

"Father! Stop!" I think this is what I heard as they struggled with me. "Father—what are you doing? You have to—" I think I may have hit someone at this point, but, let's be clear, I did not bite, did not bite at one of them. "You have to respect his wishes." A nurse held up his wrist and the Comfort One bracelet, but I couldn't see it. I know it was there, but I couldn't see it. I could only hear it clink and wink and laugh at me, and then I couldn't hear it at all, because I was running, down the hall, out the doors, into the snow, off to the wolf.

YOU HAVE THE PROOF, Ronnie said, and I do.

Proof is in my pocket, the inside breast pocket of my parka, as I race my snowmachine down the frozen river. Proof is a small book of strange paper bound in green leather. Proof is what I bring the wolf.

Proof: this is what I searched for, years later, in Anchorage.

But there was none.

Everything had changed. Every street I walked down was paved, the sidewalks were clear. New buildings had gone up. Old buildings cleared away. The Starhope still stood, or its shell did. It had new windows. In the lobby, plants, and a guard in coat and tie. And on the second floor: nothing, nothing I needed to see.

And out at the base, where the strangely frightened teenaged soldier at the main gate waved me through when he saw my collar, I could see that Fort Richardson and Elmendorf Airfield had changed as well. They were separate bases now, but more important, the mud was gone, and so too the tents, the crowds. I picked my way down new streets, around new buildings, circumscribed, incredibly, by tidy green lawns. And finally, I turned down a street that I'm fairly certain is the one that used to terminate at the front door of our Quonset hut.

And it was gone, too, of course. Which I expected, though I was disappointed. I wondered what it was like when they tore it down, what happened when neither Gurley nor I returned from our secret mission, whether the major ever searched the tundra for some proof of plague, or whether he launched a search for some proof of us.

Maybe no one noticed, or didn't notice for a while. The war was ending then. We disappeared in July, the war ended in August. And the balloon that carried that boy was either the last or among the last, or so I've deduced from the odd article or two that I've read in the decades since. They gave up, Japan. Credit Gurley, I guess, or the editors who voluntarily obeyed the press ban: until it was lifted, not a word about the balloons was printed or broadcast, and the Japanese were left to conclude that their massive undertaking had failed.

No trace of plague weapons was ever found in Alaska or farther south, though I've read there were plans for plague-laden kamikaze planes to attack San Diego in the fall of '45. Northern China, Unit 731's home, offers a glimpse of what might have been: in the years following the war, tens of thousands died in successive waves of plague, likely spread by animals escaping from, or released by, those who'd spent the war experimenting on them.

The plague failed to reach us, but the balloons did not. They rose from the ground into the clouds and flew across the ocean. They landed in Canada, Mexico, and the U.S. In Alaska, in Washington, in Oregon, in California, in a dozen other states, and who knows what's still concealed today beneath the forest floor? After the war, researchers reinflated a captured Japanese paper balloon and launched it from Southern California, just to see how hardy it was, just to see how far it would travel, having already made the trek from Japan.

It landed in Africa.

But that one balloon doesn't interest me so much as the dozens Gurley and I left behind in Anchorage. How strange it must have been in those first days without us, those last days of the war, MPs guarding a building uninhabited but for balloons.

In time, of course, the Army would have sent someone up to take inventory and look for clues of what had happened among the items that we'd left. What would they have found?

Balloons, still hanging from the rafters, crates upon crates of balloon parts, and those pieces too big to be crated, stacked along the floor, the whole place looking less like a home for decommissioned war matériel than the breeding ground of some terrible new weapon.

In his office, after they'd snapped the padlock? They'd find the wall map, of course, the pins running red across it, the clocks above. Gurley's dog-eared Japanese-English dictionary. The blackguard's tooth.

There I was, years later, half afraid some MP would finally take this long-absent soldier prisoner, and there was nothing there.

There's nothing there: Lily was as amazed as I at those final pages in the book, page after page of gray wash that I had read as blank, as failure, as proof of Saburo's inability to show Lily where he had gone, what he had done, what had happened to their little boy.

It's only now I understand that he could no more have mapped their son's death than he could the clouds, blood coursing through a body or spilling into the sea. The pattern is unknowable, out of reach, divine. It's only now I see, in my mind and in the overcast sky ahead of me, those washed gray pages for what they were. There may be no sharper map of grief than this, no more precise way to show a war's worth, a life's worth, a love's worth of ache and loss and absence.

Rest, write, my superiors told me, *almost sixty years in the bush, what stories you must have!* And this is how I would tell them, not with pen or pencil but a brush, dipped in water, dipped in paint, sweeping back and forth across an empty page.

Look how the gray gathers here, how here it stumbles into white.

Look closer, how each square inch, each speck of color is made up of smaller specks of moisture. Of water from the brush, of Ronnie's rain falling to those grieving parents' faces, of snow, of molecules, of the hydrogen escaped years ago from those balloons.

Of breaths escaped from mouths.

And the last thing I would draw or paint or write is what I see emerging now: eyes, ears, tail, snout, a thick mane. I throttle back and stop. Red tongue, white teeth.

Ronnie's wolf.

It must be: any other wolf would have run at the sound and light— or maybe this one has sized me up and seen me for what I am. An aging priest. A soldier who couldn't shoot. The one the others left behind.

The wolf paces left, then right, fast at first, then slow. I don't know what holds him at bay: fear of a gun? I do not have one. I raise my empty hands, and he stops and stares, his muscles tense, and so do mine.

I believe in God the Father Almighty and I believe in the wolves He made, their claws, their bite. But He did not make this one, so I have nothing to fear. This is Ronnie's wolf. A *tuunraq.* A spirit, a familiar, a work of the mind. Isn't he? I cannot come to harm from something imaginary.

But something in me *is* frightened, enough to hammer my heart and make me sweat in the subzero cold. Frightened and almost teary with joy, because the longer the wolf paces and pants, the more I find this proof that he is not, in fact, a *tuunraq,* he is the work of no one's imagination but God's, or that there is no such thing as imagination out here, that everything is real, that he is real, teeth and all, and this is why Ronnie sent me to meet him. To die, and in doing so join Lily, and the rest.

Park rangers say: appear larger than you are, make a noise, speak; remind the animal that you are human, not standard prey.

So I stay silent, I move away from the snowmachine, I crouch down, I put one knee in the snow. I shift my weight, the snow gives, I sink a little. I put down the other knee and sink a little more. I recover my balance, extend a hand, and then the other.

And the wolf steps closer, unsure.

I look at his eyes, and then remember: his mouth! Who or what is he carrying by the scruff of its neck? Lily's baby? Saburo? The boy from the balloon? Ronnie? I can't see. I look at the eyes again.

The wolf steps closer, close enough that our breath now clouds together, and I am on both knees, trembling, remembering: *This is what you must give him—*

Breath, cloud. Breath, cloud.

I breathe out the breath Ronnie gave me as he died, the breath Ronnie took from Lily's baby after he died.

Bring this to her son, I tell the wolf.

Breath, cloud.

And to Ronnie, breathe his life back. And the boy who flew across the ocean: fill his lungs once more, his balloon as well.

Breathe life into Lily.

Into me.

Deep in the snow, I feel a flash of how that first Yup'ik man of stone felt. A staggering jumble of blocks sinking, too slowly, into the tundra. I am cold and wet, and old.

The wolf steps closer and then around me. I can feel him at the small of my back, now my shoulder, now he's before me once more. I breathe deep; I'm ready. But then, without a look, without a sound, he leaps away, lands in a trot, then leaps again, and lands galloping, fleeing or leading me to some new and distant place.

I rise.

ACKNOWLEDGMENTS

Those interested in the historical and cultural issues raised here should consult the following sources, to which I am indebted: Robert Mikesh's definitive *Japan's World War II Balloon Bomb Attacks on North America*; James H. Barker's beautiful and informative *Always Getting Ready: Upterrlainarluta: Yup'ik Eskimo Subsistence in Southwest Alaska*; Ann Fienup-Riordan's *Boundaries and Passages: Rule and Ritual in Yup'ik Eskimo Tradition*, where I first found a version of the myth of the sobbing boy buried beside his mother; *Bethel: The First One Hundred Years* by Mary Lenz and James H. Barker; Segundo Llorente's *Memoirs of a Yukon Priest*; and A. B. Hartley's *Unexploded Bomb*.

I am very grateful to the following individuals and institutions for helping me ground this work of fiction in fact: former Comdr. Hansel T. Wood, Jr., USN; CW04 John D. Bartleson, Jr., USN (Ret.), historian of the Naval Explosive Ordnance Disposal Association, Inc.; Maj. Sean Bourke, M.D., USAF; Robert C. Mikesh, former senior curator, National Air and Space Museum; Alan Renga, assistant archivist of the San Diego Aerospace Museum; Dr. William Atwater, Ph.D., director of the U.S. Army Ordnance Museum; Dr. Amy R. Cohen, Ph.D., Randolph-Macon Woman's College; Lt. Amy Hansen and the public affairs staff of Elmendorf Air Force Base; the National Air and Space Museum Archives and Library; the National Archives facilities in Washington, D.C., and College

Park, Maryland, especially the archivists of the Motion Picture, Audio and Video collection; the Rare Book and Special Collections Room of the Library of Congress; the John Wesley Powell Anthropology Library of the Smithsonian National Museum of Natural History; the Alaska Room librarians at Anchorage's Z. J. Loussac Public Library; Aaron Micallef, director of education and public programs, and the archive staff at the Anchorage Museum of Art and History; the General Research Division of the New York Public Library; the Seattle Public Library; George Mason University's Fenwick Library and Georgetown University's Lauinger Library; and the Martha Washington Library of the Fairfax County (Virginia) Public Library System.

A wide variety of patient and knowledgeable Alaskans helped me avoid making *cheechako* errors (such as misusing the word *cheechako*); I'm particularly thankful to Mike Martz and John Active of KYUK/Bethel Broadcasting; Joan Hamilton and Michael Stevens of the Yupiit Piciryarait Museum; Grant Fairbanks; Sarge Connick; Elias and Bernie Venes; Gladys Jung; Crusty Old Joe Stevens; Olivia Terry of Island Air; VPSO Mark Haglin; the folks at KNBA; and the extraordinary Susan Oliver (and her extraordinary family) of Kodiak.

A final thanks to those who read, again and again, and offered their advice and encouragement, especially my editor, John Flicker; my agent, Wendy Sherman; my provocateur, Susan Richards Shreve; and my parents, Joan and Charles Callanan; as well as Tony Eprile, Cathy Gray, Dan Kois, Mike Pabich, Nani Power, Paula R. Sidore, and Mary Lucy Wood; along with all the staff and students of the George Mason University Creative Writing Program, including Richard Bausch, Steve Goodwin, Beverly Lowry and Carolyn Forché.

Thank you most of all to my wife, Susan, whose love, quiet courage, great patience, and ability to defuse just about anything inspired much of this book.